PRAISE FOR
MONSTERS BORN AND MADE

"An exhilarating race of willpower and defiance, set on an utterly unique world filled with glorious monsters."

—Xiran Jay Zhao, #1 *New York Times*
bestselling author of *Iron Widow*

"*Monsters Born and Made* takes well-beloved YA tropes and turns them on their heads, creating an action-packed rallying cry against oppression and a riveting tale of one girl's desperation to survive no matter the odds."

—Roseanne A. Brown, *New York Times* bestselling
author of *A Song of Wraiths and Ruin*

"Both a brilliant competition story about a girl facing down impossible obstacles and a skillful critique of the society that created them, *Monsters Born and Made* will leave you breathless and desperate for more."

—Vaishnavi Patel, *New York Times* bestselling author of *Kaikeyi*

"In this heart-wrenching tale of one girl's fight for survival, Berwah skillfully tears apart humanity's mask, revealing brutal truths about the monstrosities that lay within. An epic, page-turning debut by a brilliant new author!"

—June CL Tan, author of *Jade Fire Gold*

"Readers familiar with YA-dystopias will be at home here, among monsters who are creatures—and the human monsters who drive systems of inequality and oppression."

—*Paste*

"Fluid prose and a breakneck pace ensures a wild ride from start to finish."

—*Publishers Weekly*

"Berwah's worldbuilding is intense, depicting a cruel society in which the power-hungry elite are just as monstrous as the terrifying oceanic beasts...for dystopian fantasy fans seeking something fresh and savage."

—*Kirkus Reviews*

"Berwah's YA debut thrusts readers into a chilling world where sea creatures aren't the only monsters to fear."

—*Booklist*

"The South-Asian inspired setting is the true draw here...Koral is earnest and deeply well-intentioned...grim but compelling."

—*The Bulletin of the Center for Children's Books*

★ "Berwah builds excitement with her well-crafted characters and storyline. Her world building is superb, and masterfully weaves in elements of the South Asian caste system. This book will leave readers eagerly awaiting a sequel."

—*Youth Services Book Review*

"A gripping tale of struggle and sacrifice."

—*Lightspeed Magazine*

Also by Tanvi Berwah

Monsters Born and Made

SOMEWHERE
IN
THE
DEEP

SOMEWHERE

IN

THE

DEEP

TANVI BERWAH

sourcebooks
fire

Copyright © 2024 by Tanvi Berwah
Cover and internal design © 2024 by Sourcebooks
Jacket art © Sasha Vinogradova
Cover design by Erin Fitzsimmons/Sourcebooks
Internal design by Laura Boren/Sourcebooks

Published by Sourcebooks Fire, an imprint of Sourcebooks
P.O. Box 4410, Naperville, Illinois 60567–4410
(630) 961-3900
sourcebooks.com

Cataloging-in-Publication Data is on file with the Library of Congress.

Printed and bound in the United States of America.
LSC 10 9 8 7 6 5 4 3 2 1

For everyone who has had to pull themselves out of the deep.

ONE

*T*oday, I heave, blood streaming down my face and dripping onto the packed ground below, *is not the day I die*.

The monster I'm fighting—a red stygic—has annoyingly similar thoughts.

It screeches madly, swiping a claw at me, and I leap back. Just not in time. Red warmth fountains out from my shoulder, a small gap between my armor and helm. I skid across its belly, knifing the skin as I go. And swear. The belly is hardened, protected by strong, natural armor. My knife does it no harm. I'll have to go in for the kill if I don't want to end up with its fangs through my spine.

The spectators around the pit roar in unison, enjoying the game of blood, and urge me and the stygic both to *fight fight fight!*

And this monster takes them a little too seriously.

A long claw swipes at me. I roll down onto the packed ground and avoid getting skewered. But the stygic kicks me hard. I spin backward. Slam against the wall of the pit arena. A brassy ringing tears through my head at the impact, and despite the armored protection, pain surges throughout my body. If I wasn't wearing the helm, I'd be lying on the ground with my skull cracked open. What a sight that would be for these bloodthirsty leeches in the audience. I clutch my knives and push myself up, my vision unsteady. Up in the stands, deafening cheers echo across the space.

Dark Dancer! Dark Dancer!

I know what the crowd wants. They want me to kill it but not easily. That's what this is. A playground of death. These people come here to bet on gore and ruin, and I can't sabotage the show.

I throw my hands into the air, the blades gleaming gold from the flames in the braziers, and grin at them with bloodstained teeth. *Give them a show, Krescent*, Badger always says. And the moron is right; the stands explode with applause.

I grip my knives and face the stygic through the growing haze in my mind.

What a magnificently gross beast. It's a bony amphibian, and its whole body is covered in deep red scales. Its large head accommodates four eyes, each blinking separately, and the mouth full of long, sharp teeth that are constantly grinding against a skinless jaw. A slender body is held up by six hardened-looking claws that double as limbs. And at the rear, there's a scorpion-like tail that has a stinger.

The monster makes a horrible keening noise.

And suddenly charges to the left of the arena—away from me. I look around to see what it's going for. The sudden spurt of venom from its tail cuts so close I hear the burning hiss of the substance as it eats away at the sand. Startled, I trip backward. From this vantage, I see the red-black venom creating a hole in the ground.

Damn it, Badger. How did you get this devil thing into the arena?

I haven't given the creature a single scratch, and yet it has me soaked in blood. It rears its head, cries loudly, and charges at me. I take a stance. The dancer's stance. I throw a knife. The stygic dodges cleanly and whips its tail, sweeping me off-balance. I land on my back against the ground. Two of the stygic's claws land on either side of me, and it screams in my face. The razor-sharp fangs enclose a black hole so deep I could vanish inside.

Before I can move, it lunges.

Forgetting my knives, I grab hold of its jaw. The serrated edges of the bones cut through my skin. The weight is too much. It pushes down. So close. I can see the veins running at the back of its mouth. The foul, fleshy smell is overwhelming.

The fangs crack hard against my helm. The stygic is too strong. My arms buckle under the pressure, and the fangs clamp around the helm. Panic grabs me as I stare down the stygic's throat again.

No—I can't be swallowed whole. It's the worst death I can think of. Darkness.

Screaming, I start punching the sides of the creature's face. It howls, startled as it lets go of me, and scuttles back. I cough and cough, drinking in the stale, liquor-drenched air of the pit, my heart beating madly against my rib cage. Bile rises in my throat. The inside of my head turns into molasses.

The stygic thumps the ground with its front claws. It's only now I notice how the walls have spatters of dried blood too. Did the last fighter not yield? Did they *die*?

Such a brutal death…and all just for fun.

I grasp for my knives but I only have one left. The rest are scattered across the pit, helpless.

My knees tremble.

The stygic shakes its head, whips its tail side to side, and then rushes at me.

I position myself, holding the knife out in front of me. Today's *not* the day I die. I promised Rivan—

The stygic brings down both its front claws. I dart out of the way.

Frustrated, the large beast turns, graceless.

And I am a dancer. A swirl to the right, a swirl to the left. The dancer's way. The stygic rushes after me, stumbles, and I launch myself at it and land on the back of its long neck. The soft area where I punched it in the head is still red. That's its weakness.

I cling to the stygic. It bucks, raises its claws, and hits at the walls, but I refuse to let my grip slide. Instead, I stab at the top of its soft head. I stab and I stab. Blue blood spurts out—into my face and my mouth. I'm screaming and stabbing. Every muscle in my body lusting after the death of this creature.

Finally, the stygic collapses, and I roll off it unceremoniously.

A breath of relief mixed with regret tinged in blue blood as I rise, victorious.

Today is not the day I die.

Pain thunders through me. My knees buckle and drop to the ground with a thump, my knife still bloody and clutched so tight that my knuckles threaten to slice into the seams of my skin.

The crowd roars its approval. I gave them entertainment. A chill drips down my spine. How long will I have to keep doing this? How long can I keep cheating death?

"And look at this," Badger booms above us. "The Dark Dancer triumphs once more. An unbeaten streak!" His voice is jubilant along with the crowd. But I see the coldness in his stark white features. I've destroyed his new toy.

The next moment, without warning, the ground shudders.

I lose my balance and slam against the wall, struggling for purchase. Above me, the world bursts into screams. The thundering of the ground roars like a dragon as it quakes with an oceanic might. The crowd jostles on the stands, uninhibited, and one of the railings around the arena gives way. I forget where I am. My home—my parents—*no*, they're dead. Am I at the shoreline? Did a creature attack? Did I fall into the sea? But the wall—shaking but solid. The arena. *I was fighting.*

And then someone crashes into the arena from the stands above. A moment later, the quake subsides.

The crowd suddenly starts screaming again.

I whirl.

The stygic, crumpled on the ground and bleeding to death, manages to lift its trembling tail.

And as I try to shield the man on the ground, it shoots its venom straight at me.

TWO

I hold the compress softly against my eyes. Lot of good that does. The medic—although it's generous to call the man who bandages us after fights that—says that I'm lucky the helm caught most of the venom from the dying stygic and only the fumes got in.

My burning eyes, however, tell a different story. Still a better one than the man who fell in the pits during the quake. I glance at his body in the corner, wrapped in white.

My help made no difference. He'd fallen headfirst on the packed ground.

Tears sting my eyes. Everything's blurred. The medic doesn't care as long as I'm still seeing color. He's all I've got. No way I'll be allowed into the hospital at the Collector's compound. They don't even let injured miners out of work hours in there.

Down in the pit, the crowd dances in a rain of blood. The quake is ended, but now the anger at one more thing out of their control has sent them all spiraling worse than usual. Already two bouts have been over after me. I don't know the result of either. The medic sent me back to the fighters' shared prep room to make space for the others. I should be grateful that I'm alive after what happened, but as I stumble back in the room, my arm outstretched to feel my way in, I hear giggles.

"Dark Dancer," comes Ansh's annoying voice. "Seeing dark?" He leans against the door with his twin sister, Yara. Both of them work days at the mines and fight nights here. They were orphaned at the same time as me, and even though I've known them longer than anyone else on this messed-up island, they hate me.

"An incredible improvement from seeing your face," I call.

"You'll get what you have coming, Krescent Dune," Yara adds.

"You're probably right." I smile through the painful spasm across my face. As if I don't know why she keeps using my full name here, unlike in the arena where I'm only announced as the Dark Dancer, hoping someone still angry enough will make the connection and come for me.

Someone bumps against my shoulder—purposefully. There's enough space to avoid walking into anyone. Another one of the twins' minions. They've made it a personal mission to make things as miserable for me as they can. I lose my balance, only stopping myself from pitching face-first onto the dusty floor by catching the arm of the person next to me in a death grip. They yelp.

"Watch where you're going, *matya*!"

A monstrous fish that eats its own young. It's a creative insult, I'll give him that.

Rivan often suggests, gently if uselessly, that I make friends in the arena too—but that would be worth the effort if it could accomplish something. Something other than being ratted out or protested against, that is.

I step out of the room, before I break into a fight outside the pit, and head out into a narrow hallway. This network of tunnels beneath the hills was dug long before humans settled on the island

7

of Kar Atish. We don't know what was here before—*who* was here before. There were some who took shelter below ground before the Collector's men found the mines on the island. Tunnels and caves go far underground, like giant worms slithered through them, and those closer to the surface are walled with an unknown black metal, the likes of which has never been found anywhere on the island.

The narrow hallway is walled similarly, strangely. Pitch-black and claustrophobic. It feels like I will die buried here, under the weight of the cruel, remorseless land above.

They say it wasn't always without mercy.

The island had its terrors, but it also had beauty; when the hills above the ground of this warren had been the home of sea farmers and smiths, when humans still had humanity intact.

Kar Atish sits high above the sea, surrounded by basalt columns like a prison, its surface jagged like the fangs of an ancient dragon. Our island's mountains have been cut down by harsh winds and side-falling rain, revealing dark shades of blood and gray beneath the ashen surface of the rock. And below lie underground caverns filled with seawater. It's a grim place, black stone and ruined coasts, rising from the stormwaters defiantly.

But it's the deep underground that conceals something worse: the ore of zargunine. An alloy of an unknown substance mixed with gold. More valuable than the blood flowing in our veins.

It is zargunine that attracted our overlords.

The Collector and his men arrived from Sollonia, the biggest of the ten islands. They called themselves the Landers, an upper caste of rich, powerful people who seem to hold our world in their fists, and decided we need regulation, turning us all into prisoners in our own home. We were informed that anyone not a Lander was of a lower caste, a Renter, by birth. Our food, our clothes, our roofs— everything became the property of the Collector and his company.

There was only one way to feed hungry mouths. Work in the mines, bring them zargunine, and earn the company's scrips to exchange for food, water, and clothes.

Or die.

Death roams like a perpetually hungry beast on the island.

I shake my head.

The past is gone. The present is permanent. It is only my future that I care about...

Or I will, once the weekly installments end.

My parents may have died, but their debts have not. If I miss the installments, the Collector's office will make a slave of me, my very body chained to this island of shadows forever. I can't stop fighting in the pits any more than night beasts can stop hunting in the dark.

I walk through the door at the far end, into a cramped room the size of a rat's hole.

Oshen, tattooist and friend to us fighters, looks up and breaks into a grin. Behind the dirty goggles and beneath his mop of hair, he still looks like a child when he smiles, despite being well over fifty.

"Heard you were in the arena when the quake happened?"

"The ocean hates me."

"I wouldn't worry too much about the ocean down here," he chuckles. "New tattoo?"

I nod. The chain mail across my torso is too cumbersome to remove here, so I only take off the steel sleeve. Most of my arm is already marked anyway. There's space for one near my wrist, where it won't obscure the others. Only a pinprick of a tattoo. To mark my seventy-eighth kill tonight.

"It was a red stygic, one of a kind," I tell him, as is our little ritual every time I come here. "A deep maroon creature. In the sun, its damp scales would shine."

But I killed it. Whatever brute monster they bring to the pits is no

9

different from any other. They're all still made of flesh and bone and blood, and I still have to deal out death to them.

Before the pits, I would go down to the shoreline as a child, watch those creatures from afar, delighting in the way they moved and lived. Now I watch them bloody and beaten.

By my own hands.

"Everyone has to eat, Kress," Oshen says, noticing my expression. He brings out the needle and antiseptic, wipes the skin near my wrist, and begins his work.

"I'd rather get off this island to die than stay in this hell and continue eating. At least I won't have to watch people fall to their deaths anymore."

"How you come to terms with what you have to do to live is your business," he says, concentrating on my wrist. "But don't take on the burden of this man's death. If you do, it will be very hard to shake it off, child."

Oshen is one of the only people who still sees me as a child. Would he be this kind and forgiving of my acts if he knew who my parents were? For him, I'm only one of the many orphans of Kar Atish with dead parents and their living debts.

He continues, "Where do you wish to go?"

I usually only share that with people I'm close to. But I'm not close to *anyone* on this island. Except Rivan, who I've shared everything with for a long while now. Well, almost everything. But my mother is dead and the truth of my blood gone with her.

"Chandrabad," I tell him finally.

Oshen laughs heartily. "Big dreams, eh?"

"Never settle for anything less than your worth." I wink.

"How's Rivan?" he asks just as the needle breaks skin. The pain erupts like an exploding star. But thinking of Rivan is easier—I know why Oshen brought him up. It distracts me, draws my mind to that soft smell of rebru soap that Rivan buys at the weekly bazaar at the harbor.

"As he always is," I grit out. "Hates that I'm here fighting creatures and throwing away my life."

"He's a good one," Oshen says.

"No disagreement there." It's not Rivan's friendship I question— it's his inane need to pretend that I can continue living on this island like everything's fine.

The door at the back slams open, so close the wind whooshes inside and stings my eyes.

One of Badger's men stands there. "Here you are. Been looking for you all over. Badger wants to talk."

I take off the compress I'm still holding to my eye, blinking rapidly as tears stream down my face. "What? Why? My fight is done."

"Only passing instructions, Dark Dancer. Go talk to the boss."

"One minute," Oshen cuts in. "Let me clean this up." He gives me a meaningful look, and I could drop to my knees in gratitude. He's bought me several precious minutes to collect myself before I leave.

Badger only sees fighters after the bouts to dismiss them— reprimand them. What did I do? He can't pin the man's death on me. And I had to kill the beast, or it would have taken me out. Badger can't hold my wages for that—the fighters won't stand for it. Even if it's just me.

I get to my feet, heading toward the guard, but hesitate at the turn of the hallway.

My eyes fall on a mural of the mythical Naag dragon that covers both sides of the wall. In the stories, the dragon is a serpentine creature with scales and spikes and fins and fangs. It guards a treasure in the ocean obsessively. Even in the mural, the ferocity in the creature's large black eyes is cruel.

Maybe it's a sign.

If Badger wants to reprimand me, I shouldn't give him the chance to. That's what Rivan would say if he were here.

I start to turn back just as the wage distributors enter the hallway. The messenger's eyebrows rise. "Fumes got your brain? It's that way."

Gritting my teeth, I stalk forward, passing the pointed gaze of the Naag dragon. Badger went all out when he began earning steady profits down in the pits thirty years ago. Building a whole network of offices and even residences for himself and his close people, safe from the storms around the sea and the ashen air.

At Badger's office door, flanked by two guards, I hesitate again.

His guards do not.

They open the door and shove me in.

THREE

I trip on the rug before steadying myself. I *always* trip over this thing. Any kind of negotiations fall flat when you're already starting from a humiliated position.

Badger, lounging on a stuffed armchair, one leg on the table, doesn't look up from whatever he's reading. It's probably nothing. He likes to make—or fake—-an impression. Although it's redundant. On an island full of miners greased with grime, orphans running around in the dust, beasts warring, he stands out with his fine-boned pale face. His deep red tunic is tailored to fit, and a single gold chain holds back his hair, the only sign of his caves full of silver.

Silver that keeps the Collector's men in his pocket. Silver that he's made from our blood.

My blood.

My burning eye.

I finally take off my helm. Of all the armor, the dragon helm is my one distinguishing feature. Sharp spikes rise at the top, the spine of the Naag dragon, sleek and reptilian in look; it's wicked when it cuts. It is painted the deep oiliness of tar—perfect for the Dark Dancer. A gift from Badger when I won my tenth bout at twelve and earned the name, and a reminder that any status I have in here is his generosity.

How has it already been five years?

"Badger," I say finally. "You wanted to talk?"

He lifts a finger—*wait.*

Damn him.

Now I can't move until he tells me to. I can't speak until he lets me. I'm held hostage without even doing anything. *Stupid Krescent, so stupid.*

I continue fidgeting.

The room is lit with chandeliers. On the walls on either side of me, Badger has stuffed heads of a bixtor and a byotor—both flying amphibians—hanging like decorations. Beneath each are two rifles. Only Badger could afford Lander weaponry such as this, and only he would treat them so lightly.

"Darling," he says at last, putting the paper away, "have a seat."

I sit, one hand still holding the compress softly and the other clenched tight in my lap. My back doesn't touch the chair. My right foot refuses to stop bouncing. Badger, on the contrary, sits calm and collected. He leans back in his chair, hands locked behind his head. A picture of assurance, control. Badger must be almost fifty, but he doesn't look any older than late thirties. Whether that's due more to his wealth or the fact that everyone else on the island is constantly fighting to live—I can't say.

He smiles. But the coldness from the fight is concentrated in his eyes.

"At this rate, you won't have space on your body to keep the count." He glances at my wrist. The new puncture on my skin to remind myself what I'm doing here, what my freedom costs.

"You've come a long way from the day you stumbled in here for the first time." Neither of us could forget that day, when I, a skinny

14

eleven-year-old, refused to leave his door even when his henchmen threatened me.

Those days, I was always hungry, looking for ways to earn something—anything. I heard you could get not just the scrips that only work on this island but actual silver at Badger's pits. Money that's used on *other* places. The nine other Islands of Ophir that could mean freedom. If I had enough silver, I could escape this forsaken, ugly prison and find a life elsewhere.

A life where no one knows who I am and what my parents did.

The sound of Chandrabad was sugar sweet. Most people on that island are academics, and even the Renters, the lower-caste people like the miners here, have a better life than anywhere else. I could live an anonymous life, where no one would pry into my past.

But Chandrabad is not easy to get to.

I would need silver that only these pits could give me.

Nobody thought I'd survive my first match.

Everyone underestimated me. Most of them are out of a lot of scrips now. And I'm still here.

"Not long enough," I say finally.

"Still dreaming of leaving the island?" Badger raises a brow. "Your boy will go with you?"

I choke, something kicking my stomach from the insides with full force. "Rivan's not *my* boy. We're friends."

"Pity. I hoped he might be enough to keep you here." He shrugs. "You could make a fortune, you know. One day, someday, the pit will need someone else at its head."

For a moment, I gape at him. He can't be suggesting what I think he is. I've had enough dealings with him to know this is bait. If I'm aiming for his fortune, I'm a danger that needs to be eliminated.

"Getting away from this place is all I want," I repeat calmly.

"But you need to get out of your debts first."

"Yes." Or I will never find any peace. I will always be a fugitive, hiding wherever I go.

"Well, killing my expensive new investment wasn't the best way to clear your debts now, was it?"

A claw ticks down my spine. "What else was I supposed to do during a fight, Badger?"

I can *read* his mind now. He probably expected the stygic to finish me off once and for all. No more payment in silver that I ask for, unlike the others who are happy with scrips. No more people betting on me, and Badger forced to give away a larger share every time I fight. And no more hatred toward Badger's men from those who remember my parents for employing me.

"Of course, darling, I'm merely saying that things around here cost." He inhales deeply. "I'd hate for something to go wrong with money. You know what people can do over a single scrip. Would hate to see you in the mines or worse."

My toes curl in my boots. If I don't appease him right now, he could very well act on his threat. Throw me out so I have nowhere else to go but the mines, where one slip could mean I'm hounded and killed. Or get me jailed—the Collector's jail is simply renamed enslavement.

"I don't want to work in the mines, Badger," I say, as softly as I can. Being down there in the darkness, no way out, would ruin me before anyone even remembered whose daughter I was.

Badger puts his feet down and leans forward, hands locked. There's a glint in his cold eyes. My stomach churns at the sight of it.

Two floors below, an after-hours battle between creatures only has the late crowd roaring with frenzy. Badger's smile at the sound is imperceptible. But I know the power that courses through his veins at the reminder that within these walls, he owns blood and flesh of not just us pathetic humans but the beasts whose primal powers rule the giant seas.

It gives him the illusion that he could take on the whole Council of Ophir, the Lander leaders who decided our fate centuries ago.

Despite myself, I wince.

"You're tense," he chuckles. "What is it? The man who died? Don't take his death personally, darling. After all, you didn't plan it, unlike your parents."

Blood rushes to my head so fast I lose my remaining vision for a moment. Fuck him. *Fuck him*. I force myself to stay steady. Take a deep breath and swallow my words. He will not get the reaction he wants so badly.

"I have an offer for you, to make up for the loss tonight faster."

I wait for him to continue, my knuckles tight.

"Lose the next match."

I blink.

"After today, even I'd bet on you."

So when I lose the next match, all the money the spectators bet on me will go to Badger. That's how this works. Why should it matter to me how Badger gets his money? My only concern is my wages. No—not the only.

"They will hate me if I'm the one who makes them lose the money..."

"It will certainly help me cover my losses faster. Plus, instead of the fight money, you can get a cut. A small one, but more than enough."

It's a fair offer coming from him. Which is why a shiver scuttles through my body. I've fought in Badger's pits for far too long to not know he's saying one thing and thinking another.

"Badger, thank you for the offer," I say. "But I don't think it's a good idea for me to upset the audience."

"No trust in some good faith, then?"

Goose bumps prick my arms. "You let me fight here when I had nowhere to go. I trust you." *Never*. Badger has no one's interest at

17

heart save himself. Only reason he let me fight was because he'd seen how I fought a night beast outside his doors, how entertained his men seemed. How could he let a show go on for free? He deals in blood and tears, and they have a cost.

"I just think it's a bad time right after the stygic and the quake. Maybe there will be something else I can do to cover the loss."

Badger sighs. He leans back in the chair, hands placed at the edge of the table. "Sleep on it, sweetheart. And don't forget to take your wages for tonight before you leave." He gives me a razor-sharp smile, and with a quick wave, he dismisses me as swiftly as swatting a fly.

An abrupt silence greets me back at the fighters' room. Of course they must have heard Badger called me. So they're all still here, gossiping and theorizing. Not surprising—he rarely interacts with fighters alone. The others barely get glimpses of the owner of the pits, and only during the fights when he announces them.

"Getting increased pay, Dark Loser?" Yara calls. Ansh looms next to her, watching me.

The mood in the room is jittery. Some of them are looking for a fight, probably hating that I beat the stygic and not them, that I stole a moment of glory, or they are disappointed the quake didn't take me out too. Or whatever made-up reason they've come up with. At the end of the day, I have won every fight I've been in—I have a moniker people recognize me by. I get paid half in silver.

They hate that it's me at the top, not one of them. It's incredible that they think they deserve it, having done nothing to earn it. I pay in blood—I carry it with me.

"Between the two of us, only one is a loser, and it's not me."

"So what did he want?" Yara says without missing a beat.

"Just wanted to see how I'm doing after the venom attack."

I start walking, refusing to give them another chance to accost me. Their whispers are barely contained, their eyes digging at my back.

18

"Liar," someone hisses.

"I don't need to lie," I snap. "If you people did half of what I do in the pits, maybe you wouldn't be whining out here."

It's a moonless night, and streetlights are too good for this side of town. Perfect for the night beasts on their hunt, so I slip out my dispeller and shake the glass orb carefully. The liquid metal shimmers softly, casting a light. The feeling that someone is watching me creeps up on me. I turn, stare down the empty, rocky path. Then I finally head home.

The other fighters want me to explain, step by step, how to make Badger give them higher wages. As they always have for years now. As if I have anything to say. If I knew how to, would I still be here getting venomous fumes in my eyes? The only reason he agreed for silver in the first place is because I'm his best fighter.

I resist rubbing my eyes, blinking rapidly as tears gather at the corners. Every inch of my body hurts from today's fight. The stygic was no joke. I couldn't fight a toddler right now. I only drag myself forward one step at a time.

The fang-like spires of rock jutting out of the ground form a narrow, crooked path. Toward the left, the ground falls away sharply, revealing the basalt columns barring us on the island. Beyond, the sea is still tumultuous, drinking in any sound my feet make.

Slowly, by memory, I make my way to the eastern slum in the narrow corner where Kar Atish's land turns abruptly to the west. Most of the slum is either niches carved into the outer side of the cliff or spires around which people tie tents, teetering on the edge so as to not block the Landers' way when they travel. It's the best we have, being nonminers, to protect ourselves from the toxic air and the metallic rain that leaves bare skins raw and red in just a few hours.

Beyond the mountains and the underground river of lava called the Redwater, the westernmost side of Kar Atish belongs to the

Collector. Only the Council officers and Landers posted on the island live at the Collector's compound, although the building is so large we could all fit inside. But it's the refinery that's the biggest structure on the island. On the edge toward the north, next to the harbor. That's where the generational miners have houses too, stone quarters, stacked like dead fish together.

That's where I lived, once, when my parents were alive.

Suddenly, there's a shift in the smoky air.

I'm not alone out here. My steps slow. The dark to the right of me is impenetrable. Not even the red-eye glint of the raath, a kind of night beast that are always waiting to catch their prey off guard.

I blink, trying to make my vision clearer, but the veil of distortion has yet to dissipate. Panic surges in my throat. What if a creature from the sea has made its way up here? I'm in no condition to fight.

Pebbles clatter at my back.

I whirl. Someone stands a hand away from me.

"Yara?" I say, exhaling. "Unless you're going to pay me, I'm not telling you any secrets about seducing Badger." Her brother and their friend flank her.

Instead of answering, she lunges at me. I stumble, trying to hold my balance, but fall to the ground. The dispeller spins from my hand, rattling as it goes, its faint light circling in the dark with the motion.

I push myself up on my elbows. Pain screams along my arms, the wounds from the pit fight bleeding again. My vision, already unclear, doubles. "What the hell—"

A kick to my jaw. I land flat on my back. My mind sways, unable to make up or down. I have to fight back. I scramble—or try. My body groans with pain and panic.

"You think you're better than us, don't you?" says Ansh.

They hate you, my mind says, delirious, as my vision melts into a hexagonal shape. Six Yara and six Ansh.

"Hey!" comes a familiar voice.

"It's him." Ansh swears. "Let's go." He reaches down and snatches my packet of today's wages. Then his strong fist connects with my face. I slam to the ground face-first this time. And everything vanishes.

FOUR

I t's the good dream, again, after weeks.

There's the sun, a strangely pleasant sensation, like on rare days when the sea storms are calm and there's no rain. And without the heat that burns through my skin. I'm not on Kar Atish, but a flat, plain island surrounded by a sea that murmurs softly. Rivan and I, the children that we were, chasing one another all over the beach. The water rushes under our feet. I fall down, and he collapses beside me, laughing. The sea washes over us gently, and we stare at the sky. Nothing hurts us.

There's no one else on the island, after all.

Just me and him.

No debts, no fights, no blood, no one to hide from. Nothing to run from.

Then he gets up, looks at me with softness in his eyes, but his face is contorted with worry. He's frightened. I want to ask him what's wrong. He slips an arm around me. "Kress," he says. Then urgently, "Krescent. You have to wake up now, please."

The sound of his voice registers finally. He doesn't sound like the child in my dreams. Above us, there's no sky but a dull stone roof cast with shadows. It reminds me of when he first found me—sleeping in the niche next to his house three weeks after my parents died, and even with his brothers joking about getting a new pet, he never indulged them. He has been my friend since. He has always managed to pull me out of any misery.

But the pain exploding in my head is too much even for him.

"Rivan?" Saying his name hammers my jaw.

"Thank the ocean. Tell me what hurts."

As the room settles into focus, I feel his arms around me. And his warmth as I lie cradled against him on the floor. Rivan's clothes are soaked in blood too. I'm at his house. In the corner, his brothers are watching us with concern—very uncharacteristic for both of them.

"You look like hell," says Mayven, the youngest of the three brothers. The rings in his brows glint even in the low light. I'm glad for that tiny detail, because it helps me orient myself.

"Still better than you, I think." My voice cracks. The side of my face stings. Ansh kicked me, I remember now, and I scraped my face on the stone path. I feel for my ribs. A miracle, I think as I press my hand to my chest, my stomach. I was still wearing my armor when I left the pits, too tired to take it off. It might have saved my life.

"Nothing's broken," I murmur. "But it hurts." A shudder racks my body at the reminder of the hatred in Yara's and Ansh's eyes. "What happened?"

"Hadn't seen you all day, so I thought I'd check on you," Rivan says. "Glad I did." His arm tightens around my shoulder, and I gasp.

"You're made of stronger stuff than those cowards," says Ashvin. He scratches his brow with a thumb, dispelling the frown. He's older than Rivan and me only by a year, and yet he acts like he's responsible for the entire world.

"I bet being beaten up every day helped," Mayven says.

"Shut up, May," Rivan snaps. He turns to me. "You did bleed a lot." He shakes his head and studies the side of my face, my arm where the entire fabric is wetly red and bunched up, exposing wounded skin beneath. "But he's right. You'll be fine."

I sit up and almost fall back. Rivan's palm catches my head immediately. "Easy."

Then, my memory still rattling, I cry, "They took my money." A steel-heavy ache thumps inside my skull. My breaths come up short, painful in my lungs, like every shot of air is an arrow. "Rivan. I can't—the deadline—"

"Kress," Rivan says sharply. "Stop. Don't worry about it right now."

But I want to argue. How can I not worry? I have to go get it back. I have to fix myself.

"I want to get rid of"—I look down at my clothes wet with blood— "all this."

Rivan brings me to the bath, runs hot water, and leaves to get a change of clothes. The bathroom is a small space at the back of the room, a makeshift bath, no light save a candle lit when someone's here. No less than a luxury for people like me with barely a spit on this island to call home. I strip—or try to. Every movement sends ripples of ache through me. Taking off the chain mail alone is exhausting. My fingers start shaking, then my hands. The bones inside are jelly, wobbling. Tears spilling down my bloody face, I tear at my clothes. The wet patches of fabric collect in a heap on the floor, uncaring, unimpressed.

I lower myself into the warm water. Push my hair out of my eyes and hold my hands in front of me as the warmth sinks into me. Drops of blood drip into the water from my hair. Any energy I had deflates. I pull my knees to my chest and sit there in the candlelight, staring at my shivering fingers above my knees, sticky with blood.

I have been injured in fights before. Broken ribs, broken fingers. The time I thought my left leg would have to be amputated. None of those times left me feeling like this though.

My hands shake, refusing to be still. The water is entirely red now. I know I should move, wipe myself, put on some medicine and bandages, but my body stays exactly as it is. Curled into itself. Bearing the pain as it continues to spread. Textureless, transparent, nothing at all. If I sank beneath the water, what would happen? Would the pain go away? I am lulled by the warm waves.

"Kress?" Rivan knocks on the door, which is not a real door, just a corrugated steel sheet propped upright and a flat piece of rock tucked beneath to indicate when someone's inside.

The candle flickers, rippling the shadows.

The knock comes again.

"Answer me, Kress."

In my mind, I do. But I can't open my mouth.

"I'm coming in."

The door creaks further, and Rivan says nothing for a while. He stays at the threshold. An eternity sways from one to another before his shadow takes one step forward, merging into mine. I hear him inhale deeply. He gets inside the bathroom, adjusting the door back, and puts the clothes beside the sink. Then he sits next to me, outside the tub.

"Kress," he says softly.

A tear trails down my face. My eyes stay locked on my fingers, wrinkly from the bath, as I scratch at the skin, trying to scrape the blood off, which just makes more of it trickle through.

Rivan catches my fingers. He picks up the washcloth and dips it in the water. Gently, so gently, he rubs it across my hands. A shudder crawls ant-like on my body. He pats the cloth down my shoulder. The stinging increases. So does my fidgeting. I curl and uncurl my toes under the water. Rivan doesn't speak, doesn't tell me to sit still, and slowly, the water in the bath turns even darker.

He drips water through my hair, cleaning it off, untangling the knots. As if we're in my dream, just the two of us, and I have nothing to be afraid of. He's so gentle that it's agonizing. I'm a kicked foal, a stray, with nowhere to go unless this kind boy shows me mercy. I'm grateful for him, yet the feeling leaves me gaunt. If I had more silver, like Badger, I could be strong like him too. No one could challenge my strength. The water ripples around me.

This is karma for my parents, just like everything else in my life.

"Stop," says Rivan sharply. "You're not your parents."

I look at him, startled. Did I say that out loud?

"You are your own person. Karma is not real. This anger toward yourself is not going to save you."

There's no pity in his eyes, like I thought, like I see in his brothers sometimes, which is why I can sit here, naked, and still not feel ashamed. But even he doesn't truly understand the weight of what it means to have claws digging in your bones.

He has always hated that I fight in the pits, but it isn't his life on the line every month. It isn't his dream to collect enough money to get the *hell* off this cindered island.

Rivan gets up on his knees and puts an arm around me.

He lets me cry until I've run out of tears.

"I got you fresh clothes," he says, looking back at the sink once. I nod, and when I don't move, he sighs and gets up. "We need to dress your wounds too. Come out soon."

As he leaves, I push back against the stone wall. The rippling of the water is loud this time, as if the whole ocean outside moves with me. My fingers are clean, but there's some dried blood under the nails. I push the nail of my left thumb under the nail of my right thumb and dig the flakes out. Just like I hunted for scraps in garbage dumps.

This is what I have without the strength and without the silver—this miserable life of clawing my way out of the darkness toward light, only to find emptiness and another long tunnel. And these wretches think they can steal from me? Take what is mine, what I fought for, bled for?

I need to get the money back. Make up for the loss and insure myself against something like this happening again. Prove to them that they will not throw me into any darkness.

My stomach clenches tight. Everything I want has only one answer. Silver. And there's no other way to get that silver on this island except for the pits. No other way but for Badger's offer.

I'll have to lose my next fight.

FIVE

A week later, I walk back to the pits over broken paths waiting to catch ankles in their mouths. The dark red sheen of the setting sun casts a bloody drape on every steep slope. But I have to be early—get in, fight, get out. Before Rivan's day shift ends. I don't want to do things behind his back, but he knows how badly I was hurt, so he would have questions. Questions I don't want to answer.

My face is still darkened with bruises, body aching in protest, as if it knows what I'm about to put it through.

It's perfect, though, and believable. If I'm hurt already, nobody will wonder why I lost. I lower my helm, concealing my face. The cold metal smell sinks into my skin, fortifying me.

From the corner where I stand, the empty prep room pans out in a triangle, lit at the center by a single dim starfish, encased in a lamp with dusty glass, casting oily darkness everywhere else. The crowd outside barrels on, despite the death of that man just a few days ago, cheering wildly as the night's inaugural beast on beast fight proceeds, their own violent rhythm immunizing them against the blood and death. Badger's arena is the chosen narcotic on this island.

And if I'm contributing to it, well, I wouldn't be here for long now.

By the time the prep room starts filling, I can hear the confused mutterings in the air.

I have the room's attention.

They would have liked today to themselves. They are angry I'm back.

It's not easy to get into these pits. Even with the wins, the battles are deadly. But people caught inside die like tadpoles stomped on, so there's never a lack of fighters either. Even when most fighters are too young, too old. Scattered about, talking to others or themselves, sullenly wondering—too late—if the extra coin is worth their lives.

The new ones must be strategizing.

It's a waste of time. Agility, speed, even tricks—they work against other humans. But not the monsters that fight in this pit. You need more than physical ability.

You need luck.

Across from me, Yara and Ansh watch me like raptors. I wave at them, just to piss them off, and lean against the door, silencing my hiss of pain. A picture of unconcern. If anything, it renders them unable to gloat at my expense. No one gets the best of me—*no one*.

And today is not the day I die.

Just lose.

The evening promises a spectacle, whether I came or not, from the buzzing conversation. Badger, it seems, has grown a penchant to keep things interesting. He used to let us fight raptors and giant crabs and feathery stone lizards, but the people have gotten bored of death playing the same old cards. They've been getting enough death in the mines lately. So, they come here for the mind-numbing entertainment that promises blood where they're in control and not the victims.

It's booming business.

I already have my number ready—first, like usual, unlike the last turn I had here. It gives the spectators no time to speculate, but more scrips to bet. Coming right out of their day shifts, it's the high of watching someone else suffer that these people bet on. None of them know their meager scrips will be stolen right out of their hands tonight.

"You ready?" calls the bouncer.

For a moment, I think of the quake. Since the last time, there have been two more shudders, each lasting only seconds but terrorizing nonetheless. Some say that we have angered the island by digging in the mines deeper than we should. Not that the Collector would ever share that opinion.

What if we get hit by another when I'm in the pit again?

But what else can I do?

I swallow my misgivings and adjust my armor. Stepping into the ward toward the pit, I move my fingers in sharp motions, urging the blood flow, reassuring myself of the chain mail wrapped around the backs of my hands. My breastplate is in place, my throwing knives, and my helm too. This isn't my first fight, but this is one where my life might depend on the outcome. The thought has my heart skittish in its small cage. I hop on the spot. Open and close my fists. Bend my leg and pull at my foot.

"Never seen you so nervous," the doorman says. He chews a straw, eyeing me curiously.

Inside the pit the crowd jostles, yelling and laughing.

"Got hurt bad last time," I say, stretching my arms over my head.

"So why you back here so soon?"

"Why is anyone?"

"Well," he sneers, "have fun in there, Dark Dancer."

The roar of the crowd echoes inside my skull. The lights glare down harshly, and for a moment, I lose my footing as the door groans shut behind me. I steady myself just as the creature's gates open. Brace for whatever monstrosity I'm about to lose to.

It's a lizard—a giant dusty blue lizard with a flat face and a huge forward-leaning mouth, standing on four legs that are half my height. I gape at it, mouth slack. How will I lose to *this*? This ridiculous-looking soft creature?

Confusion ripples across the pit. Murmurs of annoyance. Until Badger's voice booms across the cavernous hall. "You think you know this creature? The sersei may look one way but—"

The lizard's collar blinks red and it shrieks. Badger's collars are notorious; green as they drip sedatives into the creature's veins to calm them and red when jolting them with electricity to make them aggressive. The lizard's giant three-forked tail lashes at the walls of the pit, sending a shudder throughout. The tail slams down on the ground, then rises in attention, completely at odds with the liquid black eyes.

Where in *hell* is Badger bringing these venom-tailed creatures from?

"Are you ready for another performance from our Dark Dancer?"

I make the blades dance in the air before gripping them tight and bending my knees. I am turned to steel. Applause rings through the pit at the display, hoots and shouts and laughter. The sersei lizard stumbles, looks around—

And locks eyes with me.

A skittering noise fills the pit, low-pitched and cantankerous. A thousand tiny insects crawling in my ear. I shake my head. The sersei chirps, this time higher, but stays. A murmur of *"Boo!"* sweeps through the crowd. Damn it, I'll have to provoke this creature. At least a few good rounds before I lose—or the crowd will completely turn on me.

I adjust my knives. And sweep to my side. The sersei skitters, mirroring me, and we end up across from one another yet again.

"Fight it!" someone yells. The audience roars, clapping and thumping. This is good because it startles the sersei. It hisses and raises its tail higher, alert.

Good girl.

The sersei leaps and slashes at me. I duck and spin, one foot rooted in place. The tail comes at me, and I block it with the hard side of my knife. A terrible, frenzied scream unleashes from the sersei as it twirls in the air, gnashing its short, sharp fangs.

The mood of the crowd has changed as well. The annoyed half-heartedness has given way to cheers of "Go, Dark Dancer!" and hoots and raining scrips into the betting bowls—just the way Badger likes things in the pit. It brings a wicked smile to me. Round one is mine.

The sersei hisses, but still with uncertainty. As if trying to scare me away without a fight. It skitters but stops a good distance away. Then it leaps again, quick and sharp, and I roll away from its path. My knife screeches against the wall of the pit as I extend a hand to stop myself from slamming into it.

Behind me, the lizard falls flat on the ground and scrambles in desperation. It finally extends its talons. Bares those sharp fangs. And unleashes an infernal scream.

The hair on the back of my neck stands. I hadn't expected the soft-looking creature capable of such a sound. I breathe deeply, tighten my grip on my knives. A small, star-shaped pain twinges in my lower back. *Not now.* I need to up my fight so I don't wind up dead—or worse, bore the spectators.

The sersei springs, and I have no way out except backing up. I shriek as I push against the wall and leap to the ledge jutting out midway to the seats. The sersei's tail sharpens. It snaps, knocking me off my feet. My back hits the spiked wood of the ledge, and a scream tears from my throat as I go tumbling down. I grab at the wall, losing my knives in the process. And suddenly I'm hanging from the ledge totally exposed. The rugged splinters of the wood dig into my palm. My knives scatter on the ground, and the sersei swipes a padded claw at them. They clang against the wall across the pit. Way out of my reach.

The sersei snarls below, its big, black eyes fixed on me. All around us, the raucous cheers fade, breaths held, awaiting what happens next. The air itself slows, filling with the wet growls of the lizard. My fingers begin to slip.

I tighten my hold, gasping, and glance up. Badger sits in the balcony, hands relaxed on the arms of his chair, one leg pulled up on the knee of the other. The small red lamp at his back lights a bloody halo around him. A king, watching over his kingdom.

I drag myself up again. Each breath a line of fire, burning red from the halo around Badger. I pull out the throwing stars from the side of my belt.

The sersei stands still, eyes focused on me. One throw and I could blind it. *How would you like that?* I remember the venom from the fight last week, and my eye twitches.

The sersei puffs itself up, readying for an attack. This bout needs to be over now. If I keep fighting this creature—or dodging it, more like—I'm bound to injure it gravely. Not sure Badger would like that after his precious stygic. The fighters' lives aren't important here; the whims of the boss are.

I throw a star to the right. The sersei leaps after it—and I have my window. I drop to the ground, firm on my feet, ignoring the shooting pain. But the sersei changes direction midway and charges back at me. I swing out of its way. The wall shakes with the impact of the lizard's head. Cries break out over us. But I'm not out of harm—the sersei's tail comes straight at me and pins me against the wall.

I struggle against the grip. It's too heavy. Any second, the lizard could turn its fangs to me. Caution wars with my survival instinct—and loses. I lock my legs around the tail, pinning its venom shooters together. A star flies out of my hand and catches the side of the sersei's face.

The crowd erupts in roars.

The sersei screeches. Tries to slam me off itself. I'm less a dancer, more a parasite clinging to its scales. My hands are beginning to get numb with the pain. We go in circles, my head slamming against the ground, the walls, and finally—my fingers slip. I tumble down the pit, and before I can get my bearings, the sersei jumps on to me.

My fingers catch its jaw. Wet flesh and fangs sink into my hands. The creature scratches down my skin, slashing its tail. And forces its head down. Its eyes are a pool of black. Panic and fear making it wild. I can't hold it back. If I don't yield now, I'll be dead. But if I yield—*no, I have to*. That's what I was building toward. The sersei is just a creature; it doesn't know what else to do but fight. It has nothing personal against me. And it's scared—this fight is square. If I hadn't pulled back in the beginning, I'd have won easily. But I had to give the creature chance to dominate. I had to—*say the words, damn it*.

"*Yield*," I shout, and the sound clangs in my skull. "*I yield*."

The sersei's collar goes from red to green. For a moment, its liquid eyes enlarge, looking at me with a sudden fear. A small whimper cuts off in the middle as the collar does its work, and the creature falls to its sides, unconscious.

I roll on my stomach, deathly pain pounding in my muscles, and try to get up. My left hand gives way. I fall flat on my mouth, jarring my teeth. Granules of sand plume with the impact, getting into my eyes and nose. Giving this match away was my choice, but now it's real, and my thoughts are careening everywhere. What am

I supposed to do now? I've never yielded before. What if the crowd is suspicious?

I sit half up, breathing heavily. It's then, the pain pulsing and rearing, that I register the silence in the pit. The absence of cheers or boos, the cursing, the foot tapping. The annoyance and anger that I'm expecting.

Instead, what comes is worse.

The hissing. It starts somewhere to the left. Sweeps through the first row, then picks up across the pit. A ghostly wind churning into a windstorm. They're hissing at me. An old tradition from the days of fishermen when the pit fighting took place near the seas, and the losers were tossed into the water to be at the mercy of the creatures who lived there. These people are not just angry; they want me erased from this fighting pit. Teeth bared, eyes raging, the spectators take on the form of a monster.

My worst fear is realized.

Badger sits still, crowned in the red light, and watches me with the eyes of a predator having finally caught its prey.

SIX

You promised!"

I stomp across the room, coming to a stop an inch from Badger. I know what I look like: filthy and battered, lip split, bruises down my face, the pit's dirt tangled in my hair. He doesn't flinch. Only stares me down, bored, leaning back on the table.

"I *promised* nothing," he drawls. "I offered you a deal."

He turns his back on me and rounds the table. Sits down in his grand chair. The ease of the movement is a giveaway that he doesn't care what I have to say or do. His whims. Always.

My heart hammers in my throat.

"Why are you doing this?" My gaze flicks to the bundle of silver on his table. What was supposed to be my cut from the fight. It's no longer mine to take—and Badger is banning me from the pits. The thought hasn't even settled in my head. Everything is a whorl of claws and fangs and Badger's voice, echoing through a fog.

"You heard them," he says. "I will not risk our whole audience for you."

I stare at Badger. At his nonchalance, at the calculated look in his eyes, an inch from true, dark malice. He's a snake ready to strike.

"That audience has grown *because* of me," I snap. "I'm your best fighter."

"You are no one," he says, cruelty flecked in every word. "My pits existed before you, and they will long after you're gone. I *owe* you nothing."

There's a flatness to his eyes that tells me he's not changing his mind. The same feeling as from the night of the red stygic crawls down my neck. He wants me gone. But it doesn't make sense. Have I offended him? I haven't seen him for months. All I do is fight and leave. The only thing I can think of is my winning. How can he be so threatened? Disgust arises in me, meeting the callousness in him.

"Besides, once the call comes from them"—he nods his head toward the door, indicating the hissing spectators—"I will not stand in their way."

Six years of my blood spilled in these pits, and this is what he repays me with. A sickening crunch rumbles in my head. Trying to get a red stygic to kill me, then luring me to *this* with silver. Badger is nothing but a sick, narcissistic man who couldn't bear me not subjugating to his wishes.

Understanding floods me.

"You weasel," I whisper. "You put your men in the audience today, didn't you? You had them start the ancient call."

"You're drunk on fighting and imagining things, Krescent," he says in his infuriating drawl. "Fighting down here changes nothing for you on the island above."

"That's why I want to leave!"

He flourishes his hands. "Well, then. Here's your chance."

I see blinding red, unable to speak, to even scream.

At the door, I pause and look back. This man, who rules the world below like those foreigners rule us above, has ruined my chances at a better life. And I hate him. "You can bribe his men to look away all you want, but I wonder how long you would keep this kingdom if the Collector himself knew what was going on down here."

Without waiting for a reply, I slam the door behind me.

You are no one. Badger's voice haunts me.

Another smaller quake had the ground swaying just after I left, tumbling rocks off the spires and blocking the closest path to the eastern slum, forcing me to double back and go...nowhere.

Which is why I find myself climbing up the toothy hills near the mines, dangerous in the slick rain. But I don't care. Anything to take my mind off wanting to wrap my hands around Badger's throat.

The lights from the mines cast a stronger redness here, unnaturally diabolical. But it's a familiar place. A few years ago, Rivan and his brothers found a tiny cradle atop the tallest hill. They sometimes spend their rare off days here, hidden from the island's constant cacophony. Often, Rivan invites me, much to May's annoyance.

From the top, I can pinpoint the exact little stone house I once shared with my parents. It sits between the countless other identical houses, little matchboxes carved out of stone for the mine laborers, but my parents had painted a side of it seaweed green—my favorite color. It is long faded under the harsh dust from the mines, but the strip of paint on the plain stones still stands out.

I pull out my knives.

If my mother were here, she would be hysterical.

But, well, she *isn't* here.

Fire crackles in my blood. Burning me.

The knives are cold in my hand. I clutch them tighter. And slash at the air and the rain. Again and again. I hurt so many creatures. Maimed and killed. I am uniquely cut out for this because I know them well. I spent much time as a child at the shoreline watching them. Observing them, learning their habits. Their weaknesses. Not so I could kill them. It wasn't what I wanted—but I *had* to.

I would make up for it somewhere, somehow. That's what I always thought. But now? All that blood, for this—to be thrown out at someone's whims? Alone in the red night, I scream and hack and pour all my fury into the emptiness. I'm a fighter. I *kill* despite myself. I will not go down so easily.

Sweat rivers down my back, merged with the rain and draining onto the rocks below. I keep slashing. Twirling and throwing the blades, except the dagger I always keep close—the katar that belonged to my father. Then the shooting stars. If I have to stay here all night to get this anger out, I will. But I won't let that smug-faced son of a bitch make a fool out of me. He's goading me so I make another mistake, so he can ruin whatever life I have left.

He can't.

Even if he already has. I have no money—and the deadline for this week's installment is tomorrow. *No*, I correct myself, *later today*.

What will I do now? The mines won't take me. The Collector's compound won't employ me as long as I have debts to clear. Chandrabad is out of the question without silver. Even smugglers would think twice before taking me aboard.

What were my parents thinking without leaving me a contingency plan? Did they not care at all? Did they say something that I've forgotten? Have I suppressed my memories?

I fall down on my knees, into a puddle of dirty water that splashes against my skin, and scream viciously, without inhibition, until everything pours out of me.

Except—a pebble slips somewhere to my right, subdued in the

sound of the rain. It rolls down, tapping against the wet rocks on its way.

Blood rushes to my ears as I stand and whirl, holding the katar out. The blade stops an inch from Rivan's throat. He raises his hands, water sluicing down his face, his eyes serious but also amused.

"Why are you here?" I ask, keeping my katar steady, my voice hoarse from the screaming before. Raindrops get into my mouth, the taste coppery and full of this island.

He ducks fast and out of the way, appearing behind me. His hand shoots out, and I dodge, falling into the pattern we started ocean knows when. He hates that I fight at the pits and yet always helps me practice. Sometimes, like now, without my asking.

He swipes at the ground as I leap back with a snarl and says, "You didn't come home. You always come home after an arena fight."

No, I don't.

Instead of saying anything, I flip the katar in my left hand, feint, and go straight at him. He catches my wrist, and I end up slamming into his chest. We stand there, heaving from the exertion. And it's not like I haven't seen his pale gray eyes a thousand times before, but they shine in the ruddy light, and for an intense moment, all I can do is stare back into them like an idiot.

He raises a brow as if he knows I'm trying to deny it. That I go *home*.

I frown but concede. He's right. Without thinking about it, I've always stayed at his place on fight nights. It makes sense. He lives closer to the arena.

He makes me feel safe. I unconsciously look for him after the battles.

I push at him, twisting out of reach. For several moments, we're locked in a game of dodging and ducking and running. I'm the better fighter, but Rivan's instincts are as sharp as blades. He guesses my move. Feinting is no use with him. I *hate* it. Fighting him is not like fighting the creatures—they can't distract me like he can.

And it's probably my rising emotions that make me slip. He catches me at the last second, and I crash into him again, his arm around me and my back pressed against the solid wall of his chest. My hair comes loose in the drizzling rain, sticking to the side of my face.

"I heard what happened at the pit tonight," he says, his voice rumbling in his chest behind me. He doesn't let go, and I make no move to step away, our breaths heavy and synced together.

"It was nothing, a bit of misunderstanding."

Rivan leans forward and whispers in my ear, warmth brushing my neck, "Your voice is never so smooth as when you're lying."

I shove his arm away and turn to look at him square in the eye.

The air between us grows taut. The red lamplight glints off the chain he wears around his neck. A single stream of rain follows a path down the center of his throat and disappears into his wet shirt. He was so gentle with me when I was broken and beaten. There had never really been any lines between us, because they didn't seem necessary. We grew up together. It makes sense that he's the one to have wiped the blood off my back.

But now it feels like something happened. Something I'm only now realizing. A kind of blurring that makes looking at him, trying to lie to him, overwhelming.

I should tell him. That my debts have grown more heads than I can slay at a time. But then what? Trouble him as I am troubled?

No.

I swallow hard. Rivan doesn't press. He watches me closely for a moment, then slides an arm around me, this time holding me more softly. I feel the knot of anxiety in my stomach unraveling and the one around my heart rising.

"We'll figure it out," he says gently against the rain.

I want to believe it, but unless Badger lets me back in the pits, there *is* nothing to figure out. I'm unwanted in the mines. There's nowhere else to go. Nowhere but the Collector's office with empty hands.

It's because I know I can't change anything that I let myself sink against Rivan. I close my eyes and let the world fade away—before I face the wrath of this island.

SEVEN

The debt clearance office is located within the Collector's compound, on the far western end of the island, beyond the tallest mountain that divides the land in two. Which is why the very air seems different here. There's still dust grating against my face but no ashy taste in my mouth. And by the time I reach the compound after half a day of trekking, it's just a cool, blue breeze off the ocean that fills in my lungs with freshness that seems long forgotten on the other side of the island. It makes the tension in my muscles relax, even if I can't stop thinking about what I'm going to say when my turn comes.

As always, the queue is long, stretching onto the rocky edge of the dry, thorny forest across from the compound. People from all over the island arrive here every seventh day of the week and are robbed of whatever little they had managed to earn. Payday—to pay *them* for letting us live in our own homes, I suppose.

The difference between the townspeople and the regulators is as stark as sea and shore. The miners have suits made of material that keeps them somewhat protected in the mines, because the Collector and his men need people in working condition. The rest of us wear loose clothes patched together with discarded fabrics, mismatched blacks and grays, ugly but practical. But when we're here, at the debt office, we're no longer miners and nonminers—we're all Renters, the lower caste, the ones who work as the Landers see fit, live and breathe as they see fit. We queue down the corner, a single file, and are forbidden to venture outside this orbit.

The regulators wear their black-and-blue uniforms, tailored precisely, with badges of authority and sneers. They move around at will, take breaks when they want, and retire inside the compound, within their offices and sectors, all protected from the harsh sun behind thick walls of stone.

By late afternoon, I'm finally beneath the compound roof. Banners flutter in the fierce winds, a golden squid on a sea of blue-black. The man in front of me takes his scarf off and wipes his weathered brown face, hands shivering. Slowly the line moves forward, and it's his turn at the counter.

"No scrips," he whispers, as if a prayer.

"This is your second strike," the officer says, almost bored. "Well, the salts it is for you."

"Is there—" the man starts, his voice already defeated, then stops. He nods and takes the papers. The normality of this doesn't faze anyone, least of all the officer. You can go once without a payment, but the second time—the salt pans it is. Day and night, unpaid bonded labor, until your last breath. And salt for the Collector and his men and Landers everywhere else. Their food gets its taste from bonded labor.

It bothers no one.

A spasm careens through my body as I step to the counter.

"No scrips," I tell him. My voice is pinched. *You're okay today. You'll go back home today.* I clear my throat and repeat myself.

"First strike? It's your share plus ten percent for next time, get it?" The officer's face is thin, but he's well fed. Healthy hair and unscarred hands that start to mark the changes beside my name in his register. He stops. "Krescent Dune?"

An icy feeling creeps down my neck at the way he says it.

Someone in the line behind me murmurs, "Kinkiller."

Someone else joins in. For a moment, they forget where we all are, together at the mercy of the Landers, and remember only that I'm the daughter of my parents. The Kinkillers, miners who killed other miners. Blood rushes to my head as I adjust my scarf, hiding my face. They can't hurt me here—the Lander guards have guns and don't tolerate disorder—but you never know.

"She's still alive?" someone else asks, confused at my very existence.

Fear turns to roiling rage within me. And I'm glad the Landers are here all anew—not for myself but for these miners. If there were no checks, the ocean knows I'd have driven my claws into them. None of these people know what it took to keep myself alive.

None of them calling me Kinkiller would survive my life.

The pounding of my heart grows and grows, even louder as the counter window shuts down and a door opens somewhere at the back. The sharpness of my ever-present rage curls back into itself, fear rearing its head again. I take a wobbly step back. And two guards emerge with guns.

"Move," one of them says, pointing back where they came from.

"Why?" I dart my eyes around. The line behind me watches us, alert. Not because they *care* to intervene but out of curiosity. "It's only my first strike. I'm not going to the salt pans."

Their guns straighten. This time, both of them say in their cold voices, "Move."

It takes all of my strength not to give in to my instinct and run backward. The laws of the pits don't matter in the real world. If I run, I get shot. And the most important thing when you're fighting is to stay alive. And fight, sure. But *first* stay alive.

So, heart hammering in my throat, I take a step forward. It's not enough for the guards. They grab my arm and march me through the back door and into a room with walls of polished stone. There's a single window, set high above, and a plain desk. I'm shoved into the one small chair at the back of the room.

"Will you tell me what's going on?"

They don't answer. At least they don't tie me to the chair.

"No funny business," says the first guard, glaring, before they shut the door behind them.

Immediately, I get up and work my way around the walls. No other exit. Not even a crack in the walls. Just a claustrophobic space of gray stone and that single window.

What's going on? If they want to send me to the pans, the cart is right outside, crammed with the newly enslaved. *This makes no sense.* The window is high, but I might reach it if I stand on the desk. Will I get through it, though? It's narrow. And where would it open? What if there are guards?

The door slams open, and in walks—

"Badger?" I cry.

Behind him, someone else enters. An old man dressed in gray-greens. He holds himself upright, but the stoop in his stance is obvious as the banners rising above the Collector's compound. Pins clasped with gold chains dangle all over the front of his clothes, which reek of wealth and assurance.

I stare from him to Badger, unsure.

"Kress, meet the Collector," Badger says. "Sir, this is Krescent Dune."

Cold cuts through me. My first thought is that Badger is having me arrested.

But no more guards follow through. The Collector studies me

with his tired eyes, then moves to the desk. Contrasted by the light behind him, his face turns into craters and shadows. He doesn't smell of the metal that everyone on the island does. He smells antiseptically clean.

"Hmm," the man says, as if unconvinced of something.

Badger shuts the door and comes to stand next to the Collector. "As I told you, one of our finest. Actually, *the* finest. She defeated a half-grown scythe crab three years ago and has never lost a single match, including the ones with the red stygic and the sersei."

"Did she?" the Collector says in his dangerously calm voice. "Most impressive."

"I didn't," I burst out, my voice high-pitched and confused, "defeat the sersei."

Badger laughs shortly. "Oh, right. She did not." He turns to the Collector. "She did exactly what I asked. She threw the match knowing it might cost her a place in the pits."

I'm a fool to think the Collector wasn't aware of what's going on in his island.

"I vouch for her," Badger continues.

"Will someone tell me what's going on?" I say out of turn again, then add, "Please?"

This time, Badger remains quiet. He meets my eye and gestures for me to be quiet too.

The Collector inhales deeply. "Krescent Dune, it is a pleasure to make your acquaintance. Your feats are legendary among my people."

"My feats?"

"The scythe crab of course, but the one we most hear about is the win over the wyrm lizards, five at once." He shakes his head in disbelief. "That was a marvel. There was even a discussion if we should consider having the Dark Dancer on our security." He laughs as if it's the funniest thing he's ever said.

As if after killing two of the wyrm lizards, incapacitating the other three, I hadn't escaped the arena and vomited my guts out. As if I hadn't cried for days for what Badger was making me do by dangling silver in front of me.

The man continues in his labored, slow voice, "We also know about you and your parents. A tragedy for such a young family. Not to mention the heavy debt you now must pay."

If I'm in a heavy debt, it's only because of you.

"As Atlas Crear tells me, you would like to leave this island."

Atlas Crear? I raise a brow at Badger. He shrugs.

It takes a few seconds for me to realize the Collector was asking me a question, not stating the obvious. "I—yes."

"But it would certainly not be possible without all your debts cleared. The penalty for defaulting is, deservedly I would say, the firing squad."

Deservedly. That word catches my attention, and for a moment, I see nothing but the hard ridges of the mountains our people live on. What we *deserve* is safety and happiness and joy. But to this man, we're a means to an end, workers for his zargunine, and anything else must be discarded.

When our ancestors, the Empyrean Elders, were shipwrecked on the shores of these islands a thousand years ago in search of a better world, is this what they envisioned? People divided into castes, forced into degrees of purity of being human by virtue of the work they were forced to do?

People like this Collector handing out death to the rest of us as easily as sipping tea?

My hesitation and nerves steel behind the indignation.

"I'm sorry. Where are we going with this? If this is about my first strike, it's the law that first strikes are forgiven as long as I pay the second time. So what are we doing here?"

The Collector runs another critical eye over me. I try not to squirm. He glances at Badger and says, "I see what you mean, Crear."

Badger nods politely. He's dressed in a black jacket with gold lining, but otherwise, he carries none of his air of self-made royalty. His shine is subdued in front of the Collector on purpose.

"Your debts can be cleared, Krescent Dune," the Collector says. "You will be free to leave the island if you so wish."

The words take a moment to sink in. I look to Badger to see if this is his idea of a joke, but he looks back impassively.

When neither of them laughs, I make myself say the words. "Why would you clear my debts?"

"Have you heard of the Tarnak expedition?"

I frown. I have only a vague memory, mostly because I've *forced* myself to forget those expeditions inside the mines. Tarnak was the most recent expedition, half a year ago, fifth overall and only the second since my parents' death. The maps of the mines are incomplete, and on the Collector's insistence, parties keep going into the mines, mapping them out farther and farther, marking the location of the zargunine and other metals. Even though there's no particular need for this—the veins that are mined are still full and will be for centuries still—and the maps unrolled so far are so close to the surface they might as well just be the same damn mines.

Lander greed is a monster the rest of us can't begin to understand.

"Didn't they end up like the others as well?" Half the expedition members always vanish in thin air, and others, well, skeletons are often found when the mine work is expanded even a little. Skeletons lying in positions of terror, of *needing* to escape. Skeletons that are half-missing... An expedition into the mine has always meant signing up for death within the labyrinths below.

"Close, but not quite," the Collector says.

"What does that mean?"

"We are about to find out, which is where you come in."

My words spill out even as the realization comes in fits. "You mean—there's a chance someone from the Tarnak group is still alive down there? How? It has been half a year if I remember right."

"The increased geological activity has changed certain echoes, and we're hearing reports of voices down below. Human voices."

I fight the shiver running down my spine. "What do you want *me* to do about it?"

"If there's someone alive, we need them back. Not only to save them but to find out what they have seen. The mines go much deeper than any of us can fathom, Miss Dune," the Collector says reverently. "What the lowest deeps hold, I can only imagine. Creatures of the dark that no one on this island could face. No one except you."

I stammer, "There are…others. Surely, Landers must have better people."

"You have a history we have followed closely. Daughter of Kinkillers, a survivor against all odds on an island of blood and storm." The Collector looks me up and down. "What makes you different is your undaunted heart."

I stare at the man.

"Accompany the party I have prepared to retrieve any survivors, keep them safe from these creatures, and the freedom you want so dearly is yours, Krescent Dune."

The door has barely shut behind the Collector when I turn to Badger. "Tell me the truth. What does he want?"

Badger raises a brow. In the second it takes for me to step forward, his demeanor shifts, from the deferential performance to a king again. He rakes a hand through his hair, and his face becomes hard as stone once more.

"The truth is what you heard. You are to guard the company that will retrieve any survivors or any information as to what happens to these expeditions. No more is expected of you." His voice is steady and lazy at the same time, like it always is, but there's a spark in his eyes.

"Fine," I say. "What do *you* want? What do you gain out of this?"

Badger barks out a laughter. "I knew you were my best choice." He keeps his smirk on as he says, "What I want is for my arena to rule the world. And for that, what I need is creatures this world has never seen."

"The stygic isn't enough?"

"You defeated it spectacularly."

Cold grips my heart. "What are you planning?"

"The one hundred and fiftieth Glory Race at Sollonia starts in a day. No one from Kar Atish will ever make it, you know that?"

The Glory Race is a chariot tournament—with the beastly, vicious maristags. A game of death and luck bigger than even Badger's blood-stained dreams. It's held every four years and brings most islands to a standstill for an entire week until a champion is crowned and showered with gold. It is also a tournament only for Landers, something that Badger seems to have forgotten.

So I remind him, "None of us *can* make it."

"A Renter is one of the ten contenders this time."

That's news to me, but then, Kar Atish is as isolated as can be. It's the most distant post for Landers this far south, and only a handful of them stay here, only for supervising the mines. The other islands don't care about us—all they want are the shipments of metal and salt that we send them. News for us is already stale everywhere else.

"Do you know who?" I ask.

"One of the Hunters," Badger smirks. "Calling herself Koral of Sollonia."

I flinch. He says it like he believes in the perversity of considering the Hunters outcasts for their work, even though they're Renters like us too. It's another delicate game played by the Landers—provide the Hunters with more resources than the rest of us, and isolate them from their community, keeping them reliant on their work, until their own people forget that the division was the point. So they forget who the real monster is.

"Our island's blood and stone build their lands. Now imagine if the biggest spectacle across the Islands of Ophir is not in Sollonia but here, on Kar Atish." Badger's eyes are black flames. "Imagine when the only source of life is not the death grip of the mines. I could hold a massive spectacle. The best fighters, the most vicious creatures. It could draw real power to this island."

Carefully, I ask, "What do you want from me?"

"Go do what the Collector wants you to. Protect the company. And as you do, find me creatures no one has ever seen. Tell me what they are and where to find them. And I'll do the rest."

Of course he doesn't want people out of the mines out of the goodness of his heart. Trading death in the mines with death in his arena. For half a heartbeat, I want to slam his face into the desk behind him and tell him he can go drown in the ocean.

As if he reads it on my face, he comes to stand a hand away from me. His face is grim, cut with stone, and terrifyingly, his eyes refuse to blink. "There are two ways to get out of your debt, the salt pans or death. I have staked my reputation and goodwill with the Collector on a lifeline for you. A lifeline you would be foolish to ignore. *Are you foolish, Kress?*"

EIGHT

Y OU'RE CHEATING!" Mayven screeches so loud I startle in the bathroom, and the bandage slips from my hand.

The boys continue arguing outside.

"Rivan, you saw it, right?"

"It's two against three!" Ashvin shouts.

"I'm done with both of you," Rivan roars.

"Me too! The Shadefolk take you both!" Mayven yells.

They're playing Seep, a weird game about striking your opponent's cowries with your own and collecting points—I don't know. I never got the hang of it.

I squint as I pick the bandage back up. The lone candle is down to dregs, flickering dangerously. The wound on my left arm is healed, mostly, but it's best to avoid any friction. I can't recall if it's from the fights or from Yara and Ansh cornering me. What would it matter? All that matters is that I'm in the best possible condition in two days' time.

I sigh and sit back, staring at the mirror. Shadows of my injuries contrast the small white birthmark beneath my right eye sharply.

It's in the shape of a horizontal crescent moon, a cradle for my eye. That's what my parents named me after.

It's been hours since I said yes to Badger and the Collector, and I still cannot think about anything else. The Collector is insane to think anyone would be alive down there after all these months. But it's his money and resources to waste. Besides, guarding a company doesn't faze me—the very air of those mines is dead. There's nothing *to* protect anyone from. What bothers me is the darkness. Like stepping down the gullet of a human-devouring giant.

But I will bear it. For what comes after.

My freedom. From the soul-sucking debt, from the pits, from this damned island.

And it's this hope that might kill me. Too sudden, too dangerous, too much.

Which is why I haven't told Rivan yet.

"You know, if that bandage was one of your opponents, it'd be pulp by now, Dark Dancer."

Rivan stands leaning against the door, arms crossed. The low, orange-tinged light of the candle makes his mouth look red and raw. A sharp pang hits my stomach. I quickly look down and realize how tight I'm gripping the piece of bandage.

"And are *you* guys done beating one another to pulp over cowries?" I say, deflecting.

Rivan says nothing, only moves to stand near me, his leg touching my knee. Already he's taller than me, and I'm sitting, so he leans forward. So close. The collar of his shirt shifts, exposing the smooth brown expanse of muscled skin.

My mouth goes dry.

He takes the bandage from me and begins dressing the wound. The brush of his fingers on my arm leaves embers in its wake. My focus narrows to the pulse at the base of his throat. It quickens even as I'm watching it, matching my own. I tighten my fingers around the edge of the seat to prevent my hand from touching his skin. He takes the scissors to the bandage, eyes narrowed in concentration. His jaw hovers near my mouth, curls of hair loose below his ears. He loops an extra bandage, not saying a word.

"There, that's better." He turns to face me, the nearness of his jaw replaced by his lips.

I should shift back.

He meets my eye, smiles a devastating smile, and stands back up.

Heart hammering in my throat, I take my time to collect the discarded bandage. Throw it carefully in the trash. And stuff the first aid kit next to Ashvin's box of menstrual pads in the tiny shelf cut into the wall. The shelf overflows with med packs. The boys can go without food for days, but they always stock up on meds. Probably so they don't have to see another family member fester to death like they did with their mother…

The warm sensation spinning in my head hasn't subsided. I stand there, staring at the shelf. Why should I feel *this* weird around Rivan? I've known him for a long while now—we've always taken care of one another. Bandaged one another's wounds, held each other's hands while the other was sick, slept in the same bed and chased away bad dreams.

But perhaps that's why keeping secrets from him contrasts so starkly.

The feeling gets worse as Rivan makes me turn to look at him. He tucks a free lock of hair behind my ear, his fingers lingering on my skin for a touch too long and at the same time not. A casual, familiar gesture. Nothing out of the ordinary.

And yet.

"Are you okay, Kress?"

No, I'm not. I have the chance of a lifetime—I get to leave this island. Be free. It's the one thing I've wanted but I'm scared it will all go away.

That it was all just a mistake. And they want someone else. Someone better.

"Yeah, just hungry," I say. "Let's go eat something."

I can *taste* Rivan's disappointment as I hurry back into the room. The cowries are spilled everywhere—it's clear the loser definitely did not lose with grace. In the middle, Ashvin and Mayven sit cross-legged, a tiny bowl of fish curry and a short pile of flatbread next to them. Food for three people. Divided for four tonight. One of the many things I will repay them for, after.

Despite being the oldest and the youngest, respectively, Ashvin and Mayven resemble each other like twins might. The same brown hair and the slight bend to their noses, as opposed to Rivan's black wavy hair and eyes made of stormy gray gemstones.

As Rivan and I join them, Ashvin throws a bit of flatbread into the air, and Mayven catches it in his mouth. He chews it down and grins with self-satisfaction.

"One day, you're going to choke," Rivan says, settling down. "And I'm going to just sit and watch."

"Okay, Officer Rivan," retorts Mayven swiftly. Then he changes topics, something about the mines, his mouth half-full and his hands wildly gesticulating. The usual gossip about disgruntled miners, another attempt at organizing a rebellion despite people's hesitation. It's hard to keep up with him. But not for his brothers, who react together at the right time, even when Mayven barely keeps his rant from spilling everywhere like the cowries.

They always exist like this, move and bicker like this, different parts of the same body. I may have been invited into their home, maybe into their hearts too, but I can never be a part of them. I would unbalance them.

An hour later, after Ashvin and Mayven have gone to bed tired from their day shifts and Rivan gets ready to leave for his night at the mines, I find myself walking in circles outside. The street is narrow, doors cut into the blocks of stony hills, only two miles from the main quarry. Kar Atish is shaped like a hand joining into a shoulder. The hand works, with its mines and harbors, and at the joint, the tallest mountains and deepest craters divide it from the shoulder—where the Collector and his compound rest in easy air.

"Kress? What are you doing out here without light?"

Rivan shuts the door behind him and shakes his dispeller brighter. The sudden burst of color turning his black hair into gold will *never* get old.

Despite myself, I smile.

Rivan raises a brow.

He comes to lean next to me. "You know at some point you'll have to tell me what's going on with you."

I look at him, wondering why I haven't told him yet. I've tried—but every time, something keeps me from saying it. Rivan looks back at me, curiosity in his eyes, and I feel the space between us shifting.

A cowardly thought rises. Maybe I never tell him. I leave, get the job done, and just vanish off this island.

And then what? Rivan goes on with his life, mad at me, but maybe with time, he'll forget me. He'll work in the mines, find someone—

Why should it matter what he does with his life?

I wouldn't be here.

Might as well tell him.

"Badger—"

"What has he done *now*?"

"—and the Collector have offered me a job."

Somewhere down the narrow, rocky alley, another door opens. The night shift miners are moving out, conversations wafting in the air. A child screeches. A mother coos. The irascible scraping of metal tools begins getting louder.

And taking shelter behind the din, I tell Rivan about the rescue mission in the mines.

"So," he says carefully, "what did you say?"

"I'm leaving the morning after next."

"I don't understand. You get sick in the dark. You hate that place."

I hate this whole island. I close my eyes, breathing deeply, and open them again. Rivan watches me, and for a moment, I can see the desperation on his face as he tries to understand what's going on. If there was time, maybe I could've put myself in his place and tried to sympathize with his confusion, but there isn't. He should know by now I'd do anything to get away from Kar Atish.

I try once more. "There's nothing for me here. I've been kicked out of the pits. The miners will kill me before ever letting me work the mines. I'll be indentured to the salt pans for not paying my debts. This is my only option. But I get it. You're worried because you're my friend."

"I'm your *friend*?" His eyes widen. "Of course I'm your friend! I—we've been through so much together. Remember when Amma was dying, and you took care of her while we worked? Piling every bit of a scrip to get her meds. And now you won't let me help you?"

My lower lip trembles. Not a mention of what *he's* done for me. "How long will you help me for?"

"What do you mean for how long?" he shouts. "For as long as it takes. Forever!"

"You would, wouldn't you?" I feel my heart break. Rivan would do this for anyone, not just me. He's a good person. But he's always taken care of the kicked and the down. He doesn't deserve feeling this obligation to help me. "I'll go into the mines, far into Kar Atish's belly itself," I say. "If it means I can get off this island, I'll do it."

Rivan jerks back like he's been burned. The look on his face constricts my rib cage, lungs twinging with guilt. This is why I couldn't tell him immediately. He's taking it personally—like I knew he would.

"I've never made my desire to get away from here a secret. I need to get off this island, and for that I need money. There's no other way out."

"But this is too dangerous!" He shoves his hands into his hair, helplessly, clutching at it. "We can—we can get away from this island another way. I'll come with you. You don't have to do any of this alone. Let me—let me help you, Kress, please."

"Stop it, Rivan," I snap and turn from him before my resolve breaks. He can't make promises he will never keep. If it was just him, it would be different. But he has his brothers. He can't leave them, and I will not put him in a position where he has to make a choice.

He doesn't understand what he's saying right now because he wants to stop me.

"Can we please stop fighting? Just go back to normal?"

"No," Rivan snaps, but his voice cracks midway. "I don't want to go back to normal. I want—" He presses his eyes closed, and when he opens them, he still looks frustrated. "Why do you want it this badly?"

It's his tone, even now so confused, and the look of betrayal in his eyes that make me burst out, "Because I hate it! I've hated every minute I've lived on Kar Atish. Since my parents died and since I was forced to live on scraps. I have nothing here and no family!"

"That's not true—"

"Of course it is! I don't expect you to understand. You have your brothers! What do I have?"

Rivan's face hardens. Suddenly, the planes of his face aren't beautiful but terrible, edged with fury. He repeats, slow and clear, "What do you have?"

The outburst has left me breathless. I can only pull my brows together.

"Fine," he says, walking away. "If there's nothing keeping you here, then go."

NINE

I trek down the steep slope, feeling like I'm underwater, as the red flash of dawn cracks the sky. The storms surrounding the island briefly turn the color of freshly cut muscle before returning to soot. If Kar Atish was a flatter land, perhaps the distance from my corner of the island to the mines would take an hour. Instead, it's a land of craggy terrain, rocky mountains, stony spires, and brittle craters that give way without warning. There are even old rail tracks for mine trains, broken, because over the years, the weather got progressively worse, loosening rocks that suddenly crashed into passing carts. The ravines throughout the island are a jumble of rusting tracks.

But that's not why I want to jump out of my skin.

I haven't seen Rivan since two nights ago, when he so unceremoniously turned away from me. I thought he'd get over it by now. See why I want to go away from here. But when I stopped by his place earlier, Ashvin opened the door.

He said, "Rivan took extra shifts and never came home last night. Hey, May, you have any idea when he'll be home?"

From inside, Mayven yelled back, voice thick with sleep, "What does it matter? It's not like the Dark Dancer cares what we think."

Ashvin shrugged. There wasn't any apology in it, just weariness. "He'll be fine, Kress. You do what you have to do." He gave me an awkward hug. "Stay safe in there, yeah?"

By the time I finally make it to the mouth of the quarry, the sky has lightened—as much as it can hidden behind the storm clouds. From the top of the peak, the mine is a wound cut in the skin of the land. The clanging of tools and the abrasive noise of miners yelling back and forth gets louder step by step along the way. The work at the mines never shuts down, only divided in shifts. All ten Islands of Ophir depend on Kar Atish for a constant supply of zargunine. To build their weapons and walls and roofs and whatever else they can think of—it's a miracle element. If we stop, the other islands stop too.

Which is why we're kept here, in this open-air prison, and given no money and no opportunity.

If only Rivan understood. This life is no life.

At the top of the face of the mine, I stop and search for Rivan. Maybe I can catch him here. Down the entire potholed way, there's a swamp of workers, dressed in shabby blue uniforms, soot-stained hands clutched around their equipment, and expressions hard as the surrounding rocky peaks. The cantankerous banging of hammers and trowels and shovels, wheelbarrows scattered around, mine trains loaded with raw metal ready to leave for the refinery, the constant din of drills, miners calling out to one another—it's worse than the lawlessness of the pits. The noise makes me so irritable that I can't even distinguish faces suddenly.

From here, it *does* look like the pits. The miners are the entertainers, and I watch them from the audience's area, open to the sky and the sea.

I begin my descent, and a few steps down, a warm breeze curls around my neck. A strange sensation, like I'm being watched, crawls up my sides. I glance around. Nobody is looking. And even if they do, they'll know me from the pits. Nobody will immediately think I'm Jar and Katya's daughter.

My parents' faces have faded like sandcastles beneath a barrage of waves, but I hope that I don't much look like them.

So no one would recognize—

"Krescent! Hey, Krescent!"

A hooded person is waving enthusiastically at me, one hand shielding their face so I can't see them. They stand relaxed, leaning on a dangerous-looking spiked polearm. I glance around, alarmed, but no one seems to care.

"I'm Aryadna. The rest of the party is waiting for you." At my expression, she adds, "It's not hard to see you're not a miner. So who else would be here this early?"

I look down at the padded blacks and armor that Badger has lent me, the four daggers along my belt, the bloodred scarf obscuring my neck and mouth, and the backpack I carry securely. Aryadna, on the other hand, is dressed in dark brown camouflage gear. It makes her blue-green eyes stand out alongside her pale hair. She smiles, and it lights up her face with an almost intolerable beauty. I grip a dagger at my belt.

We head down the rest of the way.

Aryadna keeps talking. "I only said yes when we were told the Dark Dancer was coming as our guard. We had two already, but I've seen you fight. It's like watching a demon fight, and I—"

"Wait, what other guards?" I feel foolish as soon as the words leave my mouth. Of course I wouldn't be the only one.

"There," Aryadna says, pointing.

My face falls.

Like stone statues, Yara and Ansh stand shoulder to shoulder at the entrance leading into the various mine inclines and shafts.

Did it have to be them? A sudden sense of foreboding fills the back of my throat, and I collect myself before I lose my footing. Yara and Ansh are just one more obstacle on the path to my freedom. I'll deal with them if I have to. They don't look particularly happy seeing me either—at least that's a relief. Badger must be laughing in his office.

If my test was the sersei, what was theirs? I wouldn't be surprised if it was their successful attack on me. Maybe that's why they acted after all these years.

Behind them, I can see others crowded around, easily distinguishable from the workers in their gears and backpacks. A gruff-looking giant of a man with dark blond hair tied in a thick braid stares at me with narrowed eyes. Unlike the pallor on most Landers, he has burnished skin, as if he spends time in the sun. He doesn't need to introduce himself for me to know who he is. Beyorn, the Collector's man leading the mission. He seems the type who would string the twins upside down if they caused any menace.

"You took your time. We've been waiting."

Before I can apologize, one of the miners accompanying us speaks in a no-nonsense voice, "It's been five minutes." She's dressed in a minesuit and protective padding like the others, and she holds a polearm like it's an extension of her body. A ring on a chain around her neck glints softly.

Beyorn throws her a severe look. "Five minutes could mean the death of this entire company."

"None of us are dying, Beyorn. Unless you believe the Shadefolk will come for us." Aryadna laughs shortly. She squeezes past Yara and picks up her backpack. And just as she does, a small rodent flies past us, leaping at her. Aryadna screeches—and Yara grabs the creature off her and flings it away.

A sharp cut at the back of Aryadna's hand glistens brilliant red. She swears and wipes it off on the wall.

"You'll see what the mines have to teach you," Beyorn says.

Aryadna ignores him.

"Now I know you are all miners, but even so, I expect some sense from every single one of you." His gaze lingers between me and Ansh and Yara, as if he can see that we're trouble. He should take it up with the Collector and Badger. But I keep my mouth shut. "They will keep us protected from any creature we encounter. They fight in the underground arena and are used to beasts. We can expect the same steadfastness from them is what I've been told," he adds as if he wants to wash his hands of us if we don't live up to our names.

"Are you sure you're up for it, Dark Dancer?" Ansh asks, hard gaze pinned at me. "Can you keep people *safe* instead of—"

"What are you accusing me of? The Collector might want to hear about it."

Ansh's lips curl, but he doesn't do anything inadvisable.

Beyorn watches us with a frown but then goes back to the others. He points at the woman with the ring by her neck and a girl probably a little younger than me. "Raksha will take care of expanding the maps as we go, along with Siril. Thayne," he continues with a tip of the head toward the miner man, "will be second-in-command after me should anything happen. And Aryadna will assist us in whatever we need. I command the company, and what I say is final in every way. Is that understood? If it is not, tell me now and save us from a last-minute bad decision that will risk our lives."

When no one speaks up—as if anyone would with a giant Lander looming over us like he wants to bury us—he turns and picks up a glaive. Adjusts his grip on it. "Take a good look at the sky. You won't be seeing any for a while."

We are going to be down there for days, if not weeks.

For a strange, thick moment, I stare at the mine's entrance. The rough, jagged edges, as if a giant monster had clawed at the ground. I'm supposed to leave this place, but here I am, going even deeper into the land. Into the dark, where the worst of my nightmares dance wickedly.

I want to run back. To—to Rivan.

But I breathe. If I can live through starvation and the pits and this murderous island, I can also bear the dark. I will be as entombed as I have to be if I get to survive and one day get to see skies beyond the smoke and ash of this island. And I will bring these wretched people out safely, no matter the accusations Ansh and Yara want to lob at me.

Then, with a deep breath, I step inside the darkness.

TEN

If the work had been stopped for just an hour or so, we could've made it out of the crowded areas of the mines by now. But the work never stops. The Landers probably think it might cause an apocalypse if the workers were a little rested.

So we traverse through the initial chambers slowly, move down the inclines at timed periods so the wagon tracks are empty when we're on them. And bit by bit, the daylight recedes even as the heat swells like the fiery breath of a monster, every inch reeking of smoke and decay. There are no lamps, not even starfish lights, here—the air is too bad. When it gets dark, we'll switch on our headlamps, and when it gets cold, we'll light our torches. Even if they make the walls look putrid. The thought does nothing to ease the anxiety clawing at my throat.

Beyorn leads the company, with the two older miners, Thayne and Raksha, timing us since they know the inner terrain. My job will come later, when we descend and the creatures come out.

All in all, we make good time. Compared to the spires of rock and the constant knifelike wind above the ground, the path down here is mild. But it's impossible not to feel the dread pooling into my stomach.

Is it Rivan? Or the fear of being in these mines?

The uncertainty, perhaps, is what's getting to me. Of what we might encounter underground. It hasn't escaped my notice that apart from the Collector's proclamation that we're searching for someone who might still be alive, we don't know how we're going to look for them. Even if my only work is to keep these people safe, a semblance of a plan would be good.

Maybe they just didn't share it with me.

Aryadna, the girl with the strange-colored eyes, makes things worse.

She's awed by the fights, the same way that Collector Syris was taken in by the bloody entertainment.

"When you tackled the wyrm lizards, I couldn't believe it! But I wish I could have seen you fight the scythe crab," she says reverently, as if I were freeing the island from the Collector in the pits and not playing with my life. "I could never get off work."

"You had all your work during night shifts?"

"Kind of." Before I can ask why, she adds, "I'm really honored to come here with you."

I look at her square and can't keep the irritation from my voice. "Honor has no part here. I do what I do for the same reason as you. We need money for food and clothes and a place to stay."

"We do," she agrees, immediately losing the annoying awe in her eyes. "The mines aren't enough anymore. That's why I'm here, you know?"

Our last meal before we move farther is at the mouth of an abandoned shaft, about a mile from the entrance. Beyond it lies darkness, the black, toothless gullet of a monster. We will have to make dangerous descents. It's my last chance to run back. I push my fingers through the grip of the katar, letting the cold edge against my knuckles, to stop the trembling of my hand. My father used to do this too. I didn't know at the time he was nervous. He always seemed in control of everything.

It was a lie.

I shudder and tighten my grip on the katar.

I have to bear it.

When I sit at the corner of the group, Raksha and Aryadna move closer to sit with me.

"With the way we're going," Raksha says, "it will be a miracle if we return before my sixtieth birthday."

"How old are you right now?" Aryadna raises a brow.

Without missing a beat, Raksha says, "Twenty."

I choke on my porridge, which only makes the two of them laugh.

"At least something's loosened that frown," Raksha says. "Beware of your mind when we go down. It is far more dangerous than any physical obstacle."

I shrug and return to my food. I'm not here to make friends, I remind myself. My only friend is outside. I didn't like snapping at him. But it's for his own good. If he believed there's even a small chance of me turning back, he wouldn't stop. And I can't let that happen.

I clutch my spoon tighter, my resentment turning into real anger. My fingers hurt. And it only annoys me more. I force myself to keep eating, even though the porridge tastes bitterly of ash. I have to keep my strength and my mind if I'm going to descend into unknown tunnels with ocean-knows-what down there. Rivan can stay mad as long as he stays safe and with his brothers.

I glance toward the end of the group where Yara and Ansh sit with the other two miners, Siril and Thayne.

Makes sense. The two of them work days at the mines; they must know these people.

Thayne is probably my parents' age, with a seriousness about him.

They didn't have many friends, and he doesn't seem familiar. He has short waves of slick hair that is still brown but a hard, lined face where soot has settled and made its home for years and an authoritative grimness that only older miners have, just like Raksha. He carries a spiked pole and a gun strapped down his legs but otherwise sits quietly, observing the others.

Siril, on the other hand, is young and pale as a fish's belly and doesn't know how to keep her mouth shut.

"We already know so much about the sea but not anything about the ground we walk on," she says. "Unless we know, how can we learn more about our world?"

Yara and Ansh exchange glances.

"Besides," Siril continues, waving a *book* about, "the more we learn about the underground, the better we can negotiate our rights at the mines."

"What's there to learn about?" I call out, unable to stand her idiocy. "The underground's dead."

"So why are you here?" Ansh smirks.

"To make sure you don't kill everyone in their sleep."

"Killing people is in your blood, not ours."

I clench my fist. No fighting here. Can't let these two get to me.

Aryadna, thankfully, speaks. "Where did you learn to read, Siril?"

The girl turns around to us, eyes bright. "I learned it by myself."

Huh. I narrow my eyes, studying her closer. Who is this girl? How have the mines not leached the life out of her yet?

"If you can read, what are you here for? You could get a small office job at the mines," Aryadna says.

"Small jobs don't pay," Siril says with a sudden hard glare. She doesn't elaborate, finally shutting up and turning away, which makes me even more curious. How does a young miner manage to read and happen to get on an expedition as deadly as this?

I turn to Raksha. She's fiddling with the ring on the chain around her neck and, I realize now, she also wears one on her ring finger. It must be her husband's ring. And the fact that she's wearing it around her neck tells me enough not to pry. "What have you seen?"

She has a permanent frown between her brows, which lift and turn her expression from vaguely irritable to amused. Even without the frown, she'd look unapproachable: the scars on her face outnumber the actual features. And her eyes, currently studying me, are pale green lined with thick kohl, lending a sense that she could see through to my soul. She must be above forty, maybe even fifty, but there's a very raath-like sharpness to her focus.

"It would take years to recount everything I've seen," she says.

Aryadna giggles in her soup, and I fight hard to keep myself from snapping. "You know what I mean. They told me I was needed here because there might be creatures down there."

"It's best to be prepared," Raksha agrees. "Down the dark is a different world."

"Is that where you got these scars?"

"Some. Where did you get yours?"

"Here and there," I say. If she won't answer me, I won't either.

Over her shoulder, Yara has turned away toward the tunnel, but Ansh is still watching me with a hunter's precision. Whatever animosity we may have, would the twins really jeopardize all of our safety by coming after me? How can they hope to get away with it?

"Tell me," I say to Raksha, my gaze still on the twins, "about what you know of the caves below."

"The usual," she says. "Monsters and madness."

That pulls my attention back. "You've seen these monsters?"

"I've heard stories."

"Stories from whom? No one has ever come back from the expeditions."

"You spend time in the mines, and you'll come across one or two strangers who seem to be emerging from the dark." She glances toward Thayne and Siril.

I blink as I struggle to understand what Raksha is saying. "Those two have talked to someone who returned? But no one has ever returned!"

"Not in the way that matters. It's the mad who return. The mad who are no use to the Collector except for the rough sketches they sometimes carry. How do you think the maps have been building if no one has ever returned?"

My head spins.

Badger wants me to tell him about the creatures we encounter—if they exist at all—but those imagined creatures would be ones we can fight. That he believes *I* can fight. But this? Rumors of people returning with madness. If I didn't know better, I'd think the miners made it up to lure one of the Collector's men to kill him for some sick act of rebellion. But it *is* true… If no one has ever returned, how could the borders of the maps be increasing?

"Why would any of you agree to this? It's—"

"Madness?" Aryadna cuts in, and I jump. I forgot she is with us.

"Like Siril said, small jobs do not pay," Raksha says mildly.

"Well, for this mission to be successful, none of us can go mad. Are we agreed?"

"We are," Aryadna says. "After all, we're all going down for the same reason. In that dark is the way out for our destiny."

ELEVEN

As we go farther in, Beyorn and the miners light their torches and headlamps, casting the sickly light like a flimsy veil that will make no difference if a knife comes skewering toward us. I count in my head, tighten my grip on my dagger, and keep myself grounded in the present.

With every step, the idea of descending into the network of dead shafts and narrower tunnels, buried beneath the mountains, is increasingly unnerving. An alien pain pulses beneath my lungs, not enough to slow me but making its presence known with a grim frown.

There are more than ten dead mine shafts, broken cages lying askew, rust so thick it looks as if it would scatter like salt at a bare touch. We move past them quietly, like the miners before us, like we don't want to disturb them.

And soon, we arrive at a small cave. A track cuts across from the left side to the right, a few carts discarded stationary on it. The cave looks rarely ventured into, likely just where they throw junk that is too big to carry all the way back up. At the other end, a passageway leads in two different directions. On one side, we can see in the last of the faint light, its emptiness, tracks extended into—nothing. The other side is dark as ink.

"Here be dragons," murmurs Aryadna.

Raksha swears. "Don't say that. You will make it come true."

Aryadna laughs shortly. "You don't believe that."

"I do," Raksha says firmly. "The land keeps its secrets."

There's a reverence in the way she watches the darkness, like she can will it to stay silent and let us pass untouched. My mother was the same way—a believer in the darkness and what it hides. She told me stories about the Naag dragon. But in her stories, instead of guarding treasure in the ocean, it could breathe fire and it stayed hidden in the fiery depths of Kar Atish.

A shudder racks me at the remembrance.

Beyorn gives Raksha a sideways glance, then says to me, "From here on, you lead."

I nod and tighten my gloves to hold up the torch. It would've made for easier movement if I had a lamp, but my head already pounds with the fear of darkness—I don't want to add the weight.

"And you, boy," he adds to Ansh, "you will be at the back end. Your sister will split time between you and Dune to help maintain the line."

"Ugh," I say automatically.

Everyone turns to stare. Yara and Ansh, knowing I just made myself look unreasonable, give me identical smirks.

"Is there a problem?" Beyorn growls. His eyes are two dark pits of tar boring into me.

"No, I was just looking for the match so—"

He throws a new box of matches at me that I catch out of instinct and no small shot of panic that he was throwing an iron star at me. "Get going."

Swallowing my pride, I light my torch. The flame hisses sharply, casting huge shadows across the cave, and the bright light sears my eyes. I shut them tight and turn my face the other way before slowly opening them. Even with the new light, I can't see beyond the first few steps. An oiliness clings to the void. My vision, too, remains hazy.

I take out one of my daggers, adjust my grip. From this point, this company is my responsibility.

"All right, let's do this."

The maps go on for a few miles into the incline, charting out the natural labyrinth of tunnels cutting in and out of it. We shift westward. It doesn't escape my mind that the farther we go west, the more we're moving right beneath the sea with its great waters and monsters.

There are remnants of the mines above—for one, the distant echo of the clang of tools and growl of wheelbarrows. Veins of zargunine, glimmering in the dark like iridescent water snakes, emerging along the walls every few meters. Somewhere in the deep, far beyond reach, must be the substance that mixes with gold up here to form the ore of zargunine.

Behind me, the others are quiet. Only the scraping of shoes and breaths getting laborious as we continue. So far, nothing has interrupted our way through. And I'm starting to think if anyone is alive from previous expeditions, they might have simply gotten lost. These tunnels are too narrow, too labyrinthine for any living creatures to hide and attack.

But if there are truly no monsters, there might be some truth to the madness in this chasm of darkness.

How will I keep them safe from madness? What if whatever madness took hold of my parents runs in my blood and I'm the one who hurts them?

My throat constricts, forcing me to stop walking.

There's a *whoosh*, and hot fire comes so close I feel my neck sear. Someone yelps just behind me and pulls the fire back.

Beyorn hisses, "What the hell is going on? Why did we stop?"

"Krescent, do you see something?" Thayne asks.

"No," I say, heartbeat booming in my ears. "I thought I did. Let's keep moving."

Beyorn thunders, "Then why did you—"

"It's better to stay safe," I snap. "Isn't that why you brought me down here?"

The echo of my voice makes me feel strangely powerful. Shutting up a man like Beyorn who looks like he could break me in two and pick his teeth with my bones—and doing so in front of witnesses—almost makes me forget why I stopped in the first place. The thought of madness.

Maybe it's exactly this, the *thought* circling inside minds and bringing madness on.

So there's nothing to do but continue down the catacombs, on and on into the womb of the land, beneath the ocean pressing on us, passing countless diversions down the paths, until I feel as if I've never seen the sun, as if the dark is a solid wall pressing against me.

The others murmur at the back, but I don't mind. It's a sign that I'm not here alone.

What if we never find anyone? The Collector said there were reports of human voices. But what if it's a mistake? When do we turn back?

This is beginning to look as foolish an errand as gathering seawater in hand and waiting for salt to be left behind.

"You don't look half as insane as you do in the pits," Yara breathes down my neck. "Maybe it's the dark."

I keep from sticking out a leg and letting her tumble headfirst down the tunnel.

"Maybe you're going blind." As soon as I say it, my left eye twitches, reminding me of the poison it took.

"I must be, since I don't see lover boy circling you. Or did he finally come to his senses and move on?"

I clench my teeth and ignore Yara's goading. She *knows* how to get under my skin. And I can't possibly keep off the dark's madness if I keep losing my cool over her and her brother. But the thought of Rivan *moving on*—whatever that means—sends a spider crawling on my heart.

He's just annoyed that I'm taking a risk. He'll come around. Like always.

Why couldn't he just wish me luck and get over it? If he thinks it's so dangerous, what if I never come back alive?

A faint noise cuts through the fog in my mind.

"Wait—you hear that?"

At the change in my tone, Yara drops the mockery. She looks around, then says, "Let me check down the line."

She tells everyone to stop moving. Beyorn grunts at them to gather in the center, then lifts his torch higher, a giant among mortals.

I move ahead to the corner, one step at a time, breath held. Awareness dawns slowly in my mind, the dust coating my skin moving as if it has taken life of its own. On either side, unforgiving walls slip closer. This isn't like the pits. If something attacks me, there won't be a collar around it.

I look back once. Ansh and Yara have the tunnel mouth covered.

So I creep forward, holding the torch at arm's length. The corner turn comes closer with every breath.

The tunnel opens up in a hall. The torch's flame lights up the circular roof, plunging the dark walls in shadows that seem to warp any perspective. This room shouldn't be here. The maps show a network of caves and tunnels, labyrinths crossing into one another, but not halls this big.

"Wait here," I call to the others and move in.

A high chirping to my right. I swing the torch in the air, throwing violent shadows about.

Even after years of fighting and seeing creatures out of nightmares, this new sight stops me in my tracks. A sheen of luminescence—almost the shape of eyes but not quite—gleams in a corner. I raise my dagger. The creature is small, rodent-like. It hisses.

And just as I lunge, it slips into a crack in the rock. I squint, looking for a place wide enough to slip in my hand. But the creature burrows deep blindly. It looks defenseless. A ruse, I know. But I recall the eyes of the sersei just before I yielded. This is just a creature in its home. It's not attacking us. I don't want to kill it.

It's one thing to fight in the pits for my life and completely another to take a life for nothing.

Did my parents ever think of that?

I shake my head and pull back. As if now's the time to ruminate over their sins. The creature continues to breathe heavily but stays inside, watching cautiously. Maybe I don't have to kill it. Just hurry and get out of here.

I sweep the fire around the hall and, finding nothing else, call the others in.

One after the other, they tiptoe inside—except Beyorn, who can't *not* make noise when he moves.

Yara and Ansh arrive at the end. Their identical thin, pointed faces look grim. Ansh, whose main differing feature from his sister is the permanent smirk on his face, looks around. Skeptical. He keeps his hand extended to prevent Yara from entering the hall until he's sure of safety.

"There's nothing here," I say through the pain that now lies just below my throat. And before either of the twins object, I add, "This hall shouldn't be here either, according to the map."

Siril steps up, her book tucked under her arm. "Those maps won't help us. They were rudimentary, and no one has double-checked them. There could be danger at every turn."

"If there's danger, she will deal with it." Beyorn points at me.

"I wish I had your confidence," Siril says.

Beyorn takes a threatening step toward her, and she moves back, making herself smaller. My fingers slip into my katar, but Beyorn only says, "Do you want to go back?"

Siril shakes her head.

"Good. We move west. That's it."

Siril looks at me helplessly.

What does she want from me? I can't do anything to undermine Beyorn—none of us can.

Thayne steps up next to Siril. He says calmly, "If we're going to plunge in the dark, we're going to do it with all our hearts or not at all." He continues to look at her like he's calculating the next fear she will voice, readying himself with an immediate answer.

Miraculously, she only nods and adjusts the straps of her backpack.

"Good. And we have our compass," I say, copying Beyorn's forceful tone. "So if something goes wrong, we can just trace our steps back."

Making enemies with Beyorn is the last thing I want. Who knows what will happen once the Collector's people are found? They could go back on their word. So no. I will not take a miner's side just as I know none of them would resist from calling me Kinkiller if they knew.

I will only do what Beyorn wants.

And if that means plunging in farther down this abyss, so be it.

TWELVE

We continue on, and when the creature doesn't return to trouble us, I breathe a sigh of relief. Badger wouldn't want that kind of animal anyway. If they're keeping to themselves, I'll keep the company out of their way too. Even if Yara's getting suspicious that we haven't encountered any creatures in the dark.

So when I feel the weight of someone's gaze sending a cold shiver up my spine, my first thought is Yara or Ansh. I slow down and focus on the group behind me, listening for the shift of a foot, for the hiss of a blade.

But no one charges at me. No coup takes place.

I stare into the reflection on my blade.

It's the dark, the claustrophobia of moving beneath the ground.

I keep walking, ignoring the strange feeling at the center of my chest that is pressing harder than the physical pain ever since I descended into this darkness. The feeling of someone following us. It's nothing but my paranoia, the dark cloying at the edge of my mind. No one *can* follow us down here. We've traveled too deep beneath.

Monsters and madness.

I swear under my breath, shaking my head slightly to banish the thought.

Miners' superstitions. Nothing more.

And if I fall for these tales, what difference is there between me and the ones who let my parents rot under the sky?

The ground beneath soon grows sharper, rocks turning into fangs snapping at our feet. My teeth set on an edge. A susurrating wind passes by.

"There's an opening somewhere," Thayne calls softly. "Careful."

I look back, a single drop of sweat trickling down my temple. He's squinting at the easily missed sheen of green in some of the cracks along the floor. It's probably fungi. And the reason any of the critters survive down here.

We pass some of the lakes of seawater. Knowing they exist and looking at them in real life are completely different things. The ceilings don't seem any softer than the surroundings, but they are lower. Hidden behind a haze, somehow. The water itself lies still, murky, hiding depths we don't check. If someone falls down from above the ground, they'd die simply because of the height. Every time we leave behind a lake, I breathe easier.

Very soon, we leave the range of low-roofed halls and come across another tunnel that opens up in a startlingly large cave. The ceiling gleams with tiny starlike points scattered throughout, blinking and shimmering and dancing in the dark.

"Zargunine," Aryadna breathes.

Behind each of these hundreds of stars, there's an entirely new vein of the ore, ready to be drained for a thousand more years.

The sight is as beautiful as it is surreal. Deep beneath the ground, with stone and water burying us, a hall with a starlit night for a ceiling. We stand there, gaping at it, a constellation of dancers and monsters cast against dark velvet. Each point of light a tenderness in the discordant world around us.

Until Beyorn bellows for a lunch break, shattering the illusion the stars cast on the rest of us.

"Lunch is probably long past," mutters Ansh. He and Yara immediately settle next to Thayne, who has found a boulder to lean against.

Thayne places his spiked pole beside him and crosses his arms as the rest of us scramble for a place to sit. Even Beyorn's face is smeared with dirt now. It must be over five hours since we descended into the caves.

"I do not miss the sun," Thayne says to the twins. The three of them spread their food between them, sharing. "But I would give anything to sit by the sea with Tamina's fish."

Tamina, I gather from their conversation, is a woman who routinely serves lunch to miners when her work gets wrapped up early. She charges them nothing for it. For a moment, I feel like it's just something they made up. Who has the luxury of friendship *and* free food on this island?

I catch Thayne looking at me, a frown between his brows, and he abruptly turns away. I hope it's not because he recognizes me.

But he's already turned back to Yara and Ansh.

"When do we make actual camp?" Ansh yawns, casting about.

Thayne says, "You need camp to sleep? Well, I don't. I'm so good at it I could do it anywhere with my eyes closed."

Yara groans as Ansh laughs.

Aryadna says, "If my grandfather made that terrible joke, I'd understand. You're not old enough to get away with it, Thayne."

"It's his specialty," Raksha adds in a light tone, at odds with the permanent seriousness of her face. "It's all he contributes."

They go on like this, back and forth, the humor progressively getting worse, which is perhaps what makes it better. Like a little family, all of the miners.

I'm from a miner family. I deserve this companionship too—not to be made a pariah on the island where I was born. What if I were to start screaming? Show them the insanity of what's been done to me—by my parents and the world—that I keep at bay out of sheer will, while they all moved on, bundled their feelings into anger and disgust toward a child who did nothing to them but exist.

I'm *almost* about to open my mouth. But for all I know, someone other than Ansh and Yara might also be victims of my parents' actions. I should just be grateful everyone is too busy focusing on our survival to make the connection between my last name and the people they hate.

As if Aryadna reads my mind, she calls, "Let's ask Krescent, then. What's the worst joke in your family?" Her face is flush, eyes bright, and she probably thinks she's being nice in including me in the conversation, but my heart sinks.

"No family," I choke the words out. My mind, however, drifts to Rivan and his brothers, of the many nights I spent with them, of the way I leave my things, weapons and clothes, at their place. Of the way they always make space for me, even though they fit together neatly. Perfectly. And have no need to fit me in.

"Really?" Ansh says without missing a beat. "What happened?"

"Let's keep some of the conversation for later," Raksha cuts in, saving me. "Who knows how long we have to be down here?"

Ansh locks eyes with me, smirks. *You got saved this time, Dune.*

My appetite vanishes, leaving a sour taste in my mouth.

I lean against a slope and watch the entrance we just came from. Dark as the gullet of a predator. Once I start watching, it feels irresponsible to take my gaze off it, so I stay on guard.

It helps assuage the feeling of being watched too.

Beyorn consults with Raksha and Siril on the maps. Siril is supposed to be marking the new chambers and tunnels we see and the location of new zargunine veins. I'll have to remember to sneak a copy of it later, to mark the creatures I see for Badger.

Siril edges closer to sit with Raksha and Aryadna. The trio are within hearing distance, murmuring softly about the mission.

"We knew it was going to be dangerous," Raksha murmurs.

"Dangerous, not illogical," Siril says, annoyed. She pulls at the jerky she's eating violently, as if it's offended her. "We're here to find people, build the maps farther if we can, not to jump into the ocean and kill ourselves."

"What's so illogical about it?" Aryadna asks. "We knew what we were doing when we were asked to join the party. The lack of information has always been clear."

"I'm beginning to doubt if the mission is even about finding the survivors."

"Of course it is," Aryadna hisses. "What else would *anyone* want to go down there for? Find out if the monsters are real? Then what? Wave at them and run for our lives? No, we are going to look for people and drag them back if that's what it takes."

"When you put it like that..." Siril tugs at the jerky again.

I can't keep quiet anymore. "You arrived before all of us, Aryadna. Anything you picked up? Anyone specific we're looking for?" The Collector revealed no names, but it must be someone important. This mission is too risky for just anyone.

Although I still think no one could be alive down here alone.

"According to what I heard Beyorn say, two people escaped the caverns, but I think they...died," Aryadna says, frowning, as if she isn't sure it was death that claimed them. "The deep underground turns into mazes and—well, people get lost. It refuses to let go of the people. The land is"—she looks at each of us before adding—"holding them hostage."

"The land is holding them hostage?"

"I'm sure it's just the way it feels to people like Beyorn who haven't worked in the mines." Aryadna looks at Raksha for support, but the latter is staring across the chamber, deep in thought.

I want to tell Aryadna how insane she sounds. But it's true that Landers who stay at the Collector's compound for most of their time on the island have no real sense of the world. They think everything can be explained from within their protected walls. But when your life is intertwined with the land, even to the detriment, you begin to have a more coherent relationship with it, where it warns when you transgress. The miners know the violence we cast on the land, they are guilty of it themselves, but they don't do it because they *want* to.

Just like I fight in the pits not because I want to.

"You're not afraid of also getting lost?" I ask quietly to no one in particular.

"Some. But it can't be any worse than serving them for the rest of my life," Siril says. There's no venom in her voice, just a fact. "Come into this world and spend every waking moment trying to make sure there's enough scrip to exchange for enough food so you survive only to do more work for them." She stares into her hands, her voice growing smaller with every passing moment. "Then your family gets taken away—not just the adult but a child too—and you're left with the cruel monotony of working in the grime and making one morsel of food last for the whole day so you can save the scrips you earn to pay for their freedom.

"And so you end up on the path to almost certain death. Taking on a journey from where no one returns. But if you manage it, they will reward you. Perhaps that will make the suffering and the cruelty worth it."

I sigh. Siril has the same yearning as every person on Kar Atish, but I ask anyway, "And the monsters? The madness?"

84

"There's no place in this world without monsters and madness, Krescent," Aryadna says.

To that, I have no argument.

But I can't stop myself from finally voicing my thoughts. "And how will we know when to stop?"

The chatter dies, spoons held midway. All gazes turn to Beyorn. He's not fazed or even seems like he's giving the question any thought.

"We stop when I say we stop."

The arrogance in his tone makes my mouth curl with disgust before I realize what I'm doing.

"You have a problem?" he says. His torch crackles at his side, a match for his temperament.

I glance at Aryadna, closest to me, and she's shaking her head inconspicuously. Raksha's frown is even more pronounced.

I look back to Beyorn. "No. You hold the command."

So he does, leaving behind the chambers and the small, chittering creatures watching us from their corners. Afraid of us or for us, I can't tell.

THIRTEEN

We have been underground for a little over a day now. The caverns turn larger and higher. Their ceilings are ink-dark, but the points of zargunine grow more numerous as we move. Somewhere close, a cracking reverberates in the emptiness, like ice breaking.

The feeling of being watched has pervaded everyone at last.

Even with the fire of the torches, our breaths grow colder, fogging every time we exhale. Our footsteps are loud, but the sound of the ice eclipses all. Aryadna takes my torch and walks beside me, lighting my way as I hold a weapon in each hand, and Raksha has her pike out.

Then comes the growl.

"Is that…a rock?" Thayne says. His voice is, unsurprisingly, tired and flat, testament to the years of dangerous mining he has undertaken.

I look up. The giant teeth of the cavern hang down menacingly. If one breaks, it could easily take half of us along with it. But it's not rock. The sound came with life of its own. I reach for my torch, and Aryadna silently hands it back. She's on edge too.

I turn and slowly take a step toward the way we came. A tremor rocks the cavern, and Beyorn thunders, "Gather to me, now!"

A whip-lashing cracking sound explodes in the cavern. And then a battle cry. A *human* cry.

An animal screech cuts the air, followed by the deafening sound of rocks falling, and then someone hurtles through the mouth of the cavern. Chasing them is something gleaming with malicious brightness, high up in the air, its reek filling the large hall.

And the person it's chasing, someone with black hair and—

"Rivan!" I scream.

The shock of it sends me into full tilt, and I crash to the ground, even as Yara and Ansh storm past me, their weapons drawn.

A single tentacle cuts the air, cracking like thunder, and whips at Yara and Ansh. They lunge in opposite directions to avoid it. Rivan backs away from the creature, which emerges fully. It looks like a jellyfish, a semicircular gauzy body, floating in midair. And I recognize the luminescence pulsing along its sides, the ones I mistook for eyes when it scuttled back in the niche. I left it alive. Because it wasn't hurting us.

The elongated tentacle begins buzzing with red sparks again, rearing high, ready to strike.

A second's heartbeat, and I throw a star straight at the creature.

It dodges.

Where are its eyes?

It looks sightless, mindless, but its instincts are sharp as raptor fangs. It avoids the rocky outcroppings from the walls, expertly darting through the air with speed and purpose. A singularly baffling creature. I can't stop staring, trying to figure it out. Whatever Badger was expecting, it wasn't this.

I pull out my daggers. Yara and Ansh are back up again too. They're coordinating, dodging the creature, trying to tire it, get it to cross its tentacles. *Something.*

And as they do, I take a second to study the creature. Too high for any of us to really hurt it. And too fast. Yara ducks as the tentacle grabs for her.

Except it slides beyond her and goes for Ansh.

The company behind screams. The jellyfish snatches Ansh, dangling him upside down.

"No!" Yara screams. She races at it in a flash, forgetting any pit instincts, seeing only her brother.

I run after her, and Rivan tries to stop me.

"Get out of the way!" I yell at him, my blood running hot in my veins. The sound catches the attention of the jellyfish, and it rises even higher. Ansh flails and tries to stab it, but one sharp jerk and his blade clangs to the ground. The luminescence around the jellyfish's body brightens to blinding proportions. I throw my arms up to shield my eyes.

"Ansh!" Yara yells. "Dune, help me!"

I don't know what to do. The creature is floating high up, and we can't reach it.

The creature starts squeezing Ansh, who bellows, and claws at the tentacle.

"I need someone to distract it! Rivan—" I turn again. "Thayne! Come on up here!"

Thayne jogs over with his spiked pole. Behind, Yara is still grappling with air, trying to throw blades while avoiding getting Ansh.

"Keep its focus on the two of you," I tell Rivan and Thayne.

Just as I turn, Rivan grabs my hand. "What are you going to do?"

"What I do best."

Shouting for her to get out of the way, I rush up to Yara. She momentarily loses focus and stares at me, open-mouthed. I flash past her and bang against the wall with speed. There's no time to feel the pain. The cavern's walls are craggy. I grab a jutting ledge and leap over the rocky slope.

Rivan and Thayne grab broken rocks and swing at the creature, making noise and shouting, keeping the creature from focusing on anything else.

Across from me, Yara begins climbing too.

My hand slips, and I gasp. But reach again. And climb.

The creature is now shooting red stings, aiming at Rivan and Thayne, and my heart is beating very hard in my throat.

A flare of light flashes in the corner of my vision. The next second, the side of the slope cuts off, crashing into a pile of rubble. I press against the sides as the debris continues falling. A sharp piece of rock cuts through my palm, and I gasp.

At the sound, the jellyfish bobs uncertainly, rotating in its place. Taking advantage, Ansh twists his body and makes a daring reach for the tentacle grabbing him. His hands claw at it. A wounded shriek rings along the walls, jarring through my bones. I shut my eyes tight to contain the strange sensation reverberating in my body.

"Get down!" Rivan yells.

I turn around so fast that I almost lose my grip on the rocks. Rivan shoves Thayne out of the way and gets hit by one of the red stings. My scream doesn't leave my throat. He goes flying back and slams against the wall.

My stomach drops. A violent denial tears itself from me: *"No!"*

Thayne bolts after him.

I try to climb down, but my hand slips on a rock, and I realize that I have to take down this bizarre monstrosity or there's no protecting Rivan from something even worse.

Yara reaches eye level with the creature. As I begin climbing again, she throws a dagger at it with a cry. The blade knocks into the spherical body but bounces off harmlessly. The creature jerks up and down, startled.

I reach Yara. All I need is *one* opportunity to strike.

Ansh catches the tentacle between his teeth, screaming, and the creature flashes back and forth viciously. In the blink of an eye, the creature severs the tentacle. It flies in the air—taking Ansh with itself.

Ansh crashes against the far side of the cavern.

He goes limp.

Yara screams.

The company rushes to Ansh.

In the ensuing commotion, with everyone distracted, the monster begins glinting red again, gathering steam beneath the translucent outer layer. If it unleashes those luminescent stings once more, they will strike at the group—all of them together.

I look at Rivan and Thayne; they're still huddled beneath the wall.

Yara is frantic about Ansh.

And the creature is moving toward her.

I swear and hang back. "Yara! Careful!"

She whirls to me, then the creature, and tries to get out another blade. But she's trembling. Her hand keeps slipping.

The jellyfish is vibrating now. This close, I can see the lethal-looking barbs around its body. Quickly I switch my daggers for the longest one.

With a roar, I abandon the caution of the pits, forcing myself to forget the distance to the ground, letting my body take over and do what it knows best. I grip the dagger in both hands and leap off the wall, rushing through the air toward the creature. The blade lodges itself deep in its flesh, and a spurt of blood engulfs my face, filling my mouth. I cough and hack and gasp.

The creature shrieks, circling in the air madly, trying to throw me off.

Blood makes my fingers slippery, and I grip the dagger tighter—

I scream, the sickly blood still coating my mouth. The walls blur past me as the creature begins plummeting, still moving in circles. I reach and grab at it, a handful of wet muscles. The creature shakes wildly. Turns to strike with its remaining strength.

And that's when we slam onto the ground.

FOURTEEN

T he creature's body cushions my fall. But the impact rings
through my bones, a shock of pain running through my body.
I pull in breaths with difficulty, the blood blocking the back
of my throat and filling my nose. Coughing it out lights fire through
my lungs.

I lie there, just grateful to the ocean I'm not dead.

Then I roll off the creature's squashy mass and slam on the ground,
my palms slick with blood and my eyes threatening to pop out of my
skull.

I don't know how I got from there to the edge of the wall or who
came to pick me up. The pain turns everything around me to the
deepest night that I can't see through. Only when drops of water
dribble down my chin do I gather strength in my arms and snatch the
waterskin, sucking through to the last dregs.

When I finally open my eyes and blink my vision clear, Aryadna is
wrapping my hand in a bandage.

"That was quite dramatic," she says. She reaches out, tentative,
and I don't even bother to jerk away like I would have outside this

tomb. Apart from the bandage on my hand and the painful spasms in my feet, I'm not hurt. At least not in a prohibitive way.

I search for any injuries on Aryadna, but she seems fine. Raksha sits on a rock across from us, watching me with her permanent frown, but says nothing. A short distance away, Yara is crouched over Ansh, with Siril helping them. The sight of them brings back the shock of jumping off the wall and toward the jellyfish crashing into my mind. I wince.

"Rivan—"

"New guy? Yeah, about him…" Aryadna shifts, giving me a view of the wall to my right. Rivan is hunched over, gripping his upper arm as if in pain. The sight is a gut punch. Thayne sits with him— Thayne who was about to be hit before Rivan—

I lurch from my place, even as sharp pain bites at me, and make my way to Rivan. He looks up as I approach, tries to shift, and grimaces. He has a bag and a pike, and his shoes are sturdy. He's even wearing a sensible jacket over his miner's clothes.

"You planned this." I sit down and pick up the discarded cloth that he must be using to wipe his forehead with. As I touch the cloth to his skin, he winces.

"The creature cornering me? No, I did not."

"Stop it, Rivan. Why in hells would you *do* this? Follow us down here?"

"What was I supposed to do? Let you get yourself killed so far away from—from everything?"

"And you're helping by coming here how, exactly?"

Rivan's eyebrows lower as he concentrates on me. I'm determined not to look straight at him. For days, he didn't speak to me, refusing to see sense. It was eating me inside. And now here he is, in the flesh, and I'm the one furious.

"Do Ashvin and May even know you're here?"

"May does. He'll tell Ashvin."

I swear. "What is wrong with you? You know how troubled Ashvin gets. How *could* you—and now—" I press the cloth on his forehead *hard* and he yelps.

"Okay, okay, I agree. I didn't think this through." He grabs my hand and removes it from his forehead. The touch of his callused fingers is so familiar, so precious, it takes everything in me not to burst out crying. "But I couldn't just let you be here with all these"—he looks around—"miners."

I roll my eyes, even as he still holds my hand. "How could they know anything about me down here?"

"By yourself, they wouldn't have. With those two... Come on, Kress. You'd have done the same if it were me."

Of course I'd have done the same. But I'm not going to admit that.

Rivan tries to sit up, only to gasp. His grip on my hand tightens.

"What hurts?" I say automatically.

"Nothing," he says. Then adds at the look on my face, "The whole slamming-into-the-wall thing didn't go as planned. I hate you, by the way." He directs the latter at Thayne, who sits a few feet away from us.

"You have even more of my gratitude, then." Thayne gives no indication that he's taken Rivan's words in the worst way possible. Like they understand one another.

Rivan confirms my suspicion. "I know Thayne. He's too peaceful to be here. Is this some kind of hunting mission, and you're going to use him as bait?"

"For the ocean's sake, *no*."

Rivan catches my eye finally, and just the look is enough. Despite how dire everything is, we start snickering like children. But then he quiets. I raise a brow and he gestures over my shoulder, letting go of my hand.

Beyorn stands there, watching us. From this angle on the ground, he appears a giant ready to stomp a boot on me. One after another, Thayne, Siril, Aryadna, and Raksha join us too. They're expecting something.

The realization of what happened and what might happen now finally dawns on me. It's his company, the Collector made him leader, and here we are—an attack so soon. And someone who has no business being here.

"Who are you?" he asks, jaw tight.

Rivan and I stand.

"I'm Rivan, a miner"—he gestures at the others—"like them."

"Whatever you think you're doing here, boy, you will not come with us."

"We can't leave him here alone!" I shout.

The muscle in Beyorn's jaw twitches. For a heartbeat, I feel as if he's going to hit me. And what if he does? He could leave me—and Rivan—here as punishment. He could do anything to us down here, and no one would stop him.

Yara hurtles to us, coming to a stop an inch from Rivan. She stabs a finger into his chest. "You brought that creature to us. It's *your* fault my brother is hurt."

I stop myself from correcting her. It's *my* fault that the creature came after us. If I killed it like I was supposed to, Ansh wouldn't be hurt. He's sitting half-up, a bandage around his head, a hand in a sling. I can't see him properly from this distance, but his hatred doesn't need light to cut through to me. He gets up, groaning with effort, and limps his way to us.

"If he hadn't shoved Thayne aside, one of our company would be dead." I know, of course, how flimsy this logic is, but I won't leave Rivan alone here in this labyrinth of death.

Beyorn's lip curls. "He wouldn't have needed to if you'd done your job right."

"I—"

"You have come here on the Collector's discretion. Down here, I run things."

"One more person to help can't hurt," Aryadna says timidly.

Beyorn shuts her up with one look. "He has nothing at stake here. If he slips, we would all be at risk. So actually, it will hurt."

Rivan glances at me as he says, "I have more at stake right now than anyone present."

Blood rushes to my cheeks. I scramble to draw attention away from what he's just said. "If you won't let him come, then I will stay with him and go back. You can continue on with your half-dead guard and his sister who will always prioritize him over the company's safety."

Before anyone says anything, a bark of laughter erupts from Yara. Everyone turns to her, even Beyorn.

"You speaking of the miners' safety is a bit ironic, don't you think?" she snarls. "Did you tell them who you are?" She stabs a finger toward the others. "Do they know who they're traveling with?"

"What does she mean?" Siril asks, swiveling her head from Yara to me.

"Tell them!" Yara shrieks. "Tell them who your parents are."

"Shut up, Yara," Rivan says quietly. He leans against the wall, breathing deeply, as if it's hurting him.

"Why?" Yara turns to him. "We're walking in death's mouth down here. We should have all the facts."

Aryadna glances at Beyorn, then me with questions in her eyes.

"Tell everyone you're Jar and Katya Dune's daughter!" Yara yells.

In a second, everything changes. There's an uproar of disbelief, shouts and questions ringing in the cavern.

Siril lunges at me, and Rivan shoves his way in front of me, hands outstretched as if he could single-handedly hold back the entire world from us.

Aryadna stays where she is.

"My parents died in that blast your parents set off," Yara continues. "As did so many others. Brothers and sisters and so many family members. And here you are, making more of us bleed. You are your parents' daughter after all, Dune. Is that why you came here?"

"That's a lie, and you know it!"

Siril clutches her backpack to her chest as if she's protecting herself, her eyes wide with true fear. "Why weren't we told this? She's going to kill us down here."

I didn't realize I still had the capacity to feel hurt when people see me like a monster. As if I'm not risking my life to protect *them*.

Raksha moves like lightning, her polearm held at the ready. She says harshly, "A child does not pay for the crimes of their parents."

"I don't—" Thayne starts but is cut off by Ansh.

"Raksha-ma," Ansh says. "This is the Kinkillers we're talking about. Not even the shadow of their blood is welcome in the mines. You, of all people, must see reason."

"I see reason." Miraculously, Raksha glares at him. Her free hand closes around the ring on the chain around her neck.

"Your petty miner dung business," Beyorn cuts in, his voice dangerously soft and impeccably loud at the same time, "is your business. But this mission will not be jeopardized, or none of you will see the light of the day. Do you understand that?" He directs the latter toward Aryadna, who seems to be the only one standing in no-man's-land.

Beyorn hasn't spoken much during the journey down here, but I realize now, he never needed to. The darkness that has descended on his face makes me see that this man could crush my skull with his bare hands if he wanted to. The Collector sent him alone to lead so many of us. It must mean something.

Raksha's defense, even if it's probably only because she needs me to keep the company safe, builds my courage, and I say, "We can deal with this—with *me*—when we return. But we have to return alive for that." And once I return to the land above, nothing will keep me on this island anyway. I will live beneath the better skies of Chandrabad. By myself, away from my parents' names and their deeds. I will not be called to court for their crimes.

"So our safety rests in the hands of the person whose parents basically went insane and committed mass murder for no good reason?" Siril says, dismayed.

I may not be the monster they think I am, but I can glare like one. "Basically, yeah."

Thayne is the one who relents first. Then, much to Yara's annoyance, the others follow. Ansh places a hand on her shoulder, clearly holding her back from opening her mouth again and getting decked by Beyorn. Both of them turn to give me a death stare. The expressions on their faces, grayed by exertion, are predatory. I won't be dropping my guard for the rest of this journey, any more than I would have on the island above.

Raksha lifts up her polearm, signaling the start of the truce.

And just then, a cry escapes Rivan. He crumples to the ground.

"Rivan!" I reach for him. A spasm of agony racks his back.

"What's wrong with him?" Aryadna asks, joining me.

I don't have time to think about how she's talking to me. As Rivan presses a hand to his chest, I open the zip of his jacket, then unbutton the top of his shirt.

His chest is bleached white. And in the middle of his collarbones is an angry wound with luminescent red threads pointing toward his heart.

FIFTEEN

I haven't puked all over myself," Rivan says.

I look into his eyes that are lighter than they should be before going back to the mass of red on his chest. The sting hit him square. Rivan claims he felt nothing but warmth, nothing to suggest he'd been physically hurt. But the wound sticks to him like death.

The caves are cold, burning my lungs, making my hands shake. I can't believe I didn't notice it before.

What will I say to Ashvin and Mayven if something happens to Rivan? He's here because of me.

"Whatever's going on in your head," Rivan says, breaking my thoughts, "is not going to help us."

"*Us.*" It's Beyorn who speaks, in the way of a deadly snake positioning itself to strike and leave no chance for its victim to escape. Slowly, as if from a nightmare, colors change in my vision. I remember *why* I'm here. And with who. They come into focus. Yara, Ansh, Siril, Thayne, Aryadna, Raksha.

"He's hurt," I say to Beyorn. "I need to go back and get him help."

"What you need to do," Beyorn growls, "is get up and move."

"He'll die!"

Beyorn storms forward. He stops a hand's length from me and stares down. "No business of mine. None of us asked him to come here. We have wasted enough time."

"He's my best friend, and I'm not leaving him to die."

And he won't die, not ever.

Beyorn's face hardens. "The Collector has his wisdom, and I will not question that. But if you leave now, I will make sure you have a black mark against your debts. You will see no profit from this expedition."

Which means I can never get off this island. Once a debt is black-marked, it becomes perpetual. I could pay off all the original amount, plus interest, and they will still keep my tab open as punishment for obstructing the Collector's work on the island. Soul-crushing labor and enslavement are how they run this place.

Power-tripping bastards.

I say nothing, sensibly, because I know if I open my mouth, it will only be to curse him aloud. Beyorn grits his teeth.

He digs his hand in his large pocket. Before I can step back from him, he's pulled out a gun and planted its cold barrel on my forehead.

Someone gasps.

"Whoa." Thayne raises his hands and tries to step between me and Beyorn. "We can discuss this."

Beyorn stays still, power radiating from him.

"Do what you want," I say through my darkening, angry vision. "I will take him back, or I will die. Either way, I'm not going any farther with you."

"Kress," Rivan hisses, alarmed.

I ignore him and keep my chin up, refusing to look away from Beyorn. My heart beats erratically, pounding in my ears.

Don't call my bluff.

Over Thayne's shoulder, Beyorn looks between Rivan and I, his cold, calculating gaze resting in the small space between us. I understand, at the same moment as he does, where my vulnerability lies.

He moves the gun from me to Rivan in a swift motion without taking his eyes off me. "Do what I say and move. Or he'll die much sooner."

In a second, my instincts kick in, and I lunge to snatch the gun out of Beyorn's hand. Thayne twists at the last moment, and I collide into him, but it's Rivan who grabs my hand first. I look down at him incredulously.

He squeezes my hand. Gets up.

"I'm fine. We'll dress the wound up," he says through the slightest of tremors in his voice. "And then we can go ahead."

"You are not of the company," Beyorn snaps.

"I will not leave him," I say. "And if you hurt him, you have nothing left to blackmail me with."

Flames reflect in Beyorn's eyes, turned dark with fury. It's a gamble, but it's also true. There's not a world where I could leave Rivan alone. To die.

As if the burden my parents left me with is not enough that I must live in a world where Rivan's death is my fault.

"We're wasting time," Raksha says harshly, breaking the tense silence. Beyorn turns to her as if in disbelief that someone other than him has dared to speak, but Raksha meets his eyes. "If the boy must come, then let him. Better than to stand still, neither here nor there."

Beyorn watches Raksha with narrow eyes, then looks at Rivan and me. A savageness enters his features.

The hall is large, empty—save for us and the corpse of the jellyfish creature. Yara and Ansh would *cherish* the chance to hunt us. Raksha-ma and Aryadna don't seem like people who enjoy chasing after people. And who knows where Siril's and Thayne's loyalties lie?

101

Thayne tries to keep peace, but Siril, who came here with her silly book, didn't hesitate to want me dead.

But she doesn't have any weapons. At least none that we can't fight.

No, I think as I look at Rivan, *not we.*

And…then what? Even if I manage to get Rivan and myself away from here, we'd still be hurtling in unknown territory, choked by the dark all around, with Beyorn on our heels.

Rivan and I exchange glances. His wound hasn't spread further in these past few minutes, but the direction of the strange threads is unmistakably toward his heart.

Finally, Beyorn says, "You will continue if you don't want a black mark, and whether the boy dies here or down there is your wish. But if the boy slows us down, no one is going to stop for him. Now move!" he shouts, and in an instant, the queue is reformed.

"If he has to die either way," I say, my lips trembling, "then there's nothing that you can do to make me go with you. No black mark is going to force my hand."

"You're not worth this much trouble," Beyorn growls.

"Don't do something imprudent, Beyorn," Aryadna calls sharply. "The Collector himself chose her for this mission."

The tic in Beyorn's jaw pulses as the others stand there watching with bated breath for whatever decision comes. Is this how it ends—with Rivan wounded and me unable to do anything? No more dreams of free shores and blue skies. Only the dark in my veins. And Rivan? I look at him. He never talks about *his* dreams. Nothing but the safety of his brothers for whom he labors in the mines every day. Does he die because he made the mistake of caring for me?

Killing people is in your blood, not ours.

Then, Beyorn says, "If you do your job properly, we can talk about getting him to the compound's doctors upon our return."

My head spins. It's—but Rivan needs help *now.* Before I can argue any further, Raksha steps in front of me. She drags me to a corner, away from everyone else.

"The man is right, and you know that."

"So what do we do?" I whisper angrily. "Nothing?"

"We don't know what that creature is or what this wound means. You won't be able to get help at the compound without Beyorn's endorsement."

"What if it's poisonous? It has to be treated on time to be contained."

"We don't know that, Krescent," she says patiently, her lips curling. "It's a risk, yes. A risk we have to take, or Rivan dies anyway."

"So—"

"It hasn't affected him immediately"—she looks at Rivan—"so maybe it's not a venom. Look, you can waste time trying to go back up in the dark without the help of maps or compasses or even light, or come with us and wrap up this journey as fast as we can so actual doctors might look at him."

"What kind of a cruel option is this?" I ask, tears stinging my eyes.

"The only kind we have under them," Raksha says with resignation.

We continue for several hours, going deeper and deeper down the caves. Fortunately, the decline steepens on its own, and we don't come across any descents where we need to rappel. Rivan couldn't take it if we did.

I keep at the head of the company. This time, I make no mistake— any creature that crosses our path dies. But not many do, and the ones that I'm forced to kill are only small ones. We move past stranger and stranger surroundings. The chambers get bigger, paths start forking in more directions, filled with stone pillars that seem…unnatural.

Once or twice, I feel eyes on me from the dark. But when I check, it's nothing. Nothing except the persistent pain that now hammers between my shoulder blades. I've never felt anything like it before—not restricting, only constant. As if something has gotten locked beneath my skin, trying to find a way out.

Beyorn keeps up to the west, leading us past many chambers. It's curious how he can be so sure of the direction with a compass and an unconvincing map when so many others have gotten lost.

Yara stays at the back with Ansh. I can feel their hateful gazes on me even up here. Almost as if they'd let another creature attack us just to get back at me, even if it hurts them again in the process.

At every turn, I sneak a look back at Rivan. He's managing but not without difficulty. I still keep up the speed. The sooner we can scour the caves, the sooner we can get out.

He catches me looking, and he stumbles, but Aryadna reaches out and helps him.

After what has to be hours, Beyorn calls for a break.

"Finally," Siril murmurs, shooting the leader a dark glare.

We sit in the faint light off the nearby seawater lakes. Despite the central fire, the cold stings. The cave around us bends toward the center, lower than the others, and smaller too. It's safe—but water trickles down its far wall, frozen in places. The burning eye of the sun feels like a distant memory. Even its wrath would be welcome in this cold.

I scour the perimeter as the others set up camp.

When I return to the group, I find Rivan helping them instead of resting. He's taken off his jackets. The pale shirt clings to the strained muscles on his back.

Then he turns, and the wound's void gapes at me.

I shake my head.

"You shouldn't be doing this," I say.

"And fixate on this"—he looks down—"like you?" But then he sees my face and laces his fingers through mine, squeezing them. "Sit and eat something."

104

Without the constant vigilance, hunger's claws rise up suddenly at the mention of food. I can't remember the last time I ate something. And just a few nights ago, Rivan and I were having dinner with his brothers. The thought of Ashvin and Mayven makes me queasy.

"Do you think the Lander really means it?" Rivan asks. The strange red threads flash quietly along the wound, bright in our dark surroundings. A lure, as if to say *come closer*. It may be my imagination, but the lower edge has expanded a tiny bit already.

"Yes, he does," I say fiercely. *Or I don't know what I'll do.* "I'm not going to be the one to tell Ashvin and Mayven that their brother—for the ocean's sake, Rivan. This was such a foolish thing to do."

Rivan laughs shortly. A hollow sound. "Whatever Raksha-ma told you, trust in that. She knows what she's saying."

He knows as well what it would mean for Ashvin and Mayven if something happens to him. May, especially, never got over watching their mother die the slow, painful death. It's why he's always so mean about everything. A front to protect himself.

But I don't push it. Raksha *does* seem well-respected among the miners. If she says it's not a venom—even if it sounds like wishful thinking—maybe it's true. Even Yara and Ansh don't argue with her. I glance across the cave and catch Yara staring.

Kinkiller, she mouths.

Rivan says, "She wants to roast you on a spit."

"She can get in line," I say dryly.

The others are murmuring quietly. Thayne sits with Raksha and Siril on an elevated flat stone. They're supposed to keep watch, but he's staring down the space in front of him with the meditative quality I've come to associate with him. Aryadna is talking to Beyorn. She seems strangely not afraid of anyone in this company even though we're all strangers. Mostly. But she spoke for me and helped Rivan through our journey. And that's all that matters. If these red threads turn out to be venom... If we can't get back in time... If—

The metallic taste of blood slips into my mouth, and I realize I've been chewing on my lip.

I get up for another perimeter check.

The tunnel we left behind breathes empty, the walls of the cave gleam like dark seas beneath starless nights, and I find nothing. Nothing save that strange sensation in the pit of my stomach. It's fear, I know. Fear of losing Rivan.

When I turn back, at first, I can't locate him in the group.

But then there he is—Aryadna standing close to him. To check the wound, I think.

The sight of her hand at Rivan's collar makes my stomach lurch.

"Pack up," Beyorn barks from somewhere to the left. "We continue in half an hour."

Groans erupt from the company. But everyone begins to move.

"Thought you were supposed to be on the alert always?" Yara says at my ear, startling me.

How did she sneak up on me? "I could fight you blind, Yara."

She guffaws, then adds, "Speaking of being blind, they look so good together, don't they?"

Rivan's head is bent toward Aryadna. Her hand has moved from the fabric of his shirt to the skin on his collarbone, and my entire vision tunnels on that brief touch. I feel like I'm going to be sick.

"If my *best friend* had gotten hurt by a deadly creature while he was trying to find me, I think I'd be happy he's getting something out of it in what might be his last couple of days," Yara says.

Heat pounds in my head, swallowing every sound. The compass in my hand shatters. I look down. The glass screen cuts through my palm, blood trickling onto the broken bits lying around my feet.

Yara shakes her head. "Oh, no. Looks like she's lost her direction."

SIXTEEN

By the time we range miles of empty caverns, over two days pass. I can sense the others growing lax, but the seeming calm makes my heart race faster. Keeping them all safe is my responsibility—even more so now with Rivan. Although his wound shows no obvious signs of infection, the warm red has only grown. I can't close my eyes to rest without dreaming of Rivan dying.

Things are too quiet. Except for the drip of water echoing from somewhere to our right. A row of glowing mushrooms interrupts the dark until even they vanish.

We stop at a low plateau, the drop only a few meters. Along the edge, though, are some more mushrooms, tiny and shimmering.

"They could be poisonous. Stay away," Raksha barks when she sees Siril kneeling close.

We're making good time according to Beyorn, who alone seems to know anything about where our journey stops, so he lets us have a bigger break, get some sleep.

Siril and Thayne take watch toward the cliff.

It doesn't help my jitters though. With Rivan wounded, all I want is to keep moving and hurry out of here.

All this break does is let my mind wander.

Whatever I felt on seeing Aryadna near Rivan, it doesn't make sense. It's strange, an excavation of my insides that I did not permit, and it doesn't feel good. Almost as if she was encroaching on something that was mine. Which is a silly thing to think of for a *person*.

What's even worse is knowing that doesn't change the fact that my palms have been clammy ever since.

I don't need any of this right now. Damn Yara. It's *her* fault for filling my head with pointless things. And what am I doing, letting her manipulate me like this?

Get a grip, Dune.

If anything, I should be thinking of how to help Rivan. How to get him out of here.

I sweep a glance across the company. The bags and the shut-off headlamps are heaped in the center, and everyone is curled around. The ceiling in the cave is low, and there are stalagmites along the plateau until the mushrooms begin growing at the edge where I stand, near Siril.

It would be so easy to grab these people's supplies as they sleep and leave them to fend for themselves. I'm quicker and lighter on my feet than any of them. Not even Yara and Ansh could keep them safe, nor could Beyorn lead them out if they don't have weapons and compasses. With no food and being lost, none of them would return. No one to counter any story I could tell the Collector. We were ambushed by a monstrous creature. Everyone died but me.

I'd get half the promised pay.

I'd get no black mark on my debt.

Rivan would get help faster.

Adrenaline rushes through me at the thought.

I push my bag behind a boulder, next to where Rivan is resting. With his eyes closed and the wound behind his shirt, he looks so serene. I could sit and stare at him forever.

I shake my head. It's best to let him sleep. No point in telling him before we're ready to leave. I'll wake him up at the end. And we'll run.

My stomach twists as I move to the center of the company. Most of them are already asleep, Raksha almost but she's pressed her face into her scarf so she wouldn't notice anything. I shoot another quick glance at Siril and Thayne at the edge of the plateau. Siril, who believes I'm here to kill her like that's what I do for fun.

If we're quiet, they won't even know we left.

I take the bags first—the food and water, emergency kits, extra compasses, ropes and gear. Everything from one neat heap. These people are begging to get ambushed. It takes several long minutes to take away everyone's headlamps, slowly so I won't make any noise. The weapons lying next to everyone come next. I hide them at the entrance of the hall to take them later.

Stripping Yara and Ansh of their weapons, however, is hard. They're both light sleepers; they're both used to fighting monsters as I am.

I slip out Yara's throwing stars from the side pocket of her jacket. If either of them wakes up—

But they don't.

The entire company, minus Siril and Thayne, lies on the plateau now, vulnerable. All I have to do is wake Rivan up quietly. I tiptoe to him.

"Look!" Siril says excitedly, her voice echoing in the emptiness.

I slap a hand to my mouth to keep myself from gasping aloud.

Raksha moves. But no—she only turns in sleep.

Siril lifts something to Thayne. "Have you seen this color before?"

In her hands is a rock, I think. Under the muted light from her headlamp, it shimmers. The color could be violet, but it is lighter. Like the pale shades that Lander clothes are sometimes made of. Something soft and kind. It has nothing of the hardness of miners.

Siril's whole face has lit up like that of a child. Thayne indulges her like she's his own.

The memory rushes back to me like a punch in the gut. I was five or maybe six and playing along the shore despite my parents having told me for the hundredth time how dangerous it was. That the monsters in the sea would eat me and take me away from them, and would I like that? *No*, I'd said, wide-eyed. And yet when they left for the shift, I skipped down to the shore. Curving around the spires, the cliffs. I found a newly hatched flonner, alone, which I knew wasn't possible. Flonners were incredibly protective of their young. Only death could separate them. So I picked the baby up and ran back home. My parents had come back and were worried sick, and my father was going to yell, but I held up the flonner to his face. *Look what I found. It was alone.*

I saw many emotions cross my father's face in that moment. Emotions I can now name. Anger, but terror, then relief, and maybe even joy. At the end, all he did was help me take care of the flonner until we could release it back in the sea safely a week later.

That's what Siril and Thayne look like. A daughter and a father.

They're such bad watchers. I managed to move all the gear. I could easily walk away. A vicious creature could creep up on them, and they wouldn't see their own deaths coming. They won't last a day without me.

If I leave these people stranded...

I wish I *were* the Kinkiller these people want me to be so badly. But fortunately for them and unfortunately for me, I have a thing to prove, and I will have to protect them even if the majority of this company deserves to be sersei food.

I walk away from Siril and her absurd rock, and under the pretense of checking the perimeter, I slowly bring everything back before anyone wakes up.

SEVENTEEN

The next crossing brings us to a series of narrow alleys along overlapping walls that take hours to get through.

"Be careful," I call, still sullen over losing the opportunity to get out of here. "The walls are jagged."

I go first, but my bag gets caught in the walls. We try to shift the bags, squeeze them, but there's no way we can cross the alleys with the bags and the torches while also keeping our weapons at the ready.

"I'll take you one by one," I say, examining the space between the alleys. "I'll hold your flame and any weapons. Come behind me with our bags."

Beyorn lets me take Rivan first. Not out of generosity but probably because Rivan's dispensable and it's better to leave him waiting on the other side.

It's a cumbersome, slow process. The scraping of my suit against the stone echoes through my bones, the fire from the torch making my eyes water. For the first hundred or so meters, the ground is fanged, making it difficult to walk. Every press on the ground sends a shocking pain even through the thick boots. It's suffocating, stone pressed on either side.

"If something attacks us, there's no space to fight back," I murmur.

"Let's hope nothing does, then."

I laugh shortly, only to hiss in pain when a rock jabs at my stomach.

"Tell me about the others," I say, facing forward and moving at a glacial pace. "You know them?"

"I know Raksha-ma the best," he says. "She's Harren's mother."

"Harren? The Young Scythe?" I snort. "That explains so much."

Even I've heard of her son, Harren, the leader of the younger faction preparing for a full-scale rebellion in the mines against the Collector's growing ruthlessness. All those minor blasts ruining tankers, ship damages, port blockage—causing all sorts of trouble to the Lander overseers.

People affectionately call him the Young Scythe.

I can see he takes after his mother. She may not be a rebel, but Raksha commands respect by her very presence.

"Thayne keeps to himself," Rivan continues. "I think he—he might have been there."

There. The day when my parents set off the blast in the mines. Is that why Thayne is such a peacemaker? Because he saw someone he loved die? Does he hate conflict because he doesn't know which of his own people might betray him if he doesn't keep everyone together?

"And Siril, with her books. She's harmless, if that's what you're wondering, by the way. All of them are good people."

"She calls me Kinkiller."

"It's what she's been taught to think of you as, Kress. These people have nowhere they can direct their festering anger toward. Easier to hate you than face the life they're being forced to live."

"Isn't that just great," I say through gritted teeth. How could I ever

113

prove I am not my parents if they have already decided what they think of me?

If only there were something to fight. Fighting keeps my mind busy. It's harder to think about dead parents and pathetic miners when you're focused on where the next claw swipes from. Staying angry at all these people who hate me for what my parents did works the same.

"And what about Aryadna?"

He says after a moment, "I don't think I've seen her before." He doesn't sound particularly concerned, though. Maybe he just didn't come across her. The mines are hard work. Not everyone has the same temperament of thinking of everyone else as family.

We continue on slowly, sweating and cursing.

The walls begin to grow wider, giving us respite, but the alleys are still never-ending.

More than that, though, the structure feels like it's been carved. The incline grows smoother—as if a worn passage, not the rocky terrain of the rest of the underground. And the fractured walls now are filled with silvery minerals glinting in our torch lights.

It all feels purposeful, not the action of time.

The thought keeps my mind off the other thing gnawing at me, even as the space stays narrowed.

Every time an alley ends, another begins.

We've been at this for almost an hour. I'm beginning to feel as if we're moving in circles.

"This is a labyrinth," I breathe. My voice echoes anyway. "Stay close."

"Are you sure the others are safe out there without you?"

"Yara and Ansh are with them."

Soon, the alleys begin to expand until the last one spits us into a caved-in hall leading away toward multiple passages, rubble clattered across the surface. And every passage looks the same.

I heave, sweat pouring down my back. Breathing is painful as I suck in lungs full of air, every movement a stab in my sides.

For a moment, the pain takes me back to days of running up the hills, training around the spires in the metallic rain and along the coastlines where the sea creatures weren't always docile. Terror beat me sharply at every turn in those days, but I had to get into Badger's pits. Otherwise I would sink into the very stone of this island, never to get out.

Good job not sinking in the stones of this island.

I straighten. "Wait here. I'll go back to them."

Then, I plunge back into the labyrinth.

For a while, everything seems fine. But then, without Rivan with me to talk and keep me distracted, silence prowls along the edges of my mind, slowly becoming bigger and bigger. I put each step down with care, making sure there *is* ground beneath me. Not just emptiness.

Several minutes like that, and I want to shriek, just to keep myself company.

Parts of the labyrinth are so narrow that I could simply give up on holding myself up and still gravity won't be able to pull me down. And would that be so bad? If I just didn't have to carry my own burden? Maybe I would float away. Like the jellyfish creature. My body could slowly split and spiral upward, turn into air, and vanish. I could stop walking. Just stay here. In the maze, away from everything and everyone.

My one job here was to keep everyone safe. But I failed that. Rivan might be dying.

Useless. It's how I've felt since Badger threw me out and perhaps why I even agreed to come on this journey. To have my debts pardoned but also to prove something. But what? That I'm not my parents?

And still, Siril shattered that illusion in just a moment—*kill her before she hurts us*.

I've stayed hidden for so long, and they still see me as a monster.

If I am truly no different from my parents, should I even bother leaving this island? If I will only hurt people anywhere I go, is it not kinder to stay here, quietly, in a corner? Who am I to want out of the life that I'm doomed to live?

All the guilt of what my parents did, the fear of being found out—it has pressed on my shoulders, weighing me down. No feeling survives long in me before being smothered by this weight. And now I'm beginning to think perhaps I died the day my parents did too.

Better to have died in the pits.

I should blow out the torch.

Let the dark take me...

"Krescent!"

The voice hits me hard, and a shadow flees from my mind.

I heave, breathing in air as if for the first time.

A fiery torch lights the alley's wall to sunlike brightness. Aryadna almost slams into me. Her face is red as she drags herself through the narrow maze. And she's still yelling.

"What were you *doing*?"

I swear, tasting the dust in the air with renewed vigor. "It felt like I was—I was underwater." In truth, it was worse. A voice inside my head as if it had always been waiting to strike, finally getting an opportunity. A venomous snake slithering until it had replaced me inside my own mind like I was nothing. Only a little obstacle it climbed over. And it wanted me. "Madness," I breath. "It felt like madness."

"Are you sure you're okay?" Aryadna asks. She's pressed against the wall, her arm extended to hold the torch for lack of space. She must be hurting.

"I am," I say. "And no one should do the crossing alone."

She nods and then leads me out.

Hours later, with Aryadna's help, I finally get everyone from one end of the labyrinth to the other. We pick the westernmost passage out of the hall where I'd left Rivan.

The madness does not come again. But I still feel its forked tongue inside my mind, waiting for an opportunity once more. To remind me again of the life waiting for me if I get out of this darkness and don't run from this island.

Is this something that might have afflicted the previous expeditions?

Maybe they didn't have someone to lead them out of the labyrinth.

I don't tell anyone else about it. I'm not sure what I can say that won't make me look like a coward unfit to do my job. Maybe Beyorn adds another diversion in our already flimsy plan.

"Beyorn, I need matches—" I stop speaking.

A coldness grips my spine. It sinks into my skin in a way that makes me feel like I'm standing in the pits, my back to a lunging monster.

"What's wrong?" Thayne calls.

I shake my head slowly. It's a smell—not unlike that of the pits. Of blood and violence in the dusty, stale air. Something musky within the chilled surroundings.

Something almost...human.

I glance over my shoulder. Beyorn's huge frame touches the low ceiling. He obscures Raksha, Yara, and Ansh behind him. Rivan is with them, half of him visible as he leans to the wall. My stomach lurches at the thought of what this journey must be costing him. But everything seems normal. And still I cannot shake the feeling of being watched. Of being...pursued.

The first time I felt this, it must have been Rivan. But now?

There's no wind. I wave my torch from side to side. In the moment the *whoosh* of the flame dies, I think I hear something moving over the rubble we left behind.

This time, I stop and turn.

Aryadna raises a brow.

"Do you hear something?" I ask.

She closes her eyes, listening, and behind her, Siril turns around on her spot, casting a look everywhere.

"I don't know?" Aryadna says uncertainly.

"What do *you* hear?" Beyorn asks.

"Movement," I say simply.

After that, we walk with drawn blades, and Raksha joins me with her polearm.

Still, when our stalker appears, he nearly kills one of us.

EIGHTEEN

A shadow separates from the wall and leaps at us, catching Siril by her stomach. She screams. The rest of us are caught half-way in scrambling and aiming our weapons.

"What is it?" yells Beyorn from the back of the row.

Between the shouting and the scrambling, no one answers him. Raksha and I grab for the creature, with a leathery brown skin. But we only catch air. It darts around us with inhuman speed. We grapple with it for several seconds. It claws my arm, and the outer layer of my suit rips. For a moment, we're just a mass of teeth and blood and hair.

My foot slips. I crash into a wall and my head rings.

Beyorn roars and, using his entire frame, slams into the creature and pins it to the wall.

No, I think, my vision still blurry from the hit, *not a creature at all*.

It's a man, dressed in thick brown robes. In the dark lit by nothing but flames, he looks like death has taken a form. His body is wiry, less than half of Beyorn's mass, yet he doesn't stop *rampaging*, so furiously that it looks as if he could burst out of his body and become a storm himself. He and Beyorn struggle for an elongated moment, unbridled and violent, and then—

Beyorn shouts, "My fucking ear!"

The sudden smell of blood pours in the air as the man continues to battle Beyorn madly, still trying to bite him from beneath the hood. The sheer intensity of his movements makes me think of a rabid animal in no control of its actions.

Siril stumbles back, scrubbing viciously at Beyorn's blood that got sprayed on her, at the same time as Aryadna steps closer. Her eyebrows are pulled down, as if she can't believe what she's seeing.

"What *is* that?" she says.

Beyorn, still screaming as crimson spills down the side of his face, tears off the hood with his bloody hand.

I gasp.

Beneath the hood, the man's brown skin is ashen, smooth like a carved marble. As if the man has never walked beneath the sun. Not even Landers look as sunless as this man. He spits the torn flesh of Beyorn's ear and holds his mouth open in a threatening gesture, lined with thick, hammer-like teeth currently dripping with blood. And the eyes as he darts his gaze about—unnaturally large pupils, like vats of deepest black oil.

Beyorn pulls back from the man but keeps one hand locked around his throat. He squeezes. The man makes a deep growling sound, clawing at Beyorn's hand.

"Animal," spits Ansh.

Raksha shoots him a dark look, then says, "There have been rumors...but I didn't think..."

I catch Rivan's eye. He seems as baffled as me.

"Rumors of what?" Beyorn asks, his voice strained.

"The Children of Shade," Raksha says slowly, eyeing the stranger up and down. "People who have lived in the caves for generations. They are their own clan. No connection to the world above."

Beyorn curls his lip in disgust. "A Shademan, huh? Are you worms the ones hunting the previous expeditions?"

Without warning, Beyorn punches the man full in the mouth.

The man howls and drops to the ground, holding his face and convulsing like a fish out of water.

"Stop it!" Thayne cries.

"Bind his wrists quickly," Beyorn orders.

Yara and Raksha take hold of the man, even as he continues to thrash in their grip. Ansh hurries over with a rope. The Shademan watches his movements. He turns his shoulders downward, trying to make himself small. His body shivers beneath the brown robes. Ansh is quick with the tying. The Shademan's wrists are thin, although he doesn't appear to be starving. Not like the children aboveground, at least.

He probably got separated from his group. Despite the display of violence, he's afraid.

Even if he injured the biggest of us, even if he gave us the fright of our lives, he's still only one man. At our mercy.

What stories do they tell among themselves about the people who live above?

Beyorn grunts in pain as Aryadna tends to his wound, a hole in the side of his head, just like mines cut into the island. His furious eyes remain fixed on the Shademan, oozing with evil hatred. It's almost like his anger at being attacked has erased any pain he might be feeling. He's completely hypnotized by his own rage.

Thayne takes advantage of Beyorn's silence for the next few minutes and kneels in front of the Shademan. "We mean you no harm, friend."

Somehow, I doubt that the man, covered in blood and tied like a beast, will believe that.

"Friendship with these brutes is not why we are here," Aryadna murmurs as she tears strips of bandage.

"You call him brute, yet we're the ones who tied him up," Thayne grits out as he gets up and strides away.

Beyorn frowns after him, and I know this slippery moment of empathy is going to cost Thayne.

The size of Beyorn's square, brutish face dwarfs the Shademan's whole head. The Shademan stops struggling against his ties and glowers at Beyorn. Then he smiles grotesquely with bloody teeth.

An act of defiance.

"Tell me, Shademan," Beyorn speaks softly, as if holding back all his rage. "Where are the men who came before us? What happened to them? Did you hurt them?"

Aryadna wraps up the bandages and puts the emergency kit back in her bag.

At first, the Shademan tracks Aryadna's movements, frowning at the kit. Then he eyes Beyorn's wounds. But he gives no answer. He tries again to claw at Beyorn futilely, tries to get rid of his trappings, tries to push back into the wall as if he could melt into it and escape. The rest of us watch him struggling and failing.

Then, he opens his mouth and screams.

Beyorn slaps him. "What can you expect from someone living in the rot rather than in the light?"

"What are we doing with him?" I ask, determined not to look at the Shademan.

"Was it not your one job to keep a lookout for things exactly like this?" Beyorn asks.

I think of all the times I felt someone was following the company. I chose to keep quiet. But what would it matter? The Shademan knows the terrain, the secrets of the caves, better.

"He was hunting us. He hid well."

Beyorn curls his lip. With half of his face bandaged and the other still red with flecks of blood, he only manages to look like a monster himself. "I don't know what the Collector saw in you to put our lives in your hands."

He turns back to the Shademan. "Speak, rat. Where are our people? What did you do to them?"

The Shademan growls, flames reflecting in his black eyes.

Beyorn grabs his chin, pressing his fingers with so much force that the man's resolve breaks and he cries out. "I will bring down the ocean if that's what it takes to make you squeal."

"He can't understand you," I blurt, my heart hammering in my throat. "You're wasting time."

For the moment, it's not Beyorn's ruthlessness that scares me but the implications of his threat. If he really does bring the Collector's army down here, invade the Shadefolk's territories, he could ruin an entire people.

"Is that right?" Beyorn says, frowning at the man. "I suppose, where would he learn to speak like a man when he lives like a rat?"

"He can't tell us anything. I think we should let him go," Thayne adds.

"Why do you speak on his behalf like so?" Beyorn asks dangerously.

"I'm not. I only think this is not what we signed up for."

"We will make him talk. We will take him back aboveground, and he will speak. This man"—Beyorn stops to grab the Shademan's head and shoves him toward the wall—"knows secrets about the land we live on. Perhaps he has more information about zargunine. Or other metals of use. One of you take his responsibility." He looks at each of us. His one eye gleams with the torch, the red on his bandage already crusted to brown.

No one moves. Thayne looks like he might be considering it, but Raksha subtly shakes her head, and he says nothing. He's under enough scrutiny.

"I'll do it," I say.

"You should focus on the path forward."

"All the more reason to keep him at the front with me. Maybe he knows places where creatures dwell. Self-preservation is a good motive."

I have to keep an eye on the Shademan personally—I can't trust anyone else to.

"Let her do it," Raksha says. "He'll only slow us down if he's at the back."

Beyorn nods. "Fine, then." He glares at the Shademan. "He's now our captive. And if he so much as looks in the wrong direction, I'll shoot him."

NINETEEN

As I expected, the Shademan makes scouting difficult. He drags his feet, tries to go in the wrong direction, resists walking at all. But that is also why I know keeping him with me is keeping him safe. If he troubled anyone else down the line and they said something, who knows if Beyorn might make good on his threat?

We traverse through caves, on uneven ground that makes our progress slower. To make up for it, Beyorn keeps us moving relentlessly for hours. It feels like walking inside the closed mouth of a beast, its teeth sharp and jagged beneath our feet. My legs throb with pain. Rivan is at the back of the line with Raksha, and I have to keep myself from checking on him.

Every now and then, I can clearly hear water tinkling somewhere close.

In two days, we will have been down here for a week. If we still don't find anyone, we'll go back. And I'll get Rivan to Lander doctors.

"Is this safe?" I ask, pointing a torch down a narrow path. The flames light only half of the path, while the rest remains dark. After the labyrinth, I have no intentions of stepping into unknown dark again, letting any madness into my head.

The company waits for us a few steps away.

The Shademan offers no help. He stubbornly watches me gesture down the dark. Blood has dried along the lower half of his face, and his nose sits crooked. He must be in pain with every breath, but he hasn't shown any.

"Well, I tried," I tell him. "If a creature attacks us, it'll be your fault."

I've barely turned when the Shademan breaks out of the line. He slams into Siril and, as Thayne reaches to catch him, drags him alongside and runs. He knows the terrain, while Siril and Thayne bang into stone as they try to stop him.

Beyorn fires his gun.

"You imbecile!" I shout, not knowing who I'm yelling at.

Raksha roars, "You'll hit Thayne or Siril!"

He doesn't listen, and Raksha hurtles after the trio, trying to intervene.

I swing from trying to keep up with the others to Beyorn. "She's right. Stop this!" Then, before he can kill one of our own and burden us with the blood of the Shademan too, I pull out a throwing star and aim for the low end of the roof.

Stones roll off the jutting edge from the sharp hit.

The Shademan yells, startled, and Raksha wastes no time jabbing the polearm on his chest. Siril and Thayne take his arms. He growls, still struggling to get himself free.

"All you managed to do," Thayne says wearily, "is make the man in charge angry."

"Tie his feet too," Beyorn calls. "Drag him if he doesn't keep up."

Rivan and I exchange looks. No one says anything. On the island, the Collector's men punish miners by chaining their feet and making them work. It is gruesome and inhuman. At the end of the shift, the

126

miners' feet are swollen and bloody. It happened to Mayven a year ago, and it was the only time I saw Rivan cry.

No one here in their right mind would do that to someone else.

Especially me.

"What are you waiting for?" Beyorn snaps.

Aryadna, finally, moves to the Shademan and gets to work. "You brought this on yourself," she mutters as she secures the ropes.

Thayne requests some time to pull himself together, and the others also chime in before we move forward. Probably to shake the memories of chains rather than to rest. But my insides are jittery with frustration. The more we rest, the worse Rivan will get.

Raksha comforts Siril in a corner, rubbing her back and speaking softly to her. "We get paid whether we find someone or not. That was the deal. This Shademan doesn't change that, okay?"

"I really need that money," Siril sobs.

Aryadna steps up next to me, the same grimness in her features with which she tied the Shademan. I know she did it to spare us all, but the bitterness of the act hasn't left me yet. When I glance over, Aryadna is watching Siril wipe her tears.

"It's Siril's sister and niece who work at the salt pans," she tells me. "I suppose she was always going to take any unpleasantness down here harder."

"If by unpleasantness, you mean tying a man up like he's a rabid monster—"

"Don't *you* give me this, Krescent. You're supposed to be more practical. That's why you're here. Don't you think the Shademan's existence changes everything? How can we look for our people when others might have already gotten to them?"

"*Our* people?"

She waves a hand impatiently. "You know what I mean. People from above."

I turn away from her. "He's just one man."

"It seems our lack of information about the deep is worse than we thought," Aryadna says.

Beyorn, seemingly, agrees though it's obvious he hates it. He directs his frustration at the Shademan. "This time, if you try something funny, you will only *wish* you were dead."

The Shademan says nothing, but he doesn't need to. His look drips with pure loathing as he stares at each of us. I may have imagined it but—

"Why do *you* have to be the one dragging him around? I don't like the way he looks at you," Rivan says, voicing my thoughts.

"Seems like how everyone above the ground does," I try to joke. By the flattening of Rivan's expressions, I have not succeeded.

But somehow, I know that the Shademan doesn't mean me harm. Or, at least, not singularly me. Curiosity gets the better of me, and the next time we stop, I find myself staying with our prisoner instead of leaving him in a corner.

The dried crusts across his features blunt them, but beneath, I can still imagine the ashen cast to him.

He doesn't deign to look at me when I kneel in front of him. But I can tell from the twitch of his shoulders that he's aware of me. And if he followed us for so long without detection, he's smart enough to have noticed the number of knives and weapons I keep.

I check for the others before slipping out a bottle of water. "Here. I doubt you have anything on you."

The Shademan moves with astonishing speed to snatch the bottle out of my hands and guzzles the water down. It spills over his mouth and into the layers of his clothes. The bottle is nearly empty when he stops.

"It would be for your own good if you don't antagonize Beyorn," I whisper. "He's a brutal man. He means it when he says he'll take you out of here."

128

I get no answer.

"I know you don't understand a word I'm saying, but can you not use some sense? You're in obvious danger here."

"Even if he did understand us, what makes you think he will believe anything we say?" Thayne asks, coming up to stand beside me.

I look up at him. "Like I said, it's for his own good."

"The Shadefolk are tougher than the ocean. They have to be to survive down here. You think discomfort bothers them?"

"It won't be *discomfort* if the Collector gets his hands on him." And since he works with people like Badger, I wouldn't put it past him to have learned of some choice torture methods from the master of the pits.

"We're all one second from death any moment anyway, Krescent," Thayne says. "The Shadefolk know that as well as anyone." He walks back to where the rest of them are. Beyorn is already deep asleep. The pain from his ear must have gotten to him finally.

I sit next to the Shademan, head resting against the wall. The chatter of the group is dying too.

"One time," I murmur, mostly to myself since he obviously doesn't understand anything, "they got a varmee in the pits where I fight. I don't know if you know what they are. These small mammals that live in caves beneath the shores, and their entire bodies are packed beneath slabs that are bone-hard. And when they're threatened, the slabs lock together and form a cube, and the varmee hides inside. But they've also got mean claws. One took out a fighter's eye. We call him Manzar One-Eye. Anyway, this varmee refused to fight back, no matter what I did. And then the pit master turned the collar up and gave the poor creature a shock so bad it died right there.

"It wasn't my kill, but I still got a tattoo for it. To remember." I lift my left sleeve. In the inner elbow, among many other, is the dot right at the center to represent the varmee. But unlike the others, it has a small crescent shape tattooed beneath, matching the birthmark beneath my eye. "It might have lived if I'd provoked it bad enough to fight. If it had only just realized how much danger its stubbornness was putting it in. All it had to do was to lose its pride in that moment and survive. Survive to live again."

The Shademan looks back at me dead in the eye, unmoved. I don't know why I'm telling him this. I shake my head and get up, even as the sinews down my back almost break with the exhaustion of being down here.

I leave the bottle with the strange man.

TWENTY

I find Rivan sitting on a small boulder. He pulls me close, his hands on my waist, and I rest my head on his shoulder. We stay like that, without saying anything. We've always been comfortable in the closeness. The familiarity of him turns my body from granite to sand. He knows I need this moment of peace.

When I pull back reluctantly, he says, "Are you still mad at me?"

"I don't know. Are *you*?"

"You know I can't stay mad at you for long."

Despite our situation, I smile at him fondly. "Did you know I would be this much trouble when you first met me?"

"The first time I saw you, I thought you were dead, and the raath were going to swarm, so I wanted to clear the place."

"*What?*"

"You know they can really infest places," he says mildly.

I laugh, raise my hand to playfully punch him, but stop at the sight of the wound. The laugh vanishes. I blink to clear my vision because it can't *possibly* have been pulsing.

I lower my hand until it rests next to the wound, on Rivan's skin, which is cool to the touch, and his breath hitches. "If something happens to you because of me—"

"Nothing will happen to me. Not until…" He takes a deep breath, my hand rising and falling with his chest. "Not for a very long time. I have so many things to say to you, and I'm not going anywhere until I have said every last one of them."

I look up, his arms still encircled around me. Even here, surrounded by this chaos and darkness, dimmed by the threads licking their way to his heart, Rivan's eyes hold a stunning light. There's something different about him here underground, but it's probably just the lack of sun and the unfamiliarity of the surrounding. He still has his wavy curls, the same stormy eyes, the same red mouth that—

He glances away, I want to reach up and hold his face, study it, know it, *understand* it. So when I run, I will never worry about forgetting the way he is.

"I finished my water," he says. "Can I have some of yours?"

"Yeah—" I start and stop, remembering I gave my bottle to the Shademan. "I mean, I finished mine too. I'll ask someone. Aryadna—no, I don't know. Thayne, maybe, yeah. He'll help—"

"I know you gave your water to the Shademan." Rivan pulls up a side of his mouth, amusement crinkling at the corner of his shadowed eyes.

I stare at him, dumbfounded. "Then why?"

"If I had asked you outright if you did, you would have denied it. And so no one finds out, you wouldn't have asked for water from anyone either."

"He needed it more," I say pathetically.

"And only you saw that."

And only Rivan would make it sound like I did something life-changing. He's too kind, and he thinks so is everyone else. He came here for me, and look what it got him. A wound that's eating at him a morsel at a time.

132

He raises a brow. The movement livens up the planes of his face in a different manner, and the need to be even closer than I am right now, mere inches away enclosed in his embrace, intensifies. I say nothing, only murmur something about checking if he looked unwell, and withdraw.

I turn from him and realize how hard my heart pounds in my throat, how unbearably loud it is, yet not enough to drown the voice in my head that keeps repeating one thing: making a new life on Chandrabad means losing Rivan.

The last tunnel in the labyrinth is darker even in the flame. Beyond the small circle of light from the torch, everything remains a fearful night. Beyorn makes Yara join me at the front, which she does while glaring daggers at me and the Shademan.

"I'm enjoying you being around less and less," I murmur.

"Yeah," she says, "but I have actual reasons to hate you."

Let your reason rot you from the inside for all I care. I keep my mouth shut, though. Antagonize her and who knows? She could refuse to fight when the time comes. I could've risked that before, but not now, when Rivan's life is on the line.

I speed up to get away from her, but the Shademan lags back. He glares as he looks down to his tied feet.

"Now you understand gestures?" I say, annoyed.

The tunnel begins narrowing in the middle, the walls pressing at my sides, and leads us down a steep slope, forcing me to slow down again.

I hold my daggers up in front of me, each step cautious. Yara breathes shallowly behind me. The walls seem to suck in the light, leaving no shadow, no perspective. The silence rings in my ears. It is dizzying—even worse when the path ends abruptly at an archway.

I stop walking and stand still, my torch held aloft, plunging every-thing beyond the arch into a darkness deeper than anything we've seen so far. The disorienting ringing pulses softly, fading but still there. No one asks me to move, not even Beyorn, who I can sense *wants* to. They're all staring at the arch too. And the two broken pillars on either side of it.

Despite what we know for sure, that zargunine comes from deep beneath the ground, where creatures of darkness dwell, someone built pillars of stone here. And carved into them with delicate precision.

I stare, transfixed.

The arch is twice my height, even with parts of it lying crumbling on the ground. If the sun shines on it, it could pass for a gateway at some place like the Collector's compound. But how could it be here? So deep into the ground. We have been down here for five days now. There's simply no way that—

And yet we found a man with black-hole eyes and bloody teeth down here.

Buried beneath the ground, under the sea.

Rivan's gasp tears me from the pillars. He presses near the wound, his face contorted.

"I'm okay," he says when I reach him, but he leans on me just the same as I put his arm around my shoulder. Then, looking back at the pillars, he adds, "Well, not really."

"What are these?" I murmur.

"Pillars," Yara says without missing a beat.

Rivan and I turn to her together, and she only sneers at us.

"Does she ever tire of this?" Rivan asks.

Beyorn rounds on the Shademan. Despite the bandage tied around his head, a bloody patch dried to brown where his ear should have been, he looks beastly in the dark with the flames throwing his shadow like a giant's in the narrow space. "What do you know of this?"

I start, "He doesn't—"

The Shademan spits in Beyorn's face.

Beyorn hits him again, and Raksha rolls her eyes. "That's not getting him to talk," she snaps. Then she pulls the Shademan upright, dragging him away from Beyorn. The uneven slapping of his feet against the stone is loud and uncomfortable.

"We have to keep moving," Beyorn says gruffly. Perhaps it's the wound that has left half of his face bruised, but for the first time, I notice a little uncertainty in his face.

Thayne starts softly, "When we were offered the chance to come down here in exchange for whatever we wanted, we were under the impression the Collector would send someone with some idea of what we were walking into. But it seems, as with most things Landers promise us, I was wrong."

"We are going up to the previous expeditions' mission point. We are following the map the last man we found drew for us. It is better information that anyone before has had," Beyorn spits out. "You were all promised the same thing: if we don't find anyone at the end point, we will head back."

"The map from the man who was delirious with madness?"

Beyorn turns to face Thayne, a shadow descending on him with silence burning past ash. "You think you're here because you have merit? It was I who *let* you come only because you found my brother. Don't test my patience."

Raksha and I exchange glances at this new information. So the madman is Beyorn's brother. What's he trying to prove by retracing his steps?

Yara, though, lacks all tact. "Your brother? That just means you're running on sentiment. We're out here risking our lives based on your brother's testimony, and you can't tell us anything for sure!"

"We already knew he can't," says Raksha, her beady eyes fixed on the darkness beyond the arch. "Even if that map is right, it tells us where to go but not what we will find there." She looks over her shoulder toward the Shademan. "Or who."

"My job is to get to a certain point for the Collector," Beyorn answers. "And yours is not to question if you wish to reap your rewards."

"If we return alive." Yara stands tilted toward Ansh, like she's shielding him. I'd forgotten he, too, was hurt during the fight with the jellyfish creature.

Beyorn's frown deepens. "You have grown a mouth on you, have you?"

Yara looks at Ansh and then, strangely, to me. When I give her no reaction, she shakes her head.

Thayne says, "Being a good commander and leader means picking your fights and sometimes dropping them too, Beyorn."

"And questioning the authority of your commander is not going to help you raise the silver you need to save your lover."

Thayne's jaw clenches. As if reminded of who he's talking to, he looks away and says nothing.

The corners of Beyorn's mouth rise in ugly satisfaction. He straightens his shoulders and goes back to his map for several long minutes.

None of us dare move, reach out to Thayne, and tell him we think he's right. Beyorn may have gotten some satisfaction out of using Thayne's weakness to shut him up, but he's still bristling. One strike and the match of his anger will light a fire.

We can't afford any fires.

I deliberately turn back to the arch, staring at the dead piece from a world that shouldn't exist. Only the struggling Shademan breaks the deathly silence, fidgeting and snarling every few seconds. It's a miracle he followed us for however long he did when he can make such a racket.

136

Beyorn rolls the map and snatches his torch back from Thayne.

Warily, the rest of them line up again, watching me expectantly.

Rivan looks gray now, beads of sweat lining his neck.

So I lead on at a stiff pace. Raksha switches places and comes to handle the Shademan alongside me. This time, everyone's more alert, watchful of our surroundings as we step through the arch.

Beyond the arch, we walk down a low-roofed path. On either side, the stone, which must once have been smooth, is cracking with time. The flames of our torches catch glints deep in the cracks, like the walls are stuffed with gemstones, but they vanish the second I try to look directly. I reach out and brush my fingers along the wall.

"It's a passageway," Siril murmurs somewhere at the back.

Yes, but to what?

The moment the thought comes in my mind, the passageway ends and answers. We stand on a landing, with narrow steps leading to level ground. The hall rises to heights greater than the Collector's compound, empty but so expansive that its walls remain obscured in shadows. A hollow mountain.

And in the center stands the ruins of a stupa.

TWENTY-ONE

After so long in the dark, there comes a moment, sooner or
later, when you will question your senses. Madness, halluci-
nations, visions—whatever it may be, it creeps quietly.

But the flame in my hand burning hot near my face reminds me
I'm clear-eyed.

Surrounded by derelict guardrails, the stupa stands before me,
almost grazing the roof, its middle crumbling within. The top of the
hemisphere is flattened as if a giant fist slammed at it. And yet a
monolith just inside the circumference of the guardrails, reaching
the ceiling, is perfectly circular. Unlike the texture of the ground and
the walls, the monolith is smoothed, like the ocean waves drink up
every imperfection.

I suck in a breath, unable to take my gaze away.

The pillars are one thing. Even the haunting monolith.

But here, at the bottom of the known world, beneath rock and
water, beneath caves that reign over death, there existed someone—
people in large enough numbers—to have built a damned stupa. My
mother's stories never mentioned this.

There's no other entrance in the hall from our direction. This stupa is the first thing anyone will see coming down. Going through it is the fastest way across the hall. How has no one ever mentioned this if people returned from the Collector's expeditions?

Was this the sight that drove them mad?

Footsteps stamp behind me. Beyorn booms, "Are we to spend our time staring at it? Move."

Slowly, I pick my pace down the ruined stairs. The others follow, their steps echoing in the large hall of ghosts.

The ground bears testimony to time: the once-flat plain fractured, depressions scattered along the path, and the pillars collapsing like the archway littering the hall.

"People built this?" Aryadna wonders aloud.

"Unless there are beasts capable of building with stone, yes," Raksha says.

"But who?" Ansh calls out from the back.

"Did your brother mention *this*?" Yara grumbles to Beyorn's apathetic back.

Closer to the stupa, the rubble gets worse. From this vantage, its age is clear in its smooth but worn facade. By the light of the torch, faded carvings vanish in the dark around it. Some of the myriad stones around it are my height, and even though they are ramshackle, the carvings are visible on the faded reds and blues. Waves. Perhaps the sea or the storm winds. Who knows?

Inside the stupa, the darkness swallows us whole. Every step is loud as a hammer on a rock to release the zargunine. Everyone behind me lights their spare torches. As the flames lighten our path, a horrible feeling clings to me as I lead the company through. Nothing blocks our way. The stupa is hollow, but for ledges along the walls.

And above the ledges, around the stupa, are marks and murals made in a white chalklike substance.

The mural runs from the top of the ceiling to the ledge. It seems like that of a humanoid creature—if it were made of rocks—drawn as if it couldn't bear the weight of the stupa's roof. Curling its shoulders. None of it makes sense. Maybe it just looks human-shaped to me.

"Monsters made of stone?" Aryadna raises a brow. "What are we doing wasting time here? Someone clearly had an overactive imagination once upon a time and drew some superstitions on the wall."

"Myths and stories," Siril murmurs.

Raksha says, "All stories begin somewhere in truth."

"Myth or truth, all these things are dead and gone. We're in no danger from them," Beyorn says loudly.

Then why bring monster fighters to protect you?

"Letters," Siril says, tracing the marks along the ledge at the foot of the mural. She turns to Raksha. "This is writing."

"It can't be," Aryadna says.

"She taught herself to read with letters she couldn't even identify at first," Raksha says. "I think she, out of all of us, would know best. Isn't that why you brought her?" She directs the latter toward Beyorn.

He stares at the letters. "Can you read this?"

"Not unless you give me a few years," Siril says.

"Anything from you, storyteller?" he asks Raksha, who shakes her head.

Siril says, "If we explore, maybe we can—"

"We're not here to explore," Beyorn barks. "We still have miles to go to our destination."

"And what exactly *is* this destination you keep pointing to? Where does the Collector want us to go? I thought we were rescuing people." I turn to look at him. His torch casts half his face in shadows, the bandaged side the only one in light. "We weren't supposed to walk into some forgotten part of the world as intruders—as…" I search for a better word, but my mind evades me in front of the colossal find that sits in the center of this underground hall. A structure that far outshines anything on the island, even in ruins.

Beyorn gives me a disgusted look. "Are you scared of an empty hall?"

I curl my fingers in a fist. The man stares me down, the corners of his eyes crackling with savagery. Before leaving, Badger told me that Beyorn was a ship's captain who, twenty years ago, stood alone against one of the biggest rebellions the mines had ever seen. It had come close to a success, ousting the Collector's men, if it weren't for the timely reinforcements from Sollonia.

Beyorn had stayed, steadfast, refusing to leave the harbor, fighting and killing miners on the narrow gangplank. He held Kar Atish with a broken knife to its throat even as he himself bled into the waters.

For that, he was awarded medals and titles. And if this mission fails, it is his reputation, his loyalty, that fails with it.

What does he care about the world realigning itself around us?

"Thought you wanted doctors to keep him alive," Beyorn adds, pointing to Rivan.

I take a deep breath, uncurl my fingers. "All I'm saying is we ought to be careful. We should know."

"It makes no difference what is down here if it doesn't move. We continue until we can't. Our journey here isn't to stick hands into the grime of history but find any survivors and head back. All alive and in one piece."

I'm *this* close to throwing my flame right at Beyorn when Rivan, a sheen of sweat on his upper lip now along with the sunken eyes, catches my wrist and pulls me close. "Whatever you're thinking, don't."

I turn away from him. "I wasn't thinking anything."

"Sure you weren't."

As Beyorn orders, we continue on our way, leaving from the back of the stupa.

Just as I step out, my foot crunches on something—something that isn't stone. I lower the torch to the ground.

"Bones!" I cry. I swish the fire from side to side. Mingled with the rubble are hundreds of bones. Skulls and femurs and ribs. An almost intact skeleton—if it weren't for the missing legs.

"Leave the dead," the Shademan rasps.

My mind reels so fast I almost fall to the ground among the bones. Words explode in half confusion, half shout. "You can talk?"

All this time—the things I said. The futility of the fights in the pit. He could understand that? What was I thinking, speaking at all to him? Did I say something else I shouldn't have?

"Lying bastard," Beyorn growls. His hand travels to his wound, his face reddening by the second. But other than that, he doesn't seem particularly bothered, only triumphant as he says, "*This* is why I made sure to keep him with us. He's a damned spy. He'd have run to his other rat friends and gotten us in if we hadn't captured him."

"Can you imagine the things he can tell us?" Aryadna says excitedly. "What these people survive on down here, the minerals we can find. Zargunine is one thing, but imagine something equally life-changing, or even better!"

"What is wrong with you?" I blurt.

She shoots me a frown. "It's a revelation. Don't pretend it isn't."

Beyorn grabs the man's collar. "What do you know of this?"

"Don't disturb the dead," is all the Shademan says.

Trembling still, I climb into the pile. The bones are fragile enough to start shattering into dust. They're all stripped to the last morsel. No sign of clothes or any belongings. Robbed? Or so old that...nothing's left.

That is too much for me to accept.

I turn and raise the torch so the light falls harshly on the Shademan.

"These people would have something with them. Water bottles, bags—something. If you know anything, now's the time."

The Shademan stares at me. Then bursts out laughing.

Yara kicks him in the stomach.

Though he tumbles over, he still laughs. "You think these people came yesterday? Last month? Last year? Last decade? Your ignorance is a miracle."

Nausea fills me at his tone. The Shademan is obviously trying to play games with us, trying to scare us in the dark. Of course these must be the people from the expedition. It can't be anyone else. He's just one man. And other Shadefolk like him are only a handful. My mother said so.

Your mother was wrong about many things.

I shake my head. It's probably some beast of the dark. There are creatures in the sea that can strip a man to bone in seconds. Who's to say there isn't one here too?

He wants us to get caught by surprise, right?

Fine, I'm ready.

TWENTY-TWO

Behind the stupa is the only other door in the hall.

Through it, we emerge into another large space and then begin an unnerving journey through empty chambers and passages, one after another, some with metal beams hanging with fragile fingers of rust from the ceilings where we pass quicker than ever.

There are chasms between chambers, narrow ledges for movement, connected only via bridges of twisted ropes and weightless stones. No one says anything anymore because there's no need to. We can all see it. This place was part of an ancient, underground civilization. Human hands built these bridges, these structures.

Increasingly, it feels like we are in a maze. The network of tunnels was one thing, but at least there was only one way in and out in each tunnel. Here, the chambers have multiple exits, and if any of us gets separated from the company—

Many hours of descending treacherous slopes and broken stairs later, we have our second break.

Rivan sits with Thayne and Siril, and when I join them only for his sake, the girl immediately shuts up, her glare full of spite. I'm surprised she doesn't call me Kinkiller.

But then, Thayne continues, "It's not like that, what Beyorn said. She's married to someone else."

Oh. They're talking about Thayne's...lover? The person he wants to save.

"So she's not your lover, but you love her?" Rivan asks. He glances at me with a piercing gaze that suddenly feels like a hot touch of fire that has burned my flesh and left my soul exposed.

"She's sick," Thayne says, brushing a hand along his light beard that conceals scars down his face. "Very sick. She wouldn't survive here without Lander intervention. If this mission goes successfully, they have promised me they will let her get treated at the Collector's compound."

It must be someone the miners know. Why else would he hide her name like this? What a strange thing it is to love someone and not be able to be with them, to keep your feelings buried and not tell them what you can do for them. I wonder what's worse, the one hiding or the one who doesn't even know.

"You're willing to risk your life and she can't even know? Why would you love someone like that?" Siril asks, her eyebrows pulled down.

Thayne doesn't say anything.

But Rivan does. "You can't pick who to love any more than you could avoid a tsunami splitting your body and leaving you strewn in the water."

My gaze finds Rivan. In other circumstances, somewhere else, if either of us heard someone say that, we would laugh. *Get out of the way, then,* we would say. But he's still looking at me in a way that is agonizing. Something rattles in the cage of my ribs, demanding I express it, but when I try to, the tide of words recedes. Revulsion at

145

my own lack courses through me, and yet unaware of this war in my head, Rivan doesn't look away.

"Talk of tsunamis aside," Siril says, adding wood to my fiery thoughts, "that's beginning to look bad."

Rivan pushes his shirt down. The bloodlike red has gotten darker. "I've had better luck with the raath than one moment down here."

It's been days since we entered the mines. I think. Every second feels elongated, every hour a bare moment.

"We should be heading back within a day," Thayne says.

"After what we've just seen, that's the last thing on my mind."

"Rivan…" I start but trail off. Still no words. But this time not for lack. There's so much in my head that I don't know exactly what I'll say if I continue. Maybe I shouldn't have come down here. I'm not equipped to handle this. One creature alone got both Rivan and Ansh. And now there are creatures that have carved entire grave-yards. What if there are worse things still? The emptiness only a lure to trap us.

And the Shademan.

I glance at him. He's sitting with his back to the wall, glaring at Beyorn.

"Who are you?" Siril calls to him. "How can you live down here all alone?"

Thayne looks at me at that, wearing a phantom expression. For a moment, blood pounds in my ears, like he *knows* and is about to say it. The one thing I have kept hidden even from Rivan. But then he turns in a slow, strange way.

He says, "You survive in the cruelest places because you must. You go on because that is what life demands. When you're used to life in a particular way, you find it hard to imagine anything else. Human view of life is narrow, so limited."

I think over that and how close those words seem to what my

146

mother used to say about the people "elsewhere," like she called them.

Raksha, after a while, speaks, her low voice ringing in the emptiness. "In my mother's grandmother's time, we were still storytellers like our ancestors. As one of the four Kathya families, we collected myths and folktales and songs." A small smile touches her lips and dies. "Before the Landmaster of Sollonia…" She looks at Beyorn, who frowns.

"Well, we have our stories of times even before our Empyrean Elders arrived on these islands. The great First Ones walked the deep undergrounds. They found halls of gold and rivers of milk, jewels like stars shining in the walls, floors glinting like sunlight in the skies. And they lived in harmony for many eons before the evil from beneath rose."

I watch how attentively Siril listens to Raksha. It's finally obvious to me that the two of them work together. One raises questions and the other brings stories as the explanation. If allowed, they could probably solve the mystery of the Shademan on their own.

They could be great historians and chroniclers if they were on Chandrabad.

I ask, "Evil from beneath?"

"Nameless things that live too deep, that never should be disturbed."

"Like the gods of Empyrean Elders?" Aryadna asks. It strikes me odd; only Landers ever refer to the so-called supreme beings that the first of our people worshipped as "gods."

Raksha frowns. "Perhaps. There's never been much about their nature."

Beyorn scoffs.

"Your reality is not real," the Shademan interrupts, making all of us jump. Siril gasps so loud it echoes across the hall. "The First Ones may be gods but they are not those of the Elders. They are gods only because they could not be killed." His voice is slithery and high, almost hypnotic.

Raksha addresses the Shademan, her body stance tense. "Why do you say that? What do you mean by our reality?"

The Shademan refuses to speak again, even when Beyorn kicks him. I begin to think I hallucinated his voice.

We pass several other halls with pillars and niches, each getting bigger, until Siril murmurs from the end of the line, "This is the layout of a city."

Raksha says, "The stupa hall must be the entrance."

"You don't think this could be the halls of gold, do you, Raksha?" I ask.

"Halls from thousand...ten thousand years ago?" Yara cuts in.

"Older," Raksha and Siril say together.

Siril throws Raksha a glance before adding, "It can't be the work of the First Ones. The architecture from that long would be crumbs of dust now. This is someone else's work."

"You're letting superstitions get to you," Aryadna says, frowning. "Even if there was something here before, it's so long ago that for us, it might as well never have existed. Our ancestors are the Empyrean Elders. They came here a thousand years ago. Who knows what happened back then? Maybe it's their work, something we didn't hear of before because it was abandoned."

No other miner seems convinced.

Thayne murmurs what seems like a prayer, a frightening enough idea above the ground, but here in this darkness to acknowledge that something like those gods might hear us...

The sinews of my chest tighten, the drum of my heart suddenly too loud. A civilization beneath the world I know, where we live, burning every day, working like rats fighting against the current of water. And here is proof that Badger's network of tunnels is nothing but a mere spit of what existed before.

A keening sound fills my ears.

Too loud, too discordant.

For a mad moment, I feel like ants are crawling inside my ear, but then we enter a big hall, leading into several directions, and I stop. A low, growl-like purring and the skittering of many tiny feet.

The sound isn't in my head—and it's growing louder.

"You all hear that, right?"

The company looks around warily as the sound continues to grow. The dust here is broken, thin swipes in places as if it were moved over recently.

"Up there!" Ansh shouts.

As one, we take in our surroundings, and the horrifying realization dawns: a cloudy sheet of brown-black blankets the floor. Shed exoskeletons. And above, spilling out of the holes in the ceiling, scorpions—with luminescent tails and pincers. Hundreds, maybe thousands of them.

"Run!" I shout.

Beyorn and Aryadna lead Raksha, Thayne, and Siril. Yara and Ansh follow, and I grab Rivan's hand.

A wind rises as we hurtle toward the exit—much too far. Rivan's wound slows him down, and I match his speed. More scorpions come springing out from the fractures in the wall and crawling down the pillars.

The scorpions' hissing is deafening through the hall.

"Kress, go ahead," Rivan gasps. His face is drained of blood, leaving him chalk-white.

"I'm not leaving you!"

Someone shouts. Rivan and I slam into Thayne, and the others stumble into themselves. At the top of the company, Yara is crouched next to Ansh.

She swears as Ansh's bandage reddens again.

"Get up, Ansh," she cries.

"Look out!" Siril screams, and Raksha turns, slamming her polearm into a scorpion's pincers, sending it tumbling upside down.

We're surrounded.

The many-legged creatures and their deep, empty-socketed eyes converge on us. Raksha and I have our weapons out. Yara stands in front of Ansh, who gets up even as blood drips from his broken hand.

The scorpions are vibrating, eager to sting and devour, their legs moving in quick succession, tails aiming at us. Up and down, up and down, up and down. There's no space to breathe. I dart my gaze from left to right. Rivan breathes heavily, his hand held out, as if he could push the creatures away from us.

One of the scorpions lunges. My hands work automatically, slashing it down with the dagger. It falls in a squelch at my feet. A quivering sound ripples in the air. The scorpions lean closer, their tails dripping with venom, the chitinous bodies rumbling with anticipation.

Another scorpion flies at Siril. She screams and twists free, her jacket coming up in shreds.

And then, a low-pitched buzzing fills the air.

The scorpions turn to the sound, at the back of the hall, across from where we're stranded. The buzz comes again, this time higher, almost like an electric spark.

A rush of panic grips the scorpions and they start fleeing from us. They climb back up the pillars hurriedly, disappearing through the little holes covering the ceiling.

Something is scaring the scorpions—and I doubt it would be friendly to us.

My stomach plummets. Our only hope is to outrun whatever it is.

"We need to move," I say, the words barely a whisper. "Come on!"

Ansh swings his good arm around Yara, and they run. The others follow them. Raksha and I bring up the rear, and we're the last through the gateway at the other end.

We emerge onto the side of a chasm. And a bridge half a mile away to the other side.

And just then, something large slam against the walls of the hall, shaking the ground beneath our feet.

I bring out my daggers. Yara joins Raksha and me up front.

"Everyone make for the bridge. We'll hold whatever it is!" I shout.

"*No!*" Rivan yells back, but Aryadna grabs his hand, dragging him along, and for once, I'm grateful.

Then I turn to face this new monster.

TWENTY-THREE

There is no place to retreat from the ledge beside the chasm. Only the bridge half a mile away or back the way we came. Which is currently being blocked by the monstrous—*what is that?*

Several horrifying seconds pass as it skitters forward through the arch. First the spiny, hairy front legs. Each hair the size of my arms. Two deep red compound eyes on each side of the large head, and the long spear-like mouth. To pierce its victim. Its neck is slim, easily slipping out of the gateway.

"A damned assassin bug," Yara breaths.

"Yeah, if an assassin bug was the size of a mountain," Raksha shoots back.

Yara isn't wrong—it *is* an insect. A giant venomous insect that could suck our insides with that spear on its mouth in a second.

Badger would *love* to have this monster in his pits.

For a moment, its legs slip on the ledge as the rest of its body struggles to come through the arch. Then, with a massive pull, its bulging thorax undulates in the space and all at once breaks free.

The arch crumbles behind it with a roar.

A dust cloud erupts.

I cough, grabbing for the rocky wall. In that brief moment, the giant insect lands in front of us, all six legs whirring with anticipation and its eyes forward—focused on us. The prey.

Without warning, it strikes down.

Yara and I leap in opposite directions, Raksha hurtling backward. The space where we were standing is now a crater.

The creature screeches, cutting at the nearest boulder.

Yara hacks at it with a borrowed spike. But it moves swiftly. Skittering over the ground. We're backed up against the narrow ledge with nowhere to go.

My hands hold the daggers aloft, but I don't know what to do with this monster.

It's too big. It is *impossible* to hurt it with daggers.

The red eyes loom in the dark, the faraway torches of the company gleaming brutally.

Eyes.

I can stab it in the eyes.

But how? It's too high. There's not enough foothold in the wall. And one slip—I glance to the side—will mean a long, agonizing fall to my death down in the chasm.

Out of the corner of my eye, I catch a glimpse of Raksha holding her polearm and facing the insect down.

"Yara!" I whisper. "Come with me."

She hesitates for only a second. "What are you thinking?"

"We have to go high, stab it in the eye."

It sounds so simple. But not even the pits have prepared either Yara or me to fight a monster this giant.

Just then, something whizzes past my hair. A blade. It twangs against the hairy leg and falls away harmlessly. The insect screeches, as if buzzing away a mosquito, and advances speedily.

"Well," says Raksha. "That didn't work."

A wild, hysterical laugh escapes me.

"Go," Raksha urges. "Do what you have to do. I'll keep its eyes on me."

The insect rears, screeching so loudly I'm forced to clap my hands over my ears.

Yara is already on the move, climbing the rocky wall, a dagger held between her teeth. If she gets one eye, and I come at it from the back and get the other—

For that, I need to reach the back.

I can't even feint here.

The creature shoots out its spear mouth, nearly taking my leg off. I swipe at it with a blade but only end up falling flat on my back.

"Hey!" Raksha shouts. "Come here!"

She steps backward, polearm facing front.

I take the momentary distraction's advantage and hurtle to the wall. Dagger in mouth like Yara, I grab a jutting rock and hurl myself up. There's a shriek and a clatter of metal below. *Keep climbing.* A pointed stone tears down my arm. I scream. Blood spurts from the gash, staining the black stone red. Stones go rattling past me as Yara climbs above.

And just as I reach up for another grip, the insect's spear zooms past my hair, burying itself in the stone.

I scream.

The stone comes crashing out.

And I'm barely hanging on the wall with one arm that's bleeding.

"Kress!" It's Rivan, from somewhere far behind us. The desperation in his voice echoes along the chasm.

No, go back, I think. He can't see me like this, or he'll throw himself in front of the creature.

The thought gives me a burst of speed and I haul myself up. Blood

154

spatters on the rock, some of it slipping into my mouth, and the taste of iron chokes me. A stone sails past my head and slams against the insect's head. Above me, Yara has reached the roof, now throwing rocks at the creature.

And instead of turning away from us, it screeches loudly and slams its legs on either side of me, its spear coming directly at me. Razor sharp. It will impart venom and turn my insides into mush, like a maristag's venom, and then it can suck out everything, like a spider.

With a roar, I slash at the oncoming spear with all the strength in me.

The insect's head gets thrown to the right. It screeches. Locks eyes on Raksha.

"Get away!" I shout. I try to wave—and my injured arm begins slipping from the rock.

Whether that gets Raksha's attention or not, it certainly gets the insect's. It pivots suddenly and comes at me fast, the tip of the spear slamming a hair's breadth from my ear. The impact loosens the rock I'm holding on to.

Only half a lifetime in the pits still keeps me fighting.

Yara, standing atop the wall, throws a well-aimed dagger at the insect. And gets the corner of an eye.

Red-tinged yellow blood spatters on my face.

My hand slips.

And in my desperation, I latch on to the only solid thing in my vicinity: the insect's spear mouth.

There's a moment of silence, then a buzzing. My hands tighten on the slick spear, finding no purchase elsewhere.

And then, the distance between me and the rocky wall increases suddenly.

I hear my name shouted.

But my head is spinning.

Even with my eyes wide open, I cannot make sense of my surroundings.
Everything is too loud, too fast, too dark.

My legs are swinging in empty air.

Then it hits me: the insect has taken off. It's flying.

Fear pounds in my veins anew. I grab the spear tighter, cling to it with my whole body, quivering like a fish in the sky.

Darkness blurs past me. The insect speeds down the chasm, trying to throw me off. It zooms this way, then that. And there's nothing but the deep canyon below us. I tighten my bleeding arms around the awfully thin, awfully fragile spear mouth.

The world is upside down.

Dizziness crackles in my skull.

The insect streaks around the canyon in agony. It could end up exhausting itself—falling down in the abyss. And take me with it. Horror and fear turn in my stomach. I keep spinning. My world is black rock and the darkness beneath. And then the pain catches up. Like fire, it licks through my arms, bloodied and battered.

And still, the insect flies.

I risk a look below.

There is no ground, nothing in the vast emptiness of the chasm.

"*Stupid damned insect,*" I breathe.

My hands are throbbing, the oozing blood making my grip slicker. And still the insect flies furiously, trying to rid itself of me and of the pain that must be burrowing itself deep in its head. The blood from its eye is still spiraling, spraying everywhere as it goes in circles, injured and angry. Howling wind arising out of the insect's own movement buffets us nearer the ledge once, but it keeps fighting viciously, with no mind.

The whole *point* of coming on this expedition was to finally get rid of the darkness, the way this island sucks you in and keeps its hooks in you, where you rot until you die, but here I am: wrapped in a cocoon of blood and terror slipping deeper in the ground. Is there no end to how deep these caves go? If I hit the rock bottom of this chasm, will I find another excavation beneath? Where does it end?

I tighten my hold on the spear mouth with one hand. Then, even with the pain throbbing in my cut arm, I pull out a throwing star.

I have to bring it down.

And so I aim, as much as I can, and throw the star at its rear leg.

A screech rings in my ear. The world tilts. Of course it does. The insect is wounded badly, and soon it will either stop flying or drop dead.

Whether it knows exactly what might happen to it doesn't matter. But it is losing vision in one eye, and it feels its strength weakening, and it must understand, as all living creatures do, what happens when our bodies begin to fail so fast at once, when our insides bleed and tear.

And so the creature shakes dizzyingly for a moment and, just as fast, spirals down to the bridge. A violent convulsion grips my insides. The insect swoops down, down, down, until I slam against the side of the bridge.

It hovers again but totters toward the wall of the ledge. Stone rushes at me, and with it, the rest of the company.

They hurtle back, almost falling over, as we finally come to a stop.

At the other side of the bridge.

As soon as we touch down, I try to loosen my grip, but my hands are frozen, clawlike. The insect shoves me away just the same. As I would have if there was a tiny irritant clinging to me. It comes at me, trying to pierce me with the spear, but I roll down the rocky ground.

"Come on!" Rivan grabs my arms. I scream in agony, and he immediately lets go. Raksha grabs me under the arm, and together they haul me backward.

The insect screeches and darts at us.

"Quickly!" Siril yells, waving at us to hurry. The back of the ledge is an open area, but I can't see what lies on the other side of it.

A sharp buzzing rises. It slams down in front of us, dividing the company in two. Rivan, Raksha, Yara, and me on one side and everyone else on the other. The ground is slippery with the insect's blood once more. It bears down on us.

"Yara!" Ansh shouts.

"Stay back!" she shouts.

The creature catches her around the stomach, and she doubles over. Ansh rushes beneath the insect to his sister. The fool.

But his running confuses it as it stumbles backward.

Raksha sees her chance. She drags me along with Rivan, just like Ansh, and suddenly we're in the clear on the other side.

"Come on, you two!" Siril shouts.

Yara gets up, color draining from her face when she sees both Ansh and the insect looming over them.

She and Ansh grasp hands, and I have a sudden, strong remembrance of them as children, when we used to play together, when we didn't hate one another.

They were strongest as a team.

Together, they run this way, then that, their minds working in sync. They're too fast for it. If it doubles over on itself, it will fall into the chasm below.

Yara knows that.

And just as Yara clears the ledge, running faster than I've ever seen her, the creature swipes at them from the left. Hard. The siblings' hands slam apart, and Yara goes flying forward.

The insect swipes its spear again, catching Ansh and tossing him off into the chasm.

Yara's scream rends the air.

She tries to go over the ledge, but Raksha and Rivan tackle her, dragging her back.

And behind them, the insect comes sprinting at us.

"Run!" I scream, my throat lined with flames. "Fast!"

The company turns and we race forward.

Until the other side of the landing opens up in front of us, and none of us can slow our speed, and all we can do to escape the monster on our pursuit is throw ourselves down the emptiness.

TWENTY-FOUR

The water slams into my back *hard* and breath leaves me in a single, agonizing whoosh, leaving nothing but an infernal fire thrashing and biting its way through my lungs. Everywhere around me, water splashes violently, causing a loud, echoing chaos.

I open my eyes to nothingness and everything. It takes me a moment to reorient myself. *We fell.* The ledge is far above us, a pale wound in the roof of the cavern. I cough, splutter, and try to get up—only to slip back inside the water. Fortunately, it isn't shallow enough to have killed us on impact, nor deep enough to drown us now.

The taste of sour water fills my throat.

Someone grabs my hand. I look up into harried gray eyes—Rivan. He looks just as disoriented, soaking in the water, and the red wound shining dully on his chest. Together we drag ourselves out of the water on all fours, coughing.

The lakeside is mostly jagged rock, with soft sand in places. I fall on my back, breathing hard, shaking my head to get water out of my ears and eyes. It doesn't matter. Blinding pain pierces every corner of my skull. Rivan pulls me against him, and I shiver, closing my hands around him tightly, forgetting myself in that moment.

The others crawl to the shore slowly too, slipping and groaning.

We're in a compact, circular shaft. Stalactites drip into the lake. *Plunk, plunk.* There's a faint glow from beneath the lake, enough to light the space without our torches. I check for flint, for matches, but everything is wet.

"How are we not dead?" Siril whimpers.

"Our bad luck," Thayne answers her bitterly.

Rivan and I exchange glances, then look away before we start laughing. That would be a poor display under our current circumstances.

One by one, the others sit up. Shivering with cold, muttering to themselves. I hadn't realized how cold the chamber was at first, adrenaline still pumping from the fight, but now cold rakes its claw down my back. Then I taste the blood on my lips and gag. My throat convulses with pain.

At least the water has mercifully cleansed enough blood off us that we can see.

Beyorn pushes his pike into the shore and stands up, water pouring off his back like he is a merman. His braid has finally come undone, dripping wet. He surveys us like we're the most disappointing catch of the day.

"We are in—" He barely gets the words out before Yara lashes out hard.

Claws reaching, she flies to grab my throat with animal violence. I catch her only on instinct. My left arm, already injured, buckles under the pressure.

Yara is vicious, bringing her knee to my throat. I pull myself back at the last minute, yelling at her to stop. But she's lost the only thing that matters to her. And she's now a predator without restraint, hurling herself at me with no thought.

"—rabid," Rivan shouts behind us, his words swallowed by Yara's insanity, her urge to shred me.

Because that's what she wants; I can *feel* years' worth of hatred in her breaking the dam now that her brother is gone. I block her as much as I can, but she's lost control of herself and is flinging her arms at me at a speed higher than I can manage.

"*Stop it!*" Siril yells uselessly.

Pain erupts in my body. I go crashing to the ground and immediately roll into a ball to save myself from the lashings that never come.

I look up.

Raksha and Siril have Yara by the arms, struggling as she kicks furiously in the air.

"You never wanted to protect anyone!" She whirls to Siril. "She's taking revenge on us! You were right. She's going to kill us all."

I stare at her, unable to say anything to her accusation this time.

She continues yelling, "I'm going to kill you! You hear me!"

"Whether she hears you or not," Beyorn growls, "that thing might be the one that kills us." He points upward.

The insect creature is on the ledge, leaning over, chittering and tapping at the sides of the wall. It rolls a leg, which slips on the blood streaming down its body, and a large boulder plummets down the shaft. Over the screams, the boulder splashes in the lake, drenching us again.

All of us scurry away from the lake and slams ourselves against the wall, as if that will protect us.

Beyorn says to Raksha and Siril, motioning toward Yara, "Tie that one up."

Yara snarls, but Raksha steps in front of her. She places a hand on the girl's shoulder and stays for a moment. Yara's face crumples, then loses all expression.

Together, the other two tie her hands.

Rivan watches them until they've secured Yara, then reaches to help me up. Both of us look like death, and we know it.

"How do we get out of here?" Thayne asks.

The creature is lowering itself at an increased speed now, half of its mangled thorax inside the shaft.

"Here!" comes Aryadna's shout.

She is kneeling in the corner. The ground is indented, and part of the lake drains to a tunnel, but just next to it, the ground levels once more. A rift in the stone leads away from the chamber.

"Where does that lead?" I ask, my voice strained with effort.

Aryadna frowns at me. "I—I don't know."

"So how will we know there isn't another damned monster waiting for us at the other side?"

She continues to look bewildered as if the possibility hadn't even occurred to her.

I shout, pouring all the tangled emotions racing through me into my words, "How can you still be *this* oblivious after everything we've been through down here? After one of us just died?"

Thayne breaks in, "What choice do we have? Facing death by that—" He squints above. "No, thank you. I'll risk the unknown."

I look around. The only person I could have counted on to see this my way is Yara. The one who would have to fight beside me. But she'd rather let us all get killed than take my side.

Not even Raksha seems to have much to say. And Beyorn will not listen to Rivan.

"That settles it," Beyorn says. He gestures at me. "You first."

"Send *him* first," I say, pointing to the Shademan, who is trying to make himself scarce, standing in the corner.

He scowls at me. I shrug. I sympathize with his current situation—but not enough to jeopardize my own safety.

"He may be valuable," Beyorn says.

Fury burns in me. "And I'm not? You're *alive* because of me."

Yara barks out a vicious laugh, which shuts me up.

"Would you guys like to continue arguing while that thing gets down to eat us?" Aryadna snaps.

Over the gurgling of the lake, the creature clicks above. The sound is way closer now, and I don't want to check exactly how near it has gotten.

"Fine," Aryadna says. "I'm going in first." She grabs the rope tying the Shademan up and pulls him along. "The rest of you are welcome to follow me."

She turns sideways and enters the rift, dragging the Shademan behind her. There's a scuffling sound and the scratching of stones, but Aryadna continues.

Raksha follows.

"I'll go if you go," Siril says, looking at me strangely.

It takes me a moment to realize that the hostility since she accused me of being the Kinkiller has vanished. Now, she looks at me as if I'm her personal savior.

"Fear of death can switch up every belief, huh?"

She scowls. If there were more time, I might have rubbed her face in her fear. But I'm also grateful that she hasn't strengthened her armor against me, joining Yara to call me a monster. So I turn and go in, dragging her behind me. I won't have any more deaths on my watch on this increasingly futile mission.

The rift is even narrower than it seemed, the walls squeezing tight. I tilt my head up to avoid a pointed stone cutting at me. Above, the walls simply converge. I suck in my stomach and drag forward, pulling Siril along. At the back, one by one, the others follow too.

The wall smells of water and a strange tang that has an undertone of blood. Like the air above on the island, circulating through the sea and the storms. Parts of the wall break off at the movement, startling us.

Everyone stills, clinging to the wall until the rubble falls quiet.

None of us speaks as we continue to drag ourselves. Every groan of effort is punctuated by the gurgling lake back in the chamber and the draining water in the tunnel next to us. And then, a buzzing fills the air.

"Go faster!" Beyorn, the last of us, calls. "It's come down!"

That speeds us up. Despite the claustrophobic rift and the stones starting to scratch at our faces as we press past them, we quickly push ourselves forward, squeezing ourselves and holding our breaths.

Until finally, the rift spits us out.

I drag in a desperate full breath, filling in my lungs with air, just as the others come tumbling out. Beyorn crashes into the company at last, and behind him, one giant spiny leg of the creature drenched in blood reaches out sharply.

Everyone stumbles backward, watching in horror as it tries hard to cut through the gap.

It pushes again and again, as if it wants to split the cave apart. The chittering rises deafeningly with its anger.

We hold our weapons high, waiting.

And then at last, the leg stops scratching at the walls and falls silent.

For several terrible moments, I anticipate the walls tearing and the creature flying at us, but when nothing happens, relief sends me to my knees. The monster is dead. I stay there, breathing hard, wondering if I'm just in a bad dream. Any moment now, I'll wake up and this will be over. I never agreed to the journey, Rivan never followed me, he's not hurt, and my arm is not on the verge of being severed.

And most of all, a giant oceans-damned insect wasn't after us.

The hard ground pins at my knees, bringing me back to myself. A relief so strong that I feel as if there's music in the air. Music with words I don't quite understand.

No, it's real.

"Do you hear that?" I ask.

"What?" Siril looks back to me. It's still strange to have her face stripped of the hatred she had suddenly worn. She looks confused, and I can tell she's not hearing anything. A shiver curves down me.

And cuts deep when Beyorn says, his usually gruff voice softer than ever, "We're close."

TWENTY-FIVE

The thought that we might finally reach Beyorn's destination and then get out of here spurs everyone forward faster. After the fight, no one wants to linger closer to that chasm anyway. My gasps burn my throat as I lead the company once more. Rivan insisted I take some of his water, but now I have to make it last all the way until we reach the place, at least. I can rest and ask for someone else's water during the return journey, when I'm sure no one will die of thirst.

We have lost one too many already.

Out of instinct, I throw a glance over my shoulder. Yara now trudges beside the Shademan, both of them at the center of the line.

What could I have done differently to save Ansh? I should have killed that creature faster. Stabbed it through. Something. I should have never allowed it to land on the ledge near the others.

No, stop it. It's the voice of the madness. You would have died too.

This is what I get for trying to take the easy way out. This island wants me to suffer. How could it allow me to walk in and out of its womb so simply? Of course it wormed itself in my mind. No one else seems as affected. No one but Yara—and she has an actual reason.

I keep mumbling under my breath to keep the voices in my head away, until we reach the plateau, the end of which drops down sharply hundreds of meters.

"Are you sure this is it?" I ask Beyorn. "The cliff is too steep, and if we're wrong, it could take us days to get back up."

Beyorn nods and winces with pain. "I'm sure. We get down as soon as we can, then camp for one night before moving ahead."

Seems like the harsh trek has taken a toll on him too. His injury is no better than Rivan's, but he has to put up his front. He is, after all, the captain who *saved* Kar Atish.

The cliff is longer and steeper than any we have seen since we arrived in the caves. And sharp crystalline growths jut out at irregular points between the rocks, making it even more dangerous. The rocks are also damper than any before. Close by, I can hear a rush of waterfall, unlike the faraway tinkling that interrupted our journey before.

Beyorn, though, seems excited at the idea of increased danger.

"We're close," he repeats—staring somewhere to his right. Almost like he's imagining someone there. His brother?

Raksha goes first, with Yara. Then Siril and the Shademan. Aryadna and Beyorn follow after. And finally Thayne helps Rivan down. The latter in each company needed help—a fact not lost on anyone.

I wait until Thayne yells the all-clear, then check for any bags or equipment we might have left. After scanning the area, I'm ready for my descent as well.

I wriggle my backpack closer, centering the weight, and check the clipping of the rope around my body. The sole of my shoe scrapes against the rock irascibly. I wince. Nothing emerges from the dark we've left behind. My headlamp, a necessary burden this once, isn't nearly enough to light anything, only to attract a predator. And frankly, I've had enough of predators.

Slowly, my back facing the gaping void of below, I step off the edge.

Pain bursts along my shoulder above my injured arm. The crystals stab into my feet every time I come close, scraping past my arms, making a cacophony in the large cavern. My descent goes slower than I'd like. Light from my headlamp bounces off the wall, casting eerie shadows high above but also reflecting the glimmering crystals in the rocks.

And that's what gets me.

The headlamp shines on a crystal outgrowth the size of my fist, and it glares hard right in my face. It's too bright, too close, and a sharp spike of pain slices through the backs of my eyes. I lose my grip and hurtle through open air toward the hard ground.

A scream escapes me, and I'm madly scrambling for a grip. The rope is right *there* as my fingers catch once, twice, *again*, but refuse to keep the hold. No sense of up or down. Blood rushes to my head so fast, and I know I'm dead—

At the last moment, my hand catches on an extended outgrowth, and I grasp for the rope, only a few meters above the ground. My body jerks hard as the weight slams back against me. I cough, air caught in my lungs. Pain rings down my spine so suddenly that for a moment, I fear it's broken. The shouts from the company below finally register themselves.

My vision stays dark as I lower myself on the ground and collapse, shivering with pain.

"Kress. Krescent. *Kress.*" Rivan repeats my name. He gathers me close as I kneel on the ground, the rope still tied around me. "You're okay, right? Are you okay? Are you hurt?" It reminds me of the night when Yara and Ansh cornered me, his concern completely overtaking anything else I might be feeling.

I splutter, "I am, Rivan. I am fine."

"Thank the ocean," he exhales.

As the adrenaline fades and my vision clears, I see the others gathered around me too. I nod to them. Siril helps me up, letting me lean on her as I do. I try not to, at first, wondering if she would just let me fall if I relied on her. But she only shifts closer.

"How could you not be more careful?" Rivan murmurs.

And I notice something I hadn't seconds ago. His words are slurring. My eyes drop to his collar, where the red threads burn. How many days has it been since he got hurt? I can't remember anything. The rope, still tied around me, begins to press harder. No, no, no. I need to get him out of here.

I can't let myself get killed over something so silly when Rivan needs me.

"Get up and take watch," Beyorn barks at me.

"Let her rest. She fought that monster for us," Rivan growls, forgetting it is Beyorn's discretion that's keeping him with me.

"You shouldn't be speaking at all, boy." But then, he turns to Thayne. "You take first watch. There shouldn't be any beasts from now to the end. But you never know."

Beyorn is right.

The hours are empty but colder and uneasy. Wherever we are headed to is now close. I pace around the camp slowly instead of resting like everyone advised, to keep myself occupied. These last hours are crucial, and I won't let this damned underground get into my head or hurt my body again.

Rivan tries to argue again that I should rest, but he relents easily too. Despite how low I'm running on sleep, he knows I can tell he's having difficulty with his words now.

Which is perhaps why he says, "I—don't know if—well, just tell Ashvin and Mayven, please?"

"No," I snap, a little too loud. The others look our way, eyebrows raised. I lower my voice. "Whatever you want to say to them, tell them yourself."

I turn from him and march several feet away to sit down with my legs pulled up and arms circled tight around them. The rattling spike in my breathing hurts my head as I will it to slow down. *Just tell Ashvin and Mayven.* As if he's some Lander ordering me around. No, I won't do anything he wants me to do. He can get out of here—alive—and do whatever he wants himself. I pull myself together even tighter. As if I'm turning into water and desperate to stop myself from spilling away. Why did Rivan have to come here at all? He's supposed to be smarter than his brothers and I combined.

A footstep brushes a stone. Then Rivan sinks to the ground behind me, settling and pressing his back against mine. Like we used to sit when we were children. He reaches for my hand blindly and then places our entwined fingers beside us. No-man's-land.

"Do you remember the big storm the year we turned fourteen?"

Involuntarily, I shiver. "Yes, can't forget that one." The skies had gone black for three weeks, the mines blocked, and the wind was so fierce it would cut through skin like knives through fish. Everyone who wasn't sheltered was a corpse.

"You hadn't realized it was going to be that bad even two days later when you left for the pits. None of us knew where you'd gone, because *surely* you couldn't be that ridiculous."

"But I was."

"But you were," he says, half laughing. "And I couldn't wait any longer. Anything could have happened. If you got caught in the storm, I'd never even know. So I went out. And what do I see? Krescent Dune, carrying an actual raath in her hands, crouching by the door because she didn't think we'd let her bring the beast inside but she couldn't leave it either even when it could have snapped her neck if it suddenly got it in mind."

171

"It was hurt," I say, jutting my chin though he can't see my face.

"And you saw that it was lonely and took care of it until it was better despite the storm."

"Rivan—"

What do I want to say? Why do his words make me feel exposed?

I try not to fidget, not to let him know how much the abrupt silence affects me. He's always had a memory sharper than anyone I've ever come across. He remembers every milestone in my life, every bad fight, every good fight. Everything I told him about my parents, the stories my mother told me at bedtime, the creatures my father helped me look after. And he knows all of it like I know the grip of my blades.

How can someone be like that? I barely had time to understand people before I was forced to grow up and close myself off to others. Is everyone like Rivan? Do they remember every small thing about their friends all the time, every time?

What else does he remember about me that feels like no one else ever would? Reminisce about some other weird thing I did and that he made a note of.

And of course he likes to put me at the center of it and forget about the fact that he stayed up all night taking care of the raath beast with me.

But then, he begins speaking softly again. Haltingly. As if it hurts him to say it.

"I know what you think. That we gave you a home, but what you don't see is that you held us together when we were fraying at the edges. When Ashvin felt so alone and so hurt that he couldn't protect Amma, when May didn't understand what was happening. You didn't have to do anything. Definitely not clean up after my sick mother. We should have been doing that. But you held her, and you held us. When I—I didn't know what was the ground or the sky anymore. You held our hands. My hands. You, despite how much distance you keep from everyone, were there. Every moment. You were everywhere. I wanted to die, but I kept up my face for May. And you, without even knowing, saved me from the abyss that had taken me already.

"What can I say to make you see, Kress, that if I have a home, it's because you make it so?"

That is not what I was expecting at all. I lose words; I lose all sense. Now what can *I* say to him that won't make me feel like a fool? I'm overwhelmed, and the back of my throat fills up. I need to get away. Breathe.

"I—I'll—check on the perimeter."

He shifts, releasing my hand. "Okay."

I take my torch and practically run from him.

I didn't know he was carrying these feelings inside him for the past four years? Why did he never say anything? Confusion and nerves in equal measure war in the pit of my stomach, the fight going neither way and making me feel worse.

And what was that—that *okay*?

Fine, whatever. But couldn't he have asked me to stay? We could have talked more. I could make him understand I did all that because I—well, I *do* love him. He's my best friend.

Why does he do this?

Be normal for one second, and the next, say things that confuse me so much. What does he want?

I shake my head.

Focus.

The space we're now in is beautiful, in its own way. It's a good distraction if I keep my gaze to the front and not let another thought into my mind.

The crystals along the cliff glint in the dark. At the back of the cavern, natural arches and cavern mouths are arrayed next to each other almost in a pattern. The water must be even closer given the chill in the air. The ground has indents like anywhere else, but the rock itself is smooth and level. Another part of the architecture of people from before? I shiver despite the fire held close.

What must this place have been like when the First Ones walked this world? What were they like—to live underground, away from the sun and the ocean? I wish I could ask someone, anyone, about this place. But it's been thousands of years. What we have now is either stories or people trying to be clever.

It's different for the Shademan, of course. My mother said the Shadefolk lived below out of necessity, of promises made long ago. But not everyone believed those promises. They only live down here because the older Shadefolk want to pretend they have a purpose rather than admit there's a world out there.

But, I suppose, that world is no paradise either.

And who have they made promises to anyway? What about? My mother never really clarified.

The flame throws a new shadow at the corner of one of the arches as I cross to the other side. The glimmer of the crystals dims here, the dark full, which means my torch becomes a beacon. At the end of the row of arches, the Shademan freezes.

"I thought that was you," I say quietly.

His face is caught between surprise and anger. To think he'd have escaped if I hadn't been wandering here. What would Beyorn do? Especially if this happens on Thayne's watch?

"If you go now, Beyorn will hold Thayne responsible. The man doesn't deserve the wrath of the Collector," I tell the Shademan, knowing that it doesn't mean anything to him.

"He's a madman, the big one," the Shademan says.

"He can be."

"No," the man rasps. "You don't see him truly, but I do." He hesitates, then adds, "Let me go. I cannot leave the Manibhoomi to go above."

"Tell me about the Manibhoomi, then." My words are the same as I used to say them in childhood to my mother. The Manibhoomi, land of gems, is what the Shadefolk call the underground. My mother taught me to say it right.

"What do you want to know?"

"How do you live here all alone? Alongside the monsters."

"There are monsters in the seas that surround you too. The white star in the sky burns your skin. You live up there too."

"Fair," I say.

"The world above is not for me. I will die before I speak to those people." His words are gentle, as if he's addressing a growling beast, but I can hear the determination in them too. He's not bluffing like me. He means it.

I still have so many questions I want to ask him. Who is he? How many others are there like him? Does he know of the Shadefolk who left the caves and hid among the people above? But what would it matter now? Since the moment we stumbled upon him, death has walked with us. Perhaps Thayne will be forgiven. But the Shademan will definitely see his end.

"Before you go... Can you tell me if there's any way here we can treat Rivan's wound? If a creature attacked you, what would you do? He's getting worse. I don't know if he'll make it back." Even saying it out loud stings my eyes with unspilled tears.

He opens his mouth, then closes it slowly and shakes his head. "We have our healers, you could say, who work with the—well, you know zargunine, of course. There's a unique substance that mixes with gold closer to the surface and transforms into the zargunine that you people use. We use that substance, but rarely. We just avoid

175

contact with the creatures of the deep. For it is not a substance that can be handled by any of us. Only very special people do. But," he adds as my shoulders fall, "you don't have to presume the worst. He can make it. You have to go back soon, though."

I recognize the change in his voice, that subtle urging to cut short whatever is left of Beyorn's journey. Does he truly believe Rivan will be fine, or is this just him trying to get us out of here?

"I—"

"What's going on here?"

I whirl.

Aryadna stands on a higher slab of rock, watching us with a frown between her brow.

"Nothing," I say immediately. "Just wanted to see the arches. Brought him with me in case he might know something about them."

The Shademan watches me intently.

For the ocean's sake, don't do something foolish. I plead in my mind, hoping he'll pick up on it.

"I can understand that if Siril did it, but what's gotten into you?" she says with a laugh. Almost like she's making fun of Siril. And she's comfortable doing it in front of me.

"She's on this mission *because* her insights into the underground could be helpful. She and Raksha are invaluable in building the map and helping us understand the terrain."

Aryadna shrugs. "Whatever. I just came to say that it's time for a change of watch. You're up next."

With no other choice, I follow her back, and so does the Shademan.

TWENTY-SIX

We leave the camp early and find ourselves on a fairly uneventful path. But when we duck under another ruined gateway, in only under an hour, my heart jumps into my throat.

Before me unfurls the largest cave we have seen so far, even bigger than our last camp or the pillared hall.

It takes me a moment to comprehend what I'm seeing.

Across the hall, a pale curtain of light stirs without wind, like water, like it might be...*breathing*. It stretches from the ceiling to the floor, shimmering the ghostly last light before nightfall. Huge stalactites jut out of the ceiling like fangs in the jaws of a predator, dripping quietly, each *clink* against the shallow pools loud in the large emptiness.

The curtain of light gleams softly, lighting the entire space.

And a song behind it. So, *so* faint that I don't know if it's just my mind running in circles once more.

"What's this?" Raksha asks, trying to be sharp, but her voice has an unwanted quality of awe as well.

The curtain of light seems to defy natural laws of existence. There's no foundation from which it emerges. It just exists.

Almost magical, a fantasy of the mind that shouldn't *be*.

Beyorn says flatly, "Let's get closer."

Slowly, we pick our way across. There are exits on either side of the chamber, currently standing dark and empty, but other than that, everything is bathed with the soft light from the top. Goose bumps erupt over my skin, a sense of being…*watched* tickling the base of my neck. I sweep a gaze around. The chamber is truly empty.

But then, the Shademan managed to stay hidden until he jumped us.

I unconsciously move ahead of the group, looking for any signs of disturbance. Needing to get to the curtain of light first. It is almost hypnotic. The way it moves, soft and gentle. An invitation to be touched and felt beneath your skin.

We reach the curtain far quicker than we should, given the size of the chamber. Maybe I wasn't paying attention.

Up close, the light echoes outwardly, as if the source of it is the sun through storm clouds.

"This is strange," Thayne murmurs, breaking the quiet and the flow of the music. Abruptly, the song is gone, as if it was never there, before I had a chance to acknowledge it.

"Did you hear that?" he says.

"Hear what?" Siril murmurs in a shaky voice.

I lock eyes with Thayne. *I did*, I want to say. A song without words so faint it felt like I heard it across the universe. But neither of us speaks.

"What is this?" Raksha asks, sharper than ever.

"Our fortune," Beyorn says and smiles. He steps forward, staring at the ground beyond the light. I follow his gaze and gasp. There's a circular gap in the ground rimmed with a short platform—a sort of well. It is glowing, iridescent, filled to the brim with something that looks like liquid moonlight, its crystalline beauty overshadowing everything else.

"No," Raksha breathes. "This is not what we came for."

"Is this...the other metal in zargunine?" Siril exclaims, looking from Beyorn to the others, as if for denial. The elusive metal that combines with gold to form zargunine.

I only know one thing. "Shademan, is this what you were talking about? Will this cure Rivan?"

"You folk from above are insane," hisses the Shademan. "You cannot steal from the Manibhoomi like you do from the surface."

I turn to him, and he looks genuinely frightened for the first time since we captured him. "What do you mean steal?"

"You cannot touch the Blood Well," he says. "You will bring us all to calamity."

"Be quiet," Beyorn says. He lifts his pike slowly and extends it toward the curtain of light, testing its limits. And good thing too, because the second the metal touches the curtain, it sparks with a sharp shrill and a thousand embers.

"We came to search for lost expedition members." Raksha's voice is getting higher, her grip on her polearm tightening.

She exchanges glances with Thayne who adds, "Exactly. Not for an origin well in the Manibhoomi."

"What's an origin well?" I ask, even as understanding dawns on me. We've been misled—we have risked our lives, gotten injured, and *died* for a lie. Beyorn's destination is nothing but this—this well. Not someone who needed help getting out. His brother and all of the other expeditions were searching for this place.

"This is not just a metal! It's the source of our lands!" Thayne shouts, all his soft restraint broken. "This—this raw holy substance will kill everyone if mishandled!"

"Holy? We have no gods," Beyorn says.

"There are still powers that move this world," Raksha asserts, stepping forward. "The ocean is one. And so is an origin well. You will not destroy it."

"Suit yourself," Beyorn says. "But the powers that move this world belong to Landers."

I reach for my dagger, but Beyorn is ready. He drops his pike and points two guns at us in a swift, practiced move.

"Drop your weapons now, all of you."

"What do you think you're doing?" I say, heart pounding in my throat. "We're in the depths of the world."

"Drop your weapon," he growls, pointing one of the guns straight at me.

Rivan whispers behind me, "Kress."

If it was just me, maybe I could've risked going head-to-head with someone wielding a gun.

I drop my daggers.

"Line up," he says. "And you, Shademan, and you"—he points at Siril—"step away from everyone."

Siril's face drains. "What—what did I do?"

"Let the girl go, Beyorn," Raksha says harshly.

But if he hears her, there's no stopping him. "Now do me a favor and walk into the curtain. I need to test a theory."

The Shademan recoils as if branded and gives a harsh cry. Siril, bewildered, only stares at Beyorn.

I start speaking, but Aryadna places a hand on my shoulder and shakes her head. She gestures to the guns.

"You are committing a sin," the Shademan says.

"Walk. In."

The Shademan looks at us now, all his disdain gone, replaced with the look of a creature defeated in battle, eyes large and begging for reprieve. But none of us can do anything. Even without the guns,

Rivan and I are in no position to physically take on a man as big as Beyorn. Yara is tied up. And I know the others won't move against him. They aren't fighters like me.

Siril, trembling visibly, takes a step forward to the curtain of light. It shimmers plaintively, lighting her up softly.

And the Shademan—runs.

BANG.

"What the hell?" Rivan shouts.

The Shademan slams to the ground. He looks back, shocked, at the bullet graze on the side of his bleeding foot. His face contorts with pain, his scream lodged in his throat.

"That was a warning," Beyorn says maliciously.

All I want right now is to kill Beyorn. Grab a dagger and stab him the way I stabbed that red stygic. I can feel my hands curling and uncurling at my sides. A loud buzzing fills my ears, so much so that my vision is starting to darken at the corners. How can we simply stand here?

And yet when I try to move, pain strikes like a wasp in my blood-crusted arm, forcing me to stay in place. This is not the kind of pain that became a companion—no, this is the kind that is burning me from the inside out.

Thayne, however, doesn't let anything stop him. "Let her go!" he yells as he tackles Beyorn from behind, and the two go smashing to the ground.

Beyorn swings his massive arm, but Thayne manages to escape it. Beyorn roars like a hurt maristag and dodges a kick from Thayne. As large as Beyorn is, he's uncannily fast too. Thayne, a miner with no combat experience, is no match for him. Beyorn drives an elbow into Thayne's face. Blood spurts to the ground. It all happens so fast that I don't even have time to pull myself together. Raksha barely steps forward, polearm at the ready—only to stop. Beyorn grabs a fistful of Thayne's hair and crushes his throat with his wide arm.

181

"Move," he barks at Siril, pressing his arm tighter around Thayne's neck, "or he dies."

Over the angry, humiliated tears of the Shademan, Siril's whimpers are loud too.

She looks at me. "Kress—please." Like I could save her from the entire world.

My heart shatters. I force myself to move, forgetting the fear, one hand reaching out. But Beyorn knows what to do. He keeps one arm around Thayne and points a gun to the miner's temple too, stopping me dead in my tracks.

Even as Thayne struggles against his grip, Beyorn says calmly, "Either of you disobey me and he dies."

"Let her go, Beyorn," I wheeze, tasting blood, heart hammering against my ribs with frustration. "Leave her alone. Leave *him* alone."

But the brute makes no indication that he's even heard me.

Siril watches Thayne struggling to free himself from Beyorn's grip, watches me trying to uselessly stand midway between her and the two men, and knows she's lost.

Slowly, even as I keep shouting for her to stop, she makes her way to the curtain. The Shademan, however, is still dragging. His gaze darts everywhere as if somehow he'll escape this nightmare. And then, as if out of nowhere, he grabs a pointed rock and slams it to his throat.

Or tries to.

Beyorn is there, faster than lightning. He shoves Thayne out of the way and grasps the Shademan's arm. "If you want to die so bad, why do you fear a little light?"

Then he shoves the Shademan—right into a bewildered Siril.

Both of them tumble through the curtain.

The curtain resists for a moment, stretching instead of making way, but then it does. And they vanish.

"Where did they go?" I cry, stepping forward and stopping as Beyorn turns to glare.

We wait for several chaotic minutes, Rivan by my side, Raksha cursing at Beyorn, and Thayne, a side of his face now bruised, murmuring prayers to the ocean as if it will answer so deep beneath the ground.

And even as Thayne continues to pray, the curtain ripples, the same stretching movement, and the Shademan steps out of it. He has an arm around Siril, who is doubled over and choking.

"Siril!" Raksha and Thayne reach for her.

When the girl looks up, I gasp.

The color of her eyes—black—has lightened, a film crusting over them, like a cataract blooming as we stare. And her skin is pale as milk, but it's splitting and cracking, leaving a network of bloody rivers forming silently, steadily over her colorless face. Down from her skull, along her face, hands. The blood slides down the fissures, snakes to the ground, and seeps within.

The horror of it roots us all to where we stand.

Slowly, emptied of the blood within her, Siril slumps to the ground.

I scream.

Raksha shakes her, begging her to wake up. Yelling about her new rock and her book and everything she wanted to see in the world. Beyorn is unmoved. He grabs the map, then gathers the bags with our food, water, and other supplies.

"Aryadna, tie them up," he says, barely sparing a glance for Yara who's been standing at the back, staring at the ground. A walking dead at this point. Even as he's speaking, though, the Shademan takes off. Beyorn shoots and misses. In a few seconds, he has disappeared into one of the gates.

Beyorn curses.

Aryadna looks to me, then Rivan, then takes the ropes from Beyorn. She ties Thayne, me, and Rivan together. Beyorn makes Aryadna tie herself to Raksha before securing them both himself.

"If I get out of here," Raksha growls, "I will cut your heart out."

Beyorn collects our compasses and torches. "This well is very important for us. It will transform Kar Atish. Your miserable lives are contributing to our betterment. Take heart in it."

"Then take us back," I snarl.

"And let you convince everyone not to come down here to start the excavation? I don't think so. Our Collector, his wisdom remains great, always meant for none of you to return. We needed to confirm how deadly this substance is. I suppose it is a game of luck. Some survive, while others…" He glances at Siril, then back at us. "I would shoot you and end your misery for your service, but I'm almost out of bullets, and I might need them for the journey back."

I wonder if Badger knows this. If he did, he wouldn't have asked me to report about the creatures. Not that he'll care. Yara, Ansh, and I collectively drew half of his audience, but that doesn't matter. We will be replaced. We are, always were, replaceable.

I watch as Beyorn walks away from the company, his way lit with the torch, leaving us to die.

TWENTY-SEVEN

Thayne and Raksha have been arguing for what feels like a thousand years. Across from us, Yara, her breaths slow, keeps her head bowed as if in prayers the way Thayne was doing before. Thayne, I understand, but what does she have to ask for anymore? I try to remember what I did after my parents were gone.

Nothing comes to mind except blurred skies and storms, as if I'm on the ground staring up. That can't be all I did. But try as I might, I can think of nothing else.

Soon, I will have remembered my parents more than I have lived with them. If I live.

Thickness swells in my throat, and I shake my head to get rid of the feeling.

Maybe Yara is just waiting for this ordeal to finally end.

I catch the last words from Raksha. "—and Harren wouldn't agree to this."

"How can you be so sure? Your son may be a leader up there, but if they lure them down with the promise of freedom… Why else did any of us agree? They'll be just as naive as us," Thayne barks.

Raksha snarls and looks away.

She believes Harren can keep those rebels from being swayed to come down until they see proof of Raksha's return. But I agree with Thayne. The dust of this island has a way of getting to your brain, making you believe what you want to believe. And once Beyorn reaches the surface, he can make up any story. If they bring in miners to dig in the origin well…

"Some miners have Shade blood in their ancestry somewhere, and they'll be fine, which will convince them to continue," Thayne says. "But the others?"

"They will all end up like Siril," I say quietly.

An end that no one deserved, least of all the girl who was so brilliant that she taught herself to read. So excited at the novelty of the ancient architecture and, of all things, a rock. A color she had never seen before. The rock was still in her backpack that Beyorn has taken away. My hands tremble in their confines. It doesn't matter if Siril is dead, only that I will take that oceans-damned rock back from that bastard.

All Siril wanted was to earn extra money to free her sister and niece from the salt pans. Who would inform them of their doomed fate now?

All of us should have been smarter. That need for silver—for freedom—clouded all of our judgment. Made us trust those Landers and let our guard down.

But the Shademan from before… He sensed the danger in Beyorn, of an invasion even. Beyorn said he might be a spy. So where are the others? Who has he gone back to?

The thought of Shade blood being fine is rich irony. But I can't even laugh. The Shadefolk have been dying for generations, leaving the caves vulnerable. That is what my mother always said.

If I hadn't agreed to this mission, would something be different?

Perhaps Ansh would be alive too. It doesn't matter now, I guess. All we can do is sit here and wither. Unless a creature arrives and ends our misery.

Thayne tries to move his wrist against the ropes and fails to make any significant impact. "Did you have to tie this so strongly?"

"He had a *gun* to my head," Aryadna snaps.

The panic and dread of being betrayed are gone. In their place is anger, anew. Not the kind that made me want to stab the red stygic indiscriminately but the kind I can wear and grow into. Of course the Collector planned this. Since *when* would any of them do something out of the goodness of their hearts? If there was ever any doubt, it is now incinerated.

But to sit with this knowledge and die here is not what I want.

I twist in my place, try to loosen the ropes, to pull my hands free. Until I'm exhausted and my wrists turn into useless, bloody wrecks.

"If we had something…" I begin. "No one has any weapons left?"

The pale light from the curtain washes everyone a ghostly twilight echo. Raksha, in my line of sight, looks nothing like the miner she is—stone, hard and strong. Her face is drawn, and her eyes have turned bleak. I imagine what it would be like to fear if someone I loved was being lured to the same treachery I am suffering.

But then, I glance at Rivan. Maybe I don't have to imagine so far when he's right here.

Rivan has been my strength. I can't let him become my weakness.

He's dying, and he chose it for you. You are his *weakness.*

The thought gives me vertigo, even sitting down, as if I'm falling off the cliff into the sea.

A sudden glimmer, a sudden hiss, brings me back. It catches everyone's attention. An ashy smell cuts through the sickly, metallic smell in the air.

Yara, who has stayed quiet throughout, has lit a match and holds it upside down to the ropes tying her. Excruciatingly slowly, the embers weaving into the rope dance together and form a fire. She doesn't react at all. Just lets the flame burn. Until the ropes turn black, curl, and the fire gets swallowed by the air.

Yara lifts her wrists to herself, blowing at the blackened rings left behind as if she only brushed them against a hard stone.

Then, she looks up. "What? He forgot to check me because I was already tied."

~

"Even *if* the insect is gone, we can't climb all that way up," I say, arms crossed. *What a senseless idea.*

"You want to risk the other ways? Without a compass to show us the way back—without light?" Thayne says.

"We have light." I point to Yara, who has gone back to not speaking.

"Which is what must be attracting the creatures in the first place," Raksha says.

We go on and on in circles about the way to move forward. Moving through the deep without a solid guide is a suicide mission. Staying here is death too. It is unfair and frustrating, like most of our lives, I suppose.

"Kress..."

I turn sharply at Rivan's voice.

He's leaning against a boulder, trying to stand straighter, one hand pressed over his heart. Beneath his shirt, the red has darkened. He looks up, and the pain of the corruption inside him is stark on his face, every feature twisted to an unfamiliarity.

He holds out a hand and, before I can reach him, slumps to the ground.

"*Rivan!*"

I grab his shoulders, staring at the ugly red void spreading down his chest in gnarled rivers. His face has gone white. I take his wrist, which was bruised by the ropes, and feel for his pulse.

There is none.

TWENTY-EIGHT

We haven't played children's games in years.

One of the last times was a rare calm day in the ocean. The gray cast on the island was whiter, the stripes of gray in the mountains standing out instead of merging with the black. I was seeker. Ashvin, Rivan, and Mayven hid along their neighborhood, finding fissures in the mountains and niches between cavehouses. It was fun—at least until we found Rivan lying motionless in a cove. He hadn't moved even when Mayven, then nine, bit him to wake him up. And I began panicking, crying.

He opened his eyes then and told me it was only a joke.

It doesn't feel like a joke now.

"*Rivan.*" His name rips out of me, scratching its way along the walls of my throat. "Please wake up," I say, again and again. "You can't—you *can't*—"

His face is cold marble, eyelids a deep shade of blue, and the awful wound glows—death dressed in a beautiful, inviting light.

I look up, tears streaming down and turning the silhouettes of the company into smoke. "Help me, please. Wake him up. *Help.*"

Raksha, Aryadna, Thayne stare back down at me, their eyes full of pity.

Yara shakes her head, almost imperceptibly, as if she's trying to get rid of a wisp of a thought. For the first time, I notice that she still has quiet tears tracking down her face. She never did stop crying. Perhaps she never even realized she was crying.

Is this the cost of her tears?

What will I say to Ashvin and Mayven? They will hate me.

How much more will this island take from me?

You did nothing when your father and mother died. You did nothing but hide. And now you let Rivan suffer. You let him die—

"No!" I shout and the fury echoes back, billowing the fear of losing Rivan and myself in my face. The constant, inexplicable pain of being in the dark magnifies, becoming a monster insisting on waking up with full force now.

If I don't bring Rivan back to the island with me, I will never truly leave this place. I will never be whole again.

My sobs catch in my throat, tears and breaths warring as I hold Rivan, shaking him, willing him to wake up. *Please*, I beg, the pain from my wounds washing over me anew, *let the ocean move through him once more.*

The faint light of the curtain undulates over his face, as if moonlight touching him gently, but the coldness of death bounds ahead. And even as my hands curl into claws on Rivan's shoulders, I hear Raksha as if from a great distance through water.

"Grab something, a stone, quick!"

My head throbs dully with the impossible pain, thick with many tears still to come. I make myself look up.

From the left arch of the cavern, opposite the one from where Beyorn had fled, a silhouette emerges.

Even as I stare at it, blinking rapidly to clear my vision, it splits into seven.

Seven silhouettes against the shimmering twilight of the origin well, cloaked in dark brown, hands gripping spears taller than themselves, each so sharp it glints like stars in the curtain's light. They stream through the door and cross the hall as one, drawn in a V formation, their leader setting the pace.

"Stay back," Raksha shouts, both her hands holding stones in place of her weapon.

"We don't want any trouble." Thayne holds his hands up in surrender.

They don't stop or indicate that they've heard us at all.

I look down at Rivan; if we have to run, I won't leave him. Not here, alone and in the abyss.

The newcomers halt several meters away but well within range to strike Raksha with a spear if they want to.

For several seconds, they watch us, and when the silence grows unbearable, I shout, "Who are you? What do you want?"

There comes no answer. Only the rising of a mist, a sharp rotten sweet smell, and the sudden darkening of my vision—and then nothing.

I come up to a sharp pain along the sides of my temple, an ache thudding in my ears every time I breathe. My eyes stay closed as I collect my senses.

The ground beneath my face is hard and cold but not as sharp as the ground of the caves. My mouth is parched, tongue roughened like dry leather, and hunger claws at my insides with the fiery talon of a wyrm lizard. Every breath is hard. If I close my eyes, I know what I'll see. It's why I keep them shut tight, pretending. The dark is all around me. I *know* it. And it's not like before, when I had others around me. Right now, the silence is enlarged, waiting for me to acknowledge it.

My breathing quickens.

We were ambushed by seven strangers. And now here I am.

Trapped.

You can't avoid it forever.

Reluctantly, I open my eyes to the dark looming over me, filling the expanse, grinning with terrifying smugness. *Come closer*, the dark says.

I'm hyperventilating. Trying to slow my breathing. *Focus, Kress.*

I place my hands on the wall. Drag myself up, head pounding still. Slowly I move my way around, going wall to wall. No windows. Nothing. Then I come to the door far too quickly. This is a cell. A very small, claustrophobic cell. The bars locking me in are stone, as if jutting straight out of the ground and merging with the ceiling. But that can't be—they put me in here somehow.

Those strangers.

Are they the Shadefolk? Who else could it be? Beyorn—that traitorous bastard—did say the Shademan with us was a spy. Did he bring them to us? And—

Where are the others?

Rivan? Black fire roars in my chest, hurtling through my veins. He can't be dead. No, *no*. I need to see him. Save him. Take him back to his brothers. They don't deserve this, not after watching their mother die. They need him. *I* need him.

I rattle the bars, screaming. "Let me out!"

But the bars don't budge. Even when I slam at them with everything, battering them, trying to pull them apart with as much violence as I can muster. This can't be real. I can't have been torn from Rivan like this—not at the last moment when he needed me the most. He can't be all alone, dead, here. He said he had so many things to say to me. I do too! How could I not say them? My insides burn so much I want to split myself open, lay down every memory and pain and joy that is in me, release everything I want to tell Rivan but never could.

I've lost my parents. I don't want to lose Rivan. I can't—I can't bear it.

I remember my mind used to constantly split into options—I would work in the pits, earn enough to get myself out of here, enough to even leave some silver to Rivan and his brothers. My dream of Chandrabad always on the horizon. I remember I was a Kress who fought monsters surrounded by people who cheered for death in the ugliness of that pit. But what are my options now? What would *that* Kress do? Break these bars and—then what? What is there outside these walls but more of the dark deep?

There's only one thing I can do now—cry. Cry so much that my insides melt and I dissolve into my own tears. It's my fault that Rivan died—he came here for me. It's my fault that Siril and Ansh died—I came here to protect them and failed.

I am the Kinkiller the island had always prophesized.

"Don't do this!" I yell, not knowing myself what I mean anymore.

My voice echoes in the small spaces.

I fall to my knees, crying in earnest now.

No one answers.

TWENTY-NINE

Hours later, when my face swells up with the tears, shed and unshed, I hear footsteps. A sharp crackle rends the air with the ferocity of a blade drawn, and a single candle comes to life, bobbing up and down as the person carrying it descends stairs straight across from the bars on my cell.

It's the seven strangers.

The one leading them lifts their hood. It falls back to reveal a bald brown-skinned man, a network of white lines drawn on his face like runes. In the flame of the candle, his eyes burn a brilliant green, defying any logic of light and colors. It lends him an ageless, otherworldly quality, like any second he could merge with the air, vanish.

My breath catches in my throat. The seven strangers *are* Shadefolk. A piece of history, of legend, come to life in front of my eyes. Not just a single wanderer hiding in the dark, trying to cling to civilizations lost to ages, trying to scare us into leaving his home alone. My hands shake as this Shademan, the leader perhaps, assesses me. In that one, short look, I know he knows.

He knows who I am. And whose blood flows in my veins.

My mother, the descendant of Shadefolk, the one whose ancestors left the caves and found themselves a life above the ground.

Somehow, her and my father blasting off sections of the mines while there were people inside *isn't* the worst thing about her.

"What do you want?" My words are strangled. "Why have you locked me in? Where are my friends? What happened to Rivan? Is he still alive? That Shademan said you people have healers among you. That you could help with the wound. Please, *please*, help him!"

"We make the demands here," the leader says. His voice is deep and gravelly, a strike of boulders against mountains.

I press my face against the bars, hands curled tight around them, and spit at the ground. "There's my answer to your demands."

The man on his right bristles. But the leader remains still, not even a wince. He only says, "Why were you at the Blood Well? You, specifically, with your ancestry."

My blood chills.

"You don't know anything about me."

"We know you would betray the blood in your veins for a few silver coins."

Dark anger ripples in my gut.

"You will all face the justice you deserve."

Does he mean Rivan too? "Where is Rivan? How is he? Is he—" I can't bring myself to complete the thought. Even when I try, I can't keep the tears from falling. I *hate* that these people are witness to my helplessness.

The leader turns, followed by the others, taking the only chance I may have to see Rivan.

"I'm one of you!" I scream. "Does that mean nothing to you?"

"And what have you done for us, save bringing destruction to our doors? What is your claim to the community you demand help from?"

"What are you talking about? We were *stranded* in that chamber. We don't want anything from you. None of us knew where we were going!"

The Shadefolk exchange looks, as if I said something deeply perplexing.

Then, uneven footsteps come down the stairs behind the seven. So at odds with the sharp control and elegance with which these men stand. Someone limps up from behind the seven, face half-limned in light from the candle.

"You!" I cry.

The Shademan—our spy—shrugs. "Me."

My grip on the bars tighten. "Please, where is Rivan?"

He looks at the leader, who waves a hand, and then reaches for the bars. Even as I watch, he opens them without any keys or any movement I can decipher. The stone groans as he pulls the door out. For a moment, I feel supremely foolish—if he could open the door without any keys, maybe I could have too.

"Whatever you're thinking, that's not it," the Shademan says. "Now come if you want to see your Rivan."

They take me past similar chambers in narrow halls, up a tight corkscrew staircase lit with an actual sconce at the top, and then stop in front of a large stone door. This one has guards outside. More Shadefolk. All of them living here like it's the most natural thing in the world. None of them have had to shove their hands in the dust and grime of the mines. None of them have lived under the brutal chains of the Landers.

Inside the oval room, on a slab, lies Rivan. The room is lit with thick, glossy black candles that look like they're made of stone, not wax. I hurtle across, my stomach colliding with the cold stone of the slab. His skin is pale, almost bloodless. Lifeless. Except for the shining red wound still pulsing. The floor sways beneath my feet. My hands on either side of his face, my tears slipping on his lips. As if I had been thirsty for an age and he's a well of water.

"Don't do this to me, Rivan," I breathe. "Wake up, please." Even as I say it, though, I know it's useless. He won't get up now. He's broken every promise he ever made me. But I won't leave him here, in this cold, lonely room deep beneath the ground where no one knows he's the brightness of a thousand candles. I hate him—I hate him for leaving. He *knew* how alone I would be without him. And yet.

He left me.

I clutch at him tighter. The soot of the mines, the faint smell of the rebru soap.

Pain erupts in the center of my body, and I wail like a broken bird. I cry like I never got the chance to cry for my parents.

"You saved one of us," the voice of the leader says, breaking my sobs. "We do not carry blood debts. So despite your traitorous nature, we will be willing to help the boy."

I turn to face him, letting him see the tears and the harshness. "You wasted time on purpose so he could die and then you could pretend to help."

The Shadefolk watch me impassively for a moment, then the leader says, "Creatures of the deep are not like the ones you know. They kill rarely. He's not dying. He's turning into a skinnapankh."

I blink. A whistling blasts in my ears, sharp and keen. I look back at Rivan, wipe my tears and ash from my face—leaving behind congealed blood—and *really* look at him. He hasn't moved, but the skin around the wound is cracking. The glow of the red threads, already on his heart, is now pulsing softly within the veins in his hands.

"He's—alive? Is that what you're saying? I knew he couldn't—he wouldn't..." I breathe, my mind a jumble and every word a puzzle I have to work through. I throw myself at the feet of the leader. "Help him, then, please! I'll do anything."

"It will not come without a price."

"Anything," I repeat fiercely. The salt of tears slips inside my mouth. My prices are mine to pay.

"A blood oath," says the leader, "to repay a favor when needed."

I narrow my eyes, bubbling tears stinging harshly. What are they playing at? This seems too easy. Oaths, with blood or not, are for people who put honor and trust above everything else. Maybe someone like Thayne or Raksha would be scared of this. *They* would probably come back for whatever favor is asked of them.

Why would I? For strangers, at that.

I wouldn't even be on the island if it's up to me. They could never even find me.

"Fine by me," I say quickly.

He extends his hand and I place mine in it. One of the others hands him a blade without a hilt, black and stonelike. Obsidian? This is going to hurt.

But it's nothing if Rivan will get off this deathly cold slab and walk away.

The blade pierces the center of my palm, and I hiss. Dark blood wells up in my hand, gushing toward my sloping fingers.

The Shademan places his own hand below mine and collects the dripping blood. Things like this grotesque ritual must be why my mother's ancestors left. Thank the ocean for their sense of normalcy. If these people live like this, how many of them could truly be here?

"Is it done?" I ask. "What now?"

The Shademan flicks a glare toward me before slicing the hand with my blood on it. *That* gets me worse than when he cut me. I force my retch down. He lets his blood merge with mine, then slip in a sticky waterfall toward the ground.

And astonishingly, the blood gets soaked up within seconds.

"*Now*, it is done," the Shademan says. "We will call you when we have need of you, Krescent Dune. And you will not refuse if you want to live."

Then, he delves into his robes and pulls out a crystal bottle, cut into a sharp rectangle. It contains a clear viscous liquid, made obvious only by the thick shimmering ribbons twirling softly inside.

"An antidote," he says and gestures with a graceful movement of his hand. "Skinnapankh is a formidable villain. Its poison will turn a living being into another skinnapankh, no longer a human. Death is preferable."

The leader hands the bottle to the Shademan who was our hostage. I watch, my breath held, as the Shademan raises Rivan's chin and opens his mouth. He tips the liquid in Rivan's mouth, then holds his head down and chin up.

A little of the antidote dribbles out, but the rest goes down Rivan's throat.

For several moments, nothing happens. Dread locks around my stomach. *It was too good to believe*, I think. *Rivan's gone. He's not—*

Rivan gasps.

The narrow chamber echoes with the sound.

He coughs, convulses.

The luminescence of the red pulses, once, twice. Then slowly, *slowly*, it starts fading.

Another sharp gasp. My nails dig into my palms, but I can't physically bring myself to open my fists, as if one wrong movement would cause this illusion to shatter.

Rivan takes a deep, shuddering breath. His hand trembles, and I catch it.

"Rivan? I'm here," I breathe. "Can you hear me?"

His hand moves, taking mine with it, toward his chest. He rests our hands there, breathing harshly, as if in pain. And then slowly, his eyes open and find me immediately.

It's real. It's not an illusion. Those are his eyes. I'd know them anywhere.

I launch myself at him, throwing my arms around him, my heart leaping out of its cage.

"I thought you—your pulse wouldn't—I was so *afraid.*"

He doesn't say anything, just moves his hand on my back to hold me tighter, even though his strength hasn't returned. That simple touch unleashes everything within me, and I start to weep uncontrollably. I help him sit up, never letting go of him, clutching him to me like I could fuse our bones together. We stay like that for several moments, at once long and short, holding on to each other.

THIRTY

The Shadefolk waste no time in dragging us back from the
room. I hold Rivan's hand tight as we're directed down the
hallway. His posture is unsteady, but he puts an arm around
my shoulders and manages to move—even as his confused gaze lingers on the drying blood on my hands.

From the inside, no one can tell this place is carved so deep in
the ground. It *feels* like just another walkway in the Collector's compound. But no one above the ground could even fathom how far
beneath this place exists. And how much farther into the deep this
place goes.

Walking here now, when I can think properly, see what's in front
of me, I also notice that the chambers outside are cells too. And they
hold the rest of the company.

"Raksha!" I cry. "Are you okay?"

"Krescent?" she calls, voice strong. She steps close to the bars. "I'm
fine. You? And—oh. You…" Her eyes widen as she stares at Rivan
next to me.

He nods to her.

Aryadna and Yara also come to stand at their bars, confusion plain on their faces even in the dark.

"Where's Thayne?" I ask, looking around. "What have you done with our friend?"

"I'm here," comes Thayne's voice. I whirl. He walks toward us from the far end of the hallway, coming up from the staircase behind *another* Shademan, hands tied. He was kept separate from the others like me too. I search his face for any sign of torture. Thankfully it doesn't seem like he's hurt.

Interrupting our reunion, the leader says, his forbidding voice at odds with the calm, "Normally, we would have killed you."

"*No,*" Raksha and I snap simultaneously. We look at one another. Despite being still locked up, her mouth is set in a grim line. And I nod at her. If it comes down to it, I will fight. Even if they're all armed with glaives, I have taken down beasts bigger than any of them.

Now, especially, when Rivan is okay. I have to get him back to his brothers. I have to get out of this pit. Rivan was right. Thinking that this island would spit me out only if I let it swallow my bitterness whole once was a mistake. I won't have him pay for it.

Rivan steps between me and the Shademan.

"Don't—"

"I feel fine," he says.

"But," says the leader, "this much is clear. You have not come here to seek the Blood Well."

The Shademan who traveled with us steps forward. "It was the one called Beyorn, wasn't it? He brought you here in deceit."

"Yes," Thayne cuts in, stepping up to stand next to Rivan and me. "We were told we were looking for survivors from a previous expedition. That they had gotten lost but they were alive down here."

It occurs to me now that the previous expedition met the same fate as us: the Shadefolk.

"It does not matter what their intention is or isn't. They now know where the Blood Well lies like those others," says the right-hand man of the leader. "Letting them go is a mistake. They will bring in more and make a void of the well. They will have destruction."

"We want nothing to do with the origin well," Raksha says, hands crushing the bars of her cell. "We only want to go home."

"So why do you have two Children of Shade among you?"

Blood pounds in my ears. I hope the ground opens up and swallows me whole because I—

"*Two?*" I say as comprehension dawns. I look to my companions wildly. Not Rivan or Yara. So one of Thayne, Aryadna, or Raksha are Shadefolk?

"Shadefolk aren't real," Aryadna cuts in from her cell. The Shademan from before rolls his eyes at her. "They're just stories miners make up to entertain each other."

Well, perhaps not Aryadna.

"And yet here we stand," the leader says.

A simple statement. But the miners' faces tell all: this is not a reality they want to contend with. One Shademan they can deal with, tell themselves it's just someone who has made a home down here, despite the halls we have moved through. Denial will do that. After all, Shadefolk are stories, myths, shadows in the dark. They are the demons that grab children if they play near the mines. They are monsters who will devour miners if they go in too deep. They are cloud and thunder and whispers and wraiths.

They aren't real. They aren't human.

They aren't a whole population, with their own leaders and healers, caves made to hold prisoners, much more.

Aryadna stares at the ceiling of the hallway from her cell. Then says softly, "You built all this on your own? You *live* down here all alone?"

"You live up there all alone?" the leader asks.

Rivan and I exchange glances. We have the same look on our faces. *I can't believe this is happening.*

Thayne tries again. "We told you, we are stranded. That is the only reason we are here. All we want is to go back and never disturb the—your Blood Well."

It is a strange way to refer to this origin well, from where the veins draw the viscous raw substance that merges with gold and forms the ore of zargunine. *Blood.*

The thought sends a shiver through me.

"You saved one of us, for which we thank you," says the leader, and the one who interjected before scoffs. "For only this and your oaths that you will not betray the location of this well, you may return unharmed."

"Oaths without blood?" says the second-in-command Shademan. "Flimsy words for those who breathe too much of the ash they call air."

"As opposed to the rot *you* breathe?" I say without thinking.

The Shademan lifts off his hood. There is uncommon hatred in his burning blue eyes, set in a narrow square face. He reminds me of my mother. A shiver crawls across my jaw. I wonder if somehow I'm related to any of these people.

He stares right at me while saying, "We cannot trust them. They will have to pay the price with blood like the others. That is the only way."

And that's my suspicion confirmed. They are the ones killing the previous expeditions.

"We can go back and prevent others from coming down here," I say hurriedly. It's the only thing that they seem to care about. "Look at us. We are battered and beaten." I hold out my arm. The skin has vanished behind the crusted blood. The torn sleeves clings to it, and I don't know what the wound itself looks like. I'm too scared to check.

The palm of my other hand is also wrapped in a bandage from the fight with the skinnapankh.

"We did not come here on our own. Let us go," Thayne adds.

The seven Shadefolk, in near-total silence, form a circle to confer. The remaining man leans against the wall next to Aryadna's cell. He watches her squirm under his scrutiny, amused.

I want to go back, of course, but I also can't help but wonder if that is truly the best for these people. Would Raksha, Thayne, Aryadna, and Yara really keep this quiet? A society of people living beyond the ruins of an ancient city deep in the ground of our island and seemingly guarding the origin well of the substance that forms zargunine. In caves they have transformed to live in.

How can anyone not speak of this?

And how many others on the island are like me—descendants of these Shadefolk—who are keeping this secret among themselves? The only reason I didn't know the extent of these people's lives, it seems, is because my mother died before she could tell me that her stories aren't mere stories.

After what seems like an age gone, the seven break their conference. The lone Shademan stands up and takes a deferential step back as the leader walks to us.

"You may leave," says the leader. "But to stop the one called Beyorn, not to spread news of the Blood Well. The Children of Shade are charged with keeping the well of godsblood full and intact. It is our mandate, our purpose in life since we have lived beneath the ground. The Blood Well is ours alone and will remain so. If you do not heed, we will not only continue killing every last one who steps in our domain but perhaps be forced to take this into your homes."

The ordinary Shademan slowly unlocks the rest of the cells.

Even though we're at their mercy, Raksha steps out looking mutinous, rubbing her wrists. Not at the *request*, if that's what it is, but at the way he speaks. Beyorn isn't wrong about one thing—these people will not share their resources even if anyone asked nicely. They do not need us.

Thayne, on the other hand, exhales and his tense shoulders fall. "We promise. All we want—"

"Yes, we heard," says the second-in-command, sounding bored.

Thayne swallows his words. I look at him, and his face reflects the same indignation I feel. This Shademan is dismissing us like we *chose* to put our lives at risk.

"You will allow us to wrap a blindfold around your eyes," says the leader. "For our safety, we will not have anyone who sees into our city leave. You will be escorted back to where we found you, and you may make your way back. The one who died from the godsblood will remain here."

"She has a family," Thayne says and glowers. "They deserve the peace of seeing her off to the ocean."

"And how will you explain to anyone her wounds?"

Bewildered, the company stares at each other. In the corner, Yara watches it all with dull eyes, saying nothing. As if just waiting for them to kill us if that's what it takes to end her nightmare. On the other hand, if she was at her best, we'd probably be devolved into fighting the Shadefolk with claws and teeth.

"It is best for all of you to keep your lives and leave," the second-in-command drawls. "That is more than enough."

I look at Rivan, who is still pale from the wound. The redness has stopped glowing, but it stays, a reminder of the injury. We have the whole underground to cross, filled with claustrophobic tunnels and mazes and monstrous creatures, and nothing to fight them with.

I start, "We will need help in returning—"

"That is your business. We spare your life as you spared one of ours. The debt is paid. How you keep that life is on you."

THIRTY-ONE

The back of my head is beginning to throb. Or, I guess, finally making itself known now that things are slightly calmer. Dread roils in my stomach, which interferes with my ability to focus on foraging for the mushrooms in the corners of the hall. At the far side, the brilliant light of the curtain that protects the Blood Well breathes softly.

Before leaving, the Shademan—the normal one—took off our blindfolds and told us we could collect "food" for our journey back. He meant the glowing mushrooms in the nooks, and no way of telling which ones are poisonous.

"You can't give us something from your secret city?" I asked him. And he answered the only way he always seems to: shrugging.

But Thayne insisted on collecting them anyway.

"Easy," he says now. "You're collecting fungi, not breaking the island."

I look down. My hand is red with effort as my palm grasps the head of the mushroom, meaning to wrench it out at once. Sighing, I loosen my grip and move to pick it out from the stem.

"I would if I could," I mutter. "What's this island done for any of us?"

Thayne pauses, his eyebrows drawn down. "It gave us shelter. We are always indebted to our islands for saving us when we were lost on the wild seas. The ocean might seem indifferent if not outright hostile—not in any sense we might understand but because it is a far greater power. Its vast majesty and unpredictability are not for us to ever know. Our problems, perhaps even our existence, are too insignificant for it. But these lands, they were there when we needed them."

He sounds like the Shadefolk. I open my mouth to argue but then say nothing. It's not like he's *wrong*. Admonished quietly, I continue my foraging.

Several minutes later, Rivan joins me. Involuntarily, I hold my hand back so he doesn't see the new injury from the blood oath. If he knew, he'd blame himself for getting me hurt. Even if it's not true—even if the *opposite* is true—it's how his mind works.

"Mushrooms are good," he says. "Saves us from your terrible cooking."

I scowl at him. "What are you doing? Go sit."

"I'm fine." His eyes crinkle, but I can hear the strain in his voice. "And I need to get away from Raksha's grumbling. *Harren won't do this. Harren won't do that.* It's driving me insane."

"What do you think he'll do? Harren?"

Rivan shrugs. "The little I understand, I don't think he would trust the Collector, but if his mother's missing—who knows how he deals with his grief?"

I open my mouth but he continues.

"Things aren't great at the mines, you know that. But these past few months have been especially bad. Sollonia's Landmaster has redoubled her efforts to assume direct control of Kar Atish, and it's made things jittery for everyone. Even May has been hanging around Harren and his crew."

"And we all know we can't rely on Sollonia's rebels. Their caste prestige is more important to them. They fight the Hunters and among themselves. That's all there is to it."

Rivan continues, "Which is why they are scattered, and Harren is forcing the elders to deal with things here ourselves."

We cast a glance toward the company, where Raksha is still going on to the passive group.

"We can't tell anyone what we saw here," I say softly. "It's for all our good."

There's a subtle change in Rivan's eyes, almost invisible. He smiles as if he's found what he's looking for.

"What?" I frown.

He shrugs, still smiling, and his eyes lighten up.

"I hate when you do this," I hiss. "And I hate that you're even here. If something happened to you, I would've di—" I clench my teeth. That fear of seeing him lie still had frozen all my senses. Even the dark wasn't as scary as that. He holds me in his hand, and if he dropped me, I would shatter. It is a frightening thought.

Rivan raises a brow. "You would've—what?"

Died. Where does this sentiment even come from? We were talking about rebels and miners, Sollonia and its Landmaster. We were talking about Raksha and her son.

"Finish what you were saying, Kress."

Flushed, I only say, "You should have stayed above. At least I wouldn't be worried about you and could handle things better down here."

I start walking away, a bunch of glowing mushrooms in my arms, when Rivan pulls me back to him. So close to the wound that I'm afraid I'll hurt him. His heart beats so loud I can hear it over mine, pressed against his chest. He has never held me quite like *this*, his arms circled around me like he would never let go. Heat roars through me, turning my blood to fire, as if I could burn to ashes by his only touching me. My gaze drinks in his nearness, so familiar and yet so unnerving, the plain of his chest, the column of his throat. His gaze is deep and startling and so intent that I look down again, unable to bear it all of a sudden. My heart pounds in my chest, my pulse high in my wrists pressed against him. Can he feel it? Can he hear it?

"Look at me, Kress," he says softly.

If I look at you, I will be undone.

He lifts my face, forcing me to meet his eyes. Our lips are barely a cruel inch apart. And for a moment, I feel like we would always stay this way. This close. Where nothing ever comes between us, and there's no problem in the world that we can't deal with. I don't have to think about what the tremors of my heart mean. I don't have to guess if he's good to me because that's just who he is—or if he really—

"What do you think would happen to me if something happened to you down here?" he asks, soft as seagrass. "How could I not worry out there alone?"

My voice is a bare whisper. "It's not worth you getting hurt."

Rivan closes his eyes and leans forward so our foreheads touch. Every feeling in me shoots down to this touch, this ravenous desire ripping through me. He breathes against my lips. "How long are we going to play this game, Kress?"

We've played enough games, running around, hiding and seeking, laughing and crying together as we grew up. And if this is also a game, it's not like the ones I'm used to. This game is one with stranger rules, and I'm struggling to find my footing.

Every beat of my heart is loud and almost painful, unbearable, and everything inside me is too much, my skin strained, and I want to do something terrible, something so desperate it echoes in our blood and bones—forget about why I can't let this happen, forget that I want to leave this island and I can't tie myself down—

"We have water!" Aryadna's enthusiastic shout fills the hall.

Like a whip crack, I step back from Rivan, realizing that the others are still around.

"When we get out of here, I'm going to kill her," Rivan murmurs.

I let out a low laugh, blood still pounding in my ears, and begin picking up the mushrooms that had fallen from my arms. Of course Aryadna had to interrupt.

What *would* have happened if Aryadna hadn't interrupted? What would it feel like to kiss Rivan? To let him touch me as I know he wants to. As I want him to.

Why have I been fighting this feeling—him—for so long?

Because, reminds the voice at the back of my head, *everything will be ruined if it goes wrong. Is that what you want? The thrill of a moment destroying a lifetime of friendship before you leave this island forever?*

But even that reminder doesn't stop me from filling my mind with Rivan's name as we join the others.

They huddle together, silhouetted against the curtain of light that watches them with equal attention. Aryadna has filled our skins with a trickling stream along the walls.

"The water is filthy, by the way," she says.

I sit down—Rivan doesn't, opting to stand away from me pointedly—and add my collection of mushrooms to Thayne's in the middle of our circle.

"As opposed to the water that is drenched in dirt and soot?" Raksha raises a brow. Even now, her anger at Beyorn burns in her eyes. Her mouth is pressed in a thin line, jaws clenched. It breaks the spell Rivan cast, bringing back the taste of ash and rage—because I know that she is reliving every lie the Landers told to bring us here.

A quick way to get some money, pay off any debts or get some necessary medications for family. Try to build something.

The lure of silver.

The promise of freedom.

They *knew* which ones of the miners—and the fighters of the pit—to target. Which ones of us wanted our different freedoms from their grip. Badger conspired to trap me. He probably concocted beautiful lies for Yara and Ansh too.

And where is Ansh now?

Lost in the darkness they shoved us into.

Siril? She deserved a lifetime to explore the world like she wanted, to learn everything she could, to build something new in the way only curious people like her are capable of. She deserved to see her sister and niece freed.

And Rivan? The skin at the center of his chest is darkened red still, even though the wound has been neutralized. A scar will form there, a reminder of his time in this doom.

What was I expecting? To move away from this island, I chose to go deeper in.

Because of Beyorn and whatever he needed to prove on behalf of his brother.

He knew the mission was a lie, yet he didn't relent when Rivan was hurt. I was begging him to let me go back.

I try to imagine him letting us go. My mind balks at the image. Beyorn is a venerated sea captain and war hero. He's a Lander. And for a Lander, the rest of us are barely human. It makes things easier for them if they don't see us as being worthy of the same life as them. Our loved ones could bleed in front of us, and they will still demand that we finish our jobs for them first.

Everything must serve them.

I came down the island as the protector, but I couldn't even stand up for myself.

Beyorn treated us like Badger treats the beasts in the arena.

He would have let Rivan die as easily as a mine caves in on the workers. The thought makes me feel like a fool. That I believed his promise of letting us access the Collector's doctors. All he cared about is more metal and resources his people would force us to dig for. I should have killed him that night instead of trying to sneak away with everyone's things and leaving them stranded. It would have solved everything. Ansh and Siril would be alive too.

Ever since my parents died and left me alone, helpless, I've survived through the strength of my will. To the point that I almost believed the way my mother told me I was unstoppable. That I would come out alive in every fight, no matter what monster Badger throws at me. And one day that very belief would take me away from this island of nothingness. It will have me breathe under freer skies.

Down here, that strength changed into something else, something different and darker. I don't feel as I did on the island.

Ansh dying was not the triumph I always thought I would feel when I'd fantasize about the twins losing in the arena so I would be the only champion left.

Now I have no words left for Yara. Certainly no words to taunt her.

There was no need for Siril's death either—I could have gone instead. I would survive because of my mother's blood. Like the Shademan did. But I hadn't known. And everything happened so fast.

Now there's only one thing that would make things better.

Avenge Ansh and Siril and even Rivan's hurt.

The rage simmering underneath for so long boils over, burning my throat.

This anger is useful. It has cleared my head many times before when the voices grow too loud and unconstrained. But what I need now is not just a clear head but a clear purpose.

Beyorn is my purpose.

He is the enemy.

Hurt him like he hurt you and Rivan.

But if I just hurt him, he will come back stronger. He will deploy the Collector's full power and then bring Sollonia's army behind them. Isn't that how the story of the Naag dragon goes? Cut off one head and another grows back.

I'm not the monster they think I am, but I'm no better than one either.

Beyorn has to die.

And I have to be the one to kill him.

THIRTY-TWO

The small pile of mushrooms gets even smaller within a few minutes as we gorge on, without much thought to their poisonous capabilities. All of us are exhausted and hungry. Our backpacks had enough food and water to last us over a month, but it's all in the hands of Beyorn.

It's not the first time miners have had to make a choice between satiating hunger for the moment without knowing if it might be their last morsel or die of it painfully later.

It won't be the last.

"So we're about eight days from the mine entrance," I say, the taste of the slickness in the water coating my tongue.

"Nine," Aryadna cuts in.

"Are you sure?"

"I've been keeping track. You've had a lot going on," she says gently.

"Okay, so we must leave now," I say, ignoring the sudden itchiness along my arms. The new tattoo at my wrist didn't have time to calm down, I think. "We have to stop Beyorn from getting out and luring even more miners down to their deaths."

"How can we do that in time?" Raksha says. "He has the compasses, fire—everything he might need. And what do we have except the fear of getting lost in the labyrinths forever?"

I can't deny that. We have all seen Ansh and Siril die cruelly.

"Don't forget the monsters," Thayne says.

"And the madness," I add. They all look to me at that. There's no point in hiding it from them anymore. The better we understand our surroundings, the more prepared we will be.

"When I was in the labyrinth alone, before Aryadna came to get me, I thought something had...gotten into me. Like a voice that wasn't my own. Making me think things. Almost making me want to...give up. And I believed it too. It was like I couldn't separate what was in front of me and what was that voice in my head. Well,"—I turn to Aryadna—"not until I had your torch's flame break that hold in my head."

They're all quiet. Maybe I made a mistake, and now they'll think I *am* mad and nobody would want to follow me. There are often people who stayed working too much in the mines, who lost their senses, began seeing things that weren't there, hearing voices. They were almost always let go because they weren't fit to work and would put others in danger.

Is that what I did? Admitted that I might be a danger to the others.

But Rivan only asks quietly, "Why didn't you say something?"

I shrug, not looking at him.

"But you're saying keeping a fire with us might help?" Aryadna asks.

"That's what it felt like to me."

"The problem is," Raksha says, "we don't have fire. Yara's matches won't last for nine days. Probably more, given, once again, that we do not have compasses."

"We know that we've been traveling westward all throughout the journey," I say. "If we go through the gate Beyorn left from, we will be moving north first. We go through and then find the first opportunity to cut to the right."

"What happens when we get attacked by something that will kill us with one swipe of a giant claw?" Yara asks finally.

Her face is swollen, lumpy in places, and her eyes are almost slits. She wears the haunting look of the almost dead. And I *know* she doesn't actually care whether she lives or dies, because she's aware of what happens if we come across something we can't fight.

She just wants to make sure everyone sees how ill-equipped I am to answer these questions.

But I have to convince them. "So it's a death sentence either way. We might as well try."

Rivan adds, "And we're forgetting, we still have two of the best fighters in the pit." He looks at me, the seriousness in his tired eyes softening as he does. For a strange moment, I think I see a flicker of red, but I blink and it vanishes. No, it's just the image from before still burnt in my mind.

"Beyorn cannot survive the labyrinths on his own, so he will be slow," Rivan continues. "He will want to avoid the monsters. He will wait. It's an even field. We can reach him, but we must try."

"The dead cannot try," Yara says quietly.

I swallow hard. For a long while, my only goal in life has been to escape this island, scrub myself off it and it off me. But would that have really changed anything inside? The loneliness that has plagued me for the past eight years. The anger at the cruel hand this life has dealt me.

Would leaving Rivan and escaping this place have helped me get rid of that, or would I carry it with me everywhere I go if I let even more people die and not do anything about it?

I shake my head.

Involuntarily, my gaze returns to Yara. There's nothing I can do for her. The pain that has come to her because of me. But perhaps I can keep someone else from going through this.

She, too, has suffered anew because of Beyorn.

I try to speak, but my tongue sticks to the roof of my mouth. I try again, telling them what they need to hear in this moment.

"We owe the dead, then," I say. I look each of the company left in the eye. "This is now a mission of our lives. We have to survive and make sure no one else dies down here for someone else's greed. If we come across monsters, I will fight them to my last breath if it gives anyone here a chance to escape. I won't let Beyorn win.

"I have spent my life running from my parents and their actions, but let me do something right here."

Speaking of my parents has changed the air. A wiry caution emerges in everyone again. Thayne, who might have wanted me dead when he realized who I was, watches me with a frown between his brows.

Rivan, on the other hand, has that strange, small smile once more. It's almost like he's in on a joke, something that I haven't caught up to yet.

Raksha stands. She reaches one hand to me. "We better get moving fast, then."

THIRTY-THREE

Our makeshift torches, made of the blindfolds wrapped on long pieces of stone and lit with Yara's matches, aren't half as bright as the ones Beyorn stole from us. They flicker too much, flames desperately clinging to the fabric, every second threatening to go out and leave us in the absolute dark.

Better than nothing, I remind myself as I step cautiously ahead. Behind me, every now and then, someone bumps into the wall or hits their head on an outgrowth.

The gate that Beyorn left from leads into narrow tunnels that slope upward. They are cut without logic in some places, giving the impression of broken bones in limbs that never set and now jut out of the skin like rag dolls. On the walls are drawings. In the low, shivering flame, they turn monstrous, and I have to remind myself they're only figures on the wall.

But these are not like the ones at the stupa. They are newer. White chalk human figures, beasts stranger still, and awful half man, half beasts. The thought fills me with revulsion.

There are other sketches. Rows of caskets wrapped in chains. I quickly look away from those.

Whatever stories the Shadefolk tell one another for entertainment, I don't want to know.

The Children of Shade are charged with keeping it full and intact.

Who charged them with this duty, and what does it mean? Why do they need to hoard the Blood Well for themselves?

Maybe the Children of Shade still believe in gods like the Empyrean Elders, and the Blood Well is some kind of shrine. After all, they disappeared down Kar Atish from the very first time we arrived on these shores. They never really lived in a world where people moved on, shed old beliefs, and embraced the reality of the sun and the ocean and the islands being all that governs life.

I wish my mother were alive—that she could tell me the secrets of our islands.

But... If my mother knew those secrets, were they somehow related to her trying to destroy the mines? She and my father killed so many people that day. What was that for?

So many questions. And no one I can turn to.

Raksha murmurs behind me, "If we weren't entangled in a game of invasion and hostilities, I wonder what the Shadefolk could tell us about the world below. How they crafted their homes and how they learned to build architecture like that. Stories they found out of their experiences. How they survive down here. Maybe we could provide something to them too. Our mutual exchange of ideas could have made something better of this island."

"The Landers would die before letting us make anything better that isn't immediately beneficial to them," Thayne says.

In the dark, he sounds far away. Or maybe he is. Everyone still moves slowly, each step measured.

"The Shadefolk don't want anything to do with us," Aryadna reminds us.

"For no fault of theirs," Raksha says. "There was a time when things weren't so sharply divided between the world above and the world below. We have enough stories that must have emerged somewhere in the middle."

I throw a quick glance over my shoulder. The only stories I can think of are the ones drawn across the walls. Those aren't ones anyone above the ground would know. *Should* know.

"Tell us of these stories from the middle," Rivan says. "It might help keep our minds off the dark."

Raksha hums. "Well, there is one I know well. The story of Theseus and the labyrinth."

In the time of the stone breaking, the mouth of the first cave yawned open. From within came the roars of a half man, half beast. It was a strange creature that hungered, trapped inside, for ages alone. The leader of the Atish clan descended into the cave and said, "Look, beast, what I have brought for you."

It was a stone candle, its wick lit. The creature was, it turned out, a child. And so it was enamored by the novelty of light and told the Atish leader that it would be to him as a child is to a parent if he so wished. The Atish leader laughed, for what good would a monster for a child do? Nevertheless, the Atish leader let the monster call him Father, and from that day on, he became known as the Monster Tamer.

Fools came, far and wide, to challenge the monster and claim the title. But they all came armed with knives and rocks and fists and poison. None brought him the novelty Father had. So the monster met them with its own claws and fangs, the only offering it had for them.

When the time came for Father's reign to be handed over, others called him to the next conclave to pass on the seat of the leadership. He said, "I will give up my seat if anyone here can defeat me in combat." Then, he named the monster his champion over and over until there was no one left to fight.

And so it was that Father, with his monstrous child, came to rule for years the island he named Kar Atish. He demanded tributes from all others as punishment for trying to take his seat. Not even the ocean, wandering the world and noting all affairs, said anything to Father. It did carry word to the two isles of Kuru, where a young man named Theseus was looking for his brother already lost when he was but a spark in his mother's womb.

At the ocean's request, Theseus traveled to Kar Atish, curious at the whisperings of a man and his monster. On his arrival, however, the people clamored about. They knew the ocean had brought him, and so they asked for their salvation, for their release from Father, who would lock any transgressor in caves dark and festering until his monstrous son took them.

Theseus challenged Father and was met with the same words: "Defeat my champion, and what you ask is yours!"

And so Theseus found himself down the caves with naught but a flame, a dagger, and a small wound that he used to mark the stone with blood to remember his way out. Loneliness haunted Theseus in the dark, the flames turning to little birds as they flew away, and when Theseus came face-to-face with the monster, he cried, "Brother!"

The man in the monster woke up horribly at the cry, memory flashing and dying all together, until the monster remembered he was a child once, stolen in the night by a giant of stone and changed into the half beast for play. His eyes fluttered open, his monstrosity slipping away. But with it came the dawning of his actions, of the people he devoured, of the blood he drew. Terrified of his brother's renunciation, the child monster fled into the dark.

But Theseus would not be persuaded to give up on his brother found and return from the underground. For many years thereafter, Theseus traveled into the labyrinths alone, calling out to his brother. His hair turned white and his skin turned paper, but only the dark answered until the day he faded into the dark himself.

THIRTY-FOUR

A nd this is why we must not go into the mines alone," Raksha concludes, "for it only shows us the darkness inside us, and if we cannot face it, we will be as lost as Theseus."

"Nobody is five here, Raksha," Rivan says.

I laugh.

We're marching along the labyrinths, starless and empty. After Raksha's words, our footsteps echoing in the narrow alleys break the absolute silence as if for the first time. We're moving northward and will have to turn east soon if we ever want to get out of here. Aryadna keeps track of our direction. She's confident in her ability, but I can't help but dwell on this labyrinthine underground. Monsters and madness and a life of its own. If we're not careful, we'll end up in the middle of the ocean and die entombed here.

The only consolation is that with only a single path forward for now, we're following in Beyorn's footsteps.

The mushrooms do nothing to keep the hunger away.

Or perhaps the rugged terrain is exacting its toll. Still, the years of near starvation have trained me for this. But I don't know about the others. Miners don't have a lot, but at least they get to keep their bellies full. The Collector needs strength in their arms to do the digging and dying.

When I said that we're staring at our death sentences either way, I meant it. And the others must know it too. Who else would be desperate and foolish enough to come on this trek? But I'm glad they're with me. Company is a rare gift. Trust even rarer.

The tunnels abruptly give way to a bigger cave, just as the labyrinths did when we were on the opposite side of this journey.

"Things are about to get tough from here," Aryadna mutters.

We slowly move forward, listening for every shift in the air.

The caves take on a more geometric look, similar to the city hall with the stupa. The walls are smoother too, the stone chiseled instead of the natural formation. *How big can a city be beneath the ground?*

The answer, it seems, is *very big.*

These halls aren't the works of the Shadefolk, but something—someone—even older. The Shadefolk were the first refugees, the ones who fled the shipwreck of Sollonia immediately instead of getting embroiled in wars once more. Despite the Empyreans' search for peace, they knew the islands were death, so they chose to delay theirs. All these ages, and they remained here, under our feet.

And only a handful in generations would ever venture out.

I wonder what Beyorn thinks of everything he's seen. How can anyone witness their reality breaking, finding out there are histories and existences in the world other than our own, and still only care about a thing as banal as a metal in the ground?

"It's cold," Thayne says, looking around.

"Maybe we should think about getting out," Aryadna says. "Leave Beyorn to his fate. He can't fight creatures alone."

"No," I hiss. "Beyorn doesn't get an easy death."

The moment the words leave me, I blink. The realization of

admitting aloud why I'm really going after Beyorn—to kill him—rushes at me. It *is* what I want, but it is not what I said to the others. Would they now think I am as vile as they thought Jar and Katya's daughter would be?

Someone who kills the beasts in the arena for fun—

Overwhelmed, I stop walking. The torch flickers in my hand madly, as if cackling at my shock.

"I—if he lives, he will not stop," I say in a smaller voice. They must understand. "And if the Shadefolk hold true to their words, he would only be sentencing more of us to die. I don't know what else we can do but make sure he never gets the chance to."

"Maybe you don't have to," Thayne says. "We can talk to him—"

Raksha laughs harshly, interrupting Thayne. "The Collector and his men speak the tongue of greed. Only in death will they give it up."

It's not an endorsement of *me*, but it's not an indictment either.

A large, conspicuous silence descends in the cavern, lying thickly against our skins.

Rivan meets my eye. He knows I'm looking for assurance, to know that I'm not making another mistake, and all he does is nod, which is enough.

"Fine, fine. Let's not second-guess ourselves," Aryadna says. "We have decided that we must kill him, and for that we have to catch him before he reaches the mines."

There's a murmur of assent, and we turn upward once more. The drawings fade behind us, and with them thoughts of old civilizations as we find ourselves in halls where faint noises rise again. Here and there, I think I hear a click. This time, I'm more careful and scout first before letting the others ahead. Twice, I kill small critters with nothing but a rock, holding my breath for anything bigger than me to appear. But thankfully, nothing does.

Soon, after making intelligent, if blind, guesses over the hours, we reach a cold, high-roofed space. Shallow black water lies at the center of it. On the other side of the knee-deep pool, a large door looks to a landing, a chasm, and across from it another big hall. Deep within me, I know it's the same chasm where Ansh fell, but since we came downward after a longer route, we have emerged elsewhere along it. Perhaps farther left.

And if I know, so does Yara. Her face is stark, blood drawn. As if any moment she would lash out at me.

Trying to ignore Yara, I step into the water first, and a startling shriek leaves me. "Damn the ocean, it's freezing!" I stumble back from the water hurriedly.

One by one, the others check the water, as if they don't believe me. Why would I lie about something so mundane? What would I gain out of it? As if they couldn't check for themselves. I sigh as they hiss at the cold.

"Well, it's either this straight shot or we risk getting lost to find another route. Which probably will take us back to…the scorpion cave," Thayne says.

The reminder of the scorpions—and the insect creature—sends a tremor though my heart. Absently, I lay my hand on my arm. The bone is still in its socket, holding on fiercely. But I don't think it will continue to if I have to fight a giant insect again.

"The water it is," I say with grim determination.

THIRTY-FIVE

When my mother used to say I was unstoppable, it had more than one meaning. On some days, she would say that my Shade blood might give me abilities.

"Like magic?" I had asked once, a wonder rising in my chest.

My mother laughed her bubbly, loud laugh. Even with soot settling in the lines around her mouth, she was beautiful when she laughed. She tilted her head to the right, like she always did, a lock of brown hair spiraling down, and said, "If you want to call it magic, then magic it is. But you know the thing about magic, don't you, my love? It is a secret we don't tell others, or the magic leaves."

After my parents' deaths, when I'd slept in a nook and woke up to a raath gnawing at my foot, others waiting behind, I'd fought. With a feral instinct I hadn't known I possessed. I knew of the raath. You didn't come out of their attacks alive. I didn't think I would either. But I was so angry and so sad and so alone. I wanted that fight. And somehow, I came out of it not only alive but with a strange sense that I knew exactly where to hurt the creatures. It wasn't magic, but it was something. And over the years, that sense only grew. A sense of *knowing* what's in front of me in a fight.

It's that sense that tells me my blood is stronger than this dark water's chill. Slowly, I strip off my boots and socks and pants. Lift the upper clothes a little higher. The cold's knives dig into my skin already.

A faint shadow crosses the water. I look up fast, my neck cracking. But there's nothing.

It's just nerves. And the burning cold.

I flex my fingers, tightening my hold on the torch, and burst through the pool. The water in my blood screams, and my hand freezes against the torch.

I stay still, dying of cold, and then—there's a ripple from my right.

No, I'm imagining things.

The cold has gone into my mind. Obviously. I can't think. My face is stiff and numb. Fog burns its way through me.

For a moment, I think the effort is beyond me. The chill of the water is almost unnatural. Its iron strength shackles my feet and rings in my skull. I've asked too much of my body. The blood within me is freezing. My body is going to burst.

With a panicked lurch, I yank my feet from the bottom of the pool and hurtle toward the end. My eyes burn, the cold cutting through the veins in my body, trying to engulf me. The corners of my vision darken, shrinking my sight to a narrow point of light. The water rises, and pain tightens around my chest.

Within two more steps, the light vanishes, darkness swallowing me whole.

Beyorn must have passed through here too. If that bastard could do this, so can I.

Even at this minute, he must be thinking that he's gotten away with leaving us to our deaths. That he's going to get his damned army and get the Blood Well and be honored by the overlords in Sollonia.

That he's invincible.

But I won't let him get away.

The next twenty seconds are the longest of my life. Even when I slam to the ground on the other side, my body is coiled so tight it refuses to shiver. Each moment, the cold knifes through me sharper. I pull myself up and clasp the torch tighter, letting its heat warm my face. The pain slowly subsides to a dull ache, and the shivering is brutal, teeth chattering like a thousand hammers striking at once, but I'm grateful for this thawing.

Except—that isn't—can't be—

My heart races as my vision still fights the cold.

I stare at the shore. Littered with bodies. Human bodies. Turning to skeletons. Some of them clothed, most of them ripped. Caving gear scattered about. Rusted blades. Guns lying in water, long gone bad.

The nearest almost skeleton has pits where its eyes should be. The lower half of the body, crawling away from the shore, is mangled and reeks so terribly that fat tears start spilling down my face. The other half is wearing the same minesuit and padded jackets as the miners in the company.

A scream tries to escape me, but the cold still has my throat clamped.

Shivering, I quickly dress, keeping an eye on the skeletons. A deep, primal part of me fears they might get up.

Yara and Rivan are in the pool now. Immediately, I know it's a mistake. Streaks of tears transform to ice along Yara's face. The bones in Rivan's face push against the skin. *He's in pain.*

"You can do it," I say, my voice broken and chattering. "Quickly, please."

He closes his eyes to show he heard me, but then he doesn't open them, just continues to push through.

We should've run through the oceans-damned scorpion cave instead.

All the while, my gaze darts about, searching for whatever killed these cavers. They're clearly from the expeditions. The Shadefolk must not have gotten all of them. Or maybe this is the path they took while coming down.

And something got them.

I stand up, knees burning painfully, and glance at the pool. Rivan and Yara are almost halfway through. A miracle, given how blue their faces look, how slowly they move.

By the time they slump on the shore, they're stiff as stones. I immediately place the flame between them.

What seems like hours later, the others too arrive on this side. The teeth of ice dig into each one. Raksha's stoic face is scrunched in pain, Thayne's eyes even sadder. And Aryadna looks simply *angry* as if the world has dealt her a great, personal affront by introducing her to the cold.

All of us freezing and dying on the small shore, a single flame for the six of us.

But none of us can take our gazes off the skeletons. Aryadna even pokes at one of them.

"How—?" she says, voice cut as she shivers violently. She shifts closer to the center, holding her palms up to the fire.

"A monster? What else? They look like they were trying to crawl away even as they were dying." As I say it, I cast a glance at the pool. But once again, it lies silent. I shake my head, teeth chattering anew. "We—we have to make a new fire."

"These are the Collector's men," Aryadna whispers, rubbing her hands together for the elusive warmth.

My cold breaking the fastest, I tear a strip from a small dry part of my sleeve and make a new torch. A second breath of life flares in the cold chamber, leaving me gasping. For several eternities, no one speaks as we gather in a circle with the two torches in the middle, heating our dead legs, turning the frozen red ice in our veins to liquid blood again.

"In true cold, we would be dead," Raksha says.

"The only truth I know is what's in front of me for now," Thayne replies.

I wonder where Raksha might have known "true" cold. The seas and the storms might make some days chillier, but the sun and the Redwater lava river make sure we burn. I have experienced cold air, especially during the nights, but this felt like another world. A purgatory, maybe a punishment.

"For what?" Rivan raises a brow.

I look up at him—and the others—and realize I spoke aloud. "For... for transgressing against the Shadefolk?" It's the easiest excuse I can come up with. But this place feels far vaster than mere Shadefolk living their quiet lives. This hollow ground, extending beneath not just our island but into the wider sea, is resisting us. As if with a mind and will of its own.

It is punishing us for intruding on its rest.

Aryadna watches me like I have sprouted mushrooms from my head, so I'm glad I don't share my thoughts.

I only say to deflect, "But trust me, we'll stop Beyorn, and we'll get out of here."

We decide to stay at the shore for a day, stripping clothes as they dry and adding patches to the flames, letting the heat move our blood. I sleep for only a few hours and keep watch for most of the rest, listening to the music of the fire crackling.

Aryadna sits up with me at the start of my vigil. For a while, we stay quiet and hold our palms up to the fire. Then, she watches me sideways, and by her expression, it seems like she's been dying to speak for a while.

"What's the deal with you and Rivan?"

My hands close tight. "There's no *deal*."

"Oh, come on. He came after you here," she says. "And you should've seen your face when you thought he'd died."

"His brothers would have killed me if something happened to him."

She groans. "Don't tell me that's what you've been telling him."

"What else?" I say irritably.

"You think we don't see the way you two moon at each other. If anything, *you* can't see the way he looks at you when you're turned away from him."

I choose to not say anything. My feelings—however complicated they may be—are nobody's business but mine. Not even Rivan's. I can always think clearer when he's not addling my mind.

What good would any of it do? The moment the miners found out who I was, they called me Kinkiller. Yes, things changed. But that's what my life will be if I stay here. Trying to convince everyone of my humanity every day of my life.

Rivan cares for me, I know that. The orphan girl he found shivering in her sleep.

And if I let him love me, he would do so with the kind of ferocity that would tie me here. I'd grow to resent Rivan, and I don't want that to happen to the only person who sees me and loves me for who I am. And if I disappear, it would probably be a boon to his family. One less person to share their food and supplies with. And no one questioning why he shelters the Kinkiller.

Even if I want...I want...

The center of my body twinges. Like something wants to claw out.

What do I want?

Stop it. You made up your mind to leave. Stop questioning it.

Aryadna says softly, "Of course, how could you love him when you're already in love with suffering?"

I turn to her sharply. How *dare* she?

A sudden ripple emerges in the water.

She points. "What is that?"

I gesture for her to be quiet. It expands pool-wide, touches the shore, and fades. It rose from the same side as it did when I was in the water. I stay crouched, my hands searching for a rock—*anything*.

Pebbles tumble off into the water, and I freeze.

The others are sleeping around the fire, safely away, except for Aryadna, who's moving along the shore recklessly, trying to see what it is as if she could fight it off.

Before I can get up and drag her back, a tentacle shoots out of the water past me and grabs Aryadna's ankle.

She screams as I rush forward.

I grab her arms and *pull*.

A second tentacle slams into my head, sending me crashing hard into the rocks along the shore. I hit my jaw on a big rock, and the taste of blood floods my mouth.

The shouting has woken the others.

My head rings, and another tentacle rises out of the water straight at me. I lurch out of its reach. Two more tentacles rip out of the water, and I kick madly at them.

What is this thing?

Thayne and Raksha rush forward to help Aryadna.

But they have nothing to get her out of the tentacle's grip. They scratch and kick at it while Rivan grabs Aryadna's arms and tries to drag her back.

I hurtle into the pile of skeletons and pull free the bones.

This is the weirdest fucking thing I've ever done.

"Get back!" I yell at Thayne and Raksha. Blood pours out of my mouth, garbling my words. They look up, their eyes wide, and stumble back as I slam the bone down on the tentacle. A screech fills the cavern. I keep smashing the tentacle with the bone, over and over, until dark blue blood spurts out of it, drenching me.

The tentacle slips back, and Thayne and Raksha grab at the screaming Aryadna. She falls back hard into them.

I heave, the bone still raised in my hand above my head, blue with blood, staring at the water.

And immediately, the water boils over. A grotesque black-blue creature erupts out of the water. It's not an octopus, or even close. It's something like a serpent or a lizard, with tentacles down its slender sides. Must have slithered through an opening in the walls—the pool is not deep enough to have hidden it.

Then it opens its mouth and screeches, ropes of spittle flying, giant fangs gleaming at us menacingly. Twenty tentacles slash at the air and the water, spraying us.

"Come on!" Yara shouts from the back of the chamber, almost at the exit. She's used the time to gather our temporary torches.

Rivan grabs me at the waist. "You can't fight it, Kress! We have to run!"

Wiping blood off my mouth, I hurtle out the door.

Behind us, the tentacles slam into the walls. For a terror-filled second, I think *this is it*. It's either the monster or the chasm down below.

But then, as the water monster continues to assault the cave with its tentacles angrily, trying to get us, the walls of the cavern shatter with a terrible groan. Within seconds, rocks come crashing down and block the way out, leaving us on the platform overlooking the chasm.

"What was that?" Aryadna shouts, pointing at the cave frantically, eyes still wild. "The Naag dragon?"

Raksha says seriously, "The Naag is supposed to be beneath the sea."

"We *are* under the sea. That pool probably opens up somewhere. Who knows what else it could have drawn?" I say, staring at the rocks blocking us out. Protecting us.

Aryadna laughs hysterically, and even though she's the one who brought it up, she shouts, "The Naag isn't real."

"I wouldn't bet on what is or isn't real anymore," I say. Although for all our sake's, I hope the oceans-damned Naag dragon doesn't step out of the stories now too.

"We're not safe anywhere," Thayne says.

"Death sentence either way," Rivan answers with a somber glance at the blocked cave. Plumes of dust billow in the air as the shattering echoes in the underground for many long minutes. On the other side, several feet away, the chasm yawns at us, completely indifferent.

I fall to my knees, hands trembling against the hard ground. Rivan kneels next to me. Three long scratches go up his arm too. Everything happened so fast I don't know when he got hurt. I bury my face in his shoulder, breathing in the same ashy smell clinging to every surface down here, but Rivan's warmth beneath is a comfort. He brushes a hand lightly, a feather, along my spine before pressing down on the back of my head, and I want to curl into his touch and not open my eyes ever again.

But once more, I pull back from him to wipe blood off my mouth.

THIRTY-SIX

The bridge off the platform is wider than the one before. Three of us could walk abreast comfortably. But no one wants to be next to the edges if they can help it. Especially not Yara, who stares down the darkness a touch too long. So we go one by one, with Raksha leading us for the time. Despite Yara using her quick thinking to save our meager torches, they're all useless now. Only one of them works, quivering like a leaf in the rain, and the anemic halo around Raksha is all the light we have.

I tread over the uneven bridge, arms wrapped around myself, trying to focus on the light. Growing up on Kar Atish, surrounded by storms that keep the skies away, black spires of rocks tumbling on you unannounced, mountains and hills with the black and gray bands, shadows and smoke, ash and soot, anyone would think we would embrace the dark. Thrive in it. But all being trapped in the darkness has done for me is make me afraid of the day it pushes past what thin barrier of light remains and consumes everything completely.

Hunger rears in my stomach, clawing at the walls of my body.

I wipe my mouth with the back of my hand again. My cut lip is swelling rapidly, dried blood smeared down my chin and neck. Even Badger's pathetic healers would be welcome right now. What must he be doing at this moment? Lording comfortably over the fighters and the beasts, no doubt.

A prickle scuttles down my spine, interrupting my thoughts. The dark remains absolute beyond Raksha's light. No movement on either side of the bridge. No fluttering of wings. But my stomach plummets with an unknown awareness.

I spin.

And catch Yara's hands as she rushes at me. The shock of the impact jolts through my body, pain exploding in my already-injured arm.

"What are you doing?" I yell, trying to keep my grip on her. "What's wrong?"

"*What's wrong?* You killed my brother!"

"What the hell is happening?" someone shouts from behind. My mind is so preoccupied with making sure Yara doesn't drive her fingers through my face that I can't tell who it is.

"I didn't kill him!"

My arm buckles under the pressure. I lock my jaw and *push*, sending every drop of my strength into my arms, holding strong.

Yara's foot slips.

She backs over the rough ground.

We're dangerously close to the edge.

I can't let her die too.

As the others come rushing back, I tighten my grip on Yara's wrists and snatch her forward. At the last moment, I jump out of the way, releasing her, and she crashes to the ground.

"You killed him," she cries, sprawled on her front. Every word sounds painful as she continues repeating it. "You killed my brother."

Rivan and Aryadna find me in the dark.

"Did she hurt you?" Rivan asks. His face scrunches between rage

238

and pity as he casts a glance to where Yara lies, trying to pull herself up now.

"You knew him, and you killed him anyway, Kress," she sobs.

Ragged breath catches in my throat. It's the first time she's called me Kress, not Krescent or Dune, in years.

"You let him fall into that"—she points uselessly at the chasm below—"and you *let* him die."

Bile hurtles up my throat. How many times did Yara and Ansh cry like this because of my parents? How many others? All that's left of their family now is this—a sobbing mess of a girl, capable of fighting with her teeth when she wants but completely broken now, left alone in the world. And it's my fault. For a dangerous, dizzying moment, I feel as if *I* am going to fall down the chasm. Into that darkness, that nothingness.

Aryadna steps in front of me. She puts an arm across my shoulder and turns me around, as if that will stop the echoes of Yara's wails. As we walk away, a shadow passes by, heading toward Yara. Thayne joins Rivan as the two help Yara up. The older man even tries consoling her, if such a thing could be possible.

"You couldn't have done anything," Aryadna says, like she can read my mind. "She knows that too. It's this—this bridge. This place that's making her act up."

She says it so casually that I feel revulsion shiver through me.

Yara is not acting up. She's lost her brother. Because of this journey. This farce that Beyorn forced us into. He turned us from fighters in the pit to pathetic creatures crawling in the dark. I can still feel the cold touch of the gun when I was begging him to let me take Rivan back.

Beyorn won't get away with any of it. *I* won't let him.

Slowly, we cross the wider bridge to a chamber on the other side. Luckily, it is empty of any creatures.

That's the only luck we have as the last torch burns smaller and smaller. Raksha's halo transforms into a tiny sputter, allowing us to see no more than a foot or so away.

"We know we're on the other side of the chasm, to the left of the path that we used to come down here." Aryadna traces a finger in the dust. Raksha holds the flame so close to her that her hair could catch fire.

"So we find that trail, and we can get out of here," Thayne says. Beside him, Yara watches the dust with jaded eyes.

"About that," Aryadna says. "We should consider getting on that trail at the soonest, before we lose our last light. If we find Beyorn on it, great, but if not—"

"No," I snarl. "He has everything he needs to survive. If we don't get him down here, he will come back and kill us all like he killed Siril and Ansh."

Yara jerks at that.

"We have to make him pay for getting us down here," I say. "We will find no justice up there."

"Well…" Aryadna says, annoyance in her tone. "I suppose splitting up is out of question?"

"When we find him, we can also take back our supplies. Why travel in dark and danger when we can have our torches and compasses guiding us?"

She mutters under her breath, but her shoulders drop. "Fine. Let's go."

As we move eastward once more, if farther from our original track, the chambers grow smaller again.

"There will come a break," Aryadna says. "We know we're on the other side of the chasm."

That assurance carries us through a labyrinth higher than any we've seen so far. The sight of the entrance stops me dead, my throat constricting tight. It isn't as narrow as the one with the voices. Just as the thought crosses my mind, a strange susurration blows out of the mouth of the labyrinth. My skin crawls.

"Kress," Rivan says, placing a hand on my shoulder, "you're okay?"

I place my hand above his and nod.

I can do this. It's not like last time—the alley is not restrictive; everyone can go in together. Plus, there aren't many choices in the one-way labyrinth. We know Beyorn must have also stepped off the same bridge, which means he took this path. He wouldn't be foolish enough to risk the cave of the scorpions again. He must be somewhere close.

So when the smell appears, it hits us at once.

I pull my sleeve against my mouth, gagging.

Raksha hacks, her almost-dead stone torch at the ready like a weapon, and Thayne slows his walk, checking around to make sure we aren't being ambushed.

And when I emerge into the cave at the end of the labyrinth, I can only gasp.

Hanging upside down, wrapped from toe to neck in a thick white web, blue eyes open wide in a shocked, frozen expression, is Beyorn.

THIRTY-SEVEN

The air in the chamber smells of decay and death. It is enclosed with roughly hewn rock, like angry splashes of water haphazardly carved it over ages, but there are niches, thin and sharp, that feel as if they've been clawed out. Inside each one lie many wet-looking cocoons, lit with luminescence from within, mangled together in a pile. They pulse up and down rhythmically, almost hypnotically.

Until I realize they're breathing.

I look away in terror.

The sweet rot is so overwhelming inside the chamber that it's hard to keep my eyes open.

But even with them half-closed, I can see Beyorn hanging in the corner, a stain against the whiteness.

Across the chamber, the stuff Beyorn stole from us lies scattered. Raksha and Thayne immediately grab the compasses and the matchboxes, our backpacks containing food and water and maps. I make for my daggers, clasping them tightly in my fists once before stuffing them along my belt and in my pockets. I find my katar directly below

Beyorn. Pushing my knuckles through it sends blood rushing to my head. The cold hilt sings against my skin.

I fit the rest of my things—throwing stars, two packets of edible seagrass, a waterskin—into my pockets as Raksha and Thayne also gather their weapons. Flames burst to life on multiple torches again, and warmth floods the air. Armed with the polearm, Raksha looks menacing again. Aryadna pulls on the bag full of the maps Raksha was adding to and everything else she can gather.

"Get Siril's stuff," I tell Thayne. "Make sure the rock is in there."

A pained shadow crosses his face, and he holds the backpack up; he's already got it.

Yara is the only one who remains where she is, watching us passively, no interest in taking her or Ansh's belongings.

Finally, Rivan asks, his voice restrained, "Is he dead?"

I press the tip of my dagger to Beyorn's shoulder, narrowing my eyes at any hint of breathing. There—a dangerously slow but noticeable rise of his chest.

"Afraid not," Aryadna says sullenly.

I'm not upset, I realize. Hunger courses in my veins, hunger for a fight. But in the absence of that, a killing stab would work just as well. After days of Beyorn's scorn and indifference and lies, I finally get to drive the katar's blade through him.

Rivan catches my wrist, pulling the knife back.

"What?" I ask.

"Something's not right here," Rivan says, indicating toward Beyorn. "He faced it."

Now that the torches are all lit, I look again. Behind Beyorn, the wall is a splatter of webs, remains of organic matter caught up in them. Half-bitten throats, ripped skulls, mutilated chunks of torsos.

"So what then?" I ask, tasting bitter disappointment.

"We find out what happened here. No, Kress." Rivan raises his voice at my expression. "We can do what we want later. Once we're safe. I didn't say anything before, because I needed you to keep moving."

He might as well say he hates me.

"It's one thing to defend yourself, but you're actively looking to kill someone. You, who can't even kill a creature without adding a shrine to it on your body." He grabs my arms roughly. "You're not thinking right, and I'm done pretending like I'm okay with it."

"Lower," Raksha hisses.

"He got two of us killed," I say, anger rising. "What about them?"

"And more of us will die if we don't find out what kind of monster we still have to face!"

"We can take care of ourselves," Raksha says harshly.

Thayne frowns and steps up. "We're all upset about being lured down here. But Rivan has a point. We need to make sure we will get out of here alive. If Beyorn is the one who can tell us, then we have to talk to him first. It's a simple matter of our survival over his death."

Part of me—no, *all* of me—wants to scream, to stab the blade into Beyorn and just be done with it. Letting him live any more is giving him a chance to escape. But Rivan's jaw is set tight, eyes blazing, and it's not like the usual arguments we have. It's the disappointment I've been so afraid he'll have for me one day.

Even with the anticipation, seeing it manifested is a rock in the gut. I can't make myself argue back. It's as if I'm made of stone and speaking would shatter me.

Aryadna starts, "We're wasting time—"

Yara hurtles past us, slamming her knife into Beyorn.

"Yara!" I shout instinctively and pull her back. "No!"

"You were ready to kill him!" she shouts. "He killed my brother. I should be the one to do this!"

For a second, all I can do is grapple with her, trying to get the

244

knife out of her hand as she slams a palm against my jaw. Locked into fighting and scratching and screaming. My blood pounds so loud in my head that every other sound is gone. And Yara may have grown subdued for the past few days, but she's not as injured as I am. Pain bursts in my arm as we stumble along the cavern, pushing at one another, and I've had *fucking* enough. I put all my strength into a final shove and lock her in a death grip.

"*Stop this.*"

"Let me go!" she snarls like a rabid beast with bared teeth.

"It's not going to bring Ansh back!"

"I don't care! I'm going to kill him!"

The words slam into me stronger than any physical hit. Because they're my own, held up in the defeated mirror that is Yara, finally breaking through the ugly realization that we died and bled in vain, and no amount of even righteous vengeance will change anything.

And I always did know, even if I would suppress the voice of reason, that nothing we do now will take away the pain we have gone through.

This is what Rivan has been looking at for these past few days.

I laugh—a horrible, scathing sound—and let go of Yara. She's as spent as me, falling to her knees and panting and sobbing.

I don't say anything, and I don't look at anyone. I can't face them.

So I turn and start to cut Beyorn—the monster we brought with us—loose, but the web is stronger than I anticipated. My injured arm is no help.

Aryadna steps up next to me to hold the web above Beyorn's legs.

"You'll get a burn," Raksha says and hands her strips of fabric.

Strange. I never noticed how pale Aryadna's fingers are, just like her face. No sign of soot that darkens the hands of miners. They even look soft. Not hardened with labor.

Rivan said he didn't know her.

Maybe she works with the office? They sometimes give clerical jobs of the lowest order to some lucky miner. So how did she get on this mission then? And now that I think about it, she brings in no specific expertise to the company. What did the Collector choose her for?

But these people gave me the benefit of the doubt after finding out who my parents are. I should extend some courtesy to Aryadna too. She must have her reasons for secrecy like me.

Once she wraps the fabrics to protect her palms and adjusts her grip, I begin cutting at the threads again. The repetitive movement reignites the dull ache in my arms. As if a tear is opening my skin up. This bastard's life better be worth the effort.

At last, the threads begin to give way, fraying one after another. Then, without warning, the threads break. Aryadna lunges to stop Beyorn from smashing headfirst into the jagged teeth of the ground. I drop my daggers and help. The man is even heavier than he looks.

As if he wakes out of a spell, Beyorn gasps the second he's cut out of the web. As if the web itself was holding him frozen.

He coughs and wheezes, trying to drag in breaths. His face has turned a dark shade of red. In the light of the torches, he looks like a demon I wouldn't want to fight. His hair is a tangled mess, and he has slashes down his face and neck, so much so that the previous scars seem brand new, crusted with blood.

"You all…" he starts and coughs. "How did you…"

"Never mind that," Aryadna hisses.

Reluctantly, Thayne reaches to help Beyorn up. He and Raksha remove the torn web away from his clothes and hand him water. The same water he stole from us when he left us to die.

I breathe deeply, counting down and trying to dispel the anger rising in me again. My grip tightens on the katar.

Beyorn raises his head and flexes his fingers. A strange whiteness burns beneath his skin, as if he's poisoned. It gives him the quality of almost being translucent in the light of the torches. I frown but stay quiet as he tries to speak again.

"You have my gratitude," he says.

Raksha scoffs.

"Then why would you leave us to die?" Aryadna snaps.

"Why?" Beyorn echoes, half laughing. I can't tell if he stops because he's actually thinking or if the agony of being upside down still rages in him. I hope it's the latter.

"Well, when you came down here," he says to all of us, "would you have trusted me? I wouldn't."

I say, lacing my voice with as much venom as I can, "So?"

"So I didn't trust you much either." He smiles his assured smile, which looks grotesque on his exhausted face. Good thing too. It's a reminder not to get complacent around this man.

"There is something fundamentally wrong with you," I tell him.

"Even so, my gratitude for saving me from that monster. Once we return to the surface and get the Collector out of the way, this island will be mine, and you will all be rewarded."

Raksha and I exchange careful glances. Not killing this man brutally is one thing; letting him escape out of the mines, allowing him reign over the island, completely another.

Aryadna asks, voice dangerously soft, "Out of the way?"

"An old man with low ambitions, he will never know what to really do with the treasure we have found below." Beyorn smiles, and now, a maniacal gleam in his eyes joins the translucence of his skin, making him almost glimmer in the dark. "But I do. Yes, I do. Now help me up. We have to leave before the demon returns."

THIRTY-EIGHT

Beyorn hurries us out, taking charge and asking me to watch his back. His pain is seemingly forgotten in his rush to get far away from the cave. But at times, it feels like he's walking too well. Almost running. The kind of strength that might seem in place just before the pits or a miner newly recruited.

He turns around sometimes. I see the frenzied glint in his eyes.

My fingers remain curled around my katar and my attention on Beyorn. If it is madness that has gotten in him, I will not let it take any of us.

This time, I will keep the rest of us alive no matter what.

But the farther we get from the web, the more noticeable his energy becomes. There's an unnatural way about it—like an entire life's worth of adrenaline rush pumped into him at once.

Almost like…a poison. Working its way through him, giving his body a last boost of power before leaching it all away. Like a container filled to the brim with too much until it bursts.

Because of course he must have been poisoned before being rolled into the web. That's how some creatures prepare their meal.

It's a waste of time asking him to slow down and think about what's going on with his body. Every so often, there's a whisper of a hiss somewhere in the dark behind us. A shadow stalks us since the cave. Sometimes small, but other times falling over all of us.

The spark of fear that planted itself in me when I saw Beyorn in the cocoon now burns brighter, demanding attention.

"Can you at least tell us how we can prepare to fight it if it catches up to us?" I ask Beyorn.

"You can't fight this demon, girl. All you can do is run."

What kind of creature is this? What monstrosity has venom that seems to have turned someone like Beyorn into a madman calling it a demon?

Raw fear skitters down my spine.

The lights are not bright enough, and I don't dare raise my voice to ask for more fire.

And then, something huge drops several meters away, blocking our path, shadows surrounding it like an army of ghosts, rippling without wind. There's no telling what it is, except that I have never understood what fear can be until this moment. Beyorn has gone utterly still, as if he's dead standing upright. The sheer size of whatever is behind the shadows makes our torches tiny as distant stars against the dark sky.

"The demon," breathes Beyorn.

Immediately I know why Beyorn insists on calling it a demon. Its real form remains hidden—only the endless shadows moving around it like pilgrims around a shrine. But if the brief glimpse of long legs through the curtain of dark mist are anything to go by, it might be a Maya spider. A creature with a name that no one remembers, a creature with control over illusions.

Nevertheless, if the demon towers to the sky, what does it matter what kind of creature it is?

I look back quickly once to the horrified faces and check for escape routes. The way we came only leads us back to the web cave. And beyond that, the bridge. Too risky to run over. We'd have nowhere to go after it anyway—the cave was blocked.

The many legs of the demon skitter over the rough ground. It's coming closer.

My daggers are not made for this kind of fight.

I need a larger weapon.

Before I can ask for one, Beyorn aims his glaive right into the heart of the shadows. It disappears into the darkness, and a moment later, we hear the clang of the metal against the ground and know that it made no mark.

That's it. Even if all of us were at our best, this isn't a creature to be fought.

"We can't fight shadows," I shout. "We need to retreat—now!"

As if my voice is a beacon, the monster dives straight at me. I scream and lurch out of the way. Several rocks rumble down the wall. Dust arises as the rocks hit us, and we hurtle from the walls, dividing our company in two. Me, Beyorn, and Rivan on one side and Aryadna, Raksha, and Yara on the other. Our torches are blown off in the harsh wind.

"Where's Thayne?" I shout.

Raksha curses. She digs into the rubble holding up her torch's last remaining embers. A faint voice confirms Thayne is under the rocks.

I grab Raksha's discarded polearm, but there's no time for the rest of us to help Thayne.

The shadows rise again, a menacing ghost in the sudden loss of light. An arm of shadow zooms at me, and I hack at it with the blade of the polearm. There's a short burst of black blood and a screech. I almost feel victorious. Almost. But the tiny wound doesn't slow the demon down. Instead, it turns with renewed vigor, searching for an even easier target, a familiar one.

My heart pops into my mouth. Wildly, I look for Beyorn.

The company's leader looks absolutely mad now. Blood runs down his torn clothes, eyes gleaming with true light now, like Rivan's red threads, and an animal aggression as he throws his head back to stare the demon down. He looks crazed.

"I told you," Raksha shouts from the back, "monsters and madness!"

Madness. Whatever poison went into Beyorn has stolen his mind.

Then Beyorn screams, "*Come and take me, demon!*"

Before I can throw him down to protect the madman, the ground judders. The quake sends us all tumbling across as the Maya spider floats in the air, away from the rocks. I hurtle toward Rivan, throwing my arms over my head, until just as suddenly, the shaking stops.

And the moment it does, the dust still swirling in the air, the shadows twirl and speed at Beyorn, swallowing him whole in a hurricane of whistling winds and demonic shadows.

And in that cursed moment, I know there's truly nothing I can do as death claims the man in front of me.

Maybe we should run while the demon is busy.

I look back. Raksha has half pulled Thayne out of the rubble, Yara finally moving in to help. He's awake, at least.

I turn to Beyorn and the demon, and the sudden whirling of shadows, like a hurricane rising over the sea, startles me. Beyorn uses his bizarre venom-fueled strength and hits back at the demon, twisting one of its legs. The shadows break for a second, revealing a large, hourglass black torso, but converge before I can make sense of it.

Beyorn's madness manifests into a fighter who has no self-preservation.

I've never seen anything like it. He's moving like a swift snake, as if his bulky, muscled body is made of paper. Beyorn is a man who has breathed in fair luxury for a long time now, in the cool insides of the Collector's compound, with no lack of food or water, no toil, no fights.

No Lander is capable of fighting the elements of this world.

And yet right now, he fights like a man grown in the pits of Kar Atish.

The madness has complete hold of him. But it's taken his senses too. He has no strategy and fights wildly—the demon easily deflects him. It will kill him, and then it will turn to us. I promised myself I won't let any more of the company die, and I intend to keep that promise.

My insides turn to water, but I charge forward, screaming and trying to draw the Maya spider's attention in a mad, desperate attempt. Everything in me protests, the thought of my death slamming into me, but I have faced death every day since my parents blasted open those mines. The idea of this monstrosity killing Rivan, though, lets me fight my own instincts back.

"Hey!" I yell, waving my arms. "Over here!"

The shadows turn, rippling in the air, and the demon bores toward me. A storm over the sea, rushing to make landfall. My back slams into the wall behind me.

Well, you got its attention.

I adjust my grip on my daggers. If I go down here, I will take this monster down too.

The shadows are upon me, filling up everything, and for a brief second, they part. Many black eyes, shining with insane glee, the many hairy legs big enough to skewer me at once—

Beyorn roars at the back, snatching the demon's attention. Abruptly the shadows converge. The demon whirls and screeches, as if in deep agony.

Through the swirling illusions, I see Beyorn leap upon one of the legs of the demon and slash with his glaive and a knife as he goes. Then to another and another, the Maya spider's shadows mottling with gray, until Beyorn reaches the back of the torso. And after, there's nothing but the ghastly screams that fill the entire underground of Kar Atish.

252

THIRTY-NINE

B eyorn stands over the carcass, drenched in black ichor. The shadows don't leave the dead demon stranded. They only lower themselves closer, hiding it from view still, gently undulating like waves in the sea. But the Maya spider is as far as can be from the clear waters. Perhaps it was born in another world and slipped here when no one was looking—like our ancestors. What was here before the Empyrean Elders arrived is only a whisper of legends, after all.

Raksha and Yara examine Thayne's leg that had been trapped under stone. He's in awful pain, every tortured cry loud as a gong.

Beyorn glances down at them once before disregarding them immediately. The gleam of triumph burns like lamps in his eyes, as if he's in a dream, unaware that the real world exists.

The real world, which is a tomb, lit only with one torch again, and reeking of rot and blood.

Perhaps it's a good thing. If he continues to be like this, no one will believe him about the things he's seen down here. It's the perfect outcome.

"Listen," Aryadna says to me in a low voice, trying not to disturb whatever thought consumes Beyorn. "Let me go and scout first before we move."

"I can go."

"I'd rather you keep an eye on him."

We both turn to look at Beyorn. He is still atop the corpse of the demon, hands slick with black blood. His hair, which appeared almost colorless in the sun outside, is now a tangled nest of muck. He's beginning to deteriorate finally, shaking like he has a fever. The poison in him is running its course, coming to the stage that will render him incapacitated. He grimaces at us, and his teeth, too, are covered in blood. And I hope to the all-strong ocean it is *only* blood.

"Fine," I say to Aryadna, "but be careful. Who knows what other kind of monstrosities exist here?"

When she leaves, and Beyorn refuses to look away from his kill even as his face spasms with pain, I sigh and sink to the floor. The exhaustion of this journey has carved my insides. I want to sleep for the next ten thousand years. But I don't know if I'll ever catch a wink. When we emerge, what will we do? If Beyorn truly means to usurp the Collector and manages it as well, the island will be chaos. And Badger? He wouldn't believe anything. If he heard about the existence of Maya demons, he'd want to have one in his pits.

There's only one thing we can do. The thing we set out to do when we left the Shadefolk.

Kill Beyorn.

And this time, not for vengeance but to truly keep men like him and Badger from breaking our island. This time, my mind is clearer, which is why I hate that this is the only option we have left.

"Tell me you knew it might be this bad," Rivan says as he sits beside me.

"No."

"I've never known anyone with this kind of recklessness."

"Says the one who jumped into hell without thinking."

"How many times must I tell you? I *was* thinking. I was thinking of you."

I start to turn away, but he grabs my hand, face serious. He looks tired, not the Rivan I'm used to, the one who will pick me up while I'm half-dead from a beating and walk home and patch me up. There are a thousand emotions in his eyes, each one looking for reassurance. And I don't know if I can give it to him. But here, amid all this chaos and the one coming, I know that *he* reassures *me*.

Rivan is the only constant of my life. The compass that keeps me homeward bound.

"You always do," I say quietly.

"When I said—it isn't Beyorn I care about. You know that, right? It's about you and what you would've felt after."

I nod. Rivan would have confronted me no matter who it was.

"You heard what Beyorn wants, though."

Rivan sighs. "Yes, and I know what you'll say. I just don't think it has to be you who must kill a man. Raksha could do it. We defer to her in the mines. Why not here?"

"And what would that make me?"

"Only human."

He turns my hand palm up and adjusts his grip, intertwining our fingers. This time when my heart speeds up, it's less with the unknown and more with the familiarity. The only familiarity I have in this insane place. This is a world of strangeness worse than I thought. Demons that hide in shadows exist. What else is in this world that I cannot face by myself without losing my mind?

Something in me shifts as I look at him again, as tired as he is, with the realization of his constancy. When I leave this island, I will have to leave him. Leave my bones and blood and flesh and any desire I've ever had.

It was a given, but now—now it seems like a sudden threat curled around my throat.

My parents were ripped from me by their own despicable actions. Am I letting those same actions take away the one good thing in my life again?

If I'm doing the right thing by not—not letting my feelings out, why do I have to fight them so much? How can the right thing be this painful? How can it require this much effort?

The feelings I thought would have tied me here like shackles are not what makes my breathing painful now. I lean closer, inhaling as if he's the air that would ease that pain, our foreheads touching. Every eyelash of his is coal black, framing the pale gray eyes in a beautiful symmetry. Light shimmers in his eyes again, and I want to believe it's because of me.

He brushes a thumb over my palm. And stops.

I look up and his expression is a deep map of confusion. The wound of the blood oath isn't a natural wound, and he can see that. It's too contained, too deliberate.

He continues brushing the wound. "Isn't it funny how the Shadefolk had everyone imprisoned but they also let us have this medicine?"

"Probably because the Shademan with us grew fond of us."

Rivan cocks his head to the side, exasperation on his face. "What did you do?"

"Nothing you wouldn't have."

"You drew blood in exchange for it. To what end?"

"All our safety, frankly."

Rivan drops my hand and runs his own through his hair. When he speaks, his voice is edged with frustration. "Blood isn't a joke, Kress. Who knows what they can do?"

I wince. Rivan isn't one to believe in superstitions. Him question-ing it makes my calm tremble. Just a bit, but tremble all the same. "They'll tell stories about the people above to their kids. It's what would count as normal for them."

"As if anything about this is normal," he snaps.

This time when Aryadna interrupts us, I could kiss her. She returns, shouting happily, "The tunnel ends in an empty hall just off the spider's cave. We can avoid it completely!"

I lurch back from Rivan, closing my fist and putting the thought of my blood in possession of the Shadefolk out of my mind.

"What are we waiting for then?" Raksha says.

"Exactly," Aryadna says. "Let's go in quick before some other monster arrives. I'll take Beyorn last, and, Rivan and Kress, lead us. Then you both stay and be on guard as the rest of us follow. It's just so neither end of the tunnel takes us by surprise. If someone follows us, Beyorn can handle it."

Rivan frowns. "He seems to have lost his strength."

"And his mind," Raksha breathes, eyeing Beyorn in mild confusion.

He has turned visibly weaker, a gray pallor to his skin, as he shiv-ers near one of the relit torches.

"We all have to work together. Thayne can't walk, and you and Yara have to focus on him, so can we please make this quick and not stay in one place like meat for flies?" Aryadna shouts, panic seeping into her jovial voice. She glances down at her leg, where the water beast got her.

"Okay, okay," Rivan says, holding his hands up.

I let Raksha and Yara help Thayne up first so we can keep pace. Thayne screams, then grits his teeth. Sweat lines his face as they move, as fast as he can manage. But Aryadna still hurries us up. She's truly shaken after the pool and the demon, and I don't fault her, but it's getting on my nerves. Thayne is in actual pain. It's a miracle he's held on for even this long. Any more exertion and he could *die*.

Together, we move down the tunnel. It's supposed to return upward toward the end. I can't help but think on how far back we will have to go again first. This journey has entirely been about the back-and-forth, and I'm losing any remaining sense of time. As if when I return to the island, an age might have passed.

Thayne, Raksha, and Yara are considerably ahead. Rivan and I are slower, so we can intervene if Beyorn deteriorates any further. He's seeing things now, flinging his arms around as if to catch flies.

The tunnel opens abruptly into a large hall, almost as big as the one containing the origin well.

And I know there's something very, very wrong.

The air smells of metal.

"Rivan—" I barely get his name out when a bellow erupts from the tunnel.

Aryadna has her two daggers sunk deep in Beyorn's eye sockets. He's screaming and clawing at her, but she remains unfazed, spattered with blood. Her face is a mask of red. She pulls back a blade and sweeps it along Beyorn's neck in one swift motion.

All of it happens so quickly, so unbelievably, that I stand rooted to the spot. Raksha and Yara, too, are unable to disentangle themselves from Thayne without accidentally injuring him further.

And as Beyorn thuds to the ground, blood seeping down, Aryadna snatches the gun from his pocket.

"Back up, please, all of you," Aryadna says. "Away from the door."

"What door?" I shout with disbelief at what she's doing.

She kicks at the side of the wall, and metal bars plunge down, separating us from Beyorn and her.

The cacophonous clanging rings in my ears painfully.

"What the hell are you doing?" I cry, regaining my senses. "You want to kill Beyorn—fine. Which one of us looks like we care especially about him? Why would you lock us here?"

"Oh, I don't know, Kress. Your altruism seems to get the better of you no matter what you *say* you'll do. He"—she glares at Rivan—"makes you do it. I've seen enough of it, and I'm not going to take any risks."

"Over *Beyorn*?" I can't believe this girl. Did the demon poison get in her too?

"Besides, our ends don't align. You were going to listen to those superstitious cavemen and stop us from sharing the biggest discovery in hundreds of years? No way can I let you ruin the Collector's mission."

"You're a fool, girl." Raksha bares her teeth. "Siding with those wretches over your own?"

"I *am* siding with my own," Aryadna growls. "I'm siding with my grandfather, Collector Syris."

FORTY

The next few words come from Yara, who screams and curses Aryadna, flinging herself at the bars, clawing and beating, as if she could pass through them out of sheer will.

"You're all welcome to die in here," Aryadna says, ignoring Yara's screams. "And this time, there's no exits for those little rats to come scurrying out and save you. There's probably some water in your supplies, so have fun."

And then she simply walks back with a confidence that says she *knows* where she's going.

"Fuck," I yell.

"Fuck is right," Raksha says harshly. She throws her polearm against the wall, and it clangs to the ground, echoing in the large hall.

Yara is still screaming at the empty tunnel. She kicks at the bars and beats her fists at them, tries to wrench them apart until her hands are bleeding. Her wails are moving through the ocean, like her grief over Ansh has finally been unleashed. She pulls at the bars, trying to find keyholes like the ones at the Shadefolk's city, but nothing happens.

She yanks at the bars again. But—of course—they don't give.

"We have to stop Aryadna!" Yara yells, her voice breaking. "Or it will be for nothing! It will all be for nothing!"

Raksha makes no move to stop her, so Rivan and I don't either.

"We have to get out of here," Thayne murmurs. His leg is a mass of blood and muscle, white bone shining through. He's leaning against boulders, chalk-white with the effort of staying up. No one says it, but we all know that death is circling him.

And I can't stomach that thought. No older person—no one who knows who my parents are—has brought me the sense of fellowship that Thayne and Raksha have. I don't want either of them to die.

"How?" Rivan demands. "There's no way out unless we break through."

"Then that is what we will do," Raksha snarls. She grabs a tough-looking stone and bangs it against the bars. Startled, Yara steps back for a second but follows Raksha. Both of them smash at the old metal bars, which groan under the pressure.

Blood trails down Yara's arms, seeping through torn sleeves.

Watching Yara lose her senses breaks something inside me, and all I remember is the little Yara I used to be friends with. Her parents would leave her—and Ansh—at my place sometimes, or mine would leave me at theirs, and while the elders were at work, we spent our days running around.

The memory has been seeping like water for a very long time, but it rushes back at me with full force, drenching everything.

I need to get out of here.

I turn to Rivan. "This whole underground is a connected place. There has to be a way out. We just have to find it." The desperation in my voice takes us both by surprise, and he nods.

We begin scouring every corner of the hall.

And we realize the walls are made of...zargunine. No—not

zargunine. The silvery substance from the well the Shadefolk call the godsblood. All of it, a giant case of silver godsblood, and we're trapped inside. The walls *seem* like stone, rough and jagged, but they're smooth like glass, cool to the touch. Every brush leaves a tingling against the skin of my palm. Strangely, though, it doesn't hurt to breathe near the walls, like it does up on the island. The air is full of the metallic smell of the silver godsblood, the risk of it catching fire and burning blue looming all the time. These walls are pure godsblood trapped beneath another strange substance, something that reminds me of the shielded walls in Badger's tunnels.

At the mouth of the hall, Raksha and Yara are still hard at work trying to break the bars, and the red stain on the ground beneath Thayne is growing darker.

"They're going to hurt themselves," I say.

"There's no reasoning with anyone right now, not unless we find a way out."

Suddenly the weight of my own existence is too much, and I want to sit down and cry. But if I do that now, I don't know if I'll ever be able to get up. The fury and sadness of the past few days are an ocean lapping at my feet, ready to take me under.

And that's when I feel it. A block of stone that isn't made of the silver godsblood. It merges with the surroundings, but under my fingers, its edges are rough.

"Rivan," I say, "I think I found a door."

FORTY-ONE

It seems no easier to open the circular door than it was to break down the metal bars locking us in. But we try, jamming in our weapons and applying as much pressure as we can.

I feel more optimistic than is warranted perhaps, and that optimism drives most of my strength, even when Raksha sighs and steps back, flexing her drained hands. The door is locked with rust and age, but it has to open. I won't accept anything else.

Pain spikes in my arms with the effort.

And vanishes with a gasp. Shadows move across the door.

"What was that?" I ask to no one in particular.

"What?" Rivan says, pausing from using one of the polearms as a lever. His gaze shifts to my left, on the door. He frowns. "Are those... claw marks?"

At first, I see nothing. Only the ages of dirty matter sticking layer by layer to the stone door. But then the faint, narrow track lines take shape. *Very* faint.

"These don't look like animal claws," I say, running a finger down one of the tracks and noticing that the size of the indents fits perfectly along my fingers. These aren't nail scratches. Like there might be if drawn out of recklessness and desperation, as if to escape something, but instead, they're pressed onto the door like a—

"It's a pattern," I breathe.

Rivan pauses tracing the lines and steps back to look at it whole. "It's a hand." Before I can say anything, he places his palm in the indents, fingers somehow fitting what appeared a smaller hand just a second ago.

Nothing happens.

"Well, it was worth trying," he says.

It still is, something whispers in my mind. An unknown feeling. The same as I had in front of the curtain of light when it rippled and I interpreted it as a kind of music. A song only I can hear. There might even have been words in it, but I didn't understand them. Just the feeling of a harmony.

Of someone calling me in that music.

I reach out and place my hand on the indent. Like it fit Rivan's hand, it fits my much smaller one too.

I grew up on stories of underground glories, all of which sounded like they were happening ages ago. Of the Shadefolk who had made their home in the tunnels they found. Of the heroism, the resourcefulness, and the clashes with monsters that had no name, of brilliant caves and the veins of zargunine that covered the dark ceilings like rivers of gems in the sky. Of the voices that emerged from the primordial tunnels that lay even deeper than any man had dared to venture.

And who knew who those voices belonged to or what they said?

I don't understand what the song of light says either, but I hear it. Louder than ever before.

"*Kress, get down!*" Rivan's voice is loud too, but not enough to drown out the sudden whistling that erupts from beyond the door.

He pulls me down, and the stone door explodes, shards flying everywhere.

The white smoke comes a moment later, emerging in the middle out of nowhere, as if seeping through the walls and taking the form of a thick cloud. It looks like cotton at first and then takes a marble sheen as it keeps getting bigger and bigger.

Rivan and I grab hands and run.

"Get back! Something's wrong," I shout.

We look over our shoulders as I run toward the center of the hall, and the smoke spills out faster. It reaches the ceiling now, a mushroom-shaped cloud inside the expansive space, its tail still inside the tunnel from which more of it keeps escaping.

"It could be a noxious gas!" Thayne yells, trying to get up, and gestures wildly for us to get away.

The cloud continues to grow into even thicker, almost solid-looking coils as the absolute white begins to take on shades of gray, intertwining into itself until the entire ceiling of the hall vanishes behind it, as if a grotesque storm sky. Mist and smoke and shadows curl outward, swallowing the hall. The storm builds, teeming wildly and yet hypnotically until it is closer to the color of a shining gray moonstone. The clouds still gather, swirling, and then there's a bright blue lightning.

Exactly like a storm sky.

"What is this devilry?" Raksha barks. "A shadow demon—and now—"

But she has no words to name the phenomenon we're seeing.

The clouds thicken and thicken, until their undulating sharpens, sending a dizzying pain through me. And then just as fast, it spreads out, reaching toward us now. My heart thumping, I think of Siril. How the curtain of light cut through her, leaving rivers of blood on her.

What if that's what's about to happen to the others?

For a moment, the cloud pauses, as if *looking* at us, then sways in Raksha's direction. I push her out of the way and go tumbling down sideways with momentum. There's an angry lightning. And a small crater on the ground where Raksha stood.

265

I hurtle out of the way on all fours, then stumble up and run.

And the cloud demon follows.

"Keep it distracted," Rivan shouts from across the hall. He looks over my shoulder once—Yara is still working at the metal bars. They're beginning to bend.

"On it!" I shout back.

Rivan, Raksha, and I run back and forth in the large hall, forcing the cloud to split in three directions, thinning itself. I don't know if it's going to do anything. Perhaps we'll only end up making it angrier. But I have to give Yara time to escape the way I couldn't do for Ansh.

And if I have to let this cloud devour me for Raksha to drag Rivan away, I'll do that too.

The cloud roars deafeningly, as if it realizes what's happening. Then, it regathers, and it hurtles toward Raksha.

I'm too far apart. I can only scream as I *run*, as Rivan yells at her to get away, and pain pounds in my leg with each sharp thwack of my feet against the stone floor.

But it is Thayne who reaches her first.

Thayne, who is bloodied and battered. Thayne who is unable to walk on his own right now. Thayne who throws himself in front of Raksha with wide arms as if greeting an old friend.

"*No!*" Raksha shrieks.

I reach her, unable to stop myself from slowing down, and slam into her.

We watch in horror as Thayne grabs hold of the cloud demon—like it isn't smoke but as solid as marble.

"Hurry," he shouts, sweat gleaming on his stark white face, the shadows beneath his eyes blackened to soot. "Get out of here!"

But he holds on, standing alone, slowing the cloud demon.

The demon that emerged because of my hand against the stone.

Shade blood.

266

"Rivan, Raksha," I shout to them, "help Yara!"

Then I race toward Thayne, even as he shouts, "What are you doing? Run the other way!"

"Tell me the truth," I say, panting as I come to a stop. "Are you the other Child of Shade they mentioned?"

His mouth opens, then closes. The cloud takes the moment of distraction to reassert itself. It throws Thayne off his foot but he pulls himself up, his wound forgotten, staring at me.

"You—you have Shade blood too. Katya was of the Shade, wasn't she?"

The understanding plummets my stomach. Having acknowledged it to someone else. There's no taking this back.

We both turn to the cloud demon and grab at its hand. And our Shade blood protects us from whatever this is.

The demonic cloud, startled, undulates dangerously. It feels like silk in my hand, and it's hard to keep my grip on the slippery, shady substance. But I don't let go.

"Come on!" Rivan shouts. "The bars are down. Let go and run!"

I look back and gasp. He's right. They've taken down two bars and bent two more. There's enough space for all of us to fit through.

"Thayne," I say. "You go first. You'll need more time."

He hesitates but nods, his grip still tight. "Just hold on."

The moment he's halfway to the bars, Rivan jogs up to meet him and calls out to me to let go of the demon and hurry back.

I'm ready too.

The demon roars and swells and thunders.

I loosen my grip, taking a small step back. And slip on my feet. The back of my head slams into the stone of the ground.

And the cloud comes roaring at me, swallowing me whole.

FORTY-TWO

The change before my eyes is abrupt, the darkness of the demonic shadows giving way to the darkness of a strange quality, thicker than air but not quite the solidity of a wall. Almost like the viscosity of the silver godsblood fills up the space between atoms. This dark is not like the one in the mines, not even the cells. It is the kind of dark that eats you alive.

Besides the clothes on my body, I have nothing. I turn around, my heart rising as my mind tries to place these bizarre surroundings into context. I shout, shocked and scared, for the others.

I'm not in the hall I was just in. There's no one around. Thayne, Raksha, Yara. *Rivan.* As if I've been sucked into another world in the blink of an eye. The darkness here is so complete that I'm starting to feel dizzy, my mind unable to comprehend where to move, what to process.

I make an effort to walk, but my legs are wobbly. My breaths come hard and fast. And then, in the absolute silence, I hear something I shouldn't: the rush of blood in my veins. I lose my balance and crash down. It feels no different from the sides, no dimension to make me *feel* like I'm on a floor. The loudness of my heart pumping blood fills my ears.

I shout again, to hear something other than my own body.

I crawl forward. One hand, one leg. Tentatively, checking the ground for its solidity. It's the only thing that makes me feel like I'm still alive. *What has happened to the hall we were in? What has happened to Rivan?*

But thinking of Rivan only makes my lungs burn with anxiety. The rush of blood is faster, stormier, like I'm standing at the harbor, the waves of sea loud in the air. As if my veins would burst any moment now.

Am I dead?

Can you feel touch in death? I press one hand over the other, trying to ground myself in my body. But with it, a silent wave returns my feeling in a rush. Pain explodes in my body, unbearable heat clawing into my skin. A birth into the world after being cradled in the womb waters. Trying to scream, trying to *focus* on one thing, I stumble around. Scratching at my hands but there's nothing to get away from. It's all over me, everywhere.

Something lives in the darkness, something with teeth.

Then I hear it. The music that was haunting me, a moment here and there, is everywhere. Echoing softly from everywhere. As if originating from the very ground I'm walking on—which I can't see.

I move forward without sense of space or time. The fluid air doesn't change, just flows around me in waves.

Between one moment and the next, the darkness shifts, and an arched gate appears before me.

A giant octopus-like creature is carved into the wall, its arms spreading out, with massive red eyes boring into me with the ferocity of a thousand angry suns. Its open beak stretches half the length of the wall, which makes the arch. Inside is darkness. I see it, but I hear nothing, I feel nothing.

Still scratching at my arms and my face, I rush toward the darkness of the gate. Whatever is inside it, as long as it gets this crawling feeling off me.

The threshold robs me of hearing. The air in that small space switches from having a viscous, fluidlike quality to a thin, tightly bound solidity that wraps itself around me, cutting off my breathing, squeezing my throat. Before I can act on my alarm, step back, I'm beyond the arch and standing in the darkened space.

The heat, the fangs, and the thick pressure are gone.

My gasp is audible, painful—and relieved.

And short-lived as I realize I still have no idea where I am.

Distantly, I *feel* like I'm moving downward, even when I can't tell if I'm in a room, a bigger hall, or a tunnel. There's only darkness coiling along every space that ever existed.

For what feels like a thousand years, I walk, down and down as far as the path I'm on will go. My skin prickles with awareness of being watched, like a beast from the pit is keeping an eye on me, waiting to pounce.

I wonder if there is ever an end to this, a world that has always been the rocks of the island, the ocean, and the mines. If I keep walking, will I reach the beginning of the world?

My mother's stories about the primordial tunnels are beginning to come alive in front of me. I bump into the large tomb and feel along its edge. Rough stone, carvings that I don't understand, maybe some kind of old language.

The city in the caves above, the Blood Well, and now this strangeness making me feel like I'm standing on the sharp edge of a cliff. All of this—

I know the word clawing its way into my consciousness.

If you want to call it magic, then magic it is.

"This doesn't make sense," I whisper, just to hear something. Anything. "This isn't real—"

270

Something is inside my mind, taking up space. Terrified, I try to focus on myself, keep myself inside me, not give the shadow any place to push me out. If I lose my mind here to something, I will never escape.

I will stay here, beneath the ground, lost to the dark infinity of this land.

A nudge in my mind.

No, I cry. *Leave me be!*

Another nudge. Softer this time.

Understanding floods me—it's not trying to push me out but trying to reach out.

Blood roars in my ears as a hint of red floats in my vision in the shape of an oxbow lake, the river it cut from floating in my periphery.

And now...

The explosion they had set up ripped their own bodies apart as well. Their remains, a mass of blood and flesh and bones mingled without dignity, were pressed into a single white sheet that was mottled with red and black as its insides pushed through the thin fabric. The pile was sep- arate from the other dead miners, who were laid down with honor. I did not approach. The people's wails and anger were rife in the air. I heard someone call for me. Not in a way that seemed to wonder if I was okay now that my parents were gone. But in righteous anger, voice ringing with vengeance, wishing that I joined my parents too. So no blood of theirs ever crossed into the mines again.

My body is frozen in its place in the real world, but this memory is as real as it was then. The stench of the blood and the ocean, the burning ash and the slurry from the mines, coats my skin.

And I can't hide from it.

"*Murderers,*" someone wails. "*They killed everyone!*"

I'm sorry, I think to the darkness at the edge of the memory, hands pressed against my ears uselessly. *I'm so sorry. Please don't hate me for what they did. Please forgive me.*

FORTY-THREE

The memories don't let go of me. Instead, they take hold of my mind, forcing me to live through everything all over again, even as I walk on and on, down and down.

I had wondered if I might reach the beginning of the world, but now I know there's no end and no beginning to the true darkness.

The air ripples, and then the whisper of red splits into a rainbow sheen, cutting the darkness for the blink of an eye, like a river flowing in an absolute night.

There's a shift in the space in front of me, the darkness undulating like the curtain of light, edged with the rainbow. Images made of my memories split from my mind and shimmer in the darkness before me.

My first gurgling laugh, my first knee scratch. A worn homespun blanket my parents laid me on. Yara and Ansh and me, huddled near a low fire as our parents worked late that evening. Ashvin, Rivan, and Mayven making space in their house for me. Rivan's pale gray eyes looking at me...

All the little things, good and bad, that make Krescent Dune being smothered together in a little orb that can be taken away.

And take it all away, what is left within the flesh?

The spirit that lives outside of these bonds.

The thing inside my mind is trying to talk to the spirit, the one that comes from the same darkness that makes everything else, that made this thing. The one that will exist long after Krescent Dune's body is gone, the one that has no beginning and no end.

I am insane, I think.

From somewhere in the deep, a whisper.

And what makes your reality the sane one?

The soft rainbow edges shimmer, waver, and in their faint light, I see the tomb clearer. And then, a light the size of a pinhead emerges in the middle of the rainbow river.

The soft white light enlarges slowly until it takes the form of a face, taller than me.

A monstrous face with a large forehead and an equal-sized fang-filled mouth, two infinitesimal slits as nostrils in the tiny space between them, and two eyes on each side floats in the darkness. The entire face is scarred, mountainous, and brutal. Whatever the body looks like is hidden behind its colossal tentacles, each one capable of wrapping around a ship and snapping it with a single pull.

"Who..." My voice is a smudge in the dark. I try again. "Who are you?"

The thing—the monster—speaks.

A word that I'm unable to grasp in a sound that seems like the gentle flow of water in my ear, tinkling but with a deep silence between every fall of sound.

And then, it adds in an echo in my head, "But your mind will not be able to comprehend my name, nor your tongue be able to say it. Although I have had many names since the first dark, you may call me Karavi, your vessel, so you may survive in these waves of unregulated time."

"Karavi," I breathe.

Except Karavi, I see nothing, like this monster is all that exists. It is like trying to look at the world through my throat, where there is no vision, no understanding of what vision even *is*.

"Why am I here?"

The face looms over me. Comes closer. Its tremendous fangs could cut through my head and feet at once.

I hold my ground.

In my mind, Karavi shows me.

Long ago, when the very first star was still a swirl in the river of time, cosmic beings walked this world with immense powers to bend stone, twist air, move water to their will. They commanded gravity as the ground would, they knew attraction as magnets would, and they pressed air to wind as the skies would.

Along with the First Ones, there lay nameless things beneath the water of the world, beneath even the deepest lows, in eternal darkness. It was a Nameless Being that dug too deep and fractured the abyss protecting this world of all water.

From the fracture came the New Ones who fought the First Ones. And though the First Ones were powerful, they were not many. The New Ones poured into the world of water in a deluge that never stopped until every First One was bound and brought down.

Their bodies were broken, their bones flattened, and their gods-blood flew freely. The spirits within them, however, scattered, looking for a form to cling to once more, to preserve their minds and their innate selves too.

The bodies of the First Ones did not drown beneath the great ocean but stayed afloat, ribs and hearts and bones, rock-solid, until they grew stagnant as islands in the world.

Their godsblood, a viscous, shimmering silver fluid imbued with the cosmic powers, flew from all islands toward the fracture in the world. There, it all came together in the well that connects to others, a network that both sustains and imprisons the First Ones in their slumber where they lie.

There it lies, the Blood Well, filled with powers even as the New Ones vanish, losing the battle against time and the waters of the world. And ages later, there is another exodus in another world. The ones who gave themselves a name, the Empyrean Elders, arrive. A corrupting force that excavated the bodies of the First Ones, hollowing them, sucking out the godsblood for their own use. The godsblood, as it does with the First Ones, becomes both a salvation and a poison to the Empyrean Elders.

As it drains, it gently, ever gently, begins calling the spirits of the First Ones from the prisons to the open skies.

It is then, when this godsblood reemerges above the islands, that the spirit-daemons of the First Ones arrive, attracted to the scent of powers running through the godsblood.

The daemons are vicious creatures. Rudder-like tails at the end of powerful bodies, horns growing from the head, fangs and claws to cut and tear. The original among them live still, inhabited by the spirits, and use their physical forms to give birth to more daemons—to carry the spirits anywhere in the world when needed.

The Empyreans call these the maristags.

And a daemon descended from the one that carries the spirit of Karavi has bonded with a human girl who belongs neither here nor there. A girl who fights and breaks and screams and loves and cries. A girl who has no limits and feels everything. And in her, the spirit of Karavi found a kindred, awakening the memories of hundreds of thousands of millennia.

~

The monster called Karavi is not a monster at all.

This—this image of a spirit is truly what the world of the Empyrean Elders would call a god.

What had the Shademan said? *They are gods only because they could not be killed.*

I stagger backward, catching on the tomb, and fall. A piercing ache explodes in my head, a blinding light, and my mind is chaos. *Breathe*, I try to tell myself, gasping for air. I scramble to ground myself in the *now*, panic bringing every terrible thought I've ever had to the fore. *Breathe, please.* My mind wars with trickles of love and light within me, fusing together, building into a crescendo that burns within me. A gasp escapes me, and I fall to the ground, bent over, crying.

The sharpness of the pain dulls, and my sobs become soundless.

When I came down here, I came looking for a key to my freedom. To get away from this island. But now I know. There is no running in this world of islands. Every island in this ocean is the body of a god.

And here I am, in the clutches of one of these gods, who stares at me lying on the ground with the force of a thousand fiery storms.

"Now you are here, roaming inside us, disturbing us. A descendant of our enemies who keep us trapped here. Are you here for our godsblood too?"

"N-no," I whimper.

Our enemies who keep us trapped here.

The Shadefolk.

So this is what the Shadefolk's duty means. To live down here still and keep the First Ones from arising again. This is their mandate. They want the Blood Well a secret not because they worship it but so it won't ever be drained. And my mother, when she blew up the mines, she was only trying to block the way down to the Blood Well in her own desperate way. I know it now. She was trying to protect the island. These islanders who hate her and my father, they owe their lives to my parents.

And that is what the Collector and Aryadna are now going to do—drain the Blood Well for their zargunine.

Karavi speaks in my mind. "Then heed this reminder and this warning."

There's a large silence, larger than the entire underground, before Karavi's voice blows like trumpets. "This is the reminder: This world of water is ours. We created it out of the first silence and the first dark, and we are intertwined in its very foundation. That is the truth. And here is our warning: We have slept for too long. It is time that we woke. Do what you must and drain the well as appropriate. It is time that our bodies were made whole and we taste the sky and drink the ocean once more. Do this and you will see the truth of what is and what will be. Do this and you will serve in the glory of creation from before the first dawn broke. If you do not, there will be not a spark of your blood left at the end of everything."

I don't speak. Don't betray the terror at the thought of the islands splitting apart and coming together to form a cosmic being.

It would only mean one thing: the destruction of this world, the annihilation of humans.

I sense the darkness slipping, the coils swirling and lightening even as I try to make sense of where I am. But I don't remember exactly when Karavi vanished from in front of me, from my mind. One second, she still loomed large, warning me to help the First Ones or stand aside, and the next, a sharp rainbow ripples like the wind, encircling me.

Something rushes up to meet me. A silent explosion.

And then I'm coughing, my back lying hard against the stone, and

I wake up to find Rivan, Raksha, Thayne, and even Yara crouched around me.

"Thank the ocean," Rivan whispers.

"The Shadefolk are right… My parents tried…" I heave, trying to stamp the panic down. Every breath is a knife in my lungs. The still air presses with the force of a storm against my skin, every sensation too loud, too rough, too *much*.

As if I'm thrown out of the womb waters into the world anew.

"Easy, Kress." Rivan catches my face in his hand, but I have to get the words out. I *have* to.

Raksha should know her stories are wrong. The First Ones never walked on the islands; they *are* the islands. Everything I thought—everything I *am*—none of it matters. The fights, the blood, the mines, the mountains, *this very world*.

"We have to stop them," I half cry, half scream. "We have to stop Aryadna and the Collector, or we will all die."

FORTY-FOUR

T ell me again," says Raksha, her head resting on the polearm as she holds it tight enough for her knuckles to turn white, "about the First Ones."

Wearily, I look at her over my own hands clasped fast, resting on my pulled-up knees. I've coiled my body together, as close to myself as possible, inhaling the stale metallic air of the caves. Every sensation crawls like a hundred tiny insects on my skin, visceral and hot and maddening. I want to scratch my skin open, get out of this prison of flesh if that's what it takes to stop feeling everything at once.

The others are in a similar state of disbelief as Raksha.

I don't blame them.

"It—I know how it sounds," I say, mouth dry. Speaking of it doesn't ease the weight of this cosmic truth.

"It is because of how it sounds that I am willing to believe you," Thayne says grimly. His face is pale, and his leg is tied with a cloth that has gotten black with blood again. He meets my eye, and for a brief moment, the air around him shimmers with the darkness of nothingness, the one that marks him as the blood of Shadefolk.

Trying to put what I experienced—a transcendental experience with a cosmic being—into words made me doubt my own mind, made me cry like I haven't ever before. It was Thayne, my fellow Shademan, who helped me explain the story of this world by coaxing me gently, patiently, even when his own life is slowly ebbing.

Rivan believes me, I know. And fortunately Raksha does too.

Yara locks her hands in front of her and sits across from me next to the broken bars. She watches me with a glint in her eyes, like she's assessing how hard I hit my head when I fell.

"There are men up there on the island who are preparing for our annihilation," Thayne says. "Beyorn was one thing. But Aryadna is the Collector's granddaughter. They both betrayed one another, so who knows what truly goes on in those people's minds? We have to stop them however we can. It's no longer about...mining and jobs and food and houses. It's about our existence."

"No one will believe us," Yara says gruffly.

I turn to her in surprise that she has any opinion at all. She watches me like she's *daring* me to say something.

Rivan nods. At my expression, he adds, "I stand with you, now and forever. But what we have seen down here, no one up on the island has. That smoke—the shadow demon, whatever it was. Those things are not normal. Others would want more than our words to trust us."

"Harren will trust us," Raksha cuts in.

"He's one man, Raksha," Thayne says. "What happens when they deem us insane like the others? Harren wouldn't be able to do anything."

"So what do we do? We can stall them, make up things, but for how long?" Raksha says, frustrated. "Those people haven't controlled our lives for so long by doing nothing. They can and will destroy us."

After my parents died, I wanted to escape this island and its chains exactly because I know the destruction the Collector and his people can wreak.

But now, everything is backward. We stand deep in the ground, beneath the sea pressing on us. We can still get lost in here, or a monster attacks us and this time, having given so much already, we can't defend ourselves. And if we survive, Aryadna will be ready for us. If she won't kill us, then she will cast us aside, make liars of us, anything to ensure the discovery of the Blood Well comes out in the open. The Landers are selfish and malicious. They have never once extended grace to the miners. For them, everything exists to serve them. The Collector and his granddaughter will not once stop to think that they are breaking apart the land we live on. For them, the gains come first.

Aryadna even heard the Shadefolk, but she would call them villains and profiteers who want to keep the well for themselves. The truth of our world will become a lie designed to keep them from exploiting the miners' flesh and blood.

I'm not an idiot. I can't stop them all—not forever.

But I can stop Aryadna. I have to get out of here and make sure no one comes down the mines again. Or there will be no salvation anywhere I go in the world.

"We have to get the miners to stop digging too," I say. "Everyone. I know, I know what you're going to say," I hasten as Raksha opens her mouth, "but we have to start somewhere and *fast*."

Raksha stares at me for an elongated moment, then lets out a long scream. She swears and swears until she's run out of breath. No one does anything. We all feel the same way.

Raksha straightens and loosens her shoulders. "Right," she says. "We take turns in helping Thayne. We take no chances and no shortcuts. We move east, and we move quick. It's time we get out of here."

~

The travel upward becomes strangely, maddeningly easy. Tunnels open up, chambers give way, and no creature accosts us even when the scurries come too near. It is as if the creatures are driven out of our way. The ascents give us some trouble, but only because of getting Thayne upward.

The caves are helping us, and the thought makes my legs tremble.

But the ease of the way is why the light at the end of the tunnel is so sudden, so bright that for a moment, I can see nothing save for the little circumference of startling whiteness burning our eyes. And why, when the guns surround us, none of us notice at first until I walk right into the barrel.

FORTY-FIVE

Where are you coming from?" says one of the people. The whole group has their faces covered, leaving only their eyes locked on us.

"What is going on?" Raksha steps up. "Kaden, is that you?"

The one holding the gun to my head startles. "Raksha-ma?"

Every gun lowers immediately.

"You're back?" says Kaden as he rips off his face covering. "But that girl said you were all dead. Harren thinks you're dead."

"Damn that girl to the deepest sea," Raksha curses. "Thayne needs help. Hurry up."

Kaden starts to say something but then glances at Thayne and clamps his mouth shut. His face drains of color. He swears and calls out for some of the group to take Thayne to a doctor.

As they carry him, Thayne lets out a pained gasp. He gives me an encouraging smile—at least I think that's what it's supposed to be. Under the circumstances, we tried our best to keep the wound tied and prevent blood loss, but none of us are truly healers, and all I can do is hope our best was enough to keep him alive.

His leaving makes me feel strangely uncomfortable, like I've been left alone again, and I'm too young to know what to do next. But before I have time to process that, Kaden hurries us up along one of the defunct chambers littered with mining carts.

"What's happening? Why's the work stopped?"

It's only when Raksha asks that I realize it. The usual thundering of drills and ground-movers and shouts and chaos of wheels is absent, leaving behind a large silence as loud as the music beneath the ground.

A quiet, haunting whistle blows through the shafts.

"The Collector," Kaden says.

"What about him?" Raksha asks sharply. Out of the horrendous underground, she's transformed into the veteran miner that she is, automatically a leader. She stands straighter; her voice is stronger. The strength of her focused gaze could wither the sun.

Someone like Beyorn could never match her.

"He's coming," Kaden says.

"For what?" I ask. There's only one thing I can imagine the Collector wants: to drain the Blood Well. But how can that happen so soon? He would need massive machinery and endless labor—labor only the full strength of Kar Atish's miners could provide.

Kaden narrows his eyes at me. "I know Yara and Rivan. But you're not a miner."

"She's fine," Raksha says. "Thayne and I vouch for her."

"Okay," Kaden says. With one last glance up and down at me, he turns to Raksha. "In any case, I'm glad you're here, Raksha-ma, because Harren is trying his best, but we don't know what to do. The Collector wants us ready by dawn tomorrow. He's bringing in his army, and he wants us all to invade the mines."

We emerge from the mines into a different world.

It must be late afternoon, and the sun burns. Even worse now that we've stayed for so long in the dark. Everything is cast white-hot, my skin stinging raw and red as if any moment it will catch a flame. The smell of water and ash overwhelms my senses, dust running with claws down my throat. I have to force my eyes open, even as the corners of my vision darken. Has it always been like this?

The face of the mine stands empty. At the top, though, the same uniformed miners who were busy working when we went in are now armed with every type of weapon—polearms like Raksha, close-range guns, daggers and spikes and all kinds of blades. Near the face, a pile of sticks of zargunine is amassed. A crowd of elder miners sits there hunched over, sharpening the blunt sticks into even more weapons.

Not that any of this would matter in front of the Collector's sophisticated weapons.

Kaden and the group take us through the armed miners toward the back of the open space, where the black cliffs fall abruptly into the sea. The row of squat gray chambers of the Collector's officers has been converted into gathering places.

We duck into the last one, which is also the biggest. Inside, the gray cement walls keep the oppressive heat and ash trapped despite the large window looking over the sea. Even with footsteps marking the floor, everything is layered in dust and soot.

Four elderly miners and one younger, around Kaden's age but older than me, pack around a table. The first thing I notice is how rickety it is and how fragile everyone looks. The younger guy looks up, pushing his hair out of his eyes, as we enter.

He leaps to his feet in shock. "Ma? You're—here. You're alive."

So this must be Raksha's son, Harren, the Young Scythe.

Raksha gets to him in one fluid motion, like gravity couldn't work against her in that moment. She hugs him fiercely and lets up just as quickly. The tightness in his face reduces a little as Raksha takes his place, and he steps back from the table with no more questions to stand at her shoulder instead.

"How's Thayne?" one of the elder ones asks.

"They're starting work to amputate his leg, but he will live," answers someone at our backs.

"That's good. We need him," the man murmurs. He looks back to Raksha. "What happened to your mission? Did you find anyone? It seems like the moment your company left, there was a sudden influx of the Collector's men swarming around. What is the connection?"

"The Collector fooled us," Raksha growls, pressing down on the table. It makes a cracking sound. "He wants to drain the origin well, and we can't let that happen."

She quickly summarizes our journey but takes her time to explain about that disgusting insect creature and the shadow spider. And with a glance at me and Rivan, she goes on a tangent about how deadly an invasion into the mines could be. That it will start a war with the Children of Shade, and we will all die as collateral.

I hadn't realized how tightly the center of my body was coiled, worried over how this conversation would go with the miners. Thank the ocean Raksha knows how to handle these people.

"We are also looking at an exodus of underground creatures who can and will cause destruction we won't be able to deal with. This won't stop here. They will travel elsewhere, and they will cause mayhem in addition to the toll the ocean takes. Nowhere will be safe. We are staring at our annihilation," she ends grimly.

The crowd around the table swears. But there's no immediate uproar. No one even asks her follow-up questions—they believe her. This is what the mining family has always been, trust and faith in one another. I feel out of my depth here, surrounded by miners who must have had family members killed in the explosion.

"Then it's simple. We refuse to go in and we keep them back," a man named Fahris says. He looks familiar. In another life, I might have known him, but I dare not ask him anything.

"We have rotating patrols already. The top of the mine's face is covered," Harren says. "Kaden and his group are scouring the side entries and dead shafts. Ashvin and Mayven have a team down by the shore."

"*What?*" Rivan steps up, face drained of blood.

"Well, what did you think?" Harren scowls. "They were going to sit by and wait? Just be glad they weren't here when that Aryadna girl said you were dead."

"The shore has beasts from the sea too."

"And they know that!"

This is madness, I want to say. They're trying to defend the mines from all sides, but we're too close, too unequipped. And like Rivan says, fighting alongside the ocean is a death sentence. That kind of movement along the shore *will* bring out predators. It's not like when I used to play along the shore—just a child, quietly—but a large horde of prey just waiting to be ambushed.

They keep arguing back and forth, the others joining in too. In the heat, everyone is getting more and more frustrated, losing grip on our immediate situation. Here we are, getting backed even further into the corner.

I shout, "You're all focusing on defending. We need to attack them before they can reach the mines."

A sudden silence, punctuated by the wild ocean down along the shore, sinks into the small room.

"We can't let them cross the Redwater," I say. "The ground gets softer the farther in they get down this side. They can blow it up to get below. The spires will break, and the falling rocks could cause a blockade. And we have old niches the whole way. If they find even a single way in—"

"I know who you are," Harren says, annoyed, and I freeze. "You're one of Badger's fighters."

"No—yes, that's who I am, and I know how to fight."

"What's that supposed to mean?"

"That this is not a battle you'll win cowering in a corner!"

"These are monsters *we* know better," Harren says.

"No, you *don't*." I slam my hands down on the table, almost ready to grab Harren by the shoulders and shake him so he can see the reality. We cannot match the full strength of the Collector's army—even less so if Sollonia gets involved.

I look at Rivan, who stands there with his hands crossed over his chest, glaring at Harren. It was different before, but now, knowing what's at stake, I can't leave him here. And I know if I asked, he wouldn't leave with me, and neither would his brothers. Which means I can't escape this anymore.

Leave Kar Atish. Let them all rot.

That's what I always told myself to keep going in this world. It was not my fight. I would find another island and its freer skies.

But if Aryadna succeeds in invading the mines, starting a war, and breaking our land, how long will any other island remain safe? Is this what I have spilled blood—my own and that of those innocent creatures—for in the pits of the arena? For hiding in a corner while the world shatters because of men's greed?

I'm done trying to run. I deserve the same place on this land as anyone else.

When I turn back to the table, fire licking through the ash within me, ready to start screaming, I find Fahris staring at me, eyes narrowed. And before I have time to prepare myself, he speaks.

"Jar." His voice is a whisper carrying a storm. "You're Jar's daughter."

The silent air plummets faster than I can breathe.

288

"I was thinking you looked familiar—how—" He rises, the table overturning with the force, fists clenched at his sides reddening rapidly. One by one, the others realize too, and hysteria explodes. Kaden and his group, who were at the entrance of the room, roar and stomp right into the middle.

I step back hurriedly, never taking my eyes off any of them. Which of them would hurt me first? Probably Kaden and his group. Damn the ocean—they have weapons. I gasp, air refusing to help—

Rivan closes a hand on mine, stepping up next to me, shielding me with his half-turned body. I look up at him wildly, and he meets me with a ferocious gaze. *I won't let you face them alone*, it says.

Raksha's words, loud and clear, cut through the charged air. "Stop this nonsense. We need her."

"No, we don't," two of the elders snap together.

"Kinkiller," Fahris spits.

That word. Fire rips through me as I speak. "While you waste time coming up with creative names, the Collector's army is advancing on us."

"There is no *us* here." Harren lets out a frustrated breath, then turns to his mother. "Why have you brought her here?"

"Because none of you know the real danger we are in!" I shout. Heaving, I step up, not breaking eye contact with Harren because I can see he might be young, but if I don't win over him and Kaden, we might as well let the First Ones rise this very minute and end everything in this world.

Harren opens his mouth, then closes it. Anger hardens his features. Instead of me, he continues to address Raksha. "Don't push this, Ma."

Raksha stamps down her polearm so hard the gray walls of the chamber vibrate. "You think I don't remember watching your father get blown to pieces in front of my eyes? You think I don't remember the taste of his blood as it spattered inside my mouth?"

Harren pales. "Ma—"

But he has no words. And neither do any of us. For a terrible, elongated moment, all of us stand still, staring at Raksha. She has her fist closed around the ring on the chain around her neck, so tight her bones stand out.

Harren looks away, anguish burning in his eyes.

Before I found out about the First Ones, I could have still believed that miners can fight their own fights. That I had no place with them beyond the underground mines. It had been all that I was looking forward to, a life away from here.

But now I know my parents tried to protect these people—*failed* to protect these people—and that still doesn't change what Raksha has gone through. It is the brutal truth. And I cannot turn away from it.

I look at Rivan and Yara, then at every other person in the room, meeting their angry and incredulous eyes.

"That rebellion you keep talking of, trying to build us all a better world, it will die tonight if we don't stop what's coming." The weight of everyone's gaze is heavier than I anticipated.

I swallow my fear, my shame.

"It wasn't my fault," I say softly. Incredulity runs swift among those assembled. But I raise my chin and repeat, meeting each of their gazes one by one, "What happened was not my fault. I was a child. It was *never* my fault."

There's no apology I have for them, which is what I know they truly want to hear. They don't want to hear that my parents died trying to save the world, to give me a fighting chance to live in a world that wouldn't end. Now I have to finish what they started and risked everything for. No backing down now.

So I tell them what they *need* to hear. "I can't change what my parents did, but if we let the Collector move beyond the Redwater, it will be our end for always. If—if the mines are drained, what use would we have to the Landers in Sollonia? They will destroy this island. We will die the death of mute beasts."

Fahris looks like he wants to say something, but at the last moment, his gaze drifts somewhere over my shoulder instead. To Raksha.

"So," Raksha says, "if we must attack first, the valley over Redwater is our best chance."

FORTY-SIX

By nightfall, the news has spread; the miners are marching to battle against the Collector's army.

Everyone is divided in groups. Several older miners stay behind, keeping a defensive boundary around the entrance and all the nooks they know of from experience. We can't do anything about the brute force, but anything that can delay an onslaught, even if for mere minutes, is precious.

At the center of the pit, the scorched earth is where my parents were burned. Every other miner who died that day was buried in the ocean with the respect the dead deserve. Save for Jar and Katya Dune.

I kneel at the edge of the marks on the ground.

Despite the constant activity, I can sense people slowing down, giving me sidelong glances. The miner elders have grudgingly accepted me in the fold for now. But it doesn't change anyone's feelings. They've spent almost a decade building up their hatred against my parents. And what can I say to vindicate them?

Their actions may have had noble intentions, but the results did not fulfill those intentions.

And yet they're the same parents who held me when I scraped my knee, helped me raise little creatures and then release them back in the sea, sung me lullabies, and told me bedtime stories.

The pressure of reconciling all of it almost brings me to tears again.

But I won't cry in front of these people.

Let them see that I am not ashamed of my parents. I can't forgive them, but I can stand with them.

Let them see me as whoever they want to. I am who I am.

The dark skies and silent rocks watch me as I bring my hands together, bow my head, and, for the first time, whisper the words of the final ritual for my parents.

May the Water Horse watch over you,
May you sail the ocean of stars,
May you find the home of elders,
May the end begin once more.

"Will you guys hurry?" Mayven says as Rivan, Ashvin, and I fit in weapons. The brothers have gone for guns. I take one, but mostly I pick up blades in addition to my daggers. I know my strength, and it's in close combat.

"What are you hurrying for?" Ashvin stops and asks. "You stay here."

Rivan takes Mayven's arm. "Yeah, go home, and don't worry about us. We'll see you in the morning. And if—"

Mayven rips out of Rivan's grasp. "You both have got to be kidding."

He glares at them, tightening his grip on the gun he was in the process of strapping to his chest.

"May, is this the time to—" I start but Ashvin immediately cuts me off.

"I will tie you to a maristag before I let you in active battle."

The three brothers stand across from one another, each of their faces mirroring the others' stubbornness. They look unlike themselves. The bruises from these past days, the prominence of bones over paler skin. Like they've already been through a war.

"Don't make this harder than it has to be," Rivan growls.

"Yeah, that's what I'm saying. Stop wasting time and let's go," Mayven snaps back.

Faster than I can blink, the three of them are grappling.

"What in the ocean's name!" I shout, stepping out of the way. "How is this helping?"

But they fight and throw things. Clearly, none of them actually wants to hurt anyone, so they're *all* getting their fair share of punches. I hate all three of them.

"You. Are. Not. Going." Ashvin wheezes as May grabs his throat from behind, while Rivan tries to get him off Ashvin.

The fighting and shouting draw others to us, near the mouth of the mine. Half of the younger miners just start hooting and egging them on.

And just then, in a fit to get himself out of Rivan's grip, Mayven kicks fast—and hits Ashvin, who crashes into the pile of guns with a loud gasp. He tries to disentangle himself from the pile, but his leg slips. I rush to help him, and when he sits up, blood trickles down his nose. Rivan and Mayven race across to him, their faces shocked and terror marking their shouts.

Ashvin touches the blood sliding down his face, and his fingers come away red. Someone gets Rivan a quick aid kit, and he gets to work.

With the same slippery hands, Ashvin grabs Mayven's collars and looks him in the eye. "You are not going."

For a moment, the two of them just stare at each other, the rest of the world forgotten.

Finally Mayven takes Ashvin's hand and promises to his brothers, "Fine. But when this fight is over, I will break both your bones."

As I turn away to let them have a moment, he calls, "Oy, Kress." When I twist in my place and raise a brow, he adds, "Take care of my brothers."

"On my life," I tell him.

The multiple groups that line the mines and the harbor next to the refinery are our last line of defense. If they get breached, there's no stopping the Collector's army. Which is why most people with fighting capabilities go into Kar Atish, led by Harren and Kaden, hoping to bottleneck the gorge over the Redwater and keep the army far away from the mines.

The palpable strain among those leading the charge about what might happen if they fail to keep the army trapped here pulses in the air, settling on everyone else.

It's even worse along the row I walk with; Harren put me directly next to Yara. And we both have guns, which is why Rivan splits from his unit two rows behind and marches next to us.

If this is their way of keeping me in check, I'm fine.

As long as we don't let the mines fall to the Collector and Aryadna, I'm okay with marching next to the sea devil itself.

The storm is high as we move in unison, hundreds of armed miners. The black skies are thick with clouds, rain pelting the spires. The weather couldn't be worse if it tried.

I wipe water off my face, squinting to see beyond the curtain of rain. All around me, light from everyone's headlamps diffuses in the water.

For all my life, I have lived apart from the people I now march with—shoulder to shoulder, ready to die next to them—but that distance is not enough to change what I feel down to my bones now. Anticipation, yes, but raw fear too.

We've all heard stories of so many rebellions and uprisings over the years. Legends of Sollonia's fatal attempt at legitimizing rebels as a political opposition, which ended in the entire rebel movement destroyed in a single moment, and the repercussions the rest of the islands have felt for so long.

None of us will forget the Night of the Wagon Scars even though most of us weren't even alive when it happened. Miners had gone on a strike. They camped along the Redwater valley, demanding rights to better wages, proper access to health facilities, a relaxation in the indenture policies. Seven nights in, men from the Collector's compound snuck in, got into the mine train, and drove it along the gorge, right down the middle of the miner camps, and gunned them all down. Defenseless miners and their families. Children too. The pervasiveness of that devastation on Kar Atish is so strong, so real that it feels as if every miner child is born with that knowledge within us.

The raath beasts have fled in the wake of our long, serpentine march along the uneven hills, amid the spires that the rains weaken. Every now and then, rocks tumble down, scattering us, slowing us. Our progress is still steady, but I can feel the finality in the iron-tasting rain. One way or another, we will find what the fate of Kar Atish will be within the day.

Eventually, after hours, we reach the midpoint that connects the arm of the miners with the shoulder of the Collector, a narrow gorge lined with the defunct wagon tracks littered with boulders and thorny bushes and scraps scattered like excavated fossils in the hills. Discarded mine carts and rusted mine trains, wire cages, and other junk that, although reminders of horrifying things, we can use as necessary shields since most of our so-called army carries guns filled with shrapnel.

While the rain stays away due to the direction of the wind, the terrible cacophony of the storm is magnified in the gorge.

The walk up here kept most of us distracted from the obvious fear, but now, I can feel tension ratcheting up my body.

Several meters ahead, Harren and two of his closest fighters move ahead to rendezvous with the scouts.

"This is a reckless idea," Yara breathes, shooting me a look of pure loathing.

"I'd rather not have fought too," Rivan says before I can counter. "But since we are, I rather we win. So you better pull yourself together."

"If you don't stop talking to me, the next thing to come out of your mouth will be your teeth." She walks across the gorge to place herself as far away from us as possible.

"She's going to get us killed," Rivan says. "I told Harren we shouldn't bring her."

I raise a brow. "Because she's not sticking to the place she's supposed to?"

"*I* am not behaving like I want to kill everyone and then myself."

I cannot believe the words that come out of me next, but I tell him anyway. "Have some compassion, Rivan. She lost her brother in the whole farce. She's grieving."

He sighs. "You're right. I'm sorry I'm—"

"Thinking of May? He'll be fine. He's tougher than you and Ashvin give him credit for."

Rivan opens his mouth to answer, but at that moment, there's hurried movement from up in the gorge. Harren and his men return, charging down the narrow path. Several of them take up places along the gorge, and some move in among the rest of the group.

Harren stays at the top, yelling, "Get in formation! They're moving toward us now!"

Around the corner, three tanks thunder into view, the turret of each mounted with mammoth firearms. Lander machines that we can only dream of. A keening sound fills the air, and, blood freezing in my bones, I see sharp lights rising along the sides of the firearms like red-eyed raath about to leap.

Screams and bullets echo in the night. My hands automatically know what to do even as I stumble backward into the hill, shooting across the gorge at the tanks.

But *of course*, it's no use.

There's a barrage of gunshots.

Bangs and white smoke and the sweltering gunpowder streak into the air, chaos on their heels, turning everything into a death game in the narrow pathway.

Wildly, I slam back into a nearby boulder.

They weren't supposed to be here before dawn.

"Get back!" I add my voice to the chorus begging friends and family to get out of the way, to retreat, *please*!

"Harren, back down!" someone yells.

Something *heavy* clangs against the ground, causing a ringing in my body from toe to head.

Blinking rapidly, I try to look for the source.

Instead, I see Harren standing in the center of the gorge, limned in strange light as the rain blows in the changed wind against him, and emptying rounds of bullets. One of his men flees, and then a sound gun blows the other one backward in the air.

Harren howls against the wind and storm.

"Kress!" Rivan shouts, grabbing for my hand, but I'm out of his reach. "Get back! We need to retreat!"

"Where's Raksha?" I yell back.

"I don't know!"

For everything I owe Raksha, I make a run for it. And it seems

Yara has the same thought. We crash into Harren together, slamming down with him painfully as a bullet whizzes past him and grazes the top of the boulder next to us.

Harren's eyes widen. *"What are you—"*

At that moment, a blast tears through the gorge, sending the world up in flames.

FORTY-SEVEN

The harsh whistle in my head is deafening, robbing me of every sense and leaving me floating in sharp, painful whiteness for several moments.

In a startling, dizzying rush, *touch* comes back first, searing through my body, and fire storms into my lungs, which are laboring as hard as they can. And with it, pain. Everywhere.

Gravel sticks to my tongue, sanding it bloody. I try to spit it out but only end up scratching my gums and retching as the reek of gunpowder cuts through. When I raise my shaking fingers to the side of my face, they come back red too. My heart beats painfully, struggling, as I lift my head and look around.

Next to me, Harren and Yara are faring no better. We push ourselves up slowly, holding on to one another, and sit up with our backs pressed into the boulder that saved us.

One boulder.

Or we would be lying dead like the scores of bodies now spread down the gorge.

About ten steps from me, Rivan is pressed into the wall of the hill. Alive.

It's the only thing I can focus on as my vision stabilizes, the whistling in my head still far too loud.

Flames crackle along the thornbushes punctuating the gasps and cries of the dying, the overpowering smoke and dust dancing like wraiths over the dead. The darkened bodies are scorched like they breathed in raw zargunine, separated from us by a pool of blood and torn limbs.

Rain pours sideways in sheets now, splashing into the pool and diluting the blood, which slowly runs down the gorge in dark rivulets.

Rivan waves a hand, catching my attention. His mouth moves.

Don't leave your place.

And I give him an incredulous look back. *Where will I go?*

The storm intensifies, taking away whatever little ability to see I had gained after shaking off the dizziness.

Harren moves to stand, his knees visibly shaking, and I pull him back. "What are you doing? You'll get killed!"

"You're the one who dragged us here," Yara hisses from his other side. "*We need to attack.*"

"And you must be delighted we might fail."

"We wouldn't have if we stayed at our home. But you wouldn't know much about that."

"Do you not see how prepared they are? If they bombed the mines—"

"Stop it, both of you!" Harren snaps.

We fall quiet, glowering at one another. But whichever one of us is right, it doesn't change the fact that right now, barrels are still flashing from the top of the hills ahead. A cruel silence prowls, and every time there's even a slightly recognizable movement, guns go off. The blood of miners seeps down this gorge and into the island, into the mouth of the gods beneath.

I shudder at the thought of this somehow strengthening the one

I saw. Karavi. Her face—if it *was* her face—slips from my memory even as I try to recall it.

"It's going to be light soon," Harren says. "We can't stay here like fish waiting for bait."

"We move, we die," I say. And I can't let that happen—not to Raksha's son.

Then, someone calls in a voice broken as a rusted hinge, "Harren."

In the distance, a girl tries to get up. She can't be much older than me. The blue of the miners' clothes she's wearing has turned a dark midnight, soaked with blood. She reaches out, and immediately a barrage of guns screams against the fading night. Several miss, thunking along bodies already dead, but one finds its mark and explodes. Her shocked expression frozen forever, the girl slams back to the ground.

Harren roars and rushes to her.

There's a sound of a gun being reloaded. A shot. And as Harren realizes what he's done in impulse, he turns, surprised. A single bullet rips at the side of his waist.

"*Harren!*" Raksha cries from somewhere at the back. *There, behind a broken cart.*

Before Raksha gives in to her instinct too, I hurtle away from the boulder and rush to Harren. A bullet grazes past the top of my head, burning my hair. I try to drag him away, but he's too heavy, and I think *this is it.*

The next second, Rivan and Yara are there, each helping me get Harren to the side of the hill, in the temporary safety of an outcropping.

And it still isn't enough to keep Raksha at her place. She crawls like the shadow of a snake, taking advantage of the rain, and picks her way through the dead toward us.

Harren presses a hand to the patch of red rapidly spreading at his side. "Well, this isn't great."

Raksha doesn't say anything, so I do. "We have to get him back."

"And leave my people here alone? *No*," he says, but already the bite in his voice is gone. His breathing is labored, sweat trickling along and making tracks down the soot on his face.

"You'd rather be dead, *then* leave them alone?"

"You'll bleed to death here," Raksha says. She pulls his eye down and studies him. None of us have to be a doctor to know what the paleness of his skin means. We saw it with Thayne already.

"Once it gets light"—Rivan looks up, a hand shading his face from the rain smelling violently of rust—"they'll move in and chase us down to the mines."

"We move now, we might as well just slit our own throats," Yara says. Her eyebrows lower, anger descending in her again. "If I get them to chase me, maybe you'll have a chance to take him away from here."

"You can't—"

She cuts me off. "I want nothing more than to be with my brother. And if I can help my people while I'm at it, then I will. You don't get to judge me."

"Yara," Raksha says. "This is not the way."

"If what she says about the First Ones is true"—Yara throws me a murderous glance—"do we have any other choice left?"

Rivan and I exchange glances. Perhaps it's not the way, but what is? It either ends now or we struggle and die many times over. I feel the weight of Karavi's frightening gaze. The First Ones want to awaken now. No wonder the land seems to give us no respite.

I have to do what Jar and Katya Dune tried to do and failed.

"No, it is not the way," I say. "But there is another. The Collector."

Rivan closes in his eyes with understanding.

"The Landers here operate entirely under the Collector's command. They are forbidden to act against and without his will. We get him, this all ends."

Yara stands.

"Stop it, Yara," Harren breathes, a bloody hand reaching out. But he's losing strength, and his hand falls back as he gasps. Raksha presses on his wound, trying futilely to prevent the blood loss, and looks back at Yara. Her gaze is heavy with a finality.

"Even if you're right about the Collector, we're dealing with an onslaught here right now. Once the skies lighten, we will be massacred. So you do what you have to, and I will do this." Yara hoists her two guns along her hips.

She looks at me. "I will never forgive your family for what it did to mine. So don't think this is for your benefit. This is for the family that raised me. The one you will never be a part of." Then she adds to Rivan, "Get ready to get Harren out."

She turns then, no longer listening to Harren's weak protests, and steps out in the middle of the gorge.

The shooting starts almost instantly. She directs her rage, screaming, at the massive tanks blocking the path. The renewed battle noise startles everyone down the gorge, and even those half dying stop to wonder at her.

Rivan and I carry Harren in the dark shadows, unable to take our eyes off Yara. The guards atop the tanks had gone lax and are now scrambling to get in position, howling orders across the three vehicles. She's a dark demon limned in the light from the tanks, crying and screaming and giving back the Landers everything they gave us.

And then her guns fall silent.

She drops them, even as new gunfire erupts, and gets ready to die.

FORTY-EIGHT

L ook out!" someone yells from across the gorge.

From the direction of the mines—a bright, blinding light. A mine train comes hurtling over the wagon track as the remaining miners lying across the ground to protect themselves from the Landers' firing get out of the way. Alongside the driver in the first cart, a man aims a multiple-barrel gun toward the tanks, rapidly firing.

It comes to a stop a few feet from us, covering fire for Yara, who stands there stunned like the rest of us.

Oshen sits inside, his tattooed hands clutching the giant firearm. "Get him out of there!"

Rivan and I help Harren onto the cart, Raksha climbing in behind him. As Oshen continues to cover fire, Yara hurtles back, and together we help the other injured on the train. And all throughout, the cacophony of bullets rings in the night.

"Rivan," I say, ducking as the light of the firearm flashes and startles me, "we have to go now."

Yara comes stumbling toward us and takes over covering Harren.

We quickly exchange weapons, hurriedly confirm the route to get inside the mountains.

"Oshen!" I shout. "Get them to safety!"

He looks at me confused before his eyes go wide with the realization that I'm not getting on the train. "Where are you—?"

"The Collector! Hold this gorge, Oshen. It's all we have!"

And with that, I take Rivan's hand, and we step away from the wagon track.

~

Getting away from the gorge isn't easy, but Rivan and I follow Raksha's instructions and crawl down the passage. From boulders to carts to the horrible wire cages, we take shelter as we move upward, closer to the Collector's army as bullets and shells rain down all around us in retaliation for the mine train.

The old watchtowers crumble like decayed teeth on either side of the pass, narrowing the way out. They mark the turn on the island, beyond which miners cannot live anymore. But once they stood with all the majesty of legendary swords jutting from the ground, cutting the mists and looking out to the sea.

I nudge Rivan when we're close enough, pointing to the feet of the left watchtower. "There's the gap in the hill that Yara spoke of. You ready?"

"As ready as I can be." He starts to raise the lighter, then hesitates. "We're sure, right? You didn't look great when you woke up in the mines. You're sure the First One won't find you, right?"

For a tempting moment, I am selfish enough to want to say *yes, I'm terrified. Let someone else go*. But I wonder if the fear of destruction has scrubbed away the selfish bone from my body. The same fear that drives me to descend beneath the ground once more, finish this before the battle takes a form none of us can contain. "If anything happens to me—"

"Nothing is happening to you," Rivan says quietly, fiercely.

I take his free hand. The mark of the wound peeking from his open collar reminds me that every moment is precious now, as it always has been, and I have never been more grateful for him. "I don't know if we get a choice."

"You always have a choice," Rivan breathes, close to me, and then flicks the lighter on.

I scowl at him, and by his smirk, I know he knows what I'm thinking. *You did this on purpose.*

Immediately, we get our return signal. Three flicks of flame, tiny and only if you knew where to look. A beat passes. Then seven guns from the back carts of the train fire simultaneously toward the top of the hill on the right. In that very startling, very violent moment for the Collector's men stationed atop the hill, Rivan and I make for the gap to the left.

The world is a flash of rain and smoke and gunshots as we race. And the second we sweep inside the small gap, the darkness of the island greets me again.

Pressed against the wall, Rivan and I cough, wiping the rain off our eyes and mouths.

"Sometimes choices get taken away from you by the world," I say, head resting back on the wall, panting. The dark here is only partial, thanks to the slant of light from the gap, but it vanishes within a few feet. The wall and the floors are jagged, unlike the smoothness of the city cavern below.

"Then you find new ones," Rivan says.

The warmth in this part of the cavern, so near the Redwater, is hot as full noon. Almost makes me miss the chill of the lakes below. *Almost.* I force my legs in motion, ignoring my increased heartbeat as my mind decides to dwell on the underground. It's different this time, after all. We're not going any lower than the ground level, and we will remain along the island, not the depths of the seas.

We forge farther down the tunnels, seeking the heat. This close, there are no creatures crawling around. It is tempting to let down my guard, but I don't trust the land I'm walking on anymore.

After a while of silence, I ask Rivan, "Does this world feel like it lets you find new choices?"

"Not if you close yourself up to the chance."

"The *world* never gave me a chance!" I stop walking. "Its very foundation made sure I would never walk on a ground that will just let me be! My parents are gone, the miners' council hates me, and even when I try my best, I hurt people. Look at Yara—at Harren. Look at *you* here with me rather than with your brothers, who are also fighting a battle that we don't know if we'll ever win! Everything I want gets taken from me, so I'm left with no home and no love and no one has ever—"

"What do you think I've been doing all these years?" Rivan bursts out. "Why am I not enough, Kress?"

I open my mouth and close it.

Does he not know how *much* he is for me? Is that what he thinks? That I wanted to leave because of him? That I wanted to leave...him?

"I'm sorry," he says. "I'm being cruel. First that thing about Yara, and now this. I don't know what's wrong with me." His face is hollowed out. The last few days have changed him more than I realized. He's tired and jumpy and troubled.

If there's nothing keeping you here, then go.

But he followed me down the mines anyway. Even after he knew who I was, he never held it against me. He has been my family.

I approach him, a step at a time, and he tracks my movement but doesn't back away.

If I ever accepted that I feel more than what I let on, it would have tied me here. Because I wanted to leave. Isn't that what I have told myself repeatedly? And yet every time I would wish for leaving, I would only imagine myself away from the hatred of this dark land, but my mind snagged on him, always. Shying away from the idea of leaving him as if the thought should never even exist. And my dreams. Never without him.

I stop as close as I can, head tilting back as I look into his eyes. And I don't remember if, for all our closeness over the years, we have stood like this. Baring our faces to one another.

"I don't want to lose you, Rivan," I murmur. "I can't think of being without you."

"But you are afraid."

"Very."

Rivan takes my chin in his hand and kisses my forehead. "Then we do what we came here to do. We find a way."

FORTY-NINE

The rest of the way is dark, with only Rivan's lighter for illumination. But at once, the warmth turns to the heat of a large furnace, and we step into a huge chamber glowing orange with the lava from a stream across it, backed almost into the wall. The stream will expand into the river, which flows to the cliffs and, while still inside the rocks, into the seabed. Few people have seen the entirety of the river. It is too dangerous, too treacherous to step closer, but it is also our path to the end of the island without the army trampling us.

"Finally," I breathe, salty sweat slipping inside my lips.

The word echoes over the rush of the hot flow of the river.

Which is perhaps what draws the attention of the couple of wyrm lizards.

I stop, reaching a hand to pull Rivan back. He looks at me questioningly, and I point to the glimmering red eyes that look like they're floating in the air. The wyrms are a deep black color, distinguishable only because of the eyes. They're about three feet tall, thickset with strong limbs and a powerful tail the size of their bodies—bigger than the ones I fought in the pit.

I pull out my daggers.

As if it's a signal, the two wyrms let out piercing shrieks. The echoes are loud over the bubbling of the fiery lava.

Belying their size, the wyrms leap at us in a flash, all fangs and claws.

I slash my dagger, ducking beneath the body, and go rolling to the other side. The wyrm crashes into the ground but gets up immediately. It curls into itself, forming a ball-like shape, and for a second, it looks like it's retreating before it launches at me, its outer shell ringed with spikes. I flip my dagger backward, grasping the blade, and slam the wyrm with the bone hilt.

The wyrm flies into the air, unfurling and screaming, and slips into the lava stream. Screeches fill the hall as the wyrm clasps at the edge of the stream and hauls itself back on the ground. It continues its pained shrieks and hurries back into the shadows.

At my back, Rivan is barely holding his own assailant at bay. The wyrm snaps at him madly, without thought, and Rivan slashes at it with his lighter. I hurry over even as Rivan twists free from between the wyrm and the wall at his back. The wyrm leaps into the air. Rivan ducks and throws the lighter at the creature.

They collide midair.

And the wyrm swirls as it lands, moving with a speed faster than I can blink, and slashes at Rivan. He brings his arm up to protect his face. But the talons rake his arm, and he howls.

"*Rivan!*"

But he doesn't turn—only charges at the wyrm, blood spurting everywhere, and slams it into the wall. Without the spikes out in its balled-up form, the wyrm screeches in pain as the sound of bone breaking against rock cuts the air.

Rivan drops the dead wyrm.

He steps back, swaying.

I finally reach him across the hall. "Show me your arm."

Bloody ribbons. That's what his arm looks like. My breath hitches.

"This is what I feel like every time you're in that damned arena," Rivan whispers.

I'm about to respond, to tell him it's not the same, when something happens. The skin on Rivan's arm, red and frayed, begins to... pull itself back. Beneath the skin, a red thread glows.

A shocked gasp escapes me. "What—?"

Rivan, staring at his arm, moves his other hand to the wound near his heart. The same red thread pulses there.

"What happened?" I ask, touching the skin around his wound. It's warm.

"I don't know. When I woke up, I remember—darkness. A labyrinth. Until a red thread of light directed me toward the opening, toward light." He breathes deeply. "It felt like the dream of a poisoned mind. But this..."

"They gave you godsblood," I say. "Perhaps that's what this is?"

What *are* the Children of Shade capable of?

We're so caught up staring at this bewildering marvel that we miss the pack of salamanders creeping behind us.

From beneath the rocks, they skitter out, hissing. Four, ten, twenty. All of them about the size of my arm, black bodies that gleam with scarlet veins, their bulging eyes reflecting the glow of the liquid fire flowing fast from across the chamber. Living, breathing embers of coal. Their claws are small, but they shine with the sharpness of new blades.

"Rivan," I whisper. "We can't fight so many of them."

"Run for it?"

I nod. There's only one way to run—along the boiling, burning river. "Go!"

We dash forward together, leaping over the scattered rocks as more salamanders rush from under the ground. I glance over my shoulder, and spits of living fire chase us, some of them plunging *into* the maw of flames, swiftly swimming along, as the stream expands into the river the farther we run.

The Redwater burns furiously, aiding its spawn as they leap over the lava. We hurtle along, as far as possible from the hot shore, as the river skirts along the chamber.

A sharp claw nicks at the back of my calf. Blood trickles against my hot skin. *Run faster.* The salamanders race up the walls and try to run ahead and circle us, but we manage to keep pace.

And then, the chamber begins to narrow. The liquid fire bubbles up next to us, steam wraiths grabbing for us. Hot sweat pours into my eyes as the ground becomes treacherous and my speed slows. I want to hold Rivan's hand, make sure he's next to me, but our hands are too slippery.

The smell of fire and blood swells terrifyingly.

The salamanders close in.

If we can only keep running—keep breathing. Hot air fills in my lungs. The river leads right next to the Collector's compound, making a fiery waterfall before moving beneath the sea itself. It's the fastest route to the other side of the island, devoid of the hilly terrain. We can reach—we can *escape*—

The steam wraiths grasp us by our wrists and ankles now, whispering curses in our ears, boiling the blood in our veins.

Rivan gasps. "It's hot."

"I know, I know," I sob.

The heat curls around us faster, wrapping us in the inferno, choking us.

The salamanders hurtle wildly, without control, until suddenly, they stop chasing. I look over my shoulder as I run and see the entire chamber covered in the creatures, their large yellow eyes glowering at us in unison.

I stumble as I slow down, panting with the heat. "Why have they stopped?"

Rivan looks down to the narrowing shore. "I don't know."

We resume walking, checking every few seconds if any of the creatures follow, but they seem to have turned away now. The ones in the river too have climbed back on the shore and retreated. For now, our only assailant is the thick, hot smoke snaking in the air.

Every step becomes lead heavy. I gasp, tasting the dryness of my throat.

The shore narrows to the point that Rivan is forced to walk behind me. It should feel safer, but the *lack* of immediate danger only makes my skin crawl. Sweat drips in my eyes, and I wipe at them constantly, my skin burning too. The metal of the gun sears my waist as my shirt moves a little and I yelp.

Rivan clasps a hand on my mouth from behind. "*Shh.*"

The narrow shore relents ahead, sweeping backward into a cave.

From the mouth of the cave, a dark finger, the size of a boulder, tipped with a magma-colored claw extends, rising and falling slowly, in sync with the creature's hulking breaths.

FIFTY

The claw moves.

My breath gets caught in my throat, and Rivan's hand on my mouth tightens even further.

The claw relaxes.

Whatever the creature is, it is far too large to comprehend. Its breaths that I can now hear rumble through the rocks of the cave. Faraway thunder, yet to come near and devastate.

Is this what the salamanders ran away from?

I pull at Rivan's hand. "It's asleep," I whisper.

"What is it?"

"I have an idea, but I don't want to be right." To even think of it might be to give it life so I shake my head, dislodging the thought. Deep beneath the sea, the dark is different, and the creatures that live down there stay there. For one as monstrous to breathe so near the surface of the island…

No.

We stand pressed against the wall for several hysterical seconds, the river of flames flowing fast and angry beside us. It plunges down into emptiness just ahead into a shallow pool of fire and then continues beneath the seabed, which means the way out of here is close too, perhaps just beyond the cave.

"Can we risk it?" Rivan asks.

The monstrous beast snorts. As if it hears us. As if it challenges us.

"What else can we do?" I lean forward slightly. The walls of the cave are slick even in the heat, and it doesn't feel like a creature with a claw that big will be able to get out of the small mouth. A low, sleepy growl emerges and dies just as quickly.

I back away. "It *is* asleep. Count of three?"

Rivan nods.

All right, Kress, let's do this.

Three. Two. One.

We pull in deep breaths and *run*.

Our feet echo over the angry hissing of the river, the wraiths once again trying to drag us in. The claw comes closer and closer, and I'm afraid I'll trip over it, and it's so close now, level with me, and oh no—I'm about to hit it—

But then we're racing past it.

The relief almost makes me stumble and fall. I flail and turn, trying to balance myself, and in the darkness beyond the mouth of the cave, a large, fiery eye is fixed on me. Even next to the Redwater, my blood turns to ice. I become still as death.

So does Rivan. He turned when I flailed, reaching for me, and now just stands before me like a statue, his hand extended to catch me.

Neither of us move. Our eyes remain locked, terror curling around us in waves.

A terrible moan emerges from the cave.

Something drags across the floor, the sound grating like a hundred rusty steel rods scraping against flat stone, and then the scarlet claw snakes up between us. It taps the floor twice.

As if searching for something, waiting.

316

Only one claw, protruding from a sheath of oily black scales, a hint of fire in between. The mouth of the cave is too narrow for the full paw to come out—*thank the ocean*. But if this one claw swipes either left or right, at either of us, it's the river of fire.

The claw withdraws testily. And then comes speedily at me.

I scream. Scramble. And run after Rivan.

He reaches the wall of the cave and frantically searches for the naturally cut steps into the wall of the cave. Our only way out of this hell. If he can't find them in time—

A terrible roar shakes the ground.

"They're here," he yells. "Come on, Kress."

Behind us, another loud thump and a shriek send a quake through the entire cavern, drowning out every sound in existence. Pain bursts in my ears, and I clasp my hands over them.

Rivan, on the steps already, almost loses his grip.

"Go, go!" I yell, ready to climb up.

We wrench ourselves upward over the slippery stone. In the heat, we know it's not water, but whatever the slimy substance is, it tries to fight us all the way. The steps narrow as they go up. Far ahead, I can see the small circular light of the stormy day outside.

Salvation.

The third roar loosens a few rocks in the tunnel we're climbing.

A roar of hunger, not for food but simply to *devour* everything.

A roar that is perhaps the cause of the shudders plaguing Kar Atish. Normal creatures don't make sounds like that. Only one does—one that isn't supposed to be up here.

My skull rings, agony pounding at my ears.

Rivan and I lurch upward as fast as humanly possible, driven by the terror roaring closer and closer with each step. The mouth of the cave was too small; it should contain the monster. It *must*. But what might the monster be capable of when angry?

317

I risk a glance down. And bile rushes up to my mouth.

From the fickle gray light dropping mournfully down the circumference of the opening above, the angry red strips of color stand out among the tarry blackness of the monster's scales. Half of the giant red eye watches me hungrily.

The Naag dragon.

It lurches upward, slamming against the ceiling of the cave. The whole island shudders.

Could it break stone built on a cosmic foundation?

Of course it can. It's the damned Naag.

The serpent of fire, king of the ocean, the great jeweler—so many names given to this creature of legend. One that is supposed to dwell at the *bottom* of the ocean and guard its treasure. Childhood stories warning against greed and disobedience.

"Kress, give me your hand!" Rivan calls from outside the cave, and I eagerly reach for him. As if that makes the Naag angry, another roar and thunder beneath the ground shake the sides of the cavern. My hand almost slips. Rivan grabs both my hands.

He pulls even as panic makes me scream.

I climb out of the narrow hole in the ground, gasping for air.

Down the hole, the roars continue to rise, and for several seconds, the land shudders with a quake that is coming for all of us.

FIFTY-ONE

The sun isn't out yet, only a single brilliant red edge of knife along the horizon, bloodying the storm.

Today, the air even in this part of the island carries the smell of smoke and ash, the sea splashes angrily against the basalt pillars, and the sound of guns goes off at intervals as some desperate fool tries to make a run.

Daybreak is here, and we need to hurry.

We emerge at the back of the Collector's compound, in the small thorny forest that separates it from the plunge down to the sea. The usual watchtowers stand empty, windows shut and lights off. By the number of guns that have been going off the entire night, all of the people working here have been called to arms.

We cross the thorny bushes quickly, marked with scratches on our faces and necks. Once or twice, the ground shudders. I can't help but think of the man who fell to his death in the arena, caught in the quake beneath the ground. This is what has been causing them.

A monster from the deepest nightmares of this world.

How much of this island *can* be saved?

Down by the Collector's harbor, where the Landers arrive and leave from, a large ship stands anchored.

We continue scanning for any guards and any movement. Neither Rivan nor I spy any obvious protection around the compound.

Still, I signal to Rivan, and both of us bring out our guns. There are only a few proper guns with miners, and now two of them are with us. We need to bring the Collector down sooner—before the lack of these guns is felt back at the mines.

The ground begins tapering as the forest recedes. We stay toward the back of the gray hulk of a compound. Everything has the feeling of desertion, like a giant hand picked up the compound and shook it empty. No vehicles remain either, not even the carts they stuff people in to take to the salt pans. Only the black and gold banners flutter in the storm winds.

I extend a hand to stop Rivan. "There's no security."

"Good for us."

Maybe, but dread pools in my gut.

We press on, and the nagging feeling keeps increasing. I want to stop, but there's truly no movement. Nothing stops us.

"What if we're being led inside?" I ask.

"Would it matter if we have to reach the Collector anyway?"

Okay, he has a point.

Quiet and cautious, against the wind, we find ourselves inside the compound. It is full of giant pillars and dank shadows. At the entrance hall, the several doors leading to the many offices stand shut. The sight loosens the knot in my stomach.

They're truly gone. I would think them foolish, but it is only their pride, I suppose. All of them out to take on an army of shrapnel and old tools, leaving their own homes unguarded. They cannot imagine themselves anything but invincible.

At the back of the large entrance hall, two big staircases lead in opposite directions, and an elevator stands in the middle. It can only be accessed via a key that guards carry, so we take one of the staircases. The passage down is smothered in the dark, only a hint of light from the landing below. We descend into the compound with our backs to the wall. The Collector's personal residence is two stories below. It's where we'll find him—and perhaps Aryadna.

Gritting my teeth against how easily I believed her deception, I step off the staircase onto the floor.

Rivan and I dart with careful precision across the polished glass and marble halls of the compound, taking time to hide behind the large stambha pillars. There's wood too—glossy and polished enough that we can see our faces reflected. It's likely to give us away but also warn us of anyone approaching.

A deep roar echoes in the distance. I almost leap off the ground, expecting the Naag dragon to burst out of the polished floor of the compound.

Rivan throws me a glance over his shoulder, about to open his mouth, but I shake my head and place a finger to my lips. The compound is deathly quiet, and the ease from before has given way to a strange roiling again. Perhaps it's the fear of the Naag.

Or perhaps my mind is trying to warn me like it does in the pits.

A row of passages and turns later, we arrive in a large courtyard, with a single double door across. A sign marks it as the Collector's office.

This is it.

Beyond the door is the man who can bring everything to an end.

I raise my hand to bang on the door, but Rivan catches me. "What are you doing? Knocking on his door so he gets time to run?"

"No, I was going to threaten him to open up if he knows what's good for him."

"Surprise element, Kress. That's what we're going for here."

I make a face but of course he's right. "On the count of three?"

"Okay."

We step back a couple of paces, then kick at the center of the door. It rattles loud but stays.

"There goes your surprise," I say.

Rivan frowns and then slams his shoulder against the door, which flies inward.

"Surprise," he murmurs even as he hurries inside.

I expected dust in the air from the broken door, but the chamber-wide carpet lies still as death. No speck in the cold air, an absolute cleanliness. There's no other noise—no guns, no guards.

Inside, the heavy gold and brown is suffocating. A large painting of the ocean at the back does its best to camouflage the fact that the jagged wall is part of the underground stone that they couldn't break and build over.

But the office is empty.

"His personal quarters, then," I say, looking around.

"Through there," Rivan says, moving to a door in the right corner. It has a golden knob in the shape of a squid. He turns it once to the left, then to the right, and the door squeaks open.

We enter a dark hallway with overhangs filled with plants that are shockingly green. At the end, the hallway opens in a large circular sitting room, lit dimly with lamps, with more hallways leading off to the right and the left.

No one seems to be home.

But we check anyway. First the left ones. Three doors, all unlocked and all empty. Then the right ones.

The second door down the right hallway stands ajar, and some-how, I know we will find him inside. This room, too, is lit dimly. But it is warmer than the others.

It smells lived in.

"Have you come to negotiate, Miss Dune?" comes the deceptively soft voice of the Collector just as we step in.

I whirl around, my gun pointed, and find the Collector sitting on a thick chair with velvet arms. He looks so fragile, bundled in his coat, hair undone. He looks almost harmless. This man who has sent his men to slaughter my people.

"The only one negotiating here is you, Collector."

"I see Aryadna was right to join the company. Where zargunine is involved, trust no one, she said." The Collector has the audacity to shake his head. "Miss Dune, you turn out to be a disappointment."

"Yeah, well, you lied to me."

"Tell me what you would do in my place if I were to tell you that this was the only way to make Kar Atish ready for what is coming."

"And what is that?" I snarl.

"War, Miss Dune," the Collector says grimly. "War."

I exchange a surprised glance with Rivan. "A war with *who*? All the islands are governed together. You are going to war with yourself?"

"The Landmaster of Sollonia will go to war with everyone else," he says, his face drooping. "Sollonia is all-powerful, but after the Hunter girl's win at the Glory Race—"

"*She won?*" Ice forms behind my eyes. The Hunter girl—Koral of Sollonia—rides a maristag that carries a part of Karavi's spirit. Their bond woke her up deep beneath the ground.

And now the girl and her maristag have won?

"You don't know the real danger we're in. No wars among us are half as dangerous as what can be," I breathe. If I tell him, will he believe me?

But no—I can't tell him. He and his ilk would truly think me insane. Lock me up. Spread word that I lost my mind. Maybe that will make the miners give up their arms too. I can't let that happen.

The Collector watches me impassively, a child in the massive chair. "What is it that makes you hesitate, Miss Dune? These people who live in the underground are trying to keep the origin well from us. Do you work for them, Miss Dune? Is that your idea of revenge on the miners? Playing both sides, are we? What is their interest in the mines? And are they part of or do they finance in any way the miners' rebellion?"

"Do you *hear* yourself?" I say in disbelief. He has invented an entire conspiracy in his mind, motives and actions with nothing but my silence.

"I don't hear an explanation for why someone who has such good self-preservation as you would be so opposed to this historic moment."

His pompousness is so at odds with the way he appears, fragile and harmless. He has no idea he's sitting on a land about to erupt into fire. He simply believes himself and his men invincible.

Frustration seeps into my veins. "If you drain the well, where the zargunine originates from, the islands will shatter. The Blood Well has been holding everything together for a long time. Think of it like a foundation. If it's broken, we're looking at an—an apocalypse. At our annihilation."

"I see." The Collector coughs, delicately holding a handkerchief to his mouth, then primly pats his lips. He faces me square and sighs. "You have nothing to offer me except for insanity. There have been studies about the noxious gases addling brains, are you aware? But between insanity and keeping my granddaughter safe, I may be inclined to spare your life."

"I should have let her die," I snarl.

"Call them off, Collector," Rivan snaps. "You're making a mistake."

"If only it were that easy." He gives us a pathetic, patronizing smile.

That's it.

I reach up and grab his collar. "I will kill you, here and now, if you don't stop this madness."

His eyes widen, and for a moment, I see myself frozen in them: hair tied but dirty, loose curls sticking down the sides of my face with blood and sweat. It isn't a sight completely unfamiliar, but the fire running in my own eyes is.

And perhaps the Collector sees it too.

"If I were commanding an army, surely I would not be sitting in my bedroom sipping tea."

"He's lying," Rivan rushes. "You're the Collector. You control them."

The air is suddenly hotter and rippling in my vision.

"He isn't lying," I say. "He's *stalling*."

FIFTY-TWO

Rivan turns to me, eyes wide, then back to the Collector. His face pales. And I realize that though this fight, for me, is about keeping the mines locked, for him, his brothers are out there, with their lives in their hands. One at the back of the gorge, the other at the mines.

And if we don't do something *soon*...

No, it can't all be for nothing. My mind whirs like a knife being sharpened over a wheel, sparks everywhere, and a second's distraction could mean blood everywhere.

Dizzily, I walk back from the chamber.

Think, Kress.

If Aryadna is controlling the army, she has to be somewhere in this building. She won't be too far from her grandfather. They probably don't think we would have harmed him. After all, what's the use if he's not the one pulling strings?

I find myself back at the office. With the ocean spread out below, the room is sickening in its luxury. My hair comes undone at that moment, slipping over my shoulder and becoming a nuisance. I sweep it out of the way, annoyed, and my gaze catches on the neat stack of three radios on the shelf.

My heart pounds in my chest, my body already reacting to my racing mind.

I grab one of the radios and hurry back to the Collector's chamber.

Rivan, standing guard, looks up as I almost crash into him. The Collector is surprised to see me back, his frown deepening, making the valleys of his loose skin even deeper.

Without waiting, I switch on the channel and shove the radio at the Collector. "Call your demented granddaughter off. Tell her to stop."

"No."

"None of us have to die if you just do this, Collector."

"I have to put my interests first, Miss Dune."

"Don't say I didn't give you a choice." I take a deep breath and then speak to the radio. "Aryadna? It's Krescent. I have your grandfather."

The static remains uninterrupted for several seconds.

And just when darkness threatens to crush me, a crackling noise fills the chamber. Someone speaks, voice breaking. Then comes Aryadna's voice, clear as glass. "What do you think you're doing?"

"Call off your army, or I will kill him."

Rivan looks at me, startled. And I keep my gaze locked on his, begging him to understand. I won't have the blood of Ashvin and Mayven and Harren and Raksha and countless others on my hands. Not when I can exchange it for a much lesser amount.

Aryadna scoffs. "You wouldn't dare. You will have no leverage left."

"After I kill him, I will kill you, if that's what it takes to stop you."

Aryadna laughs an ugly laugh. "Don't play that game with me, Kress. You couldn't even kill that freak Beyorn. You are not capable of it."

I don't want this. They could've listened—believed me. If they had called off their men, the miners wouldn't have needed to keep fighting and dying either. None of us needed to die if only these Landers didn't treat us like we were specks of grime in their clean and shiny world.

Rivan steps closer, one hand raised to shield the radio. "We need him for leverage. We gain nothing by killing him."

Even as he's saying it, though, I feel a prickle down my neck. The same kind of feeling I get when a creature in the pits is about to have an upper hand. When I've left an opening. My stomach plummets, every fighting sense suddenly turning into a storm.

"Rivan, someone's here."

Someone turns into multiple someones. Five of them, uniformed in absolute black, visors on their faces, storm through the door with guns at the ready.

The Collector chuckles softly, coldly.

I raise my gun too.

"Let's everyone calm down," comes a voice from the back of the group. Aryadna steps out from the space between two of the soldiers, her radio by her side as she looks at us viciously. "I'm so glad to see you both again." She turns to her grandfather. "Dada, you're all right?"

"Indeed, my love," the Collector says.

"Stay back or he won't be," I say.

"No, and now that we have that out of the way," Aryadna says, "let me come to the point."

"What is your point other than being a greedy bitch who wants to destroy this land?" I spit.

"See, that's where you're wrong. Thinking I want this only for myself, as if all ten islands won't prosper if we increase our production and can supply the zargunine at a faster speed. You're the selfish one here, Krescent, not me."

328

"You saw those—those halls and that stupa. You think we're the first people to be here? Why has no one else drained the well?"

"Someone else's incompetence is not my problem," she says, then points to the soldier standing at the back. "Get the Collector, please."

I step back and place my gun to the man's temple. "One step closer, Aryadna, and you will regret it."

"Don't do something *you* will regret."

"Why don't you let me have a fair fight with these losers?" I bark at Aryadna.

"Fair is what I decide," she says and smiles.

"What you decide holds no weight here," Rivan says. "If you think you can take us all out, you're in for a surprise."

"You're a pretty boy. You should maintain that illusion and keep your mouth shut." She sighs dramatically. "Maybe it's a curse of pretty boys, don't you think, Kress?"

I look away from her before I say something that will get me shot. Aryadna is playing with me—toying with me. I let her find my weaknesses, and this is what I get. My fingers curl even as I feel the blood flow slow down with my tight grip on the gun.

"Fine, if this is how you want to play." She waves a hand, and the guards train all their guns away from me—and toward Rivan.

"Stop it, Aryadna," I shout.

"Drop your gun, then."

If I do that, they will take both Rivan and me. If I don't—

In both cases, we're doomed.

Aryadna smirks. "You were never capable of doing what is needed anyway."

"You have no idea what I'm capable of," I say and throw my gun down.

The Collector, too, grins knowingly, like he's won a bet. With one move, I swipe the katar out of my belt and across the Collector's throat. His grin remains stuck in place for a second as the dam of his skin breaks, unleashing a red river and a gurgling scream, punctuated by Aryadna's harsh cry.

"*No!*"

He falls out of his plush chair and onto the carpet, his fingers pressing together as he tries to stop the flow of his blood. But it gushes and gushes, flowing over his hands and spilling onto the beautiful carpet. He convulses and gasps for his granddaughter.

And Aryadna falls to her knees, screaming and screaming and screaming.

FIFTY-THREE

The guards drag Rivan and me from the Collector's chamber to the living room, leaving Aryadna howling like a rabid beast. I try to jerk away, but they only slip their grips from my hands to my armpits, dragging me against the floor on purpose.

"Drown in the sea," I breathe, forced to endure the humiliation, even as their roughness grows progressively.

The butt of a gun slams into my jaw. Pain blinds me, and I fall to the ground amid the circular seats. Rivan lurches for me, getting hit in the stomach. Both of us roar and reach for one another, arms pulled to breaking point, only to be dragged farther away, across the chamber.

Rivan continues grappling with his captors until one of mine places a gun to my temple.

We both grow still.

Aryadna arrives then, full of rage, full of agony. Her eyes are rimmed with red, and her clothes are soaked in the blood of her grandfather. She looks like a nightmare brought to life.

A nightmare that *I* brought to life when I killed her grandfather.

"Miss Syris?" one of the guards speaks.

She looks at him with a burning gaze. "I am now the interim Collector of this island."

The man startles but bows his head and backs away. "Yes, of course. Collector Syris."

She doesn't answer him. A destructive darkness has wrapped itself around her. The coldness that made it so easy for her to leave us to die in the underground, the cruelty that has her overseeing the murder of an entire population on the island, the heart that loved her grandfather and is now darkening rapidly—all of it, blazing together in an inferno within her like the liquid flames of the Redwater.

She walks to me and grabs my chin, her nails piercing skin, forcing me to look up at her. There is no rationality in her features, only unseeing anger.

"He was my only family," she breathes. "And you took him from me."

"I wouldn't have needed to if you didn't wage war against my people."

"*Your* people, Krescent Dune? The same people your own father and mother tried to kill? Those people?"

"You don't know a thing about my father and mother."

"I know what I need to know. Taking others' families from them— that's the Dunes' specialty, isn't it?"

I slam my head into her face, and she goes crashing into a glass table.

One of the guards shoves me back into place, almost ripping my shoulder off.

Aryadna gets up, picks a piece of glass out of the corner of her lip, which bleeds freely, as does her broken nose. She licks some of the blood off. Then, she glances at the man restraining me, and he takes out a knife. I brace myself, but the man walks across the chamber. He grabs Rivan by his hair and puts the knife to his throat.

"Wait—stop!" I cry, struggling to get out of my captors' grip.

The guard presses the knife against Rivan's throat. A red line wells along the blade.

"Don't do this. You want *me*. I killed your grandfather, not him," I shout. "Leave him be!"

A flick of Aryadna's fingers and the soldier slams a fist on Rivan's temple. Rivan crashes to the floor, groaning. His captors hold him down, and the third one kicks at him, over and over again, and I'm screaming and crying. *"Let him go! Let him go!"*

Rage burns through me to a crescendo, and I wrench myself out of the guard's grip so fast that he goes tumbling forward. My nerves catch fire as I launch myself at the guards, grappling and clawing, fighting like it's my last fight.

The lights of the pit are bright, and the spectators howl for blood, and blood pours into the ground from both me and the creature.

I snatch one of the guns.

"Don't let her get away!" Aryadna screeches through the blood pooling at the back of her throat.

The guard from the other side of the room aims. Rivan kicks him with his entire strength and sends him sprawling. I jam the butt of the gun to his head.

"*Stop!*" shouts one of the guards, pointing his gun at Rivan. "Or I'll shoot."

I aim mine at Aryadna and spit the words out through tremors. "Go ahead. You shoot, and so do I."

"Drop the gun," Aryadna barks.

Immediately, the guards' guns go down.

"You have no idea what a mistake you've made," Aryadna says to me. "Within a week, Sollonia's army will be here, and you will have nowhere to hide."

I shove her hard. She crashes into one of the guards just as Rivan, from the other side of the crashed table, yells at me to run for it.

We hurtle toward the hallway—in the dimness missing the team of soldiers filing in. Rivan shoots out a hand and catches me around my stomach. Only a few paces separate us from the door, but half a dozen new guards block our way.

I look from the guards to Aryadna, who stands behind us with her remaining men, trapping us in a small space.

"We'll never get through this," Rivan breathes.

I think of the time I first found myself alone, a child, hungry and dazed and frightened. Nowhere to go and no one to turn to. But I kept going, hiding and crawling and *scraping*. I fought apathy and scorn and monstrous beasts that have tasted humans. The stygic and the raptors and the wyrm lizards and worse. Even these enemies of mine were impressed. I went into the deep and faced a god and lived.

I did all those things. I'm a fighter. I'm a survivor.

I flip the gun toward Rivan and pull out my daggers. "You haven't seen me fight enough."

Rivan swears softly but aims both the guns. "Ready when you are."

I leap into the air and lunge for the guard closest. Like I thought, everyone is packed too tightly to shoot. My dagger cuts through the man's throat before anyone can aim properly. He howls and pivots, unbalanced, landing on another man. Both of them go down.

Another guard lunges over them toward me. But Rivan shoots him. I attack the guards one after the other. They abandon their guns and come at me with bare hands, caging me in a closed circle. I slam my head into the face of the guard nearest, smashing his nose back into his skull, and the circle breaks. Despite the odds, my movements are fast, and I manage to injure most of them—and kill some.

And I feel nothing. Nothing but triumph. Let Aryadna see the beast that has grown in me, fighting in the pits. She will give in—she will stop her army. She has to or, the small voice at the back of my mind wonders, if this is all a mistake, an act without reason, why I don't feel worse killing people like monsters from the stormy seas?

Behind me, gunshots fire indiscriminately, and it can only be Rivan. The rest of them are packed too close.

Still, I yell even as a guard tries to kick me, and I grab his leg, twisting him and shoving him away. "Rivan! Are you okay?"

"I am!"

Thank the ocean he's alive, still standing, still fighting.

I catch sight of one of Aryadna's men taking aim and whirl to find Rivan in his line of sight.

"To your left!"

The warning has barely left me when Rivan's bullet goes through the man's throat, spraying Aryadna with blood. Rivan sprints down the chamber, still shooting, and it takes me and Aryadna almost the same instant to realize why: the door stands unguarded.

She turns and runs.

I want to block her escape, but in the precious moments I spent looking for Rivan, the guards still alive—five in all—regrouped. I adjust my grip on my daggers again. A slash here, a quick stab there, but this time, the guards too have nothing to fear. They forget their protocols and lunge at me.

I fight and try to yank myself out of their grip, screaming and reaching for any bit of skin I can bite or claw or kick. I scream defiance. But they don't let go. Only tighten their grip like I'm a demon from the bottom of the ocean that must be restrained.

Rivan roars as he realizes what's happening. Instead of pursuing Aryadna, he turns and is already moving.

"No!" I shout, still twisting myself in the guards' grip. "Get her! Rivan, don't worry about me!"

But he doesn't listen. A guard pulls himself out of the group. "Put that weapon away or she dies."

Rivan meets my eyes, and my protests have no effect on him as he slides the gun to the guard without question. My gaze drops to his neck, where the cut from the knife has sealed itself already. The guard walks up to him and knees him in the gut *hard*. Rivan doubles over, teeth gritted, but gets upright.

My shoulder joints are blistering, tired of being wrenched around, but I can't stop. It can't happen again. We were so close to getting Aryadna—so close—

A sudden slap throws my face to the left, ringing in my skull.

Aryadna stands in front of me. She flexes the hand she slapped me with, her chest falling and rising rapidly.

"Bring them to the office," she says and marches through the crowded hallway.

Rivan and I are dragged behind and shoved into the office, one step closer to the island, yet so far.

Aryadna stands below the painting on the wall. "Now, Krescent—"

At that moment, the whole building shudders. Louder than ever before. A crack in the gold paint runs through the wall to my right. Like a cannon has struck it. From the bottom of the building comes a terrible moan, then a grating worse than nails against rust. It is the sound of thousands of bones crunching together.

The crack expands. Magma rises up in it, seeking the new air. The guard holding Rivan, nearest the door, curses and stumbles away from him.

Taken by surprise, my captors loosen their grip on me too. I jerk away from them, snatching a pistol from someone's pocket, and shoot. The bullet finds the mark on the first soldier's heart. Startled, as if not quite sure whether to run from the cataclysmic shaking of the building or the bullet in his heart, the soldier slumps. And the second one stares at him.

"Kill her now!" Aryadna shouts even as the corner of the room gives, debris flying in the air.

The others who had surrounded Rivan rush into action. Roaring, they aim all their weapons at me, backing me into a corner.

I shift from one to another. Four of them. If I shoot one, I'll be shot as well. I have to stall—do what Aryadna did. Maybe the quake will scare them off.

But my hand, clasped on the pistol tightly, trembles.

And the soldier who was holding me, the one standing stunned, whips about. He slashes at Rivan with a bladed weapon in rage.

I scream, rushing forward, but the soldiers form a prison around me. Terror climbs up my spine. I thrash in the circle growing smaller and smaller, looking for an escape. Blood roars in my ears, blocking everything else, even as I scream, "Let me out!"

They shove me back, and I almost lose my grip on the gun, my fingers slipping from the trigger. So I swing indiscriminately, hitting at the guards with the butt of the gun. My terror transforms into anger, unfurling vibrant as the red magma burning in the walls now. I slam into the soldiers over and over, reaching for Rivan over the linked shoulders, but they don't budge. Instead, they step forward again, fencing me in tighter.

I forget every sense of self-preservation and throw myself at the soldier directly in front of me. Destabilize their locked grid. Like a cornered animal, I writhe and lash and keep moving, never letting any of them get a firm hold of me.

Keeping them all busy with me.

No one notices when the red threads beneath Rivan's skin burn and glow, when his arm stops bleeding. In a flash, he's up and dashing across the room behind the guards, who have all converged on me.

Aryadna's panicked scream is too late.

Through the dust swirling in the air, Rivan has his arm around her throat and a hand on her head, ready to snap her neck. His grip tightens. "Say the words, Collector Syris."

"You can't—"

"You have *no* idea what I'd do to make sure Kress walks out of here alive."

"Drop the guns," the Collector barks, fear in her voice.

Immediately, the guns go down.

"Now get out of here, and run before this building explodes," I tell them.

Only one of them waits to look at their new Collector before they hurry out.

I turn to her. "This wasn't in your plans, was it? The apocalypse."

"Don't be absurd, Krescent," Aryadna growls, her frantic gaze casting about, blood dried across her face like a maze. "And let us out before"—she stops to stare at the red crack in the wall—"whatever is happening spills over."

Rivan shoves her free and crosses the room over to me. He cups my face, gaze roving all over. "You're okay?"

"Today is not the day I die," I say through a nose stuffed with blood, still keeping the gun aimed. To the Collector, I add, "Here is my ultimatum for you. That ship down in your harbor that got your army over—get on it and leave Kar Atish. Our mines will not empty."

"Do you think you can keep Landers off this island with your broken toys and two guns?"

This time when the shock wave hits, the walls give. A barrage of stone falls into the chamber. I grab Rivan's hand and duck under the table. Aryadna screams, and suddenly, her voice is cut off in the middle.

Over the desk, dust bellows over the falling debris, beneath which half of Aryadna is buried now. Just like Thayne was down below. She wails in pain, the dust transforming the golden princess into a child of the mines. Even as the building keeps shaking and screams begin down by the harbor, I push a large piece of rock off Aryadna.

Her hand, it seems, is broken. She cries, shocked too.

Rivan picks up another radio from the stock that went spinning when the wave first hit and hands it to me. It comes slick with blood.

I thrust it into Aryadna's chest. "Enough fighting and running for nothing. Call off your men. Now. Or you will die here, buried alive."

This time, the Collector, seeing her own death dancing in front of her, obeys.

FIFTY-FOUR

Over the terrifying chaos descending on the island, the Landers' army marches backward, through the constantly shaking ground, and follows the stream of lava bounding over the rocks down to the sea. One by one, hundreds of Landers get on the ship.

I watch from atop the slope, next to the shambles of the Collector's compound, still holding the gun to its very brief ruler. There is no way I will let this girl escape us until every Lander is gone from this island.

When her turn finally comes, at noon, the Collector turns to me. Her face has hardened to stone. If there ever was a semblance of humanity in her, it's gone, along with her grandfather, along with the place she has called home until now.

"You will regret this very much, Krescent Dune."

I force myself to not pull the trigger. There has been enough blood since the dead Collector sent us down into the underground. Enough blood for me to spend a lifetime scrubbing it off myself.

"Letting your grandfather and the ones who came before rule us and ruin us is the only regret I have."

Rivan steps next to me, the blood crusting on his face looking worse in daylight, and we watch Aryadna Syris descend the slope. She holds her broken arm to her chest and moves past the old pillars and the stones, the uneven terrain and the dark strips of color alongside the hill, until she reaches the harbor.

"They're not going to take this defeat and sit quietly, you know," Rivan says. "They may be arguing among themselves, but now the Landmaster of Sollonia will answer for the Syris family."

"Should we have killed them? All the hundreds of them?"

"This thing about the Blood Well being a foundation—what does it mean for us now?"

I turn to Rivan. His face is a mess, the dark wound on his chest a reminder of what he went through and what courses through his veins now. A miracle so powerful we could never dream of it.

His fingers graze the wound. Our eyes meet. In the kind of tales that Raksha would recount, there are always words, new and old, that can describe exactly what's happening. But this is not a fairy story, and here we are, standing at a precipice, unable to articulate what happened to us deep beneath the ground, forced to carry secrets with us until we can hopefully speak of them in a way that others will understand—if we ever find the words.

Perhaps he can take another blow from the daughter of Shadefolk.

"When I had…fainted down in the underground, and saw—met—that being… It was in my mind, but it was real. Like memories made into a passage that I could walk through. Someone helped me walk through."

Rivan waits.

"But she's not whole. There are parts of her spirit out in the world. I don't know what it means for us. But if the Landers with not a fraction of their power could destroy us so thoroughly, I don't know what beings of that power would do. Would our world still be

341

our world if they were free? We have to keep them locked in there until the end of time."

Rivan breathes out slowly, shakes his head. "We can't tell everyone, can we?"

"People would call me mad."

And then, the Collector's compound comes crashing down, and the ground breaks apart.

The waves of the black sea crash into the tall basalt pillars, through the dark storm whirling madly around the island, almost halfway to the top of the hill. Below, deep in the water, something is moving and shifting and changing the course of the ship, which undulates viciously.

Rivan curses. "What is it?"

The ship desperately tries to steer away, caught in a storm that gains more strength within the water. They must be trying to get back to the harbor, but they're no match for the monster that crashes out of the waves.

Two scarlet horns, livid like fire, on a large head with a bigger lower jaw powerfully lined with fangs that could pierce through the body of the ship. The Naag dragon continues to rise above, to curses and roars of disbelief. Its giant but slender and serpentine torso is lined with fiery red between the black scales. Its four limbs and massive spiked tail are all bigger than the torso itself. Biggest of all are the two unfurling finwings—to swim, to fly. The powerful finwings pound sharply with a roaring beat, slicing through the storm, unyielding, merciless, fast as a bolt of lightning.

The Naag slashes in the air, bellows so loud the fiery wind arising from its mouth parts the gray clouds. A powerful and searing sun blazes down from the skies.

The screams are hellish. And for the first time, I find myself wishing the ocean was somehow even larger, so no monster like this could ever escape it.

Rivan's voice is hoarse as he says, "That can't be—"

"Yes, it is. The Naag broke free."

The dragon plunges into the water, for a moment disappearing entirely from view, and before I can take another breath, it spears *through* the ship.

The vessel breaks apart like a toy, crashing everywhere into the sea, its parts flying in the air.

Like ants, the Landers on the ship spill into the water, screaming and lashing and dying. The Naag attacks the ones desperately trying to escape, but there's nowhere to go but its jaws. Every Lander who knows what happened on this island is on that ship, sinking to their deaths.

"The ocean save us," Rivan whispers.

I drop to my knees, hands pressed to my mouth.

The red eyes gleam in the sun, peeking through the broken storm clouds, as the Naag rampages across the water. It slashes with its large finwings, grabs people from the water, and devours them whole.

Snake shadows float along the gray-black waters, blood that cannot shine red enough.

And when it's had enough, the Naag takes to the air even as horrified roars run wild, its powerful finwings spreading wide. A burning ember made out of cosmic matter itself.

And when it reaches high enough, it turns downward. It speeds down like it wants to crash into the ship again, but at the last moment, it breathes out fire from between its fangs.

A fountain of violent, red fire burns everything in its path.

A living volcano, it engulfs the very air along the harbor. Massive roils of steam erupt, blowing toward the island, and I'm forced to raise my hands and squint against the heat.

The parts of the broken ship still above water go up in flames. And so do the desperate people trying to reach safety.

There's only one creature that has ever defeated the Naag in stories. The Water Horse. And the Water Horse has never answered prayers.

There is no safety anywhere now.

FIFTY-FIVE

When the Naag plunges back into the ocean and the dust settles, the Collector's compound is a wreck of rubble. The gold interiors, the polished wood—none of it survives except in broken reminders of what used to be once. A beam here, a pillar there.

At the far side, trapped beyond the lava falling into the sea, blocking the usual path up, are the bonded people of Kar Atish. Hundreds of them, packed together along the salt pans, watching it all unfold with eyes wide and hands clasped.

Harren sends armed miners to gather them all up safely.

And when they do, it takes me an hour to find Siril's sister. And another several minutes to find her niece—they weren't letting the mother and daughter work together. The little girl's face is gaunt, hair bleached from being in the sun, and when she sees her mother, equally as bony and stone-faced, she just stays rooted to the spot. Siril's sister runs so fast to her daughter that she becomes a phantom wind.

The two of them cry and cry and cry, holding so tight to each other that not even air could pass between them.

For a moment, I wish the Collector's compound was still standing so I could break it with my own hands again.

I wipe my tears and clear my throat. "Sheera?"

She looks up. Her eyes. They're Siril's eyes.

I'd visited Thayne at the doctor's room, and he asked me to do this. But now, I find my words stuck in my throat, and I wish he were here.

I never did learn to express my feelings properly.

Sheera stands, holding her daughter close to her still. Her hands are ruined with the labor.

I hold out Siril's backpack. "Your sister..." Why can't the ground open up and swallow me whole? Why could Siril not be here? Maybe I can just make something up. Tell this broken woman that her sister has gone off to another island. For some work. She sent me to make sure they know about it.

But Sheera interrupts my thoughts. "Where is my sister?"

A lie would be a poor way to honor Siril's memory.

But how much would the truth hurt this woman? How can I lay the burden of Siril's death on her shoulders by telling her why her sister went down the deep in the first place?

Some truths, as I know, should remain unsaid.

"Your sister was so brave. She went down the underground to—to help us all get rid of the Collector. She fought for you and all of us until the last."

It takes Sheera a few moments to comprehend. Then, her face shatters at once. She shakes her head, hands clutching her daughter even tighter.

I push the backpack, containing the pale rock, to the two of them. Sheera clasps it to her chest, buries her face in her daughter, and howls. And all I can do is sit with her there, beneath the sky, and listen to her cries. For Siril.

Everywhere around us, smoke rises from the island, the lava

waterfall still sears through the cliff into the sea, and chaos reigns. Testament to what I did today—killed humans, not just beasts. Even if they would have killed me if I didn't. I have blood on my hands I can never wash away now.

When the tears start, I don't know who I'm crying for anymore.

~

The space in front of the Collector's compound is now being used as a temporary setup while a group of miners inspects the premises inside and sees what can be salvaged for ourselves.

In a way, the old stupa beneath the ground has had better luck with time.

I'm studying the carvings on a piece of a shattered pillar when someone mutters, annoyed, "What's he want now?"

I turn—

Badger. He walks ahead of a group of his men. His mouth is set harsher than I've ever seen. He usually doesn't let anyone see him rattled, which means he's out for blood and doesn't care who gets in his way.

With the Collector's grip gone, it's him coming to claim the fortune. He can't let a power vacuum sit idle, can he?

But he's wrong.

Behind him, so many men are ones who have taunted me, mishandled me, leered at me—all while I bled and danced with death for their entertainment.

"What are you doing here?" I say loud enough that everyone looks, from the tables being arranged to the people combing through the rubble at the back.

Raksha tilts her head, grip tightening on the weapon that she still hasn't parted with even though we've been out of the mines for days now. She looks over her shoulder to me and Yara, the arena fighters.

Following her gaze, Harren frowns at us but then walks to the threshold. It's been three days since he was shot, his skin still pale from every exertion.

Something about him standing there alone makes me move.

My knees are surprisingly steady. Though I know what Badger is capable of.

"You betrayed miners," Harren says slowly.

I stop several steps behind Harren. Even bloodied and bandaged, he cuts a figure of authority that fell on him quite suddenly if he's to be believed.

Badger flicks his calculative gaze to me. It's not the kind that would've frightened me before for its sheer sharpness but the kind that I know I will have to meet unwavering.

"I said what I was told, Young Scythe," he says in a mocking tone.

Harren laughs. "That makes you either a liar or a fool."

Badger's jaw clenches. "You're a child. Get someone in charge to talk."

"I am what you get, so speak."

Badger glances over at Raksha and next to her where Thayne and the others sit at the tables. Thayne should be resting, but despite the pain, he insisted he should be here for any decisions regarding the mines. So they dragged his recovery bed here.

I'm glad for it. I may not be able to speak on any council of miners, but he can. And I trust him.

When none of the elders seem to be reprimanding Harren for speaking for them, Badger knows he's lost before he's begun.

He still tries. "You people don't own the mines. When no cargo leaves the island for over a week, what do you think will happen? They will send in more guns and boots here."

I tell him, "We will deal with them too."

Badger laughs. "So the daughter of the Kinkillers gets a say in the future of our island now?"

Before I say anything, Harren moves swiftly, grabbing Badger's collar. "Kress fought for us. She's one of us now, and we do not tolerate anyone speaking like that about our own." He shoves Badger back into his men, who shout with indignation.

I stare at Harren, at the vein pulsing in his forehead, at the anger in his eyes as he looks Badger down. All for me. He—he really means what he said. That I am one of them.

Words get stuck in my throat.

Badger knocks back the ones trying to help him and looks at the elders with rage dripping on his reddening face. "You're going to let these children drag you all down? Fine. Not all of us want that."

At his signal, his men draw their guns. Unlike the miners, who were forced to steal from the Collector and his people, Badger has always had his own firearms ready for whichever way the wind blows. Today, he stands in front of people he would call his own on another day.

"There's nothing you will find down there, Badger," I say, finally able to draw my words out through the emotion clogging my throat after Harren's defense. "Those are not creatures we can fight. Those are creatures that will annihilate us."

"Death *is* glory. Has Sollonia's supremacy taught you nothing?"

"You are so obsessed with this idea of glory, but you'll never be one of them, Badger."

"Won't I? You see these men behind me. They can take this entire hall down, and then where will we be?"

"This is the man you work for," Harren roars. "Turning us against one another. All of us have been to his pits one time or another, and we've all been robbed faceless there. We have booted the Landers off our island, and it's time we do something for ourselves. You can choose to fight for him against your siblings, or you can join us as we move to a better life on our home!"

"Where will you build this better home?" Badger barks, annoyance marring his face.

"There's plenty of room in the tunnels you relax in. All that space and what do you do with it? Lock animals in cages and build your pathetic arenas and let us all out to rot. We can all have a place to stay. We can all sustain ourselves without needing those deadly mines only if people like you don't stand in our way."

"*Enough!*" Badger bellows, snatching for a gun from the man directly behind him.

But the gun never gives.

The man holds on to it. And he asks, "What will we do for food if we don't trade zargunine?"

"We have salt pans. We have fish and seafood. We grow algae and seaweed. It is enough to sustain us, but we will keep trying for more so none of us has to want anything again. And for the rest of it, that's what we're asking everyone to collect for. We will find solutions. Together. None of us will be left behind this time."

The man considers Harren, then looks at me. He lowers his gun to Badger's shocked face. One after another, the others lay down their weapons too.

"The winner," I tell Badger, "is not you."

He lunges, and Harren throws out an arm, catching him by the throat. "Leave, Badger. Get away from Kar Atish. Enough of you and your bloodletting."

I laugh. "And you thought you'd chain the Naag and make it fight in your pathetic pits. Your dreams are revolting, and you have nothing good to give this island."

Badger shoves Harren's arm and pins me with a glare, wrath burning in his eyes. He has spent his entire life building his fortune on our blood and tears. But even he knows when he's made the wrong bet.

Slowly, he turns, though I can feel the shackles of his wrath coiling around my wrists still.

His men part to let him pass by, and that is the only mercy any of them seems to have for him suddenly. I know this is the kind of defeat that will forever darken Badger's heart. The kind that he will not rest without avenging.

I murmur despite myself, "Go to hell and don't come back."

Hours later, when Raksha calls for Yara and me to go and release the beasts before the miners can inspect Badger's warrens, no one can find her.

"Damn that girl," Raksha growls. "Where has she disappeared?"

To most others, only Raksha's annoyance is visible. But I hear the underlying worry. We all know Yara has stopped caring about herself, and ever since the Redwater valley, we can't tell what she's going to do next.

Harren sends people across the island to look for her, but I already know they won't find her unless she wants to be found.

"I bet she went after Badger to punch him in the face." Rivan stands with his arms crossed, staring at the gates, across the commotion going on in the compound. He can say what he wants to, but it doesn't change the fact that he doesn't believe it.

Apart from Raksha and Thayne, we're the only ones who truly made it out of the dark of the underground.

"We didn't get along... No, that's not right. We hated each other. But... Ansh didn't deserve it. Yara didn't..."

"You were friends once. In another life, you might have been friends still. You mourn the loss of the Ansh you might have known, the loss of Yara who could see past her grief."

"I might not have met you in that life."

He shifts to stand in front of me, eyes so serious that I fear I've said something incredibly wrong. A large silence fills my head, and I'm about to speak, to take my words back, when he speaks first.

"Kress, not even the ocean could have stopped me from finding you. It's about damn time you accepted that."

I stare at him, a lightness in my head that makes me think I'm not actually awake but in that in-between space of dreaming and sleep. I forget words. So all I can manage is a nod, and I say the most idiotic thing I can. "Okay."

Rivan laughs, and if I could catch that sound in a shell to listen to forever, I'd be fine for the rest of my life.

FIFTY-SIX

The side of Mayven's face is cut deeply, and though the wound is now clean and stitched, he winces in pain every few minutes. They say that face cuts heal better than the ones on the rest of the body, but his might leave a wide scar. Which still doesn't stop him from wanting to laugh. His joy lightens my heart, to have him whole and hearty. I don't know what would happen to Rivan if either of his brothers were hurt in a more permanent way. He would blame himself, for one.

And I couldn't live with myself for causing him that pain.

Not—not now.

"I wish I was there to see Badger's face," Mayven says. "No, wait—*Atlas Crear*."

Ashvin snorts. "He stole that name too, I bet. Found a dead Lander somewhere, robbed his body of clothes and name."

I laugh, imagining Badger's face when he finds out the things people are saying about him behind his back. Ashvin and Mayven are making the most of this whole situation.

With Yara gone, the three brothers and I have been sent ahead to scout through Badger's entire network, the tunnels and the arena, his personal warren of halls. We are to map it all out while the miners' council begins the slow, long process of withdrawing from the mines, figuring out what to do with the zargunine already mined and now lying protected, the allocation of housing and resources. Stuff of nightmares from which I was the first to get out.

Mayven jogs forward and turns toward us, still moving. "What do you call a Naag?"

"I don't know, May, what?" Ashvin says.

"Nothing. Don't just stand there calling a Naag anything. Run."

Ashvin and I roll our eyes, and Rivan snorts.

I step through the back door of the arena. In the dark, the chamber looks halfway to a grave. Walls peeling and shadowing, boards of wood littered everywhere that we used for sitting and relaxing. That it was all the worst conditions cramped together isn't news to me, but I wonder what Ashvin and Mayven are seeing in this room now.

It makes me self-conscious.

Rivan steps out of the front door. "All clear. Come on."

We parse through the arena and its surroundings, checking for any Badger loyalists still remaining, but most have fled. Those who remain are collecting their own things and moving out. No one who has stayed here in any permanent capacity gets to keep that place simply by virtue of having lived here. It's going to be a tough road ahead, but it is fair. And after getting out of Badger's absolute shadow, the people working here understand that too.

"The beasts are down here," I say, pointing down the staircase at the end of the tunnel. "You two go on through the other side. You'll find Badger's office and residence there."

Then, Rivan and I move down into the belly of the tunnels, toward the hatcheries and the dens that have made Badger's fortune. The stone steps are slick with blood and water, and there's nothing to hold on to except the rough walls. As we go deeper in, the reek grows overwhelming. But we continue, holding on to one another, each step careful.

The platform we descend on overlooks a long, wide hall through an iron grate. Cages filled with the most vicious creatures line the walls, the controls for their doors listed on a panel up here. With thick chains and locks and the absolute lack of fresh air, the hall is choking on its own misery.

I've only been here once, and back then, I was desperate. But I can see now the horrible condition these beings have lived and grown in. Their only respite is the pit where they must fight and draw blood.

I don't realize how long I've stood still, staring through the iron grate, until Rivan places a hand on my shoulder. I reach and take his hand in mine, never more grateful for him than now.

"Let's release them," I breathe.

Rivan raises a brow. "Will that not be dangerous? Where will they go?"

"I'll give it to Badger, he thought of everything when he inherited the fights. The gates lead far down the cliff, away from the island and into the sea."

Together, Rivan and I wheel the lever, and at the far end of the hall, the portcullis grinds upward. A sea breeze wafts in, carrying thick storm and soot. There's a quiet growl here and there, confusion rising.

One by one, we push up the levers on the control panel. With great juddering noises, the cage bars draw up. And as they do, I feel my nerves crackling, a strange, light energy filling me up. The sound reverberates throughout the hall. For a moment, no beast steps out of their traps, used to leaving only for blood and fights.

Then, tentatively, a chirping noise comes from a cage.

The sersei steps out, looks up at me. And as if she recognizes me, she barks. Without taking my eyes off her, I press the off button on the collar's remote control. The collar clinks against the floor. The other beasts' collars follow suit.

Slowly, testily, the beasts begin rushing out.

Half-grown scythe crabs, mutated aquabats swooping through the hall, one-horned derinos, a baby Capricorn that is stunted and emaciated, beak-mouthed ruins of marble, fendarchers, byotors, and raptors.

And at the end, the sersei, hissing and flicking her tongue by turn, rushes through the hall and into the free air.

I push back the sleeves of my tunic, exposing each tattoo. Freeing the memory of every beast that is marked on my skin. Tears well in my eyes. Not the kind I shed on nights I shivered in the cold alone. Nor the ones of wounds and humiliation, the only kind I had known for so long. Not even the ones I wept just hours ago, ones of fire and blood.

But tears of relief.

Rivan holds me for a long time. And I listen to his heartbeat, chastened. I've fought him at every turn, fought my own feelings, all the while afraid it would weaken my resolve to leave, worried it would break his heart. Irrationally, I believed my salvation lay far away from him. But he's the bright light always illuminating my way out of the darkness of tunnels and graves and coldness. Always. Where would I go if I left him behind?

"What are you thinking?" His voice is soft, and he raises a finger to tuck my hair behind my ear. His hand lingers beneath my jaw. And that touch leaves flames in its wake.

He takes my hands in his. Kisses them. Despite the blood of people and beasts on them. He saw me kill people, he was forced to kill people *for* me, and none of it has changed his behavior. The chamber was much larger when we walked in, but right now it feels like nothing else exists save the space where we stand. A cocoon of warmth and calm.

I don't know if he moves first or I do, only that we collide hard and become bound in an absolute embrace, no space for fear or doubt or confusion between us anymore. As if the act of freeing the creatures from their confines was the last thing I needed to truly believe there is a chance to turn everything around.

Free of the fight within and the need to escape, light and life break the dams around my heart.

So I tell him, "I don't feel scared anymore."

He whispers my name over and over, filling his mouth with it, until I don't know if his voice comes from him or deep within me, until I don't know if I am me or if I am him. And then he kisses me until the weight of the world slips off my shoulders. My hands run into his hair, and I never want to stop this, never want to let go of him, never—

"Don't hate me for interrupting," comes a voice. "I did wait as long as is polite, but this is getting out of hand."

Like lightning, Rivan and I part.

From the darkness, the Shademan steps forward. In the flesh. Inside Badger's warrens, with half the island swarming around us.

My hands are still around Rivan, his around my waist, and every breath is hard and fast. So all I can do is ask, dazed, "What are you—?"

"My people are under the impression that because we traveled together as hostage and kidnappers, we're friends, and you might be more receptive to me."

"Someone could see you. How are you even here?"

"And what in oceans-damned hell did you do to me?" Rivan asks.

"A thank-you for saving your life would suffice," the Shademan says. "And as for how and why I am here, we have our ways. Nothing happens on this island that we don't know about. Also, the Naag's destruction has broken open ways that have stayed shut for ages."

"What?" I let go of Rivan and face the Shademan directly. In the distance, voices grow as the chambers in the warren begin getting emptied.

"Yes," the Shademan says, growing sober for once. "The Children of Shade want to remind you that you swore an oath. And we ask now that you hold to it."

"What oath?" Rivan says, even as his hand automatically pulls open my fist. He stares at the wound at the center, then brushes his own chest, where the threads of the healed wound stain his skin.

"With the oath and the godsblood, both of you now carry the deep with you," the Shademan says. He meets my gaze and holds it. "And I carry a message from all Children of Shade. An age of gods and terror is creeping toward us, an age we never thought would exist in this world.

"We asked your mother this, and she failed. It is now you we must rest this hope on once more. Guard the way with your life, Krescent Dune. For the entire world."

All around the warren, there are people milling about, Oshen leading the charge. Clearing old chambers and locks and chains. Tearing down the fences of the arena and opening the gates. Making space for everyone who has been left out so far.

A new city, a new island. A new people.

One that will withstand the might of Sollonia. Because Sollonia *will* come for us. In some days or some years. But it will.

Tonight, it doesn't matter.

We have brought on the change that had seemed impossible. And whatever lives beneath my feet in the abyss of this land, in the walls, it can stay where it remains, locked in the deep for all eternity. Their time has come and gone. I have sworn that I will stay here for as long as I am needed, to keep the doors of those mines shut and keep safe my home. The Children of Shade have charged me with the mandate, and I intend to uphold it. So my parents can finally rest in peace too, knowing that I am here.

And if Sollonia wants to threaten our world, this island will be ready.

I will be ready.

READ ON FOR
AN EXCERPT FROM

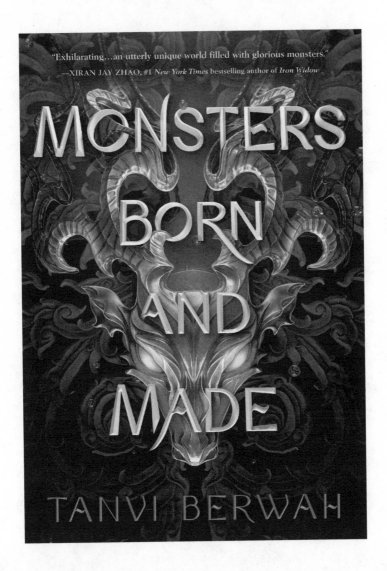

"Exhilarating...an utterly unique world filled with glorious monsters."
—XIRAN JAY ZHAO, #1 *New York Times* bestselling author of *Iron Widow*

MONSTERS BORN AND MADE

TANVI BERWAH

ONE

We hunt when the world sleeps. A risk that could kill us. A risk forced on us.

I try to awaken my brother, but he only murmurs sleepily, "Piss off."

"It's four already. Baba told us to be at the beach by now."

Emrik clutches his mattress like a crab stubbornly clinging to a rock. When I yank off his blanket, he snarls, "Get out of my room."

His shoe thuds against the door just as I shut it. I press my back against the stone wall, the chill grounding me.

Minutes later, Emrik appears. We're dressed alike: black pants, a fitted white shirt with collars up to our chins, and boots molded to our feet. Beneath, we're both wearing skaya-threaded watersuits. The Hunter siblings.

His fist tightens on the doorknob.

Being nervous before a hunt is good.

It means we're alert, not stupid.

"Koral," he says, voice hoarse. "Is anyone else up?" His hair is far past his shoulders, almost as long as mine. The single clip stuck through it shines in the anemic yellow glow of the light above the door. Before I say anything, Liria's asthmatic coughs echo in the silence.

The thought of our little sister choking on air isn't helpful as we climb the claustrophobic corkscrew staircase, leaving the safety of our underground house. But it's a good reminder of why the hunt needs to go perfectly, why we cannot let a maristag escape us tonight.

Because that's how we survive.

Capture maristags, breed them, train their offspring to tolerate land, and then sell them to the upper-caste Landers competing in the Glory Race. All at the risk of death.

Then, we dare to live. Until the next hunt.

The world outside is drenched in black ink, and the Ship of Fire constellation gleams red and yellow, taunting us. A sea wind blows in, carrying salt and storm, right as a bolt of lightning skewers the sky.

Emrik and I sprint toward the beach. It comprises the entire strip of gray sand on this side of the island. Despite the sea guzzling swaths of sand without warning, it's often stuffed with scavengers scraping at the metallic chips of zargunine on the low limestone arches that jut out of sea and sand.

Squinting for any scavengers, I end up having to sidestep a puddle of—"Skaya? Who's wasting skaya in high sun?" Do they not know how difficult extracting the jelly is and how much we need its protection against the hot sun? Though we're surrounded by water, our island is parched, and we roast with it.

Emrik frowns at the skaya puddle. The scar on his right eye, dripping like an angry tear, contorts. "Fewer people to bother with."

As we reach the U-shaped bend of the limestone cliff, thunder rumbles low. A monster waking up from sleep. The horizon, swallowed in darkness, doesn't exist yet.

Down the serrated edge, rocks shoot out of the volatile water like

364

blue-gray fangs. My face grows numb from the bite of the storm. Rawness chafes my lungs with each breath. The rocky ground beneath me is slick with dead crawlies and lichen and the water slapping against it. I must tread carefully.

"You should stay out of the sea," Emrik says.

My temper flares. Years of hunting together, and he still doesn't trust me. "Why?"

"Look at the storm."

As if you'd be any use alone. I bite my tongue. No point fighting before going into the sea. "More reason for you to have backup."

"Stay out of the water, Koral. I'll need your help to drag the maristag out." His jaw is clenched, his face thinner—its contours razor-sharp. The black tattoo on the left side of his face twists, matching mine. He looks cruel in the dark. I suppose we both do.

Emrik is three years older, but we could pass for twins when we go hunting.

I don't spot a single maristag in the black waters—not ideal on the last day of hunting season. "Can you see any movement?"

Our family, stretching back generations, has kept detailed records of the maristags. They have never been seen outside the annual upwelling of the waters. Before the sun rises today, they *will* disappear and won't return for ten months.

Their biological clocks never fail.

Last hunt's maristags fell sick and died. Emrik *says* it wasn't his fault, that he had filtered the water like always, that the maristags brought the infection from the sea. Now we have only one female left. Without a male, we'll have no fawns to sell for the remaining year.

The Landmaster will act like it's not our fault, smile, and send us away with a subsidy payment lasting maybe a month. Meanwhile, a silent warning will circulate across the island: no loans to the Hunters, no jobs.

We'll starve. Like the year I turned eight.

And this time, Liria is too sick for us to make it an entire year.

"They're hiding from the storm," Emrik says, snapping me out of the horrible memories. "Two of us will cause a frenzy. Stay here."

"Fine, go die in there."

His glare is answer enough. He strips to his watersuit, arms himself with a zargunine quarterstaff, and, before I can take back my parting words, dives into the sea. Then he's a shadow, swimming so fast he could be mistaken for a maristag.

So fast he vanishes.

The sky is getting light, a terrible dawn approaching. Emrik is nowhere. Has the sea swallowed him?

Don't be dead, Emrik, I'll murder you.

Winds pick up, hissing through the water. There's nothing but the bruised curtain of sky, cut with the menacing red light of dawn, which stains the angry foam of the sea with the color of rotting flesh.

The world retreats, enveloped in an eerie silence.

Then—a fierce cry pierces the sea, and the rancid smell of sulfur saturates the air.

I remember the first time I saw a maristag.

We learned in school about the ten Islands of Ophir and the Panthalassan Ocean, which is the super ocean that engulfs everything else. Sea creatures that are terror made into flesh breathe beneath the black ocean. Fawkeses that release a strange tarry substance, which catches fire instantly when it touches air. Raptors with saw-like teeth will carve the land to let the sea flow through so they can hunt you down. Aquabats, screeching from one end of the world to the other.

And maristags, living nightmares that move as fast on land as they do in water. The lithesome creatures are bipedal. Their front limbs are shorter. Stronger. Clawed. Made to grab prey and to tear muscles. Enormous antlers crown their heads. Their scales are luminescent and their blood green.

When maristags get angry, that's when the true horror of creation unravels.

I am five again. Kept away from the stables. That day, I remember seeing something bobbing beneath the smooth sea, water frothing around it. I stared, glued to where I stood, and the bioluminescent spots gleamed like metal in the sun and lifted. A head emerged. Sharp frillfin shot open around it, launching venomous barbs like harpoons.

One *almost* reached me.

I screamed.

That maristag vanished.

This maristag thrashes out of the water.

It's a stunning dash of green amid the cold, gray limestone. The blade-sharp frillfin along its neck have sprung open, shooting lethal barbs out. And clinging to its powerful body, bending its manefin, jerking away from the venomous blades, is Emrik—desperately digging his fingers into the scales of the maristag.

My hands are suddenly stone.

I expected to berate Emrik for stretching out the hunt until dawn.

Instead, he's wrestling with a damned maristag *in* the water.

The maristag is a glorious blur of bioluminescent green, slamming in and out of the angry black water. Between the frillfin and the antlers, Emrik has no control over the creature. One wrong snap, one treacherous slip, and it's all over for my brother.

My stupid brother.

I've seen corpses that suffered the wrath of a maristag.

I don't want him to become one.

"EMRIK!" I scream and wave. "HOLD ON!"

I leap into the freezing water.

A thousand cold needles stab at me, wrestling for control over my body, to tear it apart. The waves are crushing and dark. But I know these waters; I've grown up in them. I cut through the current, fast and smooth, forcing the water to part. Any second now, I'll reach him. I swim closer and closer, surfacing for one ragged breath.

The maristag jerks its neck. Venom, smelling like sulfuric acid, cuts the air again. Rear-curving fangs close around Emrik's arm.

My brother howls.

Coils of blood spiral into the water.

The quarterstaff slips out of Emrik's hold.

I gasp, saltwater smacking at the back of my throat. My jaw burns like it's made of metal.

The maristag is frenzied. I whirl back to the limestone. Gingerroots. I need gingerroots. Maristags are allergic to the prickly skin on the plant. Skaya vines slither over stone like fluorescent snakes, providing illumination, entangled with thick, tall grass swaying like ghosts. I frantically grab a fistful of gingerroots but their grip is too strong. I need something to cut it with.

My lungs sting and I'm forced to resurface. Lightning crashes far out in the ocean as a wave rolls toward the stones.

I brace myself.

The water still hits me like a block of iron.

The moment the wave breaks, I press my foot against the stone and pull at the bush of gingerroots. *It's not enough, it's not enough.* My fingers turn red, my grip slipping. *This isn't going to work, Emrik will die.* Blood on my hands. *Cut, already!*

The last thought escapes my mouth in a burst of air bubbles.

Pain lances my arms.

The bush snaps and I'm slammed back against the hammer-like crush of waves. I curl into myself, floating to the surface. With one deep breath, I dive back and swim into the bloodied water for my brother.

The maristag latches onto the gingerroots. It thrashes anxiously. A loose layer of tissue that forms a second skin over its iridescent scales gleams an ethereal green, blood snaking away.

I'm hands away from my brother.

"The tailfin!" Emrik's cry slips into a gasp. "Don't let go!"

The maristag closes its frills, preparing to shoot the barbs again. Right at my face.

I wheeze, water gushing into my mouth. "Let go of it, Emrik! You're going to die!" I slam the gingerroots into the maristag's neck, at the delicate place where its frills emerge, and it tosses its head in a frenzy. A painful screech cleaves the water. I wrench Emrik's bleeding arm away from the maristag—hoping that *pop* sound I hear came from the animal and not from Emrik.

Behind us, the maristag shakes its second set of fins straight. The manefin fans off along its spine and vanishes midway. I'm frozen, waiting for an attack, but the maristag turns and stares across the sea.

There's not a second to lose. The waves are strong and Emrik is still bleeding. I hold him against me and swim.

We crawl to the shore, gasping for breath. My arms tremble under my weight, fingers twitching like something alive is choking inside. "Are you—"

"Why would you do that?" Emrik cuts me off, his shout cracking midway. Sand crusts every inch of him, coloring his brown skin gray.

I'm panting, panic creeping in me as my conscience understands something before I do. "Do what? Save you?"

"I told you to grab the maristag's tailfin! I was closer to the manefin!" Red lines his swollen eyes. "We could've got it!"

Our skaya must have washed off, but he's in a far worse shape. Blood leaks from his arm, soaking his torn watersuit and darkening the sand. He looks—green. His chest rises and falls, and without warning, he vomits. I jump back. He clasps my wrist tight like a shackle.

"You were supposed to work with me! You made me lose my grip on the maristag! Koral—that was the last of them!"

"No, it wasn't." I turn to the sea. The maristag, a magnificent green, is circling farther and farther from the coast. Its antlers rise and ebb as it gallops through the water.

Today was the last day of the hunt.

The maristags are gone.

ACKNOWLEDGMENTS

First, to everyone who warned and prepared me about the beast that second books are, thank you. Going in with eyes wide open was a gift I didn't understand until I was in the middle of it.

To readers of *Monsters Born and Made*, it's one thing to publish a book, completely another to see people loving and carrying it forward. I see you, and I'm so grateful.

To Annie Berger, thank you for pointing me in the right direction always, for making this book work from that very convoluted initial idea. To Gabbi Calabrese, for loving Rivan as much as I do! To the production team—Jessica Thelander, Thea Voutiritsas, Susan Barnett, and Sabrina Baskey, thank you for taking care of this book. To the marketing & publicity team—Michelle Lecumberry, Rebecca Atkinson, and everyone who helped to bring this book to the readers. To the art team—Liz Dresner, Erin Fitzsimmons, Kelly Lawler, and the super-talented Sasha Vinogradova, for the coolest cover for this story, and to Laura Boren, for bringing this book to life so beautifully. You're all so appreciated. To Emily Luedloff, being your friend and discussing *Hunger Games* with you and Faith is an absolute joy.

To Rena Rossner, thank you for the tireless advocating of my work.

To Penguin Random House India team, especially Parul Kaushik and Sonali Arora, for bringing MBAM to my home country. To Radhika Marwah for being the coolest person I have ever known.

To Agnieszka Brodzik and the OdyseYA team for bringing to life my very first translated edition.

To Chelsea Beam, Rosie Brown, Crystal Seitz, Swati Teerdhala—cats or clowns, who knows? We started so long ago and look at us now. Almost want to put a crying emoji here but I'll refrain.

To the TheWritingFolks—thank you for rebranding, oh my god—I love you all. Angel Di Zhang and Lani Frank, for the much-needed quick reads and reassurances. You saved me from several long stressful days.

To Tabrizia Jones, for your enthusiastic support, which means the world to me.

To my dad, always. I don't know where I would be without your support and frankly if I'd even be able to persevere in this industry. And Mini, who cannot stand Dorian but it's okay because I love you, and also, your interpretation of Koral in your drawings is my absolute favorite. You win some, you lose some.

To my circle of friends, especially to Yasmin and Nikita for being the best hype girls. To Onaiza and Uday—you're both very funny, thank you for getting me so well.

To Laboni Bhattacharya, Bidisha Das, Kat Delacorte, Niyla Farook, Aimal Farooq, Margot Fisher, Sharon Sibyl Gatt, Hayley Mallary, Meg McGorry, Aishwarya Tandon, Michelle Wong—readers, writers, artists, but more importantly, friends.

And to the ones who are returning to this world of ocean for a second time or entering it for the first time—I hope you stay as we change it for the better.

ABOUT THE AUTHOR

Tanvi Berwah grew up wanting to touch the stars and reach back in time. She graduated from the University of Delhi with a bachelor's and master's in English Literature and lives in India. She is the author of *Monsters Born and Made* and *Somewhere in the Deep*. Find her at tanviberwah.com.

FIREreads

— #getbooklit —

Your hub for the hottest young adult books!

Visit us online and sign up for our
newsletter at FIREreads.com

@sourcebooksfire

sourcebooksfire

firereads.tumblr.com